Praise for the Archers of Avalon Series

Book of the Year Finalist (ForeWord Magazine)
Best Cover of 2011 (Girls on YA Books)
Top Ten Characters of 2011 "Tristan" (The Autumn Review)
Top Ten Covers of 2011 (Books Over Boys)
Top Indie Covers (YA-Aholic)

"This book enraptured me. Original. Breath-taking. Heart-breaking...in all the right ways." —UtopYA

"Entertaining, romantic, and filled with emotion, **ANEW**, is an excellent beginning to this series. The characters are lively and interesting, the plot is filled with secrets, and I couldn't turn the pages fast enough!" —Amarilys (Goodreads.com)

"Chelsea Fine has just totally set my heart on fire with this amazingly fresh love triangle and storyline. She just has a way of bringing a story to life for me with tears, laughter, beautiful romance, and a deep, strong storyline." —I Heart YA Books

"Talk about one crazy, complicated love triangle! Chelsea Fine sure knows how to pull heartstrings...I seriously need the next book. RIGHT. NOW." —Melissa (Goodreads.com)

"**ANEW** was a completely original paranormal romance...[including] witch, jealousy, love triangle, curse,

two hot brothers, most hilarious best friend ever, and immortality."
—Reading, Eating, and Dreaming

"**ANEW** is many things: a romance, a love triangle, a supernatural mystery, a race to break a curse…and all of these things weave in and out of the life of a seventeen year old girl who is just trying to live a normal life…I loved this book." —Cameron Dodd (Goodreads.com)

"Amazing, beautiful book! Just Perfect! A must-read!" —Halyna Hurdish (Goodreads.com)

"The hottest immortals to hit the shelves! It's refreshing to read a paranormal book that strays from the typical "vampire/zombie" fad…This book grabs you and holds on until the very last page. —Kiele Lauterbach (Goodreads.com)

"In **ANEW**, Chelsea Fine has created characters that are mysterious, witty, sarcastic and normal…all at the same time. They are what teenage dreams are made of." —Erin (Amazon.com)

"I needed a little break from the typical YA Paranormal Romance. This story did not disappoint!" —The Autumn Review

Also by Chelsea Fine

Sophie & Carter

Anew

Awry

AVOW

THE ARCHERS OF AVALON
Book Three

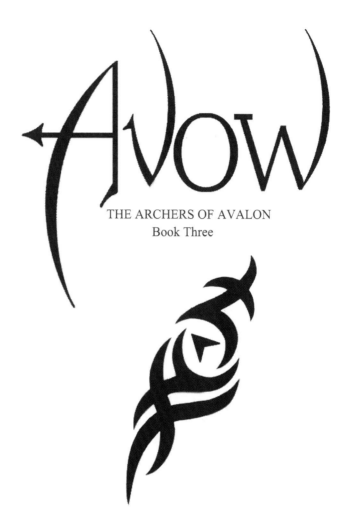

Chelsea Fine

Firefall Publishing

This is a work of fiction. All of the characters, organizations, and events portrayed in this novel are either productions of the author's imagination or are used fictitiously.

AVOW

Copyright © 2012 by Chelsea Fine

All rights reserved.

No part of this publication may be reproduced, stored in a retrieval system or transmitted in any form or by any methods, photocopying, scanning, electronic or otherwise, except as permitted by notation in the volume or under Sections 107 or 108 of the 1976 United States Copyright Act, without the prior written permission of the author.

ISBN 978-0-9885859-2-8

Contact the author via
www.TheArchersofAvalon.com
www.ChelseaFineBooks.com

Published by
Firefall Publishing
Phoenix, AZ

Cover photo by Ashley Bugg with Bugg Photographer LLC
Cover design by Chelsea Fine

*To my grandparents, Johnny and Milly.
Your encouragement has made me fearless on this journey
and your unconditional love has made me fearless in life.
I love you both with my whole heart.*

1

Scarlet had her memories back, which meant two things:

She knew where the Fountain of Youth was.

And she was mad at Tristan.

Still clutching a bloodstained knife in her hand, she marched through the graveyard and glanced over her shoulder at the green-eyed boy she'd loved for centuries. "By the way, you suck."

"Excuse me?" Tristan said.

She turned to face him. "I can't believe you tried to kill yourself."

"I was trying to keep you alive."

"Agh. Spare me your sacrificial agenda." Another memory hit her and her veins heated. "And you let me wander around with amnesia for two years?" He opened his mouth, but Scarlet cut him off. "And then you let me date Gabriel? What the *hell*, Tristan?"

A muscle flexed in his jaw. "First of all, I was supposed to die. So I didn't think intervening in your love life was any of my business. Gabriel made you feel happy and safe and I wasn't about to screw that up. And second," he raised his voice over her protests, "the reason I didn't 'meet' you for two years was because I didn't think I'd be able to follow through with killing myself if you and I were, you know...*pals*." His eyes glinted in the moonlight.

Scowling, she said, "Well that was selfish of you."

"You think *I* was selfish?" he said. "*You're* the one who shut everyone out. *You're* the one who kept secrets and stole stuff and ran away—"

"I had to run away," she snapped.

His voice rumbled in anger. "Did you have to die too?"

"I wasn't trying to die."

"But you did," he said coldly.

They stared at each other for a moment. Because of her connection to him, Scarlet could feel the hurt and fear pulsing through his veins at the memory of her last life. But she could also feel the love heating his core as his eyes traced over her in the darkness. And it was the love—that undying fire that blazed in him and burned through her—that had her lost for words as she looked at him.

He was beautiful. Even standing in a graveyard, covered in dirt and blood, he was striking. His dark hair fell wild around his face and his green eyes shone in the moonlight.

A shiver of desire ran through him—or was it her?—and Scarlet clenched the knife in her hand so she wouldn't do something stupid. Like crush her mouth to his and claw at his clothes until there was nothing between them but heat and skin. But that would, of course, lead to death.

Everything always led to death.

Tristan shifted his weight as he scanned her face. "What happened in your last life, Scar? What are you hiding? And what did you mean when you said there were 'dangerous things ahead of us'?"

Her chest tightened at his questions, none of which she knew how to answer, as millions of Avalon stars winked at them from above, reminding her of a time when she and Tristan spent their days in the trees and everything was fair; everything was simple.

Nothing was simple anymore.

Tristan tilted his head and repeated, "What are you hiding, Scar?"

She could feel his heartbeat echoing inside her soul, powerful and constant, as his emotions swam into her.

Patience. Love. Worry.

Could she tell him the truth about the fountain? The *whole* truth? The truth that would undo any hope they had of a happy ending?

She opened her mouth—

"Holy crap! Did you guys see that?" Nate jogged up to them with a knife in his hand, a grin on his face, and a trickle of blood running down his neck. "I totally kicked Ashman ass over there! I was all like *hi-yah* and *you wanna piece of me?* I was a super slayer! Buffy's got nothing on me."

Scarlet shut her mouth and shifted away from Tristan's searching eyes as Nate continued.

"It was life and death out there, guys. *Life and death.* They just kept coming at me and I just kept putting them down." Nate took a moment to catch his breath. "I mean, sure, I screamed like a girl a few times and accidently stabbed myself at the beginning, but still. I feel amazing! For the first time in five hundred years I feel *alive.*"

Moving his gaze away from Scarlet, Tristan eyed Nate's neck. "You're bleeding."

Nate touched his wound and drew back bloody fingers. "I'm *bleeding.* Ha! I have a battle wound. Oh, this is so awesome." Tucking his knife into his waistband with a smile, he looked around. "Where's everyone else?"

Scarlet's stomach churned as reality whooshed in and slapped her in the face. The last few hours of the night played through her mind like a horror movie as she remembered all that had transpired, and her heart began to race.

"Raven kidnapped Heather." Saying it out loud had emotion crawling up Scarlet's throat. She needed to save Heather. She needed to stop Raven. She needed her heart to stop pounding so she could think clearly.

Nate's face fell. "What?"

Scarlet summed up the evening's events in one breath. "Raven is actually Clare—Heather's boss at the coffee shop—not Laura. Laura was working for her, but Raven killed her and dumped her body in a grave—"

Ohmygoodness. Laura was really dead.

The pounding stopped and Scarlet's body went cold.

My guardian is dead.

There was a sudden hollowness inside Scarlet she wasn't sure how to respond to. It wasn't painful; not really. But it was tight and had her eyes stinging in the cold wind.

Laura was dead. What did that mean? Did it mean sadness? Loss? Did it mean anything at all? And why was her chest hurting so much?

Concerned green eyes roved over her features, making Scarlet feel safe enough to cry, which she refused to do.

She swallowed back the tightness and cleared her throat, focusing on the situation at hand. "Then Raven had an Ashman kick the crap out of me so she could kidnap Heather and hold her ransom for the map to the fountain. And *then* the life-force between Tristan and I shifted. So I can still feel his emotions, but he can't feel mine anymore."

Thank God.

If Tristan were still able to sense her, he'd know she was confused and scared and panicked about Heather. And the fountain. And the truth.

A sick feeling swirled inside her gut.

"And because the life-force shifted, Scarlet now has her memories back," Tristan added, sliding his eyes to her.

Nate blinked. "*What*? I go slaying for ten minutes and I miss everything—wait." His eyes shot to Scarlet and widened. "Does that mean you know where the fountain is?"

Scarlet hesitated.

It was decision time.

No truth? The whole truth? A vague truth?

"Yes," she said, going with vague. It was always safer to start vague. "But we need to rescue Heather before we do anything else."

Her heart started to hammer at the thought of her happy friend being held hostage by a vengeful witch with a drug problem. So many things could go wrong.

So many things already had.

Nate nodded. "Did you see which direction Raven took her?"

Looking around the cemetery, Scarlet shook her head and let out a groan of frustration as guilt swamped her soul. "This is all my fault. I should have stayed by Heather's side. I should have protected her."

Tristan scanned the premises. His coat was sliced open in several places and dark splotches of blood slowly seeped through the shredded fabric of the black T-shirt he wore beneath.

His immortal body wasn't healing like it should, which meant his wounds had been inflicted with Bluestone weapons.

Not good.

"Dude." Nate caught sight of Tristan's injuries. "Are you okay?"

Tristan looked down at his stained clothes and shrugged as if the slashes in his skin were more of a nuisance than anything else. "I'm fine. The cuts are shallow. Where's Gabriel?"

Scarlet furrowed her brow. "He came with me to the coffee shop, but he was gone when I came out. He wasn't with you guys?"

They shook their heads and worry crept through Scarlet's veins.

"I'm sure he's around here somewhere." Tristan looked calm as he glanced around, but Scarlet could feel concern coiling inside his chest. "Why don't you two go look for him at The Millhouse and I'll search the rest of the graveyard."

Scarlet nodded.

Good plan.

Split up. Find Gabriel. Rescue Heather.

And stay away from the fountain.

Okay, that last part might be difficult since Amnesia Scarlet spilled the beans about the freaking map, but whatever. She could still throw them off. She could lie. She'd been lying for years.

As Scarlet and Nate headed out of the cemetery, Tristan walked deeper into its shadowy depths. Distant music from the ongoing Avalon carnival drifted through the night air, making the wind sound eerily happy as it wrapped around headstones and swept through Scarlet's hair.

Putting her knife away, she rubbed her head where it still throbbed from the blow Raven had dealt her with the business end of a crossbow.

One more reason to hate the crazy witch.

Everything was so screwed up—

A sharp pain darted up Scarlet's body and twisted around her insides with liquid fire until she doubled over.

Sinking to the ground, Scarlet clutched her chest and stomach, afraid her skin might split open and empty her insides all over the grass. She tried to suck in air, but her lungs wouldn't work.

Nate dropped down beside her with terror in his eyes. "What's wrong?"

The fire turned to ice and wrapped around her organs and bones, squeezing without mercy. Scarlet couldn't help but cry out loud.

"Tristan!" Nate called, checking her pulse before pulling at the skin beneath her eyes to check their color.

Usually when Scarlet felt pain of any sort it was because her heart was failing. And when her heart started to fail, her eyes would glow and her nose would bleed. But this didn't feel like heart failure.

This felt like something else entirely.

She squeezed her eyes shut and grimaced until the agony started to subside. Her muscles loosened, her lungs started to expand, and soon Scarlet wasn't hurting anymore.

Out of pain, but still very confused, she opened her eyes to find Tristan crouched beside her.

His green eyes were glowing into the night as panic oozed from his pores. "What just happened?" He searched her face.

Good question.

Scarlet rubbed her chest to make sure all her insides were where they were supposed to be. Yep. Still in one piece.

Phew.

"She just collapsed in pain." Nate turned his eyes from Scarlet to Tristan. "Dude. You need to calm down. Your eyes are super green."

Tristan rubbed a hand over his mouth, still looking at Scarlet. "It must be the transition. Maybe when the curse shifted we switched places, putting Scarlet in pain without me, just like I used to be in pain when I was without her."

Well crap.

That would suck.

"I guess that would make sense." Nate scratched the back of his head. "Especially since her pain went away when you walked back over."

Scarlet stood from the ground and brushed the cemetery grass off her pants as Tristan and Nate rose to stand beside her.

A surge of guilt rolled through Tristan and Scarlet hurried to reassure him. "I'm fine now—"

"You're *not* fine," he snapped. "You fell to the ground in pain when I was only fifty feet away from you."

Yeah.

That was weird.

Nate pressed a finger to his lips. "If the life-force reversed your roles—"

"Oh no." Scarlet's eyes widened as the possibility sank in. "If our roles have been reversed, does that mean my touch can make Tristan sick? My touch can kill him?"

She took a step away from Tristan and felt his pounding heartbeat soften. Stepping back up to him, the pounding resumed. "Oh no. No, no—"

"Okay. Don't freak out." Nate held a hand up.

Too late.

"His heart responds to my nearness." Scarlet shook her head as her chest tightened in despair. "No, no, no."

This couldn't be happening.

"So it appears the curse has shifted," Nate said calmly. "We can handle this." He held up a calm hand to match his calm face and calm eyes as he looked at her. "All we need to do is make sure you two stay within close range of one another so you don't writhe in pain, but far enough away so

Tristan doesn't, you know, die." He shrugged. "Easy. We'll just reenact the ten-foot rule between you guys."

Nate stared at them. Waiting.

"What?" Tristan said.

Nate rolled his eyes and thrust his hands in-between Scarlet and Tristan, pushing their bodies away from one another. "Ten feet. There you go. Now let's go find Gabriel so we can get our Heather rescue on. Then we can finally find the Fountain of Youth and cure everyone of this God-forsaken and completely obnoxious curse." Turning, he headed down the street toward the Millhouse.

Scarlet and Tristan slowly followed after him in stunned silence, Scarlet biting her lip as they walked along. She was killing Tristan with her very presence.

She glanced at him under the yellow glow of the streetlamps above, running her eyes along his profile as he stared forward with a clenched jaw. He was fierce. He was patient. He was everything she loved.

And he was dying.

Divulging the truth about the Fountain of Youth was no longer an option. Tristan's life was at stake.

To hell with happily ever after.

2

After being pulled into an alley by several Ashmen, Gabriel had steadily worked through his attackers until only one remained. The final Ashman charged at him, and Gabriel swung his bloodstained knife through his chest, watching as the dead creature dropped to the ground and crumbled to ash.

Breathing heavily, Gabriel looked around the dark alley and shook his head at the numerous piles of ash at his feet.

His life was so weird.

He straightened his back and pain cut through his body. The shallow cut in his right shoulder wasn't so bad, but the deep gash just above his heart was throbbing like a mother and bleeding just as badly.

He touched a hand to the deeper wound and grimaced.

Stupid Bluestone weapons.

Stretching his neck, Gabriel headed back toward the street where he could hear the distant sounds of laughter and carnival music coming from the town fair. Was there really a happy festival still going strong just around the corner? It seemed ironic.

Let me just sheathe my zombie-killing blade and dust this dead guy ash from my hands and I'll get right back to riding Ferris wheels and trying to win ugly teddy bears.

He shook his head as he neared the edge of the alley. Hopefully Scarlet had found Heather and they were both still safe in the coffee shop.

A noise behind him caught his ear and Gabriel paused, looking down the dark alleyway in anticipation of more Ashmen. He saw nothing but shadows and—

Stabbing pain pierced his neck and his vision immediately began to swirl into darkness. He dropped the knife in his hand and felt himself collapse under suddenly weak knees.

What the hell?

Against the heaviness swarming into his veins, he tried to keep his eyes open as he scanned the street. Through his blurry vision, he made out a woman with dark hair in the distance walking towards him. He couldn't make out more than that, but he watched her walk and, dammit, he knew that walk.

Dread filled his insides as numbness overtook his body, rendering him utterly defenseless.

The figure drew close and hovered over Gabriel's face.

"Hello, lover," Raven's blurry lips said. "Did you miss me?"

Raising a gun-like weapon in her hand, she shot again at Gabriel's neck and a dart of some sort hit him. Mustering all the strength he had, he yanked the dart from his throat, but his body was too heavy to fight back and the dart rolled from his numb fingers.

His arms went numb. Then his legs. Then his whole body.

The last thing he saw before losing consciousness was the silver-eyed girl who'd once been his best friend, smirking at his weakness as she shot at him again.

****

Heather had stopped crying an hour ago, but her body was still shaking.

Raven had bound both her wrists and ankles with coarse rope before tying her body against a concrete pillar in an old warehouse. Her arms were strung above her head, her wrist ties hanging from a hook in the pillar, and her legs were pinned to the pillar, ropes winding up her calves, thighs and torso.

Squirming against her bindings, she let out a whimper. The skin on her wrists and ankles was already burned raw from her attempts at freeing herself and all the shaking her body was doing only made things worse.

The warehouse was empty save for a pillar across from her and a small table behind that. On the table were several tubes, a collection of plastic baggies, a small plastic bin, and something silver and shiny Heather couldn't quite make out.

Probably some sort of evil witch torture device.

I'm going to die. I'm going to die. I'm going to die—

No.

Heather took a deep breath and tried to think about something else. Anything else.

Like ponies.

Ponies were a happy thought. They were nice and gentle and they never kidnapped people or strapped them to cold warehouse pillars.

Ponies, ponies, ponies—

"Tie him up by the girl and for God's sake don't kill him!" Clare's—er, Raven's—voice was like nails on a chalkboard as it floated into Heather's ears.

Any attempts to think of ponies came to an abrupt halt.

A thud. Some shuffling. And soon three Ashmen emerged from the warehouse shadows with a large, unconscious Gabriel in their hands.

Dragging him to the pillar across from her, they tied Gabriel up in the same fashion as Heather and stiffly exited, leaving them alone.

Heather perked up and hope soared in her chest.

Gabriel is immortal! He can totally bust out of his ropes and find a way to get us out of this hell-hole-warehouse-dungeon place before the wicked witch comes back—

Drool dribbled from his mouth and ran down his chin.

Heather slumped back against the pillar.

Or maybe not.

Sighing in despair, she shook at her impossible ties again. Was this Raven chick an ex-sailor or something? These were like ninja knots.

Giving up on the ropes, she stared at Gabriel's body and whispered as violently as she could, "Gabriel!"

He made an *mmph* noise.

"Gabriel!" she whispered again.

He slurped up the drool, but didn't respond.

Heather turned her voice up full volume. "Gabriel Michael Archer, wake up this minute!"

With his eyes still closed, he grumbled, "My middle name isn't Michael."

"I don't care. Wake up!" she snapped. "We need to get out of here before crazy Raven and her dead minions of ash come back."

He opened his eyes and blinked in confusion. "What the hell?" He looked up and tugged at the bindings on his hands. "Where are we?"

"Raven's den of horrors," Heather said. "Turns out my boss—you remember sweet ol' Clare from the carnival?—yeah, she's Raven and she's addicted to fountain water and she's *cra-zy*." She sang this last word. "She kidnapped us and now we're her captives. Which is not sexy, despite the very spy-like feeling this whole situation has to it."

"Raven is addicted to fountain water?"

"Really?" She glared at him. "That's what you took away from everything I just told you? Focus, Gabriel. We need to get out of here!" She shook her ties again, biting back another whimper at her burning skin.

Gabriel kicked at the ropes around his feet and growled in frustration when they wouldn't loosen. He turned his attention to his wrists, hung from a hook above his head like Heather, and started twisting against the crappy rope that bound them, grunting and yanking.

Heather gave up on her ties, her skin too raw to withstand any more friction, and watched Gabriel try to bend his body out of the knots for several minutes. Without success.

With a curse, he stopped wrestling with the ropes and fell back against the pillar.

Heather looked him over, taking in his appearance. "Why is your shirt all bloody?"

He exhaled. "Because while you were at the carnival passing out coffee and smiling at clowns, I was getting jumped by a crew of Ashmen with Bluestone weapons."

Heather lifted a brow. "I'd feel sorry for you except I spent most of the night tied to a tree in a *graveyard* while my boss shot and *killed Laura* and then proceeded to beat the *crap* out of my best friend. So yeah. I'm fresh out of sympathy."

His eyes shot to hers. "Is Scarlet okay?"

"I don't know." Heather swallowed. "I hope so."

She tried not to think about Scarlet unconscious in the cemetery. Scarlet was tough. She was fine, right?

Right?

Heather's body started to shake again. She tried to calm down, focusing on a new splotch of blood seeping through Gabriel's shirt.

"You—you haven't started healing yet," she noted.

"Nope," he said bitterly. "I will soon, though. Hopefully." He grit his teeth as he shifted against the pillar and they hung in silence for a few minutes.

Heather's body stopped shaking.

Gabriel kept scouring the warehouse like some magical escape plan was written on the walls.

Looking down at her bare feet, Heather frowned. The expensive pink heels she'd had on earlier had been casualties of all the ashy kidnapping and mayhem.

So sad.

She pressed her lips together as she watched Gabriel's eyes dart around the room. "Any awesome escape plans yet?"

"The only plan I had was the wrestling out of the ropes thing. So no."

Drat.

More silence.

Heather licked her lips. "You know what would be really nice right now? Coffee. I could really go for some coffee."

Just the idea made her salivate.

He scowled. "How can you even think about coffee right now?"

"I don't know. Maybe caffeine is how I cope." She thought for a moment. "Although usually I'm a crier. Are you a crier?"

"No."

"Not even at sad movies or weddings?"

"No."

"What about commercials with little puppies that need a home?"

He blinked. "Please stop talking."

"Hmm," she said slowly. "Maybe *talking* is how I cope." Her hands started falling asleep. "You know what else would be really nice right now?"

"An off button?"

"Super powers," she said. "It would be really helpful if your immortalness came with super powers. Like maybe super strength or the ability to burn rope with your eyeballs."

"Yes, well, I'll be sure to ask for the upgraded package next time." He stretched his neck and Heather noticed a red mark next to his Adam's apple.

"What happened to your throat?"

"Raven shot me with some kind of dart."

"They were tranq darts." Raven's high heels echoed through the large room as she entered and came to a stop between the two pillars. She looked at Gabriel. "I had to use a few of them, actually, because you heal so quickly. Very inconvenient." She sighed. "But it worked and you looked so peaceful, all passed out and vulnerable on the way here. It made me miss the old days. Watching you sleep beside me."

Heather wrinkled her nose.

Gag me.

Wait no. I've already been gagged tonight and it's not pleasant.

Sometimes Gabriel's eyebrows were happy. Other times, they were concerned or annoyed. But right now, poised above his brown eyes like batwings, Gabriel's eyebrows were mad. Mad eyebrows.

"What do you want, Raven?" His voice was lower than usual. Meaner.

"You haven't seen me for half a millennium and that's your opening question?" Raven put a hand on her hip. "Aren't you curious as to what I've been up to? Don't you want to know where I've lived and all I've seen?"

"I want to know how you're alive. Especially since I killed you."

Heather blinked.

Gabriel had killed Raven?

Well, *that* certainly had never come up at the lunch table before.

A little heads up would have been nice.

Hey Heather, since we're history partners and all I figured I should tell you I'm a murderer. But I'm hot, so it's okay.

From now on, Heather was going to do background checks on all her buddies.

"You *tried* to kill me," Raven corrected. "But since I had fountain water in my veins when you broke my neck—real classy, by the way—I managed to survive."

He narrowed his eyes. "Where did you get fountain water?"

She gave him a secretive smile. "In the wall of my family's house."

"You stole the vial?"

"Is it really stealing if the vial belonged to my family? I think not."

Gabriel stared at her. "How have you survived this long on a single vial of fountain water?"

She shrugged. "Magic." She pulled a syringe of something blue from her bosom—apparently her bra also doubled as a purse—and held it up. "I thinned out the fountain water and multiplied it with spells. And now I'm down to my last dose." She looked at the syringe with hunger in her eyes.

Like it was heroin, Raven set the needle tip to the inside of her elbow and injected herself with the blue water. Her eyes rolled back into her head for a moment before she blinked her way out of the bliss and tossed the empty syringe on the table.

She turned back to Gabriel. "It must be so depressing to see me alive after all these years. You were so *angry* the night you broke my neck."

He had his evil eyebrows back on. "Yes. Because you killed my father."

"Well, he was awful."

"And you shot Tristan."

"Complete accident."

"And then you cursed me and killed Scarlet."

She shrugged. "Those last two may have been a bit rash of me."

"Rash? *Rash*? I haven't been able to fall in love for five hundred years."

"You could have loved me." She spread her palm against his bloody shirt and five purple-painted nails crawled their way up his chest to his face.

He thrust his face away and smacked his head into the pillar.

Raven pouted her lips. "Poor thing. You're not nearly as magnificent when you're all tied up." She winked. "Not like this anyway."

Nasty, nasty, nasty.

Heather was judging Gabriel on so many levels tonight.

Pulling her hand back from Gabriel's chest, Raven made a face at the blood that now stained her fingertips. She wiped her hand on his jeans until the blood was all gone.

Gabriel watched her with narrowed eyes and slowly said, "You look *old*."

Heather's mouth fell open.

Good God. Don't anger the crazy lady.

Raven slapped him, hard. "That's what happens when your supply of fountain water starts to run out and you have to dilute it. You *age*. Magic can only do so much."

"Sucks to be you," Gabriel said.

Clearly, he did not value his life.

Raven looked Gabriel up and down for a moment, then walked to the table behind his pillar and retrieved the shiny, silver object Heather had spied earlier.

Scissors. Not a torture device.

Not *yet* anyway. Gabriel was doing a pretty good job of provoking the witch, so there was a good chance she was about to cut him into bite-sized pieces of immortal deliciousness and feed him to the myriad of black cats she no doubt had stashed in the back alongside her broomstick and bubbling caldron.

Raven walked back up to Gabriel and started cutting off his shirt.

WTF?

If things got kinky, Heather was totally going to vomit.

Gabriel's eyes followed Raven's hands as she peeled the shirt off his bloodied body. Some of the matted fabric caught in his chest wound and Raven ripped it out.

He winced. "What are you doing?"

She tossed the stained shirt to the floor. "I need to make sure your cuts aren't deep enough to kill you."

"How very thoughtful of you," Gabriel said between his teeth as she prodded the cut on his shoulder.

With a satisfied nod, she went back to the table and grabbed a needle, some tubing, and a baggie before heading back to Gabriel.

Was she going to play doctor now?

Sweet mercy.

Worst hostage situation ever.

Raven shoved Gabriel's head to the side and sank the needle into his jugular, hitching the tubing to it so blood could pump from his body to the plastic baggie at the end of the tube.

Okay weird.

Gabriel stared out the corner of his eye at where blood flowed from his neck, wisely keeping his mouth shut as the crazy witch took his blood. When Raven decided she had enough, she withdrew the needle and unhooked the tubes.

Sealing Gabriel's blood into the bag, she placed it in the bin on the table and turned to leave.

"Oh. One last thing." Raven stopped in her tracks and walked back to Gabriel. Reaching for his head, she broke his neck in one swift twist.

Heather blinked in shock as Gabriel's body went limp against the pillar and his head lopped to the side in an unnatural way. A small trickle of blood oozed from his neck where the needle had just been as Raven's heels tapped their way out of the room.

Heather knew a broken neck wouldn't kill an immortal, but she couldn't seem to keep her body from shaking as she stared at his lifeless form. If Raven had no problem hurting Gabriel, how much more callous would she be with Heather?

Ponies, ponies, ponies.

3

Gabriel was not at the Millhouse. Or the fair. Or anywhere else that made sense, and Tristan's fear was mounting by the minute. Walking along the perimeter of the coffee shop, he followed the sidewalk and tried to retrace his brother's steps.

A small patch of ash caught his eye and he followed it around a corner to find an alley dotted with more piles of ash.

But no sign of Gabriel.

Nate came up behind him with Scarlet. "Where do you think he went?"

Scarlet said, "Maybe he went to find us."

Tristan spied Gabriel's knife discarded on the ground and his gut churned as he picked it up. "He wouldn't have left unarmed."

Nate caught sight of something else on the ground and bent to retrieve the small object.

"What's that?" Scarlet stepped closer.

"I think it's a tranquilizer dart." Nate turned it over in his hand.

More churning.

"Do you think someone drugged Gabriel?"

"Maybe Raven wanted to take him hostage," Nate said slowly. "Like Heather. The tranq dart is a good sign, though. It means she doesn't want to kill him."

Tristan fisted his hands and Nate eyed his white knuckles. "Don't stress, man. We'll find him."

"How?" Tristan snapped, his chest hot with fear. "How are we going to find him, Nate? With our Gabriel tracking device?"

"Ooh! A tracking device would have been a good idea." Nate nodded. "Next time."

Tristan started pacing. Why would Raven take Gabriel? *Where* would she take him? And why the hell wasn't she dead?

From the corner of his eye, he saw Scarlet run a shaky hand through her hair. He stopped pacing and tried to feel her, forgetting the curse had shifted and he was no longer privy to her feelings.

Funny how he used to think of his connection to her as punishment, taunting him with what he could never have. But now, without her emotions running through him, he felt empty and lost.

Her eyes moved to his and their gazes locked for a brief moment. A flicker of unease crossed her face and she turned away.

Tristan's chest tightened.

She was hiding something. Something big.

"Raven probably has Heather and Gabriel in the same place," Nate said, "so we just need to narrow down possible hiding spots. I say we do a background check on 'Clare' and see if she owns any dungeons or other bad guy haunts.

Avalon's not that big. We'll find Gabriel and Heather in two, three days tops."

Tristan pulled his eyes away from Scarlet and stared at Nate. "Two or three days in captivity with a psychotic witch might kill them. We need to find them now." He exited the alley and headed for his car.

"And your plan is what?" Nate said as he and Scarlet followed after him. "You're just going to drive around until you see a sign that says *Raven's Secret Hostage Lair*?"

Tristan wasn't sure what he was going to do, but hanging out in an alley all night certainly wasn't going to bring Gabriel back any faster. "What's the alternative? Go back home, eat some Lucky Charms, and get some sleep? I don't think so."

"Why are you hating on my cereal?"

"I think Nate's right," Scarlet said as they reached the car. "We can't just drive around aimlessly. We need a plan. At least we know from the tranq dart that Raven doesn't want to kill them, so that buys us some time to find them."

"Yes." Nate nodded. "Let's go back to the cabin and *plan*."

Tristan didn't like this idea. Not at all.

But he also didn't know where to look for Gabriel, so any argument he hoped to have on behalf of his driving around aimlessly plan fell dead.

"Fine," he muttered, climbing into the driver's seat.

Nate jumped into the backseat while Scarlet slid into the passenger's seat and tried to buckle her seatbelt. It wouldn't latch. The passenger's seatbelt had taken a beating when Tristan had remodeled the shack and now the latch only worked if you jiggled it the right way.

Scarlet wasn't jiggling it the right way.

Tristan reached over to help her and she swatted at his hand. "I can put on my own seatbelt."

He pulled his hand back and rested an arm on the steering wheel as he watched her struggle with the clasp.

"Mother of Pearl," she muttered, fighting with the belt.

She jiggled. She jaggled. Then she groaned in frustration and dropped her head against the seat.

Tristan waited a beat. "Are you done now?"

She sighed. "Yes."

He held out his hand in the dark car. "Give me the seatbelt."

She yanked the belt across her body and handed it to Tristan with a huff, careful not to touch him. He had to bite the inside of his cheek so he wouldn't smile. She was just as stubborn as the seatbelt.

He eased the seatbelt into the broken latch and it clicked effortlessly.

She rolled her eyes as he started the car. "So where should we start with Raven?"

"We could find out where she lives?" Nate suggested.

Tristan shook his head. "She wouldn't take Gabriel and Heather to her house. And she wouldn't leave any clues as to where she *was* taking them at her house either."

Nate frowned. "What makes you so sure?"

He shrugged. "Because I wouldn't do those things if I was going to kidnap someone."

Nate blinked at him. "Sometimes I worry about you."

"If I were to kidnap someone," Scarlet mused, "I would probably take them someplace nearby to cut down on travel. And it would probably be someplace in the middle of nowhere where Ashmen could come and go without drawing too much attention."

Nate stared at them. "Now I'm worried about both of you."

Scarlet continued. "Maybe Raven rented a house or a car—"

"Or a dungeon," Nate said.

"If we could see where she's spent her money in the past few months, we might have a better idea of where Gabriel and Heather are," Tristan said. "But we'd need access to Raven's financial records."

"Ooh! There's an app for that," Nate said cheerily, reaching into his pocket.

Tristan and Scarlet turned to stare at him.

"Just kidding." He grinned as he pulled out his phone. "But I can probably hack into Clare's bank accounts."

"You can?"

Nate shrugged as he started tapping things into his phone. "You can do anything with hacking software these days. You can even figure out the code for beating the water demon in the new Warrior Vikings game." He tapped a few more buttons. "So jj514hero can suck it."

Scarlet wrinkled her nose. "Who's jj514hero?"

"My arch nemesis in the gaming world who *claims* to live in Tokyo, but I tracked his user ID back to San Francisco." He muttered, "Little liar."

More button pushing and soon Nate held up his phone and smiled. "Tada. The Avalon bank account of a Ms. Clare Blackbird. Clever last name." He scoffed. "*Not*."

"Let me see that." Scarlet took the phone and started reading through the charges. She sighed. "There's nothing unusual in her purchase history."

Nate took back the phone. "So we'll start looking through other Clare Blackbird things." He shook his head. "Seriously. Worst name ever."

When they reached the cabin, they went inside and Nate immediately headed upstairs. "I'm just going to take a quick shower to rinse all the ash and blood off my skin and then we'll start our Raven investigation."

Scarlet looked down at her dirty shirt and hands as Tristan walked to the kitchen.

He pulled off his coat and threw it on a barstool, grimacing at the sharp aches in his back and chest where his Bluestone cuts were. Knowing it was probably going to be a long night of research and nothingness, Tristan started making coffee.

A quiet gasp—almost too quiet to hear—came from the stairs and he frowned. Who was—

Dammit.

He rushed to the stairs and found Scarlet halfway to the second floor, eyes squeezed shut and a hand braced against the wall. At his nearness, she opened her eyes and leaned against the wall in a casual way. Like she hadn't just been in excruciating pain.

"What's up?" she said pleasantly.

He glared at her. "You're supposed to stay by me."

"Don't scold me," she snapped.

He pursed his lips. "I can't feel you anymore, Scar. There's no way for me to know if you're in pain unless you tell me."

"It's not your job to keep me out of pain. And I should certainly be able to be a few rooms away from you without being in agony. Agh." She shook out her hands. "Is this what it was like for you?"

He looked at her sympathetically. "No. The pain might be the same, but I was never as bound to your proximity as you are to mine. Why are you going upstairs?"

"To take a shower."

He lifted an angry brow. "In Gabriel's bathroom?"

She put a hand on her hip. "The main floor bathroom doesn't have a shower."

Tristan tried not to clench his jaw. "The basement does."

"Yes. But the basement is yours. And since I'm like your own personal Grim Reaper, I thought it would be smarter if I showered upstairs."

He crossed his arms. "Well it's not smarter. It's painful. Come back downstairs."

"Don't tell me what to do."

He shoved the heels of his palms into his eyes with a groan. "I couldn't tell you what to do even if I tried. Which I have." He dropped his hands and gave her a hard look. "Many, many times."

She smiled tightly. "And yet you're still ordering me around."

He jutted his jaw. "Would you stop arguing and come down the stairs? You can take a shower in my bathroom and I'll stay in the basement so you're not thrashing about in pain. Come on."

She didn't move.

God, she was stubborn. And wonderful.

"Please?" he said.

With a drawn-out exhale, she stepped down the stairs. Their eyes briefly met as she moved past him and she darted them away just as fast.

Tristan felt the uneasiness in his chest return as he followed her to the basement. He watched her fingers trail down the handrail as she descended the stairs.

"Why are you standing so close behind me?" she said.

"Why are you hiding things from me?" he countered as they reached the basement floor.

She flipped around, her long hair brushing his dirty shirt as she faced him with blue eyes filled with determination. "I'm not."

He stared at her until she took a step back and met the wall, her eyes just as hard as his.

He closed the distance between them and rested his forearms against the wall on either side of her head, caging her in as he brought his face close to hers.

"I don't have to feel you," his said in a low voice, "to know when you're lying."

He watched her hard eyes flicker with something—pain, maybe? Sadness?—before falling to his mouth.

His heart stopped beating.

Bad idea. He was way too close to her. Close enough to feel her hot breath feather across his chin as she exhaled. Close enough to see the beating pulse at the base of her throat.

Close enough to touch her...

Her eyes shot back to his with renewed hardness and she ducked underneath his left arm. "Let it go, Tristan." She marched to his room.

"No." He pushed off the wall and followed her to his bedroom.

Another poorly thought-out idea.

He crossed his arms and focused on the situation at hand. "Not until you tell me what's going on."

She glowered at him. "Nothing is going on. I'm just nervous about Heather. And Gabriel. And Raven and everything."

"Right."

Her eyes flared. "Why are you mad at me?"

"I'm worried about you."

She threw her arms in the air. "There's nothing to worry about!"

"Bullshit." He moved past her into his master bathroom and turned on the shower so the water would warm up. "I can't protect you if you won't be honest with me—"

"I don't need your protection!"

He shook his head with an angry smile as he left the bathroom and walked to the dresser by his bed. "That's right. Scarlet doesn't need anything." He pulled out a soft T-shirt and a pair of running pants. "Scarlet can do whatever she wants and keep all her little secrets to herself and run away and die." He gave a jerky shrug as he turned to face her. "Because who cares who you hurt in the process of all your deception? It's all about Scarlet, after all."

"You should talk." She narrowed her eyes at him across the bed. "Just last year, you tried to *kill* yourself!"

"To save you!"

"I don't need you to save me, Tristan! I need you to trust me!"

"Trust you? The last time I *trusted* you, you disappeared and died!" His voice nearly cracked. "You died alone and terrified and there was *nothing* I could do about it." Fear clogged up his veins as he threw the T-shirt and pants on the bed. "I don't want to trust you, Scar. I want to keep you alive!"

"What are those?" She pointed at the clothes.

"Your pajamas!" He turned and left the room, slamming the door behind him.

****

Gabriel regained consciousness and rolled his neck as his bones mended themselves. Now he was pissed.

He opened his eyes and found Heather still hanging across from him, her eyes squeezed shut as she muttered something about ponies.

"Why are you chanting about horses?"

Her eyes flew open. "Gabriel! Oh, thank God! I thought you were almost dead or something."

"Nope." He felt his neck finally crack back into place and winced at the last sharp pain of healing. "Still alive."

"I can't believe Raven did that to you. What a beast. When we get rescued by a crew of hot SWAT guys—because that's how it goes down in my head; a shirtless SWAT team will rescue us—"

"A SWAT team is not going to rescue us—"

"A *shirtless* SWAT team," she said, raising her voice, "will rappel into the warehouse and rescue me and my pink shoes—but not you, because you don't believe in shirtless SWAT teams—and when they do, I'm totally going to slap Raven The Beast with a piece of this sandpaper rope." She jostled her arm restraints.

"Yeah. That'll show her."

"B-T-W," Heather said. "What's with the death wish?"

"What are you talking about?"

"I'm talking about provoking the wicked witch of the west. *You look old?* Are you trying to get us both killed?"

"She does look old. Or at least older than she used to."

"It doesn't matter! Two things you never comment on when it comes to girls: their age and their weight. That's male survival 101. Come on!"

Gabriel rolled his eyes and tuned her out as he started wrestling with the ties around his wrists again, twisting and yanking in the hopes they might snap under the tension and free him.

"That's right," Heather said dryly, watching him with bored eyes. "Just keep jiggling the ropes. Maybe they'll magically untie themselves this time."

He growled. "I have to try. I don't like being Raven's plaything."

"You mean you don't like being her plaything when it's not consensual." She wrinkled her nose. "I can't believe you slept with her, Gabriel. That's so gross."

"It was five hundred years ago."

"Still gross."

He concentrated on the ropes around his body. He was going to kill Raven. No. First he was going to break her neck—again. *Then* he was going to kill her.

He struggled a minute longer before falling back against the pillar in annoyance. They hung in silence, but every few minutes Heather would sigh heavily or make a throaty noise.

He looked her over for a minute. Her blond hair hung in matted curls around her head and the pink dress she wore led down to a pair of bare feet with matching pink toenails, making her look like a large, dirty baby doll.

She made another throat noise.

Gabriel stared at her. "Must you huff and puff every two minutes? Can't you just hang in bitterness and betrayal like me without making throaty sounds?"

"Oh, I'm sorry. Are my *throaty sounds* bothering you? I'll be sure to zip them right up so your stay at the Hostage Hotel from Hell is more enjoyable," she said. "I'm dirty and tired and I'm pretty sure I'm starting to hallucinate because, a second ago, I saw a cup of coffee hovering above your head. So I'll huff and puff if I want to!"

"Wow." He nodded. "Your coffee habit is ridiculous."

"Shut up."

He looked around with a sigh. "Why do you think Raven kidnapped us?"

"She wants the map to the Fountain of Youth. I think Scarlet is supposed to hand the map over to Raven in return for our lives. Or at least, my life. I have no idea why Raven kidnapped you—other than to take off your clothes and feel you up."

"Hello children," called a deceptively friendly voice from the other side of the warehouse. Raven stepped into sight and winked at Gabriel. "Hanging in there?"

He sneered at her.

"Don't do that, lover." She tsked. "It distorts that handsome face of yours." She looked at his neck. "Looks like you're all better. Now we're even."

Not even close, whack job.

She skimmed his neck with her fingers.

"Stop touching me," he said.

She gripped his throat and squeezed for a moment, her sharp nails sinking into his skin as she cut off his oxygen.

"Be nice, Gabriel," she said with a smile as he choked. Then she released him.

Walking over to the table, Raven picked up the needle and tubing she'd used on him before and injected the needle into him again. Soon a steady stream of red flowed from his neck into a second plastic blood bag.

He tilted his head to better watch her. "What are you going to do with my blood?"

"Get my every wish."

Cryptic.

Awesome.

Finished with his blood, Raven undid the needle and tubing from Gabriel's body and glanced at the door. "Guards!"

Five Ashmen entered the room and obediently stood guard in a circle around Heather and Gabriel.

"Nighty-night," Raven said before exiting the room.

Heather's mouth hung open. "She's leaving us here all night?"

Gabriel pursed his lips. "I'm pretty sure that's how the whole kidnap/ransom thing works."

Heather wrinkled her nose at the nearest Ashman. "Well this sucks."

A few minutes of silence passed before Heather made another throaty noise.

Gabriel blinked at her. "Seriously?"

"Shut up," she huffed.

It was going to be a long night.

****

Scarlet's body was clean, but her conscience felt dirty. Very dirty.

Tristan knew. Well, he didn't *know*, but he knew. And Scarlet didn't know how long she'd be able to keep his curious eyes from diving into her soul and coaxing out her secret.

Judging by how very much she'd enjoyed the Tristan tent he'd trapped her in when they'd been in the basement hallway, not long.

They were in the office now, with Nate sitting at the desk staring at a computer screen and Scarlet and Tristan standing behind him on either side. They'd been trying to pinpoint possible Raven locations for the past hour.

Tristan stood with his arms crossed. He'd showered after her and was now wearing a black T-shirt and faded jeans, and his dark hair was still wet and fell around his head in a tousled way that was too sexy for his own good.

Scarlet wanted to run her hands through it—but oh wait. That could kill him.

Definitely too sexy for his own good.

He looked up at her with his green *don't-lie-to-me-woman* eyes and Scarlet dropped her guilty gaze to the mahogany desktop, searching around until she found a paperweight shaped like a pyramid to stare at.

"I'll keep looking," Nate said. "But it might be a good idea to head to Laura's house tomorrow and ransack the place looking for any clues as to where Raven might hole up with an immortal guy and an overdressed, blond barista."

Scarlet could still feel Tristan's eyes boring into her.

Paperweights were so interesting.

Nate sighed and looked at the time. "It's only three hours until morning and we haven't really made any progress, so I think it's best if we all try to get some rest so we're not completely useless tomorrow."

Scarlet blinked away from the pyramid.

Right.

Like she was going to get any sleep knowing her best friend was probably in the trunk of Raven's car. At least Gabriel was with her, probably, so Heather wasn't facing the crazy witch alone.

As everyone exited the office, Scarlet headed for the stairs. She'd had to roll over the waistband of Tristan's pajama pants four times to keep them from falling off her small hips, but still they dragged on the floor.

And his shirt—his *shirt*. It smelled like him and wrapped around her body like warm hands gliding over her skin, swishing as she walked. It was all she could do not to shove the material into her nose and inhale like a crazy person.

Why did he have to smell so good? Why couldn't he smell like burnt toast or nail polish remover? It would be a lot easier to keep from shoving the shirt up her nostrils if it smelled like rubbing alcohol.

But this leather smell...

This nostalgic *I live in the wild and hunt in my free time and bathe in rushing rivers* smell was going to kill her. It was literally going to waft into her lungs and kill her with want and need and lack of oxygen.

She yanked at the large shirt, pulling it as far down from her nose as she could as she walked down the hallway and descended the stairs to the basement.

Tristan followed so close behind her she could feel his hot breath on the back of her neck. Again.

"Ten foot rule," called Nate.

"Bite me!" Tristan hollered back, more hot breath caressing her skin with his words.

A wonderful shiver ran through her body.

Damn him and his beautiful mouth and hot breath and his leather-smelling shirt.

She assumed he was headed to his own room in the basement, but when she walked into the guest bedroom, he followed her inside. She turned around to tell him to leave her alone, but his bright green eyes derailed her words.

He was so pretty...

No! No. He was not pretty. He was in danger of dying.

Focus on the danger, Scarlet.

She glared at him. "What are you doing?"

"I'm sleeping with you."

Was he insane?

She lifted a brow. "I thought you were mad at me."

"I'm *concerned*. Not mad."

"Huh. Well either way. you're not sleeping with me."

"Yes, I am."

He was insane.

"No," Scarlet repeated. "You're not. You could die, Tristan. We can't touch and we certainly can't...sleep together." She felt her face flush.

A look of amusement crossed his face. "I meant *sleep*, Scar."

"Oh. Well." She cleared her throat. "I don't want to wake up next to a corpse, so, like...scram."

"No."

She moved to push him out the door—on the off chance that she'd suddenly obtained superhuman strength and would be able to move his big body—but he reflexively drew back from her hands, keeping himself from her reach.

He froze for a moment and stared at her hands in a weird way.

"What?" She suddenly felt nervous and dropped her arms.

His lips parted in awe as he tilted his head to the side and looked her over.

Happiness. Relief. Wonder... His emotions were all warm and fuzzy.

"Tristan, why are you—"

"I don't have to keep away from you anymore," he said in realization. "My touch no longer hurts you."

His eyes traced back down her neck and he reached his hand out.

Oh crap.

Scarlet opened her mouth to protest, but his soft fingertips stroked along her jaw and she forgot what speaking was. Liquid warmth slid into her skin beneath his hand, swirling into her stomach and drying out her throat, and Scarlet had never felt anything so amazing.

His fingers trailed down her neck and softly stroked up and down her throat, his eyes watching the movement in complete fascination. She absently lifted her chin, giving his fingers more room to roam as her eyes fluttered with the curse-granted pleasure his touch brought.

"This," he moved his hand to her mouth and ran his thumb across her lower lip, "doesn't hurt you." He spoke softly and every fiber in Scarlet's body tightened with desire. "My touch isn't dangerous anymore."

Oh, his touch was dangerous. Very, very dangerous.

He could die.

Scarlet's eyes fell shut as his hand trailed down to the collar of the shirt that smelled like him and drew a hot line along the exposed bit of her collarbone.

"You have no idea how wonderful it is to be able to touch you without hurting you." The pads of his fingers moved back up her throat.

She was starting to sink into a deep and dreamy pleasure...

He could *die*.

With a strangled inhale, Scarlet opened her eyes. "Stop," she commanded. "You could die."

His fingers halted their traveling and he slowly drew his hand away. Scarlet willed her body to calm down as Tristan continued to stare at her in wonderment.

"So, yeah." She swallowed. "Why don't you back up like two hundred feet and go sleep in your own bed, and I'll stay here." *And try to get my heart under control.*

He took one step back—not two hundred—and frowned at her, all wonderment gone from his face as he shook his head. "The pain is worse at night, Scar. If I stay with you, you won't hurt so much and you'll be able to sleep."

"If you stay with me, you'll get sick." She shooed him away with her hand, growing irritated. "Quit trying to die. I can handle pain."

"I know you can, but I don't want you to."

She sighed. "Your bedroom is right next door. I'll be fine. Go."

He didn't move.

"Tristan. Come on."

He hesitated, looking her over. *Fear, concern, love, frustration.*

"Fine," he finally said and turned to leave the room. At the doorway, he stopped. "But I swear to God, Scar. If I hear you in here crying or something, I will break down your door and tie you to my body."

Her cheeks flushed again.

"Thanks for the warning." She smiled tightly. "Now, get out."

Scarlet locked the door behind him before crawling into the big, white guest bed, images of being tied to Tristan's body floating through her head.

Damn him.

She wrapped herself under the plush comforter, but knew it was useless. She wouldn't be sleeping.

Too much had happened. Too much was yet to come.

With a heavy sigh, she stared at the ceiling and tried to figure out what she was going to do about the fountain. She stared and thought and stared and thought. She shifted uncomfortably as pain slid up and down her body like a slab of cheese on a grater, growing more intense by the minute.

She stared and thought and ignored the cheese grater for an hour before she couldn't help but bunch her body into a ball against the pain and bite back a curse. The white bed creaked as she tried to get more comfortable.

It felt like her muscles were twisting together and pulling apart at the same time. Her head hurt. And her lungs were tight—like air was impossible without Tristan. But he was only one room away.

Certainly he hadn't been in this much pain when she'd been so close in the past. Right? Why was her connection to him so much more intense than his connection had ever been to her?

She tossed and turned, the bed creaking with each of her movements, until she heard Tristan's bedroom door open. She froze, afraid he'd break down her door and try to snuggle or something. Which would be...well, it would be awesome. But it would also be stupid. He'd better not try to be stupid.

Scarlet listened for a few more minutes, but when there was nothing but silence in the basement and she was sure Tristan had gone back to bed, she let out a long exhale and went back to staring at the ceiling again.

Her pain subsided a bit. Not much, but enough for Scarlet to stop thinking about cheese graters.

She inhaled deeply, smelling Tristan on her shirt and fighting back the sharp pain of sorrow that bit into her heart as she thought about the Fountain of Youth.

The minutes dragged on and—against every desire she had to stay awake and worry about Heather and Gabriel and the curse and the fountain—Scarlet fell into a fitful sleep.

Tristan would never forgive her for what she was going to do.

4

England 1539

It had been five days since Raven had killed Scarlet and Tristan was drunk.

Again.

It was late in the evening and Gabriel sat in the throne room, watching his twin brother stumble through the doors with a jug of wine.

Tristan pointed a wobbly finger at Gabriel. "You may be in need of a new court healer. Your current one just ran away."

Gabriel hung his head. "What did you do to him, Tristan?"

He chugged at the wine. "I merely asked him what form of magic could make a body disappear." He took another swig. "I may have also threatened his well-being if he refused to tell me all he knew."

Gabriel pinched the bridge of his nose. "You cannot continue threatening the servants. They do not have the answers you seek."

"But they do!" Tristan swung his arms out and wine sloshed from the jug onto the floor. "They must! Bodies do not disappear, Gabriel! They wither and dry up, but they do not vanish!"

Two mysterious things had occurred after Raven had shot Scarlet.

The arrow she'd shot had first gone through Tristan's body—which he'd thrown in front of the arrow to protect Scarlet—yet he was fine, save for the abnormally green hue his eyes had taken on since that day.

And Scarlet's body—which had been pierced through her heart despite Tristan's best efforts—had fallen dead. Yet shortly after, her body completely disappeared.

Gabriel could not explain either phenomenon. A body that healed itself was almost as mysterious as a body that vanished. But Tristan seemed to care little about his ability to self-heal.

"Bodies do not vanish!" Tristan repeated, and the ring of desperation in his voice had Gabriel drawing in a long, patient breath. Tristan had loved Scarlet and, when he was sent away from her, asked Gabriel to marry and care for her on his behalf.

Only to have Scarlet die on their wedding day.

"You should go to bed, brother," Gabriel said. "You are too drunk for conversation."

"On the contrary, brother. I am not drunk enough." He turned his attention to the wall and muttered, "I am never drunk enough."

Gabriel watched as Tristan walked the length of the side wall, his footfalls echoing around the room as he stared intently at the royal weapons hung in pride alongside tapestries and flags.

"*I know you're in pain, Tristan. And I know you loved Scarlet. I loved her too—*"

Tristan's eyes shot across the room and ran through Gabriel like a blade. "*You do not know love as I know love.*"

Gabriel sighed and leaned back in the throne. "*Are we going to be dramatic now? Maybe I shall call for some wine of my own and we can both wallow and aimlessly fight through our miserable drunkenness.*"

Tristan turned a hazy smile to him. "*Ah, yes. You are the earl now. I forget this sometimes.* Earl Archer.*"* Though he tried to pronounce the title carefully, it slurred on his lips.

Tristan's eyes went back to the wall and he reached above his head to lift a sword from its hook. He took another pull of wine before tossing the jug to the floor, a trickle of red liquid dripping from its spout.

"*I enjoy weapons.*" Tristan turned the sword over in his loose hands. "*They make me feel powerful. Capable.*"

Curse the stars, was he rambling now?

"*Yes, well, that particular weapon is an heirloom, so if you would be so kind as to replace it—*"

"*Did you touch her?*" Tristan's lax body language stiffened, but his eyes stayed on the blade.

"*What?*" Gabriel tried to sound exasperated, but his stomach tightened ever so slightly. This was not a conversation he wanted to have with a drunk Tristan—especially when that drunk Tristan was holding a sharp object.

"*Scarlet.*" He ran a lazy finger down the edge of the sword. "*Did you touch her?*"

Gabriel paused for a long moment. "*Does it matter?*"

Tristan inhaled long and slow through his nostrils as he looked up at the ceiling. "*I haven't decided.*"

Rubbing the side of his face, Gabriel said, "You are drunk. Now is not the time—"

"Did she touch you?"

Oh, for the love.

"Tristan, we were engaged. And might I remind you, it was your idea for me to marry her."

"Yes." Tristan shifted the sword to his other hand. "I believe I asked you to care for her. To protect her."

Gabriel moved uncomfortably in his seat.

"Yet somehow," Tristan continued, looking at the hilt of the blade as he squeezed the handle, "Scarlet ended up dead."

Tension filled the room.

Tristan's voice was deceptively soft as he looked at Gabriel. "You let your whore kill the woman I loved."

"I did not let Raven do anything. Scarlet was my wife—"

Just like that, Tristan was upon him, the sword pointed right at Gabriel's throat and held by the very steady hand of a very broken man.

Tristan's voice was low and hard, his slur completely gone. "She was not your wife." His eyes darkened. "She was not yours at all."

Gabriel did not breathe for fear the movement would bring his throat against the blade. He knew Tristan would never harm him, but he also knew what it felt like to lose a loved one.

Just months ago, when word had come that Tristan had died in battle, Gabriel had been turned inside out and made hollow and fierce with the notion that he would never again see his brother. To lose his best friend—to lose a piece of his blood and soul—had been unfathomable. Tristan's "death" had nearly destroyed Gabriel.

And it seemed Scarlet's death was wreaking the same havoc upon Tristan: breaking him down, emptying all he was, driving him to desperation.

It was not Tristan who stood with a blade to Gabriel's throat, but rather his broken heart. Gabriel understood this, even if Tristan did not.

Calmly, slowly, Gabriel answered, "I did not touch her."

It was the truth and, although he knew it would not ease the ache in his brother's chest, Gabriel knew it would at least remove the sword from his neck.

Tristan paused. Then whipped away from Gabriel, dropping the sword to the ground as he started for the throne room doors.

Gabriel ran a hand across his face. Whatever would he do with his wrecked, unstable brother with new, green eyes and a body that could magically heal itself—

"Wait." Gabriel called after Tristan, a memory hitting him. "Do you remember when we were young and we saw that boy by the caves nearly cut his hand off?" Gabriel leaned forward in his seat. "It was a bloody, mangled mess and we watched him hold his hand in place while it healed. Do you remember?"

Tristan turned around and squinted. "Vaguely."

"What if your body's ability to heal itself is somehow linked to whatever that boy was able to do?"

"I do not care about my body, healing or otherwise."

"Perhaps not now, but someday you may." Feeling reenergized, Gabriel stood from the throne and made his way to the doors. "Sober up, brother. Tomorrow, we are going for a ride."

****

Damn the happy sun.

Tristan's head ached for wine as he rode alongside Gabriel to wherever the hell they were headed, the rising sun biting into his eyes.

A new day. A new nothing.

"Is it not nice to leave the castle?" Gabriel took a deep breath. "You lived as a dead soul this week, brother. Wallowing in darkness, consumed with sadness. I think this outing will be good for you."

"I was not dead," Tristan said, though he wished he were.

As a memory of Scarlet snaked inside his chest, he clamped down on the tight emotion it brought. He would not think of her.

Alive or dead. In his arms or gone forever.

He would not think of her at all.

Gabriel scoffed. "No, you were just in a drunken haze that lasted five days and cost me eight servants and two court healers. Who knew you were such an awful drunk?"

Tristan glowered at his twin. Awful or not, being drunk kept the memories away and, therefore, kept him sane.

"Here we are," Gabriel said as they came upon a large house. He quickly dismounted his horse.

Tristan followed suit, but not as quickly, his sluggish body unaccustomed to being upright with the sun. "Where are we?"

"The Fletcher home."

"The house of witches?" Adrenaline shot through Tristan's body. "Is this not where Raven lives?"

"It was. But she is no longer here." Darkness clouded Gabriel's eyes. "If she were, she would already be in shackles."

"If that horrendous woman is not here, then why are we?"

"Because her cousin, Nathaniel, is the boy from the caves. And he may have answers for us." He strode to the front door and knocked.

Tristan followed after him and watched as a small, square panel in the center of the door slid to the side, revealing a pair of nervous eyes.

"Earl Archer," said the eyes, blinking rapidly.

"Are you Nathaniel Fletcher?"

"I am." The eyes widened. "But I do not know where my cousin is. Please do not kill me."

"I am not here for Raven," Gabriel said.

Nathaniel's eyes shifted to the side. "Are you here about the pheasants? Because that was an accident."

"What pheasants?"

"Nothing." Nathanial seemed relieved. "One moment."

The small panel slid back into place and the door opened to reveal an odd-looking fellow with bushy brown hair that stuck out on one side and a pair of eyeglasses caught in the mess. Despite the warm weather outside—and the fact that he was, indeed, inside—Nathaniel Fletcher wore a thick, black cloak that hung too long for him and dragged across the dirty floorboards.

"Welcome to my home, Earl Archer." Nathaniel nodded at Gabriel as they entered and shut the door behind them. He then eyed Tristan and took a step back, stumbling over his cloak. "You must be the earl's twin brother. But your eyes...how are they so green?"

"They were brown until your heathen of a cousin shot me through the heart," Tristan said crossly.

"Ah." Nathaniel nodded. "She used magic on you."

"No. She used an arrow."

"Then it must have been laced with magic." Nathaniel examined Tristan's eyes more closely. "Only powerful magic can alter physical appearances such as that. Perhaps a spell or a curse—oh! You were shot through the heart! And you are not dead?"

"Unfortunately, no." The snaking started around Tristan's heart again.

Bloody hell, he wanted wine.

"That is why we are here," Gabriel said. "My brother's body is able to heal itself and I've seen yours do the same."

"But I—but that—"

"I am not here to threaten you," Gabriel continued, "but I need to know what witchcraft allows you to heal. I believe the same magic has been used against my brother and may be responsible for the disappearance of my bride's body."

Nathaniel sucked in a breath. "Then it is true! She did disappear? I had heard the rumor, but was not certain."

"The arrow went through Tristan's heart first, then struck my bride before her body vanished. Do you know of this magic?"

Nathaniel scratched the back of his head. "I know of magic, but this...." He retrieved his spectacles from the nest of his hair and put them on before tripping his way over to a tower of books. "Was she human?"

Gabriel blinked. "Pardon me?"

"Was your woman human?"

"She wasn't his woman," Tristan said.

Gabriel slanted his eyes at Tristan before answering Nathaniel. "Of course she was human. What else would she be?"

Nathaniel shrugged as he pulled a thick book from the stack in the corner and shuffled to a nearby table. "A demon. A shape-shifter. A nymph. A mermaid." He turned through several crinkly pages. "A vampire. A ghost. A siren. A sea creature—"

"A sea creature?" Gabriel looked incredulous. "You want to know if my bride was a sea creature?"

"Yes," Nathaniel said seriously. "Did she have webbed feet?"

"No."

"Are you sure? Because women wear those awful shoes and you really wouldn't know unless she were to take them off—"

"She was human," Tristan said.

Nathaniel looked at Tristan, perplexed. "You saw her feet?"

"Yes."

Nathaniel's eyes darted from Tristan to Gabriel and then back to Tristan. "Right. In that case..." He turned another page and started reading. "Bodies only vanish after death for two reasons. Either they are called up to heaven by God." He looked at them over his spectacles. "Did you see any heavenly staircases or large groups of angels looming about her dead body?"

"What—no." Gabriel rubbed his face impatiently.

"Then the only other alternative," read Nathaniel, "is that she was infected with immortal blood prior to death." He reached for something from the table.

Gabriel blinked. "But how—"

Nathaniel grabbed Tristan's hand and pricked it with a small blade.

"Are you mad?" Tristan snatched his hand back from the over-cloaked boy.

Nathaniel looked at Tristan in confusion. "You seem unfriendly. I thought you were the kind twin. Aren't you the brother that feeds the hungry and plays with children?"

Tristan jutted his chin. "You just stabbed me, witch."

"I am not a witch. I am a wizard."

"I do not care."

"You'll have to excuse my brother," said Gabriel. "He's had a difficult week and is not used to being sober, so *perhaps you should ask for his permission the next time you feel the need to draw his blood."*

"I meant you no harm," explained Nathaniel. "You said the arrow pierced your heart before striking the bride—what was her name?"

"Scarlet," the brothers said at the same time.

"Right." Nathaniel drew out the word, eyeing Gabriel before looking back at Tristan. "I needed a bit of your blood to do a test." He spread blood from the knife onto a glass plate before retrieving a small vial of blue liquid from a false board in the wall.

Returning to the table, he added a drop of the blue liquid to Tristan's dark blood on the plate and the blood instantly brightened, turning from a deep crimson to a brilliant red

Nathaniel looked up at Gabriel and grinned. "It appears that the magic that healed your brother is the same magic that stole your bride—er, Scarlet. You, my friend," he turned to Tristan, "are filled with immortal blood."

Gabriel's brow furrowed. "That is impossible."

"On the contrary," Nathaniel pointed to the bright red spot of blood. "Immortal blood has a darker hue than that of mortals and brightens when mixed with this blue solution. I have immortal blood—which is why I can heal—and it seems Tristan does as well."

"But how?"

Nathaniel shook the small vial. "Water from the Fountain of Youth."

"Magic blue water," Tristan said, remembering the story that Scarlet's mother had told him about magic blue water being brought back from the New World by Scarlet's uncle. "It gives eternal youth, but it is highly addictive."

"Yes. And as it turns out, water from the Fountain of Youth also negates immortal blood, making it just the same as mortal blood." Nathaniel pointed to the bright red blood on the glass.

"How do you know—bloody hell!" Gabriel turned furious eyes on Nathaniel, who had just sliced his hand with the same knife he'd used to cut Tristan. "You could have asked first."

"You said I only needed to ask Tristan for permission—because he is grumpy."

Gabriel stared at Nathaniel. "Just because I am not drunk and angry with the universe like my brother—"

"I'm not drunk," Tristan said. "Not yet, anyway."

"Is your wound healing?" Nathaniel asked Gabriel.

Gabriel examined his hand, his sour face morphing into one of awe as he watched his wound begin to heal. "Incredible."

Nathaniel added a drop of the blue water to Gabriel's dark blood and it brightened just as Tristan's had.

"It seems all three of us carry immortal blood," Nathaniel said. "Which means we cannot be killed. Ever." He grinned. "Isn't that wonderful?"

Tristan frowned, not sure if he wanted to live forever.

He hadn't even wanted to wake up that morning.

Forever seemed a bit ambitious.

Gabriel continued watching his healing hand. "How can you be sure our ability to self-heal means we are immortal?"

Nathaniel shrugged. "Because that is the magic of the Fountain of Youth. A magic so rare I know of no other immortals in existence. We are not created, you see. We are born—to mothers addicted to the fountain's blue water. Very rare indeed. The fact that our mothers survived their addiction long enough to have us is astonishing."

"Are you saying our mothers were poisoned with this water?"

"Not intentionally," Nathaniel said. "Our mothers were pregnant with us during the time of the plague and both became quite ill. My uncle Eli traveled to Spain and purchased three vials of the legendary fountain water from a Spaniard named Francis. He then gave one vial to my mother—his sister—and sold the second to your father, Cornelius. Eli and Cornelius were good friends at the time and your mother's illness was breaking your father's heart. Eli wished to alleviate this pain from Cornelius. Sadly, the water only brought more.

"Upon drinking the water, our mothers were instantly cured of their sickness, yet began craving the water. They drained each of their vials just weeks after we were born and, without more to sustain them, they soon grew mad and, eventually, perished."

"But what of the third vial? Why not give them that to extend their lives?"

"The third vile," Nathaniel shook the vial in his hand, "was my uncle's last resort. He did not want to poison his sister further so instead he attempted to make a spell to cure her, using water from the third vile. But he was not successful. After my mother's death, Uncle Eli hid this potion away in the walls and spoke of its wickedness, forbidding us all of touching it.

"The day I realized I could heal, I began to wonder if the blue water had somehow changed me in my mother's womb. After years of research, I learned of the fountain's ability to grant immortal life to the unborn and it was then that I realized I my blood was composed differently than that of mortals, making me immortal.

"I found this to be a wonderful discovery, yet my uncle was not pleased and he forbid me from speaking of it or indulging in my fascination with immortality and the Fountain of Youth. Naturally, I did not heed his command, which is why I know what I do of immortality.

"Dangerous water, this is." He shook the vial again. "Although it has its benefits. We, of course, have the privilege of living forever. So that's brilliant." He glanced at Tristan. "And according to my books, your immortal blood may even bring Scarlet back to life someday."

"What?" Tristan said, his heart instantly beating against his bones with a ferocity he'd not felt in ages. "What did you say?"

Nathaniel shrugged. "Scarlet was infected with immortal blood before she died, which explains why her body disappeared. Immortal blood, if put into a mortal body, will always fight to stay alive. So you, essentially, have made Scarlet semi-immortal. And semi-immortal beings do not ever truly die. They vanish and return to the earth at a later time in the same body."

Skepticism and hope warred madly inside Tristan.

"How can we bring her back?" His palms were sweaty and his heart was on fire but, God help him, he would do anything, kill anyone, and break any rule to bring her back.

Nathaniel said, "Her return is dependent on the magic in her veins. It could take decades—"

"I can wait decades," Tristan said.

"Or it could take a hundred years," Nathaniel said.

"I can wait a thousand years."

The wizard cocked his head at Tristan. "I'm confused. Did you know Scarlet? Because I was under the impression you were gone when she first came to the castle. You seem to care deeply for Gabriel's wife—"

"She wasn't his wife."

Gabriel gave a long-suffering sigh and turned to Nathaniel. "Tristan and Scarlet were...close."

"I see." Nathaniel glanced back and forth between the brothers. "Well, either way, you cannot control her return.

But since you are immortal, there is a good chance you will live to see her again." Nathaniel grinned.

"That is not helpful," Gabriel said.

"I never said I would be helpful. I said I would ask permission before stabbing you."

Tristan was no longer listening because his heart had flown from his chest and was soaring in the sky. Scarlet would return.

He no longer wished to be drunk. Or dead.

5

England 1540

Justice was within reach.

Standing in the shadows of night, Gabriel gazed upon the old, stone house that was Raven's current hiding spot, and steeled himself for what he had to do. Everything inside of him wanted to break down the door and rip her to shreds for all he'd lost.

Well, almost all.

Raven had been his childhood ally and partner in adventure. She had challenged him and excited him, and always made him feel alive and wanted. There was a small bit of friendship lingering in his chest, reminding him of the girl he'd grown up with, the girl he'd plotted to rule the world with, his friend and lover. Surely, there was still something good inside her; something redeemable.

He exhaled slowly, remembering his role as earl did not allow him to be emotional with the law. Raven had committed great crimes and it was his responsibility to have her arrested for her transgressions.

Straightening his shoulders, he knocked on the door.

He did not expect her to answer, but the door slowly pulled back and Raven stood before him. Her long, dark hair hung around her shoulders and her gray eyes glinted in the moonlight as they stared at one another.

She did not look afraid, but rather sorrowful, and it caught Gabriel off guard.

"You found me," she said.

"Yes."

"Have you come to kill me?" She raised her chin a notch higher, looking at him with forced bravery.

He wanted to hurt her. He wanted to punish her. He wanted to go back in time and save her from herself.

But he did not want to kill her.

"No. But I need you to come with me."

"Why?" She swallowed. "So I might undo the curse?"

He'd hoped the wizard had been misinformed about the arrow being magic, but fear gripped Gabriel's muscles as the possibility sank in. "You did, indeed, cast a curse?"

She nodded and the fear around his muscles became anger.

Raven had cursed him. The only person in the world he'd trusted outside of Tristan had cursed him.

He tried to keep his voice even. "And what, exactly, does this curse entail?"

"I cursed you so you shall never know love without Scarlet."

Gabriel stood perfectly still as hate crawled out of his heart and slowly clawed its way through his chest. "Can the curse be undone?"

Did it matter? Would undoing the curse change the betrayal he felt? Would it make Raven any less malicious?

No.

She shook her head. "You shall never love another woman, nor will any woman ever truly love you, aside from Scarlet—who is dead—or me. And I am very much alive."

"You're lying."

"I am telling you the truth."

Darkness invaded his lungs and throat. "Was that your plan all along? Cursing me into loving you?"

"No. My plan *was* to rule alongside you as your partner and friend." *Her eyes hardened.* "But you abandoned me for your brother's girl."

"So you killed my father? You killed my *bride?*" *he growled.*

"She wasn't even your woman."

Why did everyone feel the need to remind him of that?

She put her hands on his chest and slid them up to his shoulders. "Do not be angry, Gabriel. Your father was awful and the peasant girl was wrong for you. Don't you see? Everything I did, I did for us. Now we can be together."

She was mad.

She was wicked and wretched and all things terrible. Had she been this way always? Had he been blind for all these years?

Darkness filled his insides with a warmth he knew he shouldn't welcome. "I would rather live an eternity of loneliness than ever love something as vile as you," *he sneered, watching the insult cross her face like a sharp slap. He reached for her hands.* "You are under arrest—"

A wall of magical flames shot up between them, burning Gabriel's outstretched hands. He yanked them back with a curse. "What are you doing?"

Raven shook her head, reaching for something he could not see beside the doorway. "I did not want to do this." *She* shoved something sharp through the wall of fire and into Gabriel's chest.

Blinding, white-hot pain split through his core and the breath whipped from his lungs. Looking down, he saw a giant knife protruding from his chest.

She had stabbed him.

His childhood friend had just stabbed him.

All reason left Gabriel's heart, leaving a hungry void in the center, and he began to shake with rage. Hate, thick and black, continued to coat his insides, slipping into the void, with hot comfort.

He slowly he withdrew the blade from his body and tossed it aside as Raven looked on in bewilderment.

Her words were quiet. "How did you...?"

"I'm immortal," he said, fury pressing against his heart.

He could feel his body start to instantly heal, pieces of pain coming and going as his skin knit itself back together.

"But you are not." His hate was more powerful than he realized and, with one swift movement, he snapped Raven's neck, breaking it with a sickening crack before dropping her lifeless body to the ground.

He blinked.

He watched the life drain from her face and felt a cold rush of remorse swoop into him. The darkness he'd just moments ago clung to evaporated from his chest; leaving a whirlwind of fear, shame, and agony in its place.

He stared down at the lifeless body of the girl he'd once cared for.

He was a murderer.

6

London 1613

Gabriel let himself into Tristan's home and sank into the nearest chair, rubbing the side of his face.

"Please, come in," Tristan said dryly, looking up from the knife he was sharpening in the corner.

"It is official, brother. Raven's curse is real." Gabriel sighed, trying to not let thoughts of the long-dead girl get the best of him. Seventy-three years had gone by since he'd taken Raven's life, but he still carried guilt.

Had she deserved to die? Yes. But at his hands?

No.

It did not matter that being earl had given him the right to execute a criminal. It was still murder.

The only thing that seemed to offset his remorseful heart was the curse Raven had bestowed upon him. A curse, it seemed, that was far more effective than he'd originally given the silver-eyed girl credit for.

Perhaps a loveless life was exactly what Gabriel deserved.

"I cannot fall in love," Gabriel said. "I've tried courting dozens of women and none of them truly fall for me. Oh, they will marry me. They will take my money and my fine food and my horses, but they do not care for me. And what's worse, I feel nothing for them."

"You have no horses," said Tristan.

"Exactly! All these bloody women keep taking my things. It's exhausting."

Tristan smirked. "Is that why you spend all your free time in taverns and gambling rings? To soothe your exhaustion?"

Gabriel leaned back in his seat. "No. I do those things to distract me from the emptiness." *And the guilt.*

Nathaniel let himself into Tristan's house as well. "Good day! What are you two talking about?"

Tristan answered, "Well, Gabriel was just complaining about love—again—and I was wondering why I even bother having a door."

"Ah, yes. The never-ending search for true love. Ooh! Food." Nathaniel snatched a chunk of bread off a plate on Tristan's desk and began eating.

"You do not know what it's like," Gabriel said. "I have not felt anything for a woman in decades. Decades. Not since—"

Tristan looked up as Gabriel swallowed Scarlet's name. Even though a century had passed, Scarlet was still an uncomfortable subject between them.

Gabriel pulled at his ear. "It's just been a long time since a woman has loved me and I miss it."

Hoping for Scarlet to come back to life was a cruel game, and Gabriel had quit playing long ago. Tristan, however, lived for the cruelty.

Scarlet might not be alive, but her presence was; her memory was. And that was enough to keep Tristan hoping. God help his poor soul.

"It is a rotten curse." Nathaniel nodded. "And also quite stubborn in its structure."

Nathaniel had tried many counter-hexes—all of which failed miserably and left sticky, smelly messes in their wake.

He wasn't a very skilled wizard. Entertaining and knowledgeable, yes. But magical? Not so much.

Gabriel groaned. "Is this what my eternity will be? Empty of love and companionship, and filled with greedy damsels?"

"It could be worse," Tristan said. "It could be filled with those who enter your house without knocking and eat your food."

Nathaniel shoved a very deliberate piece of bread into his mouth and looked at Gabriel. "You have me as a companion. What more could you want from eternity?" He chewed with his mouth open.

"Something prettier," Gabriel said, "and less disgusting."

Nathaniel swallowed. "If it helps, I've never been in love either. I'm beginning to think true love might not exist."

Tristan turned his eyes back to his dagger with an amused expression.

Gabriel sighed. "I am doomed."

"No," Nathaniel said. "You are cursed."

"Are they not the same thing?"

"Not at all. Doomed means there is no hope. Cursed means you will have to struggle to find hope, then struggle to keep it, then struggle to undo said curse with the hope that you have kept."

Gabriel blinked. "Being doomed sounds less taxing."

"Indeed." Nathaniel smiled.

"Relax, Gabriel," Tristan said. "Do not be impatient for companionship."

"This coming from the man who breaks hearts he's never even met before. Women flock to you and beg for your attention, and you ignore them all." Gabriel hung his head.

While he spent his days drinking and gambling, Tristan devoted most of his time to helping townsfolk. Providing food to the orphans, giving money to the churches, letting whoever and whatever find shelter in his large home for indefinite periods of time. It was truly impossible living alongside a brother with such a bleeding heart. And that bleeding heart was like a beacon for women everywhere, drawing them to his presence only to be sent away.

"It's truly sickening, brother," Gabriel said. "You, at the very least, should marry one of the poor girls."

"Why, so I can lose my horses?" Tristan smiled.

"Yes! Then you could join me in my misery," Gabriel said.

Tristan went back to his knife. "I have my own misery to bear."

Gabriel rolled his eyes.

Poor soul, indeed.

7

London 1684

Immortality, Tristan decided, was only magnificent for those who had a reason to breathe and, for him, that reason was lost somewhere in-between worlds. Until Scarlet returned, his every breath was just a laborious means to an end.

So he existed. But he did not live.

Waiting on love will do that to a man; keep his heart suspended in a state of thin hope—just bright enough to want to live and heavy enough to envy death.

Music played into the large, ornate room where he and Gabriel stood among dozens of other well-dressed Londoners.

Laughter, merriment, movement.

Life, breath, hope.

Mortality.

Tristan was envious of it all.

He stretched his neck, trying to ignore the mysterious pain in his limbs.

"Remind me again." Gabriel leaned into Tristan to be heard above the music. "Why are we at the Trevena Ball?"

"Because we were invited," Tristan said.

Gabriel took a deep swig from the goblet in his hand. "Yes, but why did we come?"

"Because we are young, wealthy gentlemen and that's what young, wealthy gentlemen do." A woman across the room batted her lashes at Tristan and he stifled a sigh, his lungs pulling uncomfortably tight.

"I feel that is a poor reason." Gabriel took another drink.

A group of ladies by the back doors stared at them in-between their whispers and giggles.

Tristan exhaled. "I think us standing side-by-side is drawing too much attention. People do not know what to do with twins. They see us as a circus show."

"They do not," said Gabriel. "Now, maybe if we both had tails, we'd be a sideshow. But we do not have tails. We have strong bodies and godlike faces. If we're a show of any kind, we're a show of beauty."

Tristan shook his head. "Your confidence is disgusting."

"A hundred and fifty years of female affirmation has made me this way." Gabriel's smile faltered for the briefest of moments and Tristan felt heavy, knowing that who Gabriel was and who he wanted to be were warring enemies.

His brother's behavior had not changed much in the last century: drinking, gambling, breaking rules, breaking hearts. He embraced his immortality as an opportunity to exploit life as a whole and Tristan acted as his peacemaker and babysitter, trying to keep the wild Gabriel from causing more damage than could be undone in a lifetime.

Tristan had considered leaving London and moving someplace far from his brother, but his conscience never *allowed him to leave. Gabriel was a reckless star, casting about wherever he may, exploding into whoever made him feel alive, and burning casualties in his wake.*

Lord only knows what that star would burst into next if Tristan were not there to remind Gabriel of those annoying bits of humanity called morals.

Gabriel's fruitless search for love had left him a bitter brute who swam in booze and slept beside whoever welcomed him, his mood always bleak.

Tristan was worried for his brother's state of mind and wished, more so now than ever before, that he could change Gabriel's circumstances.

Reaching for his wine goblet from the nearby table, Tristan winced. He'd been experiencing a pain that came and went, sometimes sharp and cutting, other times a dull ache, for some time now. It had come on suddenly nearly two years ago, and the pain he'd experienced that first day had felt like death itself was ripping him apart.

But it slowly subsided and he'd been living with an on-again-off-again ache ever since. Tonight, however, his muscles were throbbing and growing tighter by the minute. And he had no idea why.

"*That young lady seems to admire you.*" *Tristan pointed to a girl in pink who was smiling at Gabriel, and tried to ignore the pressure building in his head.*

He nodded. "*She does.*"

"*You might ask her to dance.*" *Tristan took a sip.* "*Less people would probably stare in this direction if there were only one of us standing here.*"

"*I could ask her to dance.*" *Gabriel took a drink from his own cup.* "*I could also feed my heart to wild boars.*"

He rolled his eyes. "*You cannot completely give up on companionship, Gabriel. That's absurd.*"

A slicing pain cut through the center of Tristan's chest and he clutched at his heart.

"What is wrong?" Gabriel asked.

"I don't...know." He couldn't breathe. It was as if all the air in the room had been replaced with fire, filling his lungs with a merciless burn.

"Let's get you outside." Gabriel led Tristan out the back doors and into the night air.

Once outside, Tristan crumpled to the ground. Every piece of his body was wringing from the inside out, killing him for certain.

"Tristan." Gabriel crouched down beside him, panic in his voice. "What is this?"

Heat, ice, fire, knives, everything born of hell was ripping through Tristan's core. And the Devil himself was clawing away at his head.

Tristan gasped. "I can't...breathe...."

Gabriel swallowed and pulled Tristan up from the ground. "We need to get you out of here and..."

Tristan didn't hear the rest. The pain closed in on him and pulled out his insides. He was dying. There was no other explanation as the world around him went cold and black.

****

Two weeks later, Gabriel shook his head as he looked down at Tristan's face, contorted in pain. "He's dying, isn't he?"

"I highly doubt that, considering he is immortal," said Nathaniel.

Tristan shoved his face into the bed and groaned against a pillow.

Nathaniel twitched his lips. "Where is the doctor you called on?"

"He should be here soon." Gabriel shifted his weight as Tristan punched the bed with a howl.

The pain had not let up for several days, rendering Tristan mad with torment and Gabriel completely helpless to relieve him.

Nathaniel rubbed a hand across his face. "This is not normal. I knew that he had been experiencing pain off and on for quite some time, but how long has it been like this?"

"Three weeks," Gabriel said.

"Three weeks and four days," Tristan corrected through gritted teeth.

Nathaniel said, "Ah, yes. Since the night of the ball."

A knock sounded at the door.

"Finally," Gabriel muttered as he hurried to the front of the house.

"Sorry I am late." The doctor was a round, balding man with a bright red nose and spectacles that were too thick and large for his face. "There are too many patients in this area lately. I am all but dead myself from all this running around and add on top of that all the cats that roam these streets making me sneeze with their dirty hair, not to mention the stench—"

The doctor continued mumbling as Gabriel led him back to the room where Tristan lay in agony. "The last patient I called on was allergic to peaches. I had never heard of such a thing, though I do suppose that isn't too great a problem around here. I've never really cared for peaches myself, though my mother was fond of peach pie. Oh, dear!" the doctor exclaimed. "What is the matter with this young fellow?"

Gabriel glared at the doctor, already annoyed with his presence. "We don't know. That is why we called you." He explained to the physician how Tristan had been in agonizing pain.

"Oh my." The doctor pushed his spectacles up further, pressing them into the skin between his eyes, and began examining Tristan. "The human body. So fragile. So many sick people everywhere. Just the other day, I treated a woman named Agnes who gave birth to the largest baby I'd ever seen and her pain, while quite intense, did not seem as debilitating as what this gentleman suffers from here." The doctor raised Tristan's arm in the air and dropped it. It crashed down to the bed, before forming a fist and punching the sheets again.

"Hmm..." The doctor shuffled about, checking Tristan's pulse and his forehead, looking in his eyes and listening to his chest. "Very odd. Very odd." He shook his head and then—foolish man that he was—the doctor pinched Tristan's bicep. For what reason, Gabriel was not sure.

Tristan lashed out from the pillow and pinned the doctor against the wall, wrapping a hand around his throat and squeezing until the man's face turned purple.

Slow and low, Tristan bit out, "Do. Not. Pinch. Me," before releasing the stunned physician and returning to miserably groaning into the bed.

Coughing and gasping, the doctor hurried away from the bed and looked at Gabriel and Nathaniel with wide eyes. "My, my. He is not well at all. He seems healthy—at least healthy enough to kill a man. Lots of muscle. Healthy skin color. But this apparent pain he suffers from—and his violent temperament—is perplexing."

Nathaniel looked at the doctor. "Do you have any solutions?"

The doctor sighed. "None other than lavender water and prayer."

Doctors were useless.

"Then I believe we are through with your services." Gabriel tried to sound polite.

"I must say," said the doctor as he gathered his things, "this has been a most perplexing month. I treated a monkey with a liver infection, if you can believe that. Monkeys make the most atrocious sounds. And I had to perform surgery on an old bloke named Henry who thought he could cut out his chronic toothache with a knife—that one was rather gory. The human mouth is madness."

Gabriel wanted to strangle the man for all his nonsensical chatter.

The doctor continued, "And then there was the young girl without her memories. Poor thing was lost, scared, and completely mad. I put her in a carriage and swiftly sent her far away. Named Scarlet, though I thought she looked more like a Mary. I nearly missed the ball because of her and I hate missing a good ball feast. And now I have this young man with an invisible pain, punching the bed sheets and choking me—"

"What did you say?" Tristan whipped around, obviously forgetting about his great pain as his wild green eyes stared at the doctor.

The doctor scoffed. "I was merely stating that I am mystified by your impossible pain and a bit offended at your attempt to kill me—"

"No." Tristan sat up in the bed. "What did you say about the girl named Scarlet?"

The doctor paused in the doorway. "Oh. She was found wandering the woods a couple of years ago, quite close to here. Sad, really. She does not know anything but her name. I gave her some lavender water, but I hardly see how that will help her remember or help her temper. She was a mean little thing—"

"What was her full name?"

The doctor rubbed at his beard in thought. "I believe it was Jacobs. Yes. Scarlet Jacobs."

Gabriel was lost for words.

Could it be?

"She was a pretty thing," the doctor said. "But feisty and not ladylike in any way. I wouldn't be at all surprised if she were raised in the wild."

"Neither would I," Tristan said slowly.

Gabriel saw the raw hope in Tristan's eyes and felt a similar emotion stir in his own chest.

Was Scarlet truly alive?

8

Tristan's heart was pounding. Joyous, terrified, excited, nervous—there was no emotion within the spectrum of human existence he wasn't currently experiencing.

He knew it. His heart, his soul, his pain-stricken body knew Scarlet was alive. And she was close.

Gabriel, Nathaniel, and Tristan rode in Gabriel's carriage to a small inn far outside of town where the doctor had said Scarlet would be.

Tristan rolled his shoulders, willing the ache from his bones as they rode along. When they'd first left, Tristan's body had been so filled with pain that he'd groaned at every jostle and bump in the road. But the longer they rode toward Scarlet, the less he hurt. It was as if the mere idea of Scarlet being alive was curing him.

He ran both hands through his hair, his nerves jumping like feet on hot coals.

When the carriage finally pulled up to a large inn, they jumped out and headed for the front door of the old building. Upon entering, the three of them stopped in their tracks.

There were people. Everywhere.

"Brilliant," Tristan muttered.

"The inn-yard must be hosting a play today." Nathaniel strained his neck, trying to see above the crowd to the courtyard beyond. People lined the halls and outside balconies drinking, singing, and laughing. It was chaos.

"How will we find her in this mess?"

"We'll split up." Nathaniel looked at Gabriel. "You take the right wing. Tristan, you take the left. Since I do not know what she looks like, I'll ask the people upstairs about the girl without her memories."

Gabriel nodded and headed down his designated wing, while Nathaniel clutched Tristan's shoulder and gave him a brief smile, as if he understood Tristan's desire to run around the inn and knock people over until he found Scarlet. "Deep breath, my friend. If she is here, we shall find her."

Before Tristan could respond, Nathaniel headed upstairs.

Tristan strode through the left wing of the inn. People, people, people.

No Scarlet.

At the back of a large gathering room, he found the innkeeper counting a handful of coins he'd collected from play-goers, dropping them into a pouch one by one.

"Pardon me." Tristan hoped his smile looked warm rather than impatient. "I'm looking for a young girl named Scarlet Jacobs. I believe she was sent to work here a few weeks ago."

The innkeeper looked up. "The mad girl?"

Tristan almost hit the man. "The very same."

"What do you want with her?"

Life. Love. A reason to breathe again.

Tristan said, "I have something of hers."

This was true.

The innkeeper waved toward the right wing. "The back of the washrooms."

Tristan gave a nod and turned away, fighting through crowds of people lining the right wing. He picked up his pace.

Gabriel was going to find her first, dammit. And he would probably say something wildly inappropriate or have the poor girl drunk by the time Tristan's feet carried him to the washrooms.

Bloody Gabriel.

As he hurried along, a strange sensation came over him. Strange and warm and...wonderful.

Love.

A happy love—a safe love—blossomed in Tristan's chest, spreading like serene fog through his body. Love for...Gabriel?

Tristan stopped walking. Maybe this was part of his illness. Maybe he'd contracted a sickness that began with excruciating pain and then morphed into a ridiculous love of one's sibling.

No. That did not sound right.

And come to think of it, he was no longer in horrific pain. Very odd. In fact, the atrocious pain he'd suffered just that morning was almost completely gone from his veins.

Shaking his head, Tristan moved forward, nearly running as he made his way to the other side of the building, rounding corners and knocking into people shamelessly.

Soon, he found the washrooms and skidded across wet floors until he managed to connect his feet to the solid ground. He paused and headed for a small room off to the side. Why, he wasn't sure, but something was pulling him that way.

He turned into the room and his heart stopped. And then it sang.

Scarlet.

He sucked in a long, deep, God-given breath of redemption and miracles and all things heavenly. Never was there a better sight than this.

She was more beautiful than he remembered, her face flushed and her dark hair loose and wild around her face, but her eyes were the same. Blue and severe, showing the strength and stubbornness she housed inside.

As he suspected, Gabriel had found her first and was speaking to her in hushed, comforting tones. The room was empty, save for the three of them, but Scarlet had not yet seen Tristan.

Her voice matched the smile on her face as she looked into Gabriel's eyes and excitedly said, "I remember, now. I remember, I remember. When you said what year I was born it was as if all my memories woke up." She put a hand over her mouth, bouncing on her toes a bit.

An odd soiree of emotions suddenly began to swim through Tristan.

Confusion, hope, love, fear, safety, confusion...

He paused. Why was he feeling these things?

It did not make sense.

Ignoring the odd twinge in his chest, Tristan opened his mouth to call out to her when Scarlet threw her arms around Gabriel and started kissing his cheeks and his forehead giddily.

Tristan's insides went empty as sharp jealousy cut through him and drained him dry. She was kissing him.

Possessiveness was coursing through his veins, but suddenly he felt safe and happy.

What the bloody hell? This was all too strange. He could not understand what was happening to him or why he was feeling such things. It was almost as if...as if....

Realization dawned on him.

Scarlet.

Somehow he knew he was feeling Scarlet. He was sensing her gratitude for Gabriel; how Gabriel made her feel happy and safe. How he made her feel loved. And how she loved him back...

There was no more air and no more light; there was only hollow blackness clouding Tristan's vision and pressing down on his chest as the jealousy swirled into sadness.

She loved him back...

Scarlet's eyes turned from Gabriel, caught site of Tristan and, suddenly, his black world burst into color. The love in Scarlet's chest exploded into a sensation more powerful than words, expanding inside Tristan in indescribable colors.

Her love for him was safe and dangerous. Passionate and soft. Wild and fierce.

It was its own being, held captive for ages and now released into new life. And it made Tristan want to shout.

Which was exactly what Scarlet did.

"Tristan!" Rushing over to him, her face flushed with awe and eyes brimming with tears, Scarlet crashed her body into his and wrapped her arms around him.

An unbelievable pleasure flooded his veins at her touch, but his mind did not care to ponder the bliss. Scarlet was in his arms. Nothing else mattered.

****

Scarlet clung to Tristan, shamelessly pressing her body against his as they kissed and embraced.

How was she alive? How was Tristan alive?

Ah! She did not care. Whatever had happened—whatever was happening now—did not matter. She had her Hunter. She had everything.

Her heart swelled so large it felt as though it might burst. Actually, it felt like it was bursting already. Harder and harder it beat against her ribcage.

He tucked her against his chest and wrapped his arms around her, kissing the top of her head as she pressed herself against his body.

She inhaled deeply and the scent of leather and water met her nose, reminding her of Hunter and the time she shared with him in the forest and how he had loved her and how she thought she'd lost him. She was so happy she could cry.

She'd been floating through this strange world for two years, so lost, so hopeless. And now she felt at home, safe and loved and happy. She buried her face even more into his chest, wanting to hide there until her world forever made sense.

The fierce pounding inside her grew almost painful and she put a hand to her chest to keep her heart from leaping out.

Tristan shifted away from her with a concerned expression and, almost instantly, the pounding softened.

"I see you've found her," said a voice behind Scarlet. "Fantastic."

Turning, she saw a stranger with messy brown hair approach them with a smile.

Suddenly aware she and Tristan were not alone in the room—somehow, she had forgotten about Gabriel, oops—Scarlet dropped her hand from her chest and took a reluctant, yet socially appropriate, step away from Tristan.

She looked at the stranger. "Who are you?"

His brows lifted. "Oh. Oh, right. You do not know me."

"This is our friend, Nathaniel," Tristan said.

"And I'm a wizard." Nathaniel smiled.

"Barely," Gabriel corrected. "He is barely a wizard."

"Hey now," Nathaniel said in mock offense. "I'm getting better."

"No. If anything, you are getting worse," Gabriel said.

Scarlet was confused. "Will someone please tell me what's going on?"

"Well, you were dead. And now you are alive." Nathaniel smiled.

"Right," Scarlet said. "And how is that possible?"

"Immortal blood." He nodded. "It's a long story."

Scarlet crossed her arms. "Then start at the beginning."

****

Scarlet leaned back against the desk in her small quarters at the inn, her servant's dress catching on the corner and tearing slightly.

Nathaniel had spent the last few hours explaining Scarlet's past and the boys' immortality to her. It was a lot to take in and most of it was disturbing.

Gabriel smiled at her from his post by the door, no doubt trying to make her feel comfortable. She smiled back at him, confusion winding through her head. He had practically been her husband in her previous life, yet somehow he seemed like a stranger to her. Like he was a warm, soft dream that had existed in one reality, but had no place in this one.

She rubbed her pounding chest for the third time that hour. "So I am semi-immortal?"

"Correct." Nathaniel watched Scarlet clutch at her heart again. "How does your heart feel?"

Confused. Anxious. Unstable.

"Fine." Scarlet dropped her hand. "It's beating rather fast but otherwise it's fine."

From across the room, Tristan's eyes slid to her and Scarlet's nervous feelings vanished. Tristan was alive. Everything would be fine.

She tried to memorize his new green eyes. They suited him better. The brown had been handsome, but the bright green was...alive. Like living fire, burning emerald as he looked at her with an almost-smile. She wished they were alone so she could touch him and smell him and taste him—

The emerald flames brightened.

"—start happening?" Nathaniel's voice pulled Scarlet away from Tristan's hot gaze.

She blinked. "Come again?"

Nathaniel cleared his throat. "I asked when you felt your heart begin to race."

"Oh. Uh..." Scarlet knew exactly when her heart had started to pound, but she didn't want to announce to the room how her heart had become a hungry drummer the moment she ran into Tristan's arms.

"Today." That was a safe, non-embarrassing answer.

"Before or after we found you?"

"After."

Tristan turned to Nathaniel. "Are you concerned about her heart?"

"I don't know." He frowned. "I feel like I've read something about ferociously beating hearts, but I cannot recall..." He trailed off for a moment, then shook his head. "Oh well. The most important thing," he said, smiling at Scarlet, "is that you are alive and well and have your memories back."

She smiled back at Nathaniel. She wasn't sure what to think of him. He was quirky and awkward, and not at all what Scarlet would have expected a wizard to be, but he seemed genuinely pleasant.

Gabriel looked out at the night sky through the window. "It is too late to travel tonight, but perhaps we can purchase rooms here for the evening and head back home first thing in the morning."

Home.

The word had Scarlet's soul aching. She'd been dead for over a hundred years. Her home no longer existed. A deep sense of loss overtook her as she thought about her mother and the hut they'd shared and how Scarlet had hunted and lived in the trees.

All that was gone. What would become of her now?

Nathaniel and Gabriel headed downstairs to speak with the innkeeper with Tristan right behind them. But when he passed Scarlet, Tristan paused.

Kissing her forehead, he whispered, "Everything will be fine, Scar."

And the aching in her soul immediately vanished.

****

Scarlet waited until nearly midnight before tiptoeing from her room. She'd had a few hours to think and realized two things that made her belly flop.

She needed to sort things out with Gabriel—which was sure to be uncomfortable.

And she was upset with Tristan for leaving her as Gabriel's fiancé in her last life.

Since she would most likely not be getting any alone time with either of them, Scarlet decided to do the least ladylike thing imaginable and visit both their doors at an ungodly hour. Oh, the horror.

She crept to the door of Gabriel's room and tentatively knocked. A moment later, his boyish face appeared in the dim light of the corridor.

"Hello, Scarlet."

"Hello." Her nerves jumped. "Um...I just wanted to apologize for...earlier...with Tristan." She swallowed, feeling guilty for clinging to Tristan in front of Gabriel when the boy had done nothing but love and care for her in her previous life. "I was not trying to hurt you or offend you—"

"Scarlet," Gabriel said smiling, "you do not need to apologize."

"But I do." Her heart squeezed. "I was nearly your wife and, while I don't know what that means for us now, my behavior today was still shameful—"

"Do you still want to be my wife?" He asked this casually, as if asking if she enjoyed kittens.

Scarlet hesitated for the briefest of moments. Not because she didn't know the answer, but because she didn't know how to explain that, no, she did not wish to be his wife, but she did still love him. She was not sure she could explain it even to herself.

He shook his head. "I love you very much—"

"I love you too," she blurted. What she did not blurt out were all the gray areas inside her love for him. The hidden places, the compromised pieces, the tempered facades.

Was love supposed to be gray?

He was smiling, but it did not reach his eyes. "I know you do. But we were together because of our dedication to Tristan and our belief that he was no longer alive." He paused. "You are not mine, Scarlet. And—as my brother so often reminds me—you never were."

"I belong to no one," Scarlet said.

"Precisely. So you have no obligation to me." He shifted his weight. "I love my brother deeply and wish to see him happy. If your heart takes you to him, so be it. If it does not, that is fine as well. You will not lose my love or friendship either way." He leaned in and kissed her cheek softly. "Good night, my Scarlet."

He gently closed his door, leaving Scarlet speechless in the dark hallway with the gray parts of her heart floating in the darkness as she pondered her relationship—or lack thereof—with Gabriel.

But thinking of Gabriel brought her thoughts back to Tristan and, therefore, her pent-up anger at his flippancy in handing her off to Gabriel. And then, of course, there was his complete stupidity in trying to save her life by sacrificing his own.

All gray areas ceased to matter as she headed down the inn's large staircase with her argument face on. Once she reached the lower floor, Scarlet found several drunken patrons walking about the lobby and halls. Some singing, some stumbling, and some hiccupping their way through tall tales only other drunks would believe. The play seemed to have put everyone in a jovial mood.

Careful to avoid a swaying man with flushed cheeks and two missing teeth, Scarlet ducked her way toward the corridor of guest rooms and tried to act natural. Well, as natural as a young lady with her hair undone could act while walking the halls of an inn at midnight.

She turned into the back corridor, the hallway growing darker as she left the bright candles of the lobby. When she came upon Tristan's shadowed door, she found it unlatched. Scarlet steeled herself for the carefully-constructed rant she had planned.

How would Tristan feel if she tossed him to her sister to love and wed? She shuddered. The very idea of sharing Tristan made her skin boil.

Slowly pushing his door open, Scarlet quietly stepped inside his candlelit room and saw him standing in the corner. Waiting. His green eyes lit as he took her in, but *otherwise his face remained unreadable. Handsome, and filled with a thousand lovely memories, but unreadable.*

No. I will not think about his face. Or his memories.

I am angry.

She lifted her chin to speak, but no words came. He lifted his chin for no reason whatsoever, but the movement had Scarlet's eyes traveling over the dark scruff along his jaw and the thick contours of his throat and—

No. No throat-gazing.

I am angry. I do not belong to anyone. Tristan had no right to offer me up to Gabriel.

She took a nervous step back and accidentally brushed against the door, causing it to fall shut and close them into his room. Her throat went dry as they looked at each other across the dark space. The flickering candlelight made his whole body seem alive with shadowed movement, but he remained perfectly still.

Was that amusement on his face?

She stared at him, hoping her hard features still looked convincing as her mind insisted on thinking of non-angry things.

Hunting with Tristan in the morning and sparring with him in the afternoons. Dinners with him and her mother and splashing with him in the river. Deep kisses in the night...

Tension filled the space between them and Scarlet inwardly groaned.

Bloody hell, she was no longer angry.

Something about the candles and the scruff and the unsolicited memories had worn her down. And now she was standing silent in Tristan's room like some ridiculous statue intruder.

She turned to leave. She would be angry with him tomorrow.

"Scar," Tristan said.

As she turned around, she opened her mouth to excuse her odd behavior with a brilliant lie she had yet to come up with, but lost her voice when she saw the softness in his eyes. Her heart filled with love and all she wanted to do was kiss him—anger be damned.

In an instant, his unreadable expression turned to one of longing and, with two swift strides, he crossed the distance between them and crushed his mouth against hers.

Scarlet immediately sank into his arms, relief, love, and joy flooding her soul as she kissed him back.

He pulled back and ran his eyes over her in awe. Cupping her face in his hands, he gently smoothed his thumbs over her cheekbones. "God, I love you."

Scarlet stared into the magical green eyes she was not yet used to, but already enchanted with, as she ran her hands up his chest. "I love you more."

"Never." He smiled and began to kiss her with a hunger that made her insides tighten. She curved her body into him and parted her lips, letting his tongue slide into her mouth.

Her hands roved over his broad shoulders and to his back, gripping his thin shirt for a moment before sliding a hand into his hair.

She loved him so much. She wanted him so much.

He pulled back from her with a curious look, his chest rising and falling with heavy breaths.

"What is it?" She was out of breath as well.

He tilted his head at her. "I think...I think I can feel you."

"Feel me?" Her thoughts went to several inappropriate places and Tristan's eyes lit again.

He swallowed. "I think I can feel your emotions. I can feel how you are happy and confused and...how you want me." His voice was hoarse on these last words.

Scarlet's cheeks grew hot.

"And I can feel your heart beating as if it were my own." He glanced at her chest where her unruly heart was going wild.

"But how is that possible?"

He shook his head. "Perhaps this is part of my blood living inside you. Perhaps," he swallowed again. "Perhaps you are a piece of me now."

At the thought of being a piece of Tristan, Scarlet's heart nearly spilled over with joy.

"You're pleased." He smiled. "I can feel that you're pleased."

"That is remarkable." Scarlet's mouth fell open. "You can truly feel me."

He nodded. "And when you touch me, it feels...euphoric."

"Euphoric?" The idea of her touch giving him pleasure made her feel powerful, and suddenly she wanted to touch him all over.

His eyes fell to her chest again. "Your heart is racing."

He placed his hand over her heart, his palm resting against the fabric of her dress while his fingers pressed into the bare skin above her neckline. They stared down at where her heart pulsed beneath his hand. Heaving. Demanding.

A warm tremble ran through her and his eyes darkened.

Was his breathing heavier than it had been a moment ago? Was hers?

"Hunter." Her voice was breathy and damp. She wasn't sure what she wanted to say, but it didn't matter. Tristan swept her mouth into his before words could form, kissing her deeply. His lips enraptured her, his tongue running along the soft inner flesh of her mouth. Hot. Wet. Desperate.

He ran his teeth up her jaw and stopped below her ear, a lick searing her sensitive skin. It was all Scarlet could do not to claw her way into his clothes. She wanted to be closer to him. So much closer.

His hands ran along her body and up the sides of her ribcage as his mouth came back to hers. Scarlet rubbed her hips against him, sliding her palms down his back to the hem of his shirt. She slipped her hands underneath and felt his warm skin against her fingers. His hands moved around her body, gripping her hips, brushing her curves—

A loud thud sounded against the door and they both stilled.

Tristan slowly pulled his mouth away from hers and looked at the closed door as if it were a great enemy.

Loud, drunk singing came from the other side of the door as, what Scarlet assumed was, a drunken guest stumbled his way down the hall, knocking into walls and other closed doors with more thuds. His off-pitch song carried on without shame, interrupted only by the occasional hiccup.

A door across the hall squeaked open and a cranky voice yelled, "Would you shut up?"

The drunkard sang louder and Scarlet couldn't help but whisper-laugh at the nonsense in the hallway, Tristan joining in with her.

"Shut up!" the neighbor squawked.

More hiccups, followed by a horrendously loud encore, and the cranky neighbor slammed his door.

Scarlet shifted, unintentionally loosening herself from Tristan's warm arms as they tapered their laughter and listened to the drunkard's song fade down the hall.

Then silence.

Their eyes met and Scarlet swallowed. "I should probably get back to my room."

He ran a hand over his head and nodded. "Yes. Of course." He moved to open the door, then stopped. "Oh. I almost forgot."

He retrieved a small object from the table beside his bed and set it in her palm, his dimples sinking into his cheeks as he grinned.

Scarlet looked down at her mother's brooch and blinked in surprise, her breath catching in her throat. "Oh, Tristan. How did you...?"

"After Nathaniel said you might someday return, I went to your room at the castle and found it for you."

"And you kept it all this time?" She looked up at him in awe.

He nodded. "I wanted you to have a piece of your family."

Scarlet kissed him, passionately and fully, as his arms gently wrapped around her. He'd hoped for her return. He'd kept a piece of her mother for her.

He'd loved her for all these years, even through death and uncertainty.

She was completely his.

9

Every nerve in Tristan's body was on edge as he stared at Nathaniel. "What do you mean we cannot touch?"

"I did not say you cannot touch. I said you should not touch. Not until we understand how your blood affects Scarlet or find a way to undo the blood connection between you two."

They had all left the inn that morning and come back to Nathaniel's estate when he'd insisted he needed to research Scarlet's heart condition. And now Tristan stood in Nathaniel's library and watched him comb through old books.

"It seems your immortal blood is straining Scarlet's heart." Nathaniel closed the book in front of him and moved on to another.

"Yes, but what does that mean?" Tristan said. "Is she sick? Is she weak?"

"I don't know. I'm not a doctor. But that's not a bad idea. I could certainly do a better job than that mumbling *fellow you pinned against the wall the other day."* He smiled.

"Would you please focus, Nathaniel. How much danger is Scarlet in?"

He sighed. "I could be wrong. Her strained heartbeat might be nothing at all. But if I am right, your immortal blood might make her very ill. Perhaps even bring her death."

Tristan's stomach dropped as he whispered, "My blood might kill her?"

"Possibly. Which is why we must find a way to break the blood connection between the two of you—"

"The fountain potion." Tristan was desperate. "That blue water you had—you said it negates immortal blood. If we were to have Scarlet drink some, would my immortal blood cease to thrive inside her chest?"

"Yes. And I've already thought of that. But that vial was stolen years ago."

"Dammit!" Tristan began to pace. "Then we must find a magic peddler with more fountain water."

Nathaniel nodded. "I will start asking around."

"Does Scarlet know that our connection may be...harmful?"

"I told her just before you came in. She did not take it...well."

Tristan turned to go find Scarlet, who was probably cursing herself into a fit somewhere.

"But until we find a cure," Nathaniel's voice stopped Tristan at the door, "or at least until we know how strong your blood connection is, you two should not touch. At all."

****

Walking through the leaf-littered woodland behind the house, Scarlet let the sour mood she'd been biting back for the past few hours sink in. *Not touching Tristan for an indefinite amount of time was preposterous, but not having a cure for his immortal blood—not having a way to stay alive—was terrifying.*

Hearing a twig snap, she turned to see Tristan coming up behind her, a dagger in each hand and a sympathetic look on his face.

Dryly, she said, "Better stay back, Hunter. I am apparently at the mercy of your immortal blood."

"If it helps, I did not know I was immortal until after you died. It's not as if I was keeping a great secret from you and allowed this to happen on purpose."

He stood a generous distance from her, his pleasant countenance an odd contrast to her bitter heart.

"So you jumped in front of an arrow assuming you would die in my place?"

"I did."

Her insides bubbled at his lack of self-preservation. "I do not wish for you to die for me. Ever."

He smiled. "I make no promises."

"Do not joke." Her veins heated. "I thought you were dead once before, Tristan, and it was hell. And then you suddenly reappeared on my wedding day only to sacrifice your life—"

"You're angry with me?" He furrowed his brow.

"Yes!"

Standing apart from him in the forest, in all the confusion of her new life, she grew furious. Furious with Tristan. Furious with all she'd suffered in her last life. Furious that her current life had not yet proved to be any less tragic.

"Why?"

"Because you gave me away!" she shouted, her fury turning into hurt. "You handed me off to Gabriel like I'm some plaything of yours and then you just disappeared."

Wind rustled the trees around them as a muscle flexed in Tristan's jaw. "I was trying to keep you safe."

She scoffed.

"What was I supposed to do?" His green eyes flashed defensively as he dropped the daggers to the ground and took a step forward. "Let you get captured by the earl? Let you be harmed by his men? Was I supposed to let you die?"

Scarlet threw her hands up. "You certainly weren't supposed to give me to your brother and fake your death!"

"I wasn't giving you to him, I was protecting you! And I had no choice but to fake my death—there was no other way out. You can't be angry with me for wanting to return to you."

"I'm not angry that you returned. I'm angry because I thought you were dead!" Her eyes stung. "I thought you were dead, Tristan. And I was barely alive—barely breathing! I was half a soul and I wanted to die. I lost my home. I lost my mother. And then I lost you." Her voice cracked as she thought back to the impossible sorrow she'd suffered without him. She shook her head and repeated, "I thought you were dead."

For several moments, neither of them spoke. The forest air filled with wind and leaves and singing birds, but no words. Tristan stared at her with sadness in his eyes and rubbed a hand over his mouth.

"I'm sorry I ever let you believe I was dead," he said quietly. "And I'm sorry for all you lost." He swallowed. "I swear I was only trying to protect you."

Scarlet sighed, her anger and pain immediately gone with his words. "I know you were." She blew air through her lips. "I'm just a mess."

He smiled. "I like messes."

Not yet ready to be in a good mood, she glared at him. "You don't understand. Everything is a mess." She started listing off her woes. "I'm lost and confused and I don't know where I belong—or if I belong—anywhere. And now I might die, which is bloody perfect. I'm scared and angry and frustrated and agh!"

He stepped forward as if to embrace her, but stopped short.

"And you and I can't even touch!" Scarlet groaned, tossing her head back in defeat. "My life is a complete disaster."

He stared at her for a moment, a small smile playing at his lips.

"What?" she snapped.

"Are you finished?"

"No." She glowered at him, desperately searching for something else to complain about. Finding nothing, she rolled her eyes. "Yes."

Taking a deep breath he stepped closer to her and gave her a reassuring look. "We will find you a cure, this I promise you. It may take time, but I will do anything to keep you healthy. A wise monk once told me there is no victory without a battle." He paused. "So we shall battle to find you a cure until we are victorious. And as far as not touching each other..." He shrugged. "Who cares? We can be together without touching. In fact," he grinned as he bent to retrieve the daggers from the ground, "I have a no-touching plan."

Scarlet eyed him skeptically. "A no-touching dagger plan?"

"Yes. It's brilliant." He handed her one of the blades, his eyes brightening. "We are going to spar. Since the point of weapon sparring is to avoid the other person, it's safe for us to interact this way—unless of course one of us loses an appendage."

"Well, naturally." Scarlet turned the dagger over in her hand.

He leaned into her and his expression became very sincere. "And as far as where you belong..." He put a hand over his heart. "Right here. Always. In life and death and everything in-between." He paused. "Never question it."

Never had a more peaceful feeling flooded Scarlet's heart than at that moment.

He stepped back, his good mood lighting up his face again. "Let's begin, shall we?" He weighed the knife in his hand. "I'm sure your dagger skills have grown rusty in your years away, so I'll go easy on you."

"Rusty?" She threw her dagger, handle first, into the tree beyond Tristan, pegging two overhanging leaves to the bark.

He smiled. "I stand corrected."

Scarlet couldn't help but smile back. She did not belong to anyone, but she belonged with *Tristan. She was home.*

10

Six months later

Tristan glared at Scarlet. "You're doing it wrong."

"I'm not doing it wrong," she bit out. "I'm doing it differently."

They both had been irritable all morning, snapping at one another and bickering. Tristan was starting to think that sparring with sharp knives might not have been a wise choice today. Especially since Scarlet—despite her stubbornness to learn new defense tactics—was incredibly talented.

With his dagger raised, Tristan moved through the trees and swung down—precise in his movement so as not to hurt her—and waited for her to block him correctly. She didn't.

He rolled his eyes. "Would you at least try to learn?"

She jabbed at him again. "I'll try learning as soon as you try not being jealous."

And there it was. The reason for all their morning animosity.

Tristan had made the mistake of telling Scarlet how Gabriel was cursed to be without love outside of her. And Scarlet's emotions had gone wild in sympathy, anger, and love.

She loved Gabriel.

It wasn't the same kind of love she felt for Tristan, entangled in devotion and desire and absolute resolve, but it was love nonetheless. And Tristan hadn't taken it well.

He blocked her incoming dagger with his own.

"I'm not jealous." He was a little jealous.

"Ha." Scarlet thrust her dagger at him again. "You practically accused me of being unfaithful with my emotions."

He blocked her blade and grimaced at her words. "Right. Well. It's difficult to feel you care for someone other than me."

"Then stop feeling me." She swiped at him.

"I can't turn it off—ugh. Quit trying to stab me, woman." He knocked the dagger out of her hand, then threw his own weapon on the ground.

They stared at one another.

"You're being ridiculous, Tristan, I love you. Not Gabriel. You."

"Yet you won't marry me."

Months ago, he had suggested they resume their marriage plans, but Scarlet refused. That, along with her emotions for Gabriel, had Tristan feeling a bit crushed.

She rolled her eyes.

He said, "I was good enough for you to wed in your last life, but somehow I'm no longer fit to be your husband?"

She thrust out angry arms. "Fine! Let's get married! Let's dance at our wedding and sleep by each others' sides and have children and live happily ever after." She dropped her arms. "We can't have those things, Tristan. And if we don't find a cure, I may die. I will not wed you only to die and leave you bound to me for hundreds of years until I return. I will not trap you into a lonely commitment like that."

She started walking through the trees.

Tristan paced behind her, dumbfounded at her reasoning. "You think 'commitment' magically happens upon wedding vows? I'm already bound to you—and have been for years."

"Yes. And I am committed to you. Which is why I won't marry you until I'm cured and no longer a burden."

"You could never be a burden."

"I'm already a burden."

"How?"

She spun around. "You can feel my emotions. You can feel the most honest things inside me and it's driving you mad!"

"I'm not mad," he said. "I just don't want to share your heart with Gabriel."

"You're not! My heart is completely yours."

"But you care for him."

"And I *love* you!" She looked incredulous. "Why are you so threatened by your brother?"

"Because he can touch you!" Tristan yelled, his heart going hollow in sadness. "He can hold your hand and kiss your lips and dance with you and keep you warm. He can do all the things I cannot."

His chest tightened.

"Hunter." Walking up to him, Scarlet stood a breath away and stared into his eyes. "There is no replacing you. Not ever. But I cannot keep fighting like this. Every day is a struggle between us. I want to kiss you and slap you at the same time. It's exhausting and it's breaking my heart."

Tristan looked at the ground and nodded. "Then perhaps we should spend some time apart. Until you're cured."

Anger and hurt flared inside her, but her face remained expressionless. "Perhaps we should."

****

"Have you told Scarlet about your curse yet?" Nathaniel's question caught Gabriel off guard as they waited for Tristan in the library.

They had been actively searching for more magic water since Scarlet's return. Nathaniel had called upon friends and acquaintances, Tristan had bought countless potions, and Gabriel had ventured to the harbors to see if word from the New World brought any news of the Fountain of Youth or its water. But nothing.

"No." Gabriel shifted. "And I don't plan to. She is happy with Tristan. I do not wish to burden her with my loveless heart."

A quiet pang of jealousy shot through Gabriel. Ever since Scarlet had come back to life, his soul had been...more. Scarlet eased the emptiness inside him and, while he understood and respected her love for Tristan, he couldn't help but envy her affections.

But he was grateful for her friendship.

He enjoyed spending time with her, introducing her to the current world and informing her of the history she had missed. She seemed pleased to live in such an advanced time, but disappointed that hunting had gone out of fashion. Tristan seemed to sympathize with her and Gabriel figured that to be perfect.

Tristan and Scarlet spent nearly every afternoon in the forest, playing with weapons and returning in the late afternoon, usually arguing. The two fought as much as they swooned. It was obnoxious.

"If you do not wish to tell her, that is your prerogative." Nathaniel looked around the library. "I wonder what it is Tristan wished to speak with us about. Where do you suppose he is?"

"He and Scarlet were arguing over how to make pancakes when I left them earlier, so who knows? They may very well be slaughtering each other with table knives as we speak."

Scarlet and Tristan stuck fast to Nathaniel's warning and carefully existed alongside one another without touching, though they occasionally exchanged looks more intimate than any touch could be.

Gabriel tugged at his collar.

Striding into the room, Tristan said, "I think we should schedule a passage to the New World as soon as possible."

"And hello to you too." Nathaniel smiled.

"From what I gather," Tristan went on, "it will take us approximately three months to make arrangements. Once we reach the wild land, we can begin asking locals and natives about the Fountain of Youth and find the damned thing ourselves."

Gabriel scoffed. "Right. We'll pack up and travel to a land where everyone dies and there is no food. And then we'll blindly hike our way to a fountain that may or may not be there. It's a huge risk, Tristan."

"So is letting Scarlet die," he snapped.

Nathaniel held up his hands. "Perhaps a trip to the Americas would be helpful. I shall look into it and, if it seems beneficial, I will start making arrangements."

"Soon," Tristan demanded.

Gabriel narrowed his eyes. "Why are you so eager?"

"We are all eager."

"Yes. But Scarlet hasn't shown any sign of illness so it is safe to assume she is still healthy." Gabriel paused. "What has you so raggedly desperate?"

"Because we have nowhere else to look and I do not want to waste another day without the cure. And also," Tristan paused, "I can feel her."

Gabriel blinked. "What?"

He cleared his throat. "I can feel her emotions and it is becoming hard to keep myself from responding to them."

The pang returned to Gabriel's chest.

"You can feel her?" Nathaniel said. "How long has this been going on?"

"Since we found her."

Gabriel stared at him. "And you're telling us just now?"

"I did not think it was important before," Tristan said impatiently. "We need to cure her and get her feelings out of me. Immediately."

Nathaniel twitched his lips. "Does Scarlet experience your emotions as well?"

"No." Tristan rubbed the back of his neck and muttered, "Thank God."

Well, this was just awkward.

Nathaniel slowly nodded. "I will start making arrangements immediately."

11

Ten weeks later

Scarlet was tied into a God-awful corset that cinched beneath a God-awful dress that billowed out around her in far too many layers of God-awful skirts.

Gabriel had taken her to the tailor that morning.

She still had not forgiven him.

"Funny. You are dressed so pretty, but you look so furious." Nathaniel smiled at her as she entered his house, Gabriel coming up behind her.

Everyone had been staying at Nathaniel's house for the past month, planning the details of their trip overseas.

Scarlet frowned at her corset. "You try squeezing your bones into one of these contraptions and keeping a pleasant face."

"No, thank you," Nathaniel said. "I feel I'm already a hazard in my trousers and top hats. I do not need to add lace and ruffles to the madness."

Gabriel shut the front door behind them and sighed at Nathaniel. "Fair warning, friend. Do not take this spitfire of a woman to a tailor. She will do nothing but complain and curse."

"Then perhaps you should not try to dress her up as if she were a doll," Tristan suggested from the back hallway.

Gabriel said, "We are heading overseas to a new land. I thought it would be prudent that Scarlet had something to wear aside from servant dresses and men's clothing." He shot her a pointed look.

Scarlet shrugged. "I enjoy my servant dresses. They are thin and practical and they do not threaten my life. And I find men's shirts far more comfortable than anything I own."

She'd developed a habit of stealing Tristan's shirts from the clothesline and spending her days dressed as him. It was comfortable and she enjoyed smelling him on her skin. She stole a glance at Tristan, thinking about how she'd rather be in his arms than in his clothes, and found him flicking his eyes over her.

Heat rose between them, invisible and dangerous, and Tristan took a precautionary step away from her.

Ever a gentlemen, that one.

Scarlet managed not to curl her lip at his behavior. To say things had gotten worse between the two of them was an understatement. They had stopped spending time together in the forest, and the little time they spent together outside the forest was always tense. They drifted further apart from one another. Physically. Emotionally.

A few days of silence led to a few weeks of avoidance, and now here they were. In the same room, not speaking to one another.

Gabriel and Nathaniel did not seem to mind the contention between Scarlet and Tristan—probably because it was insurance that she would not be exploding into death anytime soon—but Scarlet's heart could barely cope.

She missed Tristan. She wanted him. And she hated the curse that prevented her from satisfying either need. But not speaking to him, not hearing his voice flutter over her skin and bring her soul to life, was almost easier than the constant fighting and near-touching.

Almost.

"We leave in two weeks. Are there any other preparations we must make?" Tristan changed the subject to business, per usual.

Lately, he was focused and determined. She missed his lighthearted demeanor. And his smile.

He glanced at her and she quickly looked away, feeling his eyes on the back of her bare neck where her hair was pulled up. Warmth spread across her shoulders and down her chest under his perusal and Scarlet stifled the shiver that wanted to sprint through her core. He may as well slip his hands into her dress for all the reaction her body was having.

Tristan cleared his throat.

"I believe we are all set," Nathaniel said. "Our ship leaves from the south port, so I will ensure transportation for us and then we shall be off on a new adventure and on our way to a cure." He grinned around the room, taking note of the tangible tension buzzing between Scarlet and Tristan. "And won't that be pleasant? Or at least less uncomfortable?"

The only thing more uncomfortable than her tension with Tristan was her God-awful dress. She shifted and could almost hear her bones crack.

Corsets were the devil.

Tristan's green eyes were on her again and Scarlet's stomach fluttered. Yes. A cure would be marvelous.

****

Later that night, Tristan sat in his guest room at Nathaniel's house, stretching his neck against the emotions he felt coming from the girl upstairs.

Scarlet was in a fit. He did not know what was responsible for the erratic feelings inside her, but they were not letting up and seemed to grow more intense by the second, blossoming inside her and darting into him.

Frustration.

Tristan could ignore that one. When was the woman not frustrated?

Helplessness.

That was a harder feeling to push aside. Scarlet was nothing if not independent. But he could not—no, he would not—*check on her.*

Sadness.

At this, Tristan rubbed his eyes, cursing the legs that pulled him up from his chair and walked him out of his room and up the stairs.

He stood outside Scarlet's door, debating within himself. He and Scarlet had not spoken for weeks, which had greatly reduced the number of times he had to pull himself away from her company, but had left his heart starving. And he wasn't sure, even now, if Scarlet would even want him to show concern for her.

Helplessness. Anger.

He should probably go back to his own room and try to sleep through her feelings—a task far more trying than it sounded.

Sadness.

With his resolve vanishing into thin air, he quietly knocked on her door.

He heard a huffing sound on the other side and then, "Who is it?"

"Me."

A moment passed. Then two. Then the door peeked open to reveal a very frustrated pair of blue eyes.

"What is wrong?" He looked up and down the hallway for any sign of Nathaniel or Gabriel.

"What do you mean?"

He lifted a bored eyebrow.

Her face became stubborn for a moment, then turned to a look of surrender. "I need help."

She bit her lip and Tristan knew he was already done for. It didn't matter what she needed help with, he was completely at her mercy.

"With what?"

She glanced up and down the hallway before opening her door and pulling him inside. He stood by her bed as she closed the door and sealed them into her candlelit room.

Already, this was a poor idea.

With another huff, she said, "I need help taking my dress off."

This was a very poor idea.

"What?"

Glaring at him, Scarlet made her way to the vanity. "Scoff all you want, but you are a man and your clothing makes sense." She flailed her arms out helplessly. *"There are so many ties and clasps and strings on this holy damned dress and I cannot for the life of me figure out how to take the nonsense off."*

He tried to cover his smile.

"I'm being serious, Tristan." Her cheeks reddened at the crest and she wiggled in her top, trying to loosen its deadly grip around her ribcage. *"The woman at the shop tied me into this ensemble today, but she failed to teach me*

how to find my way out of it and I have been trying to free my body for an hour. I simply cannot do it alone."

Tristan smiled openly now.

"Do not laugh," she warned.

He laughed.

"I need help." Desperation. "I don't how to live in this...time. The clothing is ridiculous and the shoes are horrendous and I don't know what I'm doing! And this dress is just the end of it all!" She let out a frustrated cry.

Tristan wanted to wrap her in his arms and laugh at her tantrum at the same time. He nodded with mock seriousness. "Dresses are evil things indeed."

Temper flared in her eyes. "Get out of my room, you insufferable man."

He softened his voice as he walked up to her. "I'm truly sorry, Scar. First thing tomorrow, we will secure a handmaiden for you so you will have help dressing. And undressing."

"That's brilliant. But can you loosen me from the horrid dress tonight?" She looked down at her many skirts and wiggled again, her cleavage jiggling with the motion and derailing any sane thought Tristan hoped to have.

He cleared his throat. "Maybe you should ask Nathaniel or Gabriel for help."

She futilely tugged at a loose tie at her back. "I hardly know Nathaniel. I felt it would be highly inappropriate and incredibly uncomfortable to ask the poor man to strip my dress from my skin."

A very valid point.

"And I did not want to go to Gabriel."

Tristan tilted his head, sinfully gleeful at that. "Why not?"

Dropping the tie, she crossed her arms. "Would you like me to ask Gabriel to take my dress off?"

Hot possessiveness shot down his spine, but Tristan tried to keep his face blank. "It would definitely be a safer option."

"When have you ever known me to be safe?"

"Not once, actually."

Scarlet started twisting around again, yanking on various strings. "Are you going to help me from this bloody contraption or not?"

She lifted her eyes to him. Desire burned through her body and traveled across the room into Tristan. Hot, thick and foreboding, the atmosphere crackled and suddenly it was hard to breathe.

He slowly said, "I think I need to say no."

She sighed. "Fine, then." *She rummaged through the drawers of the vanity until coming up with a dagger.*

One of Tristan's *daggers.*

"Is there anything of mine that you do not steal?"

She wiggled the knife. "You left this on the downstairs table. It was fair game."

"And what do you plan on doing with my *dagger?*"

"I am going to cut my way out of this maze of material."

"You're going to destroy the expensive dress Gabriel bought you just today? That seems rude."

"Then perhaps you could help me before I tear this dress to shreds." *She held the dagger to the top of her ribcage and pulled at a piece of material until she had the blade positioned to cut into it.*

Tristan debated for a moment then sighed. "Turn around."

Relief flooded her body as she slowly turned around.

Maybe this would not be so bad after all. Maybe Tristan could pull at her ties and make his way out of her bedroom in a gentlemanly manner.

Another flash of desire rushed through Scarlet and into Tristan.

Or maybe not.

He stared down at her half-opened dress. "Try to hold still so I don't touch you more than necessary."

"Because Nathaniel says not to?"

"Because I don't want to hurt you," *he snapped. He began undoing the few unbroken clasps than ran down her back and watched her outer garment slowly come undone.*

"I know Nathaniel thinks your touch can make my heart sick, but what if he's wrong? I've been alive now for nearly a year and have shown no sign of illness. There is no reason to continue to believe that your blood is hurting me."

This was true. Scarlet had not been ill at all and her heartbeat, while still forcefully beating in his presence, did not seem to threaten her life. Perhaps his touch was not as dangerous as Nathaniel had feared.

Two…three…four more clasps, and the outer garment was fully undone. It fell from her shoulders and gathered at her waist. Scarlet freed her arms from the ivory material as if it were shackles and let the outer dress fall to the floor, leaving her in only the corset and a single slip skirt.

He began to gently unwind the tangled ties of her corset, brushing strands of her long dark hair to the side so as not to snare it. Scarlet swept her hair over her front shoulder, baring her shoulders and upper back, and Tristan tried to keep his eyes on the ties in his hands.

"I have missed being close to you," *she said quietly.*

Tristan's heart twisted. "I have missed you as well."

His hands felt hot as they pulled at corset strings, slowly loosening their tightness around Scarlet's body until patches of her skin peeked through the crisscrossed laces.

She shifted beneath his careful tugging and his fingertips brushed against the naked skin of her back. A visible shiver went through her and Tristan lost all coherent thoughts.

He'd pulled apart all but the top tie, so the only thing holding the corset to her body was the lace below her shoulder blades. He paused, not sure what to do with his hands now that his task had ended. But his fingers seemed to be content trailing up her spine.

No.

He needed to leave and keep Scarlet safe. Now.

Just as he lifted his fingers from her skin, a tendril of her hair escaped the mass swept over her shoulder and swung against her back. He deftly twisted it in his hand and wrapped it to the side with every intention of releasing it. But with the back of her neck exposed beneath the lock in his hand he couldn't seem to let go.

He absently leaned forward, his mouth just inches from the delicate spot where her neck met her shoulder, and exhaled against her skin.

Another delightful shiver ran down Scarlet's body as she leaned back until her body was up against his. Fighting between the desire to keep her safe and the desire to hold onto her forever, Tristan stood frozen.

He slowly, carefully pressed his lips to the very spot he'd breathed upon and reveled in the soft gasp that escaped Scarlet's mouth.

She tilted her head to the side, granting him access to her throat and shoulder, and he trailed whisper-soft kisses along the skin she shared with him.

Releasing the lock of hair from his fingers, Tristan slid his hands over her bare shoulders, lightly traced his fingers down her arms, and settled his hands against her hips, barely holding her as he kissed her.

She shifted against him, her corset lifting away from her body so his hands were now on the warm, bare skin of her waist beneath. He paused for a moment, his mouth right beside her ear as he tried to talk some sense into himself.

He brushed his lips against the sensitive spot above her jaw, felt Scarlet tremble with the touch, and all sense was lost.

There was something he wasn't supposed to do, but he couldn't remember what it was. Something about this was dangerous, yet his mind failed to acknowledge anything aside from the feel of Scarlet in his arms.

****

Eyes closed against the warmth of Tristan's mouth, Scarlet found herself short of breath as she leaned against him. Reaching her hand back, she slid her fingers into his dark hair, holding his head against the curve of her neck where he was burning kisses into her skin.

Under her loose corset, his hands slid from her hips to her bare stomach, stroking her skin.

And suddenly it wasn't enough.

His mouth, his touch. She wanted more.

Twisting around, she moved against the warm hands on her belly until they pulled out of her corset and she and Tristan were face to face. He slowly brought his hands up, cradling her face in a gentle way that brought back long lost memories.

For a moment they stared at each other, green eyes piercing blue eyes, chests rising and falling with heavy breath. He brushed his lips against hers, kissing her. Softly at first, then deeper. Then hungry and breathless; lips against lips, tongue against tongue. Scarlet moved her hands to his back, pulling him as close to her body as possible, pressing herself into him.

Sliding her hands under his shirt, Scarlet pulled the material up his hard muscles, trying to remove it from his body. *He pulled his mouth away from her long enough to pull off his shirt and toss it to the floor, before putting his hands back on her hips and bringing her back to him.*

But Scarlet gasped, stunned by what she saw on his body.

A dark design started at the top of his left ribcage, crawled down to his hip, and disappeared into the front waistband of his trousers.

Tristan followed her gaze to his torso.

"My drawing," she whispered. "You have my drawing on your skin." *She reached a hand out and tentatively touched the dark image, not believing what she was seeing.* "How is this possible?" *She couldn't pull her eyes away from the design she had long ago marked onto his body with the sap of a leaf.* "How has it not washed away?"

All at once, a thousand memories were called up in her mind. She and Tristan in the forest, hunting together, swimming together, laughing, running, loving, living—all with reckless abandon.

"It is called a tattoo and it is a permanent ink." *Tristan let her fingers trace the lines, standing still for her perusal.* "I had it stitched by a monk when I went to war in your last life."

Her lips parted. "You darkened my drawing to remember me?"

He nodded. "I wanted a piece of you to be a piece of me."

She stroked her fingers up and down the lines, pulling his waistband down so she could see more of the drawing. Her heart swelled knowing Tristan had been wandering the world for over a hundred years with a memory of her inked into his side.

She looked up at him as emotion flooded her soul and, for the first time since she'd come back to life, she was grateful he could feel her emotions. She wanted him to feel every part of her that felt deeply for him and know she loved him just as fiercely as he loved her.

With devotion in his eyes, he smiled at her and Scarlet kissed him with every fiber of her being. Her mouth went wild against his and she ran her hands down his bare chest.

She pulled back from their kiss, just far enough to breathe, their mouths so close every hot, damp breath of Tristan's feathered out against her cheeks. She opened her mouth to—well, she didn't know, exactly...beg, perhaps?—but his lips were against hers again, silencing any words she may have had and driving need through her veins.

Running his hands past her hips, Tristan lifted her onto the flat surface of the vanity behind her and stood between her legs. His lips traveled across her collarbone as his fingers pressed into the bare skin of her lower back and hips.

She held his head against her throat as he kissed her, the loose corset around her chest shifting with every ragged breath she took. With her legs wrapped around his waist, she pulled him closer and pressed her body against his.

He groaned and moved his hot mouth back to hers. "You are going to kill me, woman."

She whispered, "Never."

His hands slid down to her thighs, running the length of them until he had the hem of her slip in his fingers. He slowly pulled the slip up, his hands brushing against her bare legs.

She ran her hands down his hard stomach muscles; he ran his teeth along her jaw. She tugged at his waistband; he slid his hands under her thighs and lifted her so their bodies were even closer.

Scarlet was overwhelmed with pleasure and love and sensation and heat. She tilted her head back and her eyes fluttered open.

Suddenly the room lit up.

Bright blue light illuminated the room, glowing against the sparse furniture and Tristan's large body above her.

They both froze, the only movement between them their heavy breaths and pounding chests. Tristan pulled back from her and looked as confused as she felt.

Where was the light coming from?

"Scar." He searched her face in bewilderment and fear, his hands coming up to cup her cheeks. "Your eyes are glowing."

"What?" She blinked.

Her eyes were glowing? Glowing?

She blinked again, trying to ease the burning in her eyes. "Why are they glowing? What is happening?"

Tristan cursed under his breath and lowered his hands.

Scarlet kept blinking until the light faded, completely confused and slightly terrified. She had no idea what was going on, but she was painfully aware of the fact that Tristan was no longer touching her.

Her hands started to shake.

What was happening?

He stepped back and ran a hand over his mouth, inhaling deeply through his nose with a panicked expression on his face.

She swallowed. "What do you suppose that was?"

"A mistake. A very big mistake."

Fury lit her veins. "What just happened was not a mistake."

"I should not have touched you until you were cured."

"Why? What do my glowing eyes mean? Am I getting sick?"

"I don't know." He started pacing the room, running a shaky hand over his head as he muttered curse words.

Was she...was she dying? A swamping fear settled on her and Scarlet's pulse started to race.

"Calm down, Scar," Tristan said.

"Don't tell me to calm down! You calm down. You're the one cursing and pacing."

"Because I'm scared!"

"I'm scared too!"

Tristan's face softened and he took a deep breath. "Do not be afraid. I'm sure you will be fine. We just need to keep from touching—completely—until you are cured."

Scarlet nodded, but fear still gripped her.

He swallowed.

"Don't leave me," she said, somehow feeling him slip away from her even though he hadn't moved.

"I have to go back to my room, Scar."

She was so afraid. And confused. And afraid.

Looking at her with emerald eyes filled with love and concern, he said, "I do not wish to leave you, but I cannot stay. It isn't safe. Clearly, my touching you has done something. I need to stay away."

She shook her head.

"I cannot stay, Scarlet," he whispered, his voice pained. "Please don't ask me to stay. I do not want to hurt you more than I already have."

"Go," she whispered.

He quietly slipped out her door and Scarlet's eyes started to burn again.

12

Scarlet bunched up another linen and shoved it into the top drawer of the small desk in her room. Her nose had been bleeding off and on for the last week. She'd managed to conceal it the first few days, writing it off as a symptom of stress or fatigue, but this morning it had bled nonstop.

She and Tristan hadn't spoken a word since the night in her bedroom, keeping their contact to only passing in hallways and stolen glances across the room, but Scarlet could tell he was on edge. Always watching her, his brow always creased.

Their trip to the New World was quickly approaching and everyone—including Nathaniel—seemed anxious in some way. The last thing she wanted to do was parade a bloody nose in front of them, adding another worry to the long list of things that hovered over their heads. But she was starting to worry herself.

Her heart pounded in fear and she pressed a hand to her chest to keep the beating madness contained. She needed to tell someone about her nosebleeds, but she didn't want to alarm Tristan. Perhaps she would tell Nathaniel.

Yes. That was a good plan.

Standing up, she wiped her sweaty palms on her skirt and opened her door to find a very upset-looking Tristan standing in the hall.

"What's wrong?" he demanded, looking her over before glancing into her room.

"What do you mean?"

His eyes shot back to her. "I can feel you, Scar. I know you're scared and you've been scared all morning. What's wrong?"

Oh, damn the connection.

She stepped forward, forcing him to take a step back. "I'm fine."

"Is it your eyes? Did they glow again?" The edge in his voice disappeared.

"No," she said sternly. "This is not about my eyes. I'm fine." Her palms started to sweat again and Tristan's eyes widened.

"I just felt fear flood into you, Scar. What the hell is—" He sucked in a breath as blood dripped from her nose. Again.

She immediately tried to wipe it away, terror darting through her and making her angrier than anything else.

"Oh, Scar," Tristan whispered as he stepped forward. "Oh, no."

"I'm fine," Scarlet said beneath the hand that was actively holding her nose up. Dear God, let the blood stop.

Tristan ran terrified eyes over her face. "Is this because of me? Did I do this?"

She shook her head and tried to reassure him so he'd stop looking at her like that. "I'm sure it's something else."

"We have to tell Nathaniel," he said.

"Tell me what?" Nathaniel's voice came from down the hall and Scarlet turned to see him standing outside his door, messy brown hair matted to his head and a curious expression on his face. But the curiosity vanished as he took in Scarlet's bloody hand and, now, dress.

"What happened?" Nathaniel walked over to Scarlet, pulling her hand away from her nose. "Go find a rag," he commanded Tristan as more blood fell.

Scarlet pointed to her desk where a stack of fresh linens still sat.

A burning sensation formed behind her eyes and Nathaniel gasped as blue light reflected off the walls.

No. No, no, no.

Tristan cursed.

"Your eyes..." Nathaniel waved a hand at Tristan and sternly said, "Back away."

Tristan stepped away and the blue light disappeared from the walls.

Scarlet looked at Tristan. "It happened again?"

"Again?" Nathaniel whipped his head to Tristan. "This has happened before?"

Tristan looked panicked. "It happened the other night. I didn't know what it meant."

"You should have told me." Nathaniel cursed and returned his attention to Scarlet, studying her face like it was a puzzle. His forehead wrinkled. "Walk back over to Scarlet," he said to Tristan.

Tristan obeyed, stepping forward, and as soon as he neared, blue light shot from Scarlet's eyes. The minor burning intensified and a shot of pain cut through her insides.

Tristan cursed again. "I'm hurting her." The light faded as he moved to stand against the opposite wall, hands fisted at his sides. "I'm causing this."

Nathaniel nodded. "It appears that way."

"What is this?" Scarlet asked with a cracked voice. "What is happening to me?"

Nathaniel shook his head with a somber look, but said nothing. He did not need to, Scarlet already knew the answer.

She was dying.

****

"There has to be something else we can do." Tristan hurried around Nathaniel's library, panic and dread filling his soul.

"She's semi-immortal," Nathaniel said. "I cannot change what she is."

Gabriel—who was supposed to be with Scarlet, taking care of her through the bloody noses and eyes that were now flashing nonstop—stood in the doorway. "You need to calm down, Tristan."

He whipped his head to Gabriel, fury racing up his throat. "Calm down? Scarlet is dying. She's *dying.*"

"I know, but you need to calm down."

Tristan rubbed his jaw and looked back at Nathaniel. "We need to leave for the New World today."

"There are no ships departing—"

"Then we will buy our own ship and go alone."

Nathaniel raised his hands. "You're not thinking clearly—"

"No, **you're** *not thinking clearly!* She's going to die and I will be without her for another hundred and fifty years!" His throat closed up on this last sentence, causing him to clamp his mouth shut and wish he could tear out the heart inside him that hurt so much.

An impossible pain drove into Tristan's chest and, at the same moment, a cry came down the stairs and into the library.

Scarlet.

"Why the hell did you leave her alone?" *Tristan yelled at Gabriel as he rushed out of the library and up to Scarlet's room.*

Tristan froze when he saw her.

She was on the floor, curled into a ball as she clutched her chest, blood falling from her nose. She was in severe pain—unbearable pain cutting straight through her heart and filling Tristan's gut. She was groaning and gasping and crying and—

"Scar." *He dropped to the floor beside her, all reason gone from his mind as he lifted her gently and held her against him.*

"Do not leave me, Hunter," *she begged.* "I do not want to be alone. I am scared and—ah!" *She clutched at her chest again and Tristan felt her torture echo in his body.*

"There has to be something that will take away her pain!" *Tristan yelled at Nathaniel who was rushing into the room.*

He shook his head and hurried to Scarlet's side, looking into her eyes as she cried. "You need to leave, Tristan. Your nearness is making it worse."

Dammit, he was right.

Tristan kissed her forehead once, then twice, wishing he could take away her pain, before reluctantly releasing her body and walking to the door.

Disbelief, fear, horror, helplessness.

This was all his fault.

Scarlet shook her head. "I do not want Tristan to leave me—" *She whimpered as her pain intensified and, without another thought, Tristan turned from the room and left the house.*

Out the door and into the backfield, he put as much distance between himself and Scarlet as possible so her heart would stop breaking. But her pain stayed with him, biting into his chest with every pulse.

He wasn't far enough, he wasn't fast enough.

He began to run, but her pain was still there, reverberating in his chest.

Picking up speed, he ran until the night around him was a blur of shadows and wind and Scarlet's pain was soon overshadowed by his own pain, his muscles pulling tight and hot, sucking the air from his lungs in his distance from her.

He pressed on, through the trees and wind, until his physical pain had him gnashing his teeth, burning from the inside out. The piece of his heart that lived in Scarlet was screaming at the expanse between them, but he could not give in. He needed to run...farther...away...

His limbs started to shake, his body broke into fever and his organs began to twist until he thought he was in hell.

He felt for her and grunted at the pain that still lingered in her chest. Through blinding torment and retching muscles, Tristan pushed forward before falling to his knees. He began crawling through the dirt. Farther away. He just needed to get...farther...away... He dug at the earth, trying to force his gnarled body to obey his wishes and then—

Nothing.

The pain vanished, leaving numbness in its wake.

Scarlet was gone.

He could no longer feel her.

Letting his body fall completely to the ground, he untwisted his limbs and roared into the night.

He had killed Scarlet.

13

London 1695

Far past midnight, Gabriel stumbled into the house he shared with Tristan—months of gambling had robbed him of his own house—the bright moon giving away his shadow even as he tried to keep in the dark.

He closed the door behind his drunken body and winced at the heavy sound it threw into the room. The last thing he needed was a lecture from Tristan about his depraved lifestyle.

No one had responded well to Scarlet's shocking and horrible death. Nathaniel had locked himself in his home across town, determined to study medicine so he could heal her when she returned.

Tristan barely spoke a word and rarely made eye contact, spending his every waking hour in the forest shooting arrows and throwing weapons at innocent trees.

And Gabriel was back to feeling the full weight of the curse, painfully aware of the absence of joy from his chest. An absence alcohol, cards, and women seemed to temporarily soothe.

In two weeks time, they were leaving for the New World. Nathaniel was hopeful about this venture, as was Gabriel, but no one knew Tristan's thoughts on the matter, since the brute rarely spoke more than a single word at a time.

Maybe a new land was just what they all needed to get back to normal. Whatever normal was.

Gabriel crept softly down the hall and breathed a sigh of relief when he saw no sign of his twin.

"We need to talk." Tristan's body appeared out of nowhere.

Startled, Gabriel jumped back. "Dear God, man. Why must you insist on hiding in the shadows? I'm beginning to think the vampire rumors about you are true."

"This is no time for jokes. I need help." Tristan sniffed and gave Gabriel a despairing look. "Are you drunk again?"

Gabriel cursed under his breath, knowing he smelled of alcohol and smoke and wishing Tristan were a little less good and a little more fun. "No?"

"Right." Tristan moved past him and into the parlor, striking a few matches and lighting the room's lanterns.

"Oh, so now *light is appropriate.*"

"Shut up and listen."

Gabriel sighed and plopped down into the nearest chair, almost falling out of it as he miscalculated the center of the cushion and sat on the edge of the armrest instead. He quickly regained his balance and smoothed his hands down his jacket.

He was not drunk.

"Scarlet is going to come back to life again."

"Uh-huh."

"And I refuse to cause her death. Again." Tristan ran a hand through his disheveled hair. "But I cannot be trusted."

Gabriel squinted as Tristan's tall frame went out of focus for the briefest of moments.

"Which is why I need you." Tristan pressed hard against Gabriel's chest until he had no choice but to give him his undivided—albeit blurry—attention.

Plucking his brother's hand away, Gabriel said, "Right. Let's hear it, then. What is it you need?"

Tristan looked at him for a long moment, his green eyes more ablaze than usual and the hairs on Gabriel's neck began to prickle. He scratched at them in a desperate attempt to soothe his nerves. Something was off.

Tristan inhaled slowly. "I need you to keep me from Scarlet."

Gabriel blinked. "I don't follow."

"Do you still love her?"

Well, now that was a loaded question.

Narrowing his eyes, Gabriel leaned back. "Is this a trap?" He tugged at his collar. "Are you planning to punch me?"

"Just answer the question."

Gabriel twitched his lips. Confessing that you still loved your brother's girl was a dangerous move. And it almost always merited a punch in the face.

Ah, what the hell. How bad could a fist really hurt a numb face?

"Yes," Gabriel admitted. "Yes, I love her still."

"And she loves you," Tristan said more to himself than to Gabriel.

Gabriel blew through his lips. "Well, that's debatable. I mean, there was a time, maybe—"

"She loves you, Gabriel." Tristan's eyes cut into him. "I felt it when she was alive. I felt her love for you."

Ah, yes. Tristan could feel Scarlet. A lovely side-effect of their semi-immortal connection—wait, what?

Scarlet loved Gabriel?

Gabriel's ears and cheeks heated. He tried to swallow, but his throat was too dry. "She does not love me as she loves you."

"Not yet."

"Not ever." Regardless of what Tristan had felt in her, Scarlet loved Tristan and he loved her and blah, blah, blah.

"It doesn't matter what Scarlet feels for me," Tristan said. "I need you to take her away from me."

At this, Gabriel tried to sober up. "Hold on there, brother." He stood, pleased with himself for not wobbling. "I will not take Scarlet away from you. And she wouldn't let me even if I tried."

"If you don't remove her from my reach, I will grasp onto her in every fragile life she has, bringing her immediate death."

Gabriel scoffed. "No, you won't."

"But I will," Tristan said. Warning clouded his voice and a sharp shine in his eyes had Gabriel questioning just who, exactly, was standing before him. It certainly was not the same Tristan he'd grown up with, carefree and happy. And it was not the Tristan who was so typically rational and generous.

No. This Tristan was desperate and wild, with a darkness Gabriel had never seen before.

He rubbed the side of his face. "Are you telling me you have such little control over yourself that you can't keep your hands off of Scarlet—even to save her life?"

Doubt flashed in Tristan's eyes as he rubbed a hand across his mouth. "It's not just my hands that are dangerous. It's my presence as well. I don't trust myself."

"It will never work, brother. Without a cure, Scarlet will die anyway. Me 'taking her away' from you won't heal her heart."

"No. But it will allow her to live longer. In her next life, I will leave so she cannot find me. I will go somewhere far away where I cannot hurt her and leave Scarlet in your care. All I need you to do is keep her from loving me."

Gabriel crossed his arms. "And how, pray tell, shall I do that?"

"I don't know. Convince her I'm not worthy. Convince her to fall in love with you."

Clearly, Tristan had lost his mind.

"Convince her?" Gabriel stood with his mouth open for a long minute. "Have you not met Scarlet? She does not convince easily. She's stubborn and temperamental and obnoxiously independent. No." He shook his head. "I cannot do what you're asking. It feels wrong."

Well, there's a sentence Gabriel never thought would come out of his mouth.

"You must," Tristan insisted. "Do you understand what's at stake here? Death. Scarlet's death. Again and again until we find a cure or the damned fountain and the chances of either are slim. Do you want her to die again?"

"No."

"Then take her away from me. Do whatever you must to change her affections."

"Why me?" Gabriel said. "Why not have her fall in love on her own with some other poor fellow who is doomed to always be second place in her heart?"

"Because you I will not kill," Tristan said. "Some other 'poor fellow' would get his bones crushed."

The hardness in Tristan's eyes left little doubt in Gabriel's mind that Tristan would, indeed, kill any other poor fellow.

Gabriel shook his head. "You cannot possibly mean what you're saying."

"I do."

"Really? And what if she wants to kiss me?" Gabriel lifted his chin.

"Then kiss her." No emotion on Tristan's face.

"And if she wants to touch me?"

"I won't stop her." Tristan eyes flickered for the briefest of seconds.

Gabriel needed to push harder, he needed Tristan to see how preposterous this idea was. Tilting his head, Gabriel slowly said, "And if she wants to sleep by my side?"

Tension swamped the room.

"Sleep with her and I'll kill you." There was no mercy in Tristan's voice.

Gabriel smiled, relieved as he took a step back. "See? I cannot do this Tristan. It's not what you really want."

Tristan flexed his jaw. "How is it that you seem to have no sense of decency when it comes to your personal life, yet when I ask—practically beg—you to take the girl you want away from me, you suddenly have a moral compass?"

Gabriel shrugged. "You must be rubbing off on me."

One point for Tristan.

Damn him.

"Very well," Tristan said, renewal in his eyes. "You do not need to convince Scarlet to love you. Just promise me you'll love her in my absence. Promise me you'll protect her and provide for her and keep her happy."

"I feel we've had this conversation before..." Gabriel tapped his chin in a mocking way.

"Then promise me again."

He pursed his lips. "The last time you left Scarlet in my care, a witch killed her. And I distinctly remember you shoving a sword against my neck afterward."

"That was before my touch was deadly to Scarlet." His voice cracked. "Please, Gabriel."

It was in this moment, at the sound of Tristan's vulnerability, that Gabriel folded. *He had been selfishly trying to protect himself from going through the pain of loving—but not quite having—Scarlet, again. But when Gabriel saw the pain in Tristan's face, he made his decision. For Tristan. Not Scarlet.*

"I will do it." Gabriel exhaled. "This could end us, Tristan. You and I."

Indecision flashed in Tristan's eyes and, for a moment, Gabriel thought Tristan was going to revoke his proposal—an idea that brought Gabriel both joy and disappointment—but Tristan didn't budge.

"You are my brother," Tristan said with resolve. "Nothing could end us."

Avow

14

Charleston 1741

Tristan knocked on Nathaniel's door and waited impatiently on the doorstep. Having been in the New World for over fifty years now, Gabriel, Nathaniel and Tristan had set up homes for themselves and had fully assimilated into the rugged and adventurous land. They had gone on many quests to the lower regions, spurred on by rumors of the eternal fountain, and had traveled to the northern regions where the established cities held whispers of magic and immortality. But they were still without a cure for Scarlet.

Which was unacceptable.

The great door opened. "I would say this is a pleasant surprise," Nathaniel said, "but since you've been in an awful mood for fifty years I'm assuming you are not here to sing or dance or anything jolly like that."

"I'm afraid not."

"Well, then by all means," he gestured him inside, "come in and depress me."

Tristan smiled at his tolerant friend. He tended to be his darkest around Nathaniel. Why, he wasn't sure. But still the chap was always pleasant. "I will try to keep my depression contained today."

"And wouldn't that be a feat?" *Nathaniel smiled.* "So. What can I do for you?"

Tristan paced farther into the foyer. "I would like to go through all your books on immortality."

Nathaniel led him back to his office—which was half medical and half magical—and bustled about, retrieving books from shelves and tables and under the legs of otherwise-wobbly desks.

"What exactly are you looking for?" *He began stacking his collection of books upon one of the wobbly desks.*

"An alternative cure for Scarlet," *Tristan said.*

"I'm afraid my books may disappoint you on that end, but you are welcome to borrow them anyway."

Tristan nodded. He would read. He would scour. He would do anything to find a pebble of hope amidst the rocks of despair that sat upon his shoulders.

Nathaniel added another volume to his pile and the desk wobbled, spilling the books all over the floor.

Tristan bent to help Nathaniel gather the books and his eyes caught on a page that had fallen open. The words "true death for an immortal" *were scribbled at the top.*

He jerked his head to Nathaniel. "We can die?"

Nathaniel waved a hand at Tristan. "Supposedly. If our hearts are cut in half. But it is not true. You yourself were shot through the heart with an arrow and did not die. Clearly, the splitting of an immortal heart is not fatal."

Tristan's mind began to race and, for some reason, hope flared in his chest. "What if it was not the splitting of my heart that failed, but the arrow itself? Do you think immortal death would be possible with the right weapon?"

Nathaniel shrugged. "I suppose anything is possible."

"Interesting." Tristan wasn't sure what this new information meant, but for the first time in decades, his heart beat with a purpose.

****

Several weeks later, Gabriel patted Nathaniel on the back and hollered above the noise of the crowded bar, "Another round for the good doctor!" before winking at Greta, the bartender of his most-frequented pub.

And by "most-frequented" he meant daily. And nightly.

They had been hunting for the Fountain of Youth without success for decades now, and still had no cure for Scarlet and, therefore, no cure for his curse.

So Gabriel was still without love—a plight he endured with endless women, plenty of card games and, yes, booze. Which was why he'd wrangled Nathaniel out of his home filled with medical equipment and insisted he come out to play in the taverns tonight.

Where Gabriel had spent the last few decades gaining and losing wealth, and Tristan buried himself in books and, lately, an unnatural interest in weapons, Nathaniel had dedicated his time to his pursuit of medicine—and was actually becoming quite a skilled physician. Medicine suited him much better than witchcraft.

Greta poured another two shots for them and Gabriel lifted his glass to Nathaniel. "Drink up, my friend."

Nathaniel smiled and drank along with him. "You are in good spirits tonight." He set his empty glass on the bar.

"Yes, well, thanks to those lovely women," Gabriel nodded at the group of colorfully-dressed ladies batting their lashes in the corner, "and my beloved Greta," he smiled at Greta, whose only response was a "Hmmph", "I am in good spirits most every night."

"So I hear."

Gabriel rolled his eyes. "Has Tristan been complaining about my activities again?"

"No. He simply takes note."

"Yes, well, I wish he would throw away his note pad and join in on the party every once in a while." Gabriel waved a finger at Greta for more liquor. "It is a draining thing to be the only happy family member."

Nathaniel laughed. "Is that what you are?"

"I am certainly not the disgruntled family member." Gabriel drank up what Greta poured.

"No. I suppose you're not." Nathaniel watched Greta pour more into his glass and drank as well. "Have you noticed a change in your brother lately?"

"Yes. I've noticed he's no fun at all. He used to be pleasant, you know. Friendly and content. The bastard."

"No." Nathaniel wrinkled his brow. "I mean, have you noticed a darkness in him? He seems...different."

Gabriel shrugged. He did not have enough alcohol in his body for this conversation. "His love died. Who wouldn't be dark at that?"

Nathaniel scratched his jaw. "Yes. I think that may play into why he has withdrawn from the world as he has. Scarlet's death was horrendous."

A sharp pain shot into Gabriel's chest and he waved at Greta again to numb it away. He did not want to think about Scarlet and the hope she brought him when she was alive. He did not want to think at all.

"Now, no more talk of Tristan, he is souring my pleasant mood and he's not even here," Gabriel said. "Let us speak of other things. Like the card game being held later tonight."

Greta refilled both their glasses.

Nathaniel smiled. "You have already lost your fortune twice since we've been in South Carolina. I'm not sure a card game is wise."

High stakes made Gabriel feel alive and, without Scarlet, he mostly felt dead. "I have an eternity to win and lose my fortune, so I shall play until card games go out of fashion."

"You are truly reckless."

"Why, thank you." He smiled. "Now, drink up!"

15

Charleston 1789

Scarlet shivered against the cold chill the wailing wind brought to her body. She slowly opened her eyes to the cutting sun of a winter sky shining off the snow-covered ground, and blinked.

Where was she? And why had she been sleeping outside in the snow? She could not remember anything about her whereabouts and had just started to panic when she saw him.

A boy—a beautiful boy—stood a few yards away from her wearing a pair of low-slung pants and an open black coat over his bare chest. He was breathing heavily, like he'd been running, and he looked at her with relief and fear on his face.

"You're safe," he assured her, looking like both protector and predator.

But staring at him, Scarlet realized she did, indeed, feel safe.

Slowly, she stood up and took him in. He was not dressed for winter at all and his shaggy dark hair was tousled and wild. But his eyes...his eyes were breathtaking.

Green and piercing, they looked into her and held her captive. Her heart started to pound and somehow Scarlet knew she knew this boy. She just couldn't...remember....

A commotion behind the beautiful boy broke out and two other figures slowly approached from the forest beyond.

"Scarlet." A boy identical to the one Scarlet had been staring at carefully neared her, carrying a large blanket in his hands as he smiled.

The third boy, who looked nothing like the other two, said nothing but smiled broadly.

Unlike the first stranger, the other boys were dressed for winter, with coats and gloves and clothing covering their chests. And they both looked pleased to see her, which was more than she could say for the quiet stranger in black, standing off to the side now, but never taking his eyes from her face. She had the sudden urge to touch him.

His eyes darkened for a moment before her attention was called away by the twin boy who was now standing before her.

"Scarlet," he said. "Do you remember who you are?"

"Yes. I'm Scarlet Jacobs," she said automatically.

"Do you remember us? Or when you were born?"

She thought for a moment, fear creeping under her skin as she realized she had no recollection of ever being born, let alone when.

Shaking her head, she took a step back.

The twin boy who, she now realized, had brown eyes and not green, smiled at her lovingly. "We are your friends and you were born in 1523."

Click.

A burning began behind her eyes and the forest disappeared as she slowly went blind with memories.

Hundreds of memories. Swooping into her mind, each memory clicked into place against another one and, suddenly, Scarlet remembered everything.

Struggling to get back to the present, she blinked until the forest returned. "Gabriel!" She threw her arms around him with joy and an overwhelming sense of relief.

But then she remembered Tristan and his green eyes and open heart...and the way he'd loved her and how he had fled from her when she had started to die—

"Tristan!" Her arms fell from Gabriel as she whipped around in search of her Hunter, desperate to embrace him.

But he had vanished.

"Where is he?" Scarlet looked first to Gabriel, then to Nathaniel.

"He has left in order to keep you safe," Nathaniel said.

"If it is so critical to keep us apart, then why did he come to the forest to get me?" Scarlet put her hands on her hips, determined to argue her way into Tristan's arms, if only for a moment.

Gabriel wrapped the blanket around her. "Tristan is the one who found you, Scarlet. Because of your connection he can feel where you are."

"Oh." Right. Tristan could feel her. Could he feel how she wanted to run after him right now?

Nathaniel cleared his throat, his smile a bit too bright. "You're alive again. Isn't that wonderful?" He spoke with a strange accent. Odd.

"How long was I dead?" Scarlet asked.

"About a hundred years," Gabriel said pleasantly, as if skipping a century of time was good news and not severely bizarre.

His voice held the same accent as Nathaniel's, no longer sounding English. It sounded...less soft.

"Come," Gabriel said. "Let us take you back home."

The boys chatted away endlessly as they led her through the trees, telling her about the new land they occupied and what the world was now like. Scarlet was barely listening.

A hundred years. She'd lost a hundred years. She was overwhelmed and confused. And she was impatient to get back to Tristan, where she always felt at home.

They came upon a large house nestled in a thick clump of trees with tall, white pillars in front and shrubs lining the drive.

"This is Gabriel's home," Nathaniel said.

"And it shall be yours too." Gabriel smiled at Scarlet.

She raised a brow. "I will be living with you?"

"Yes," Nathaniel said. "And I live not far away, so I shall be able to check on you every few weeks, to ensure you are healthy."

"Nathaniel has become a doctor in your absence," Gabriel explained. "And, unlike magic, he is actually quite good."

Nathaniel glared at him.

They entered the house and took Scarlet to a large open room where Tristan was waiting for them. His arms crossed, his face expressionless. He looked older than before, and more wearisome. He stood on the farthest side of the giant room while Gabriel placed a gentle hand on Scarlet's arm to keep her at the exact opposite side of the space.

"What is this?" She looked down at where Gabriel was latched onto her, annoyance pricking her insides.

"This is us, keeping you safe." Nathaniel said.

Nathaniel stood casually in-between Scarlet and Tristan. "Since we now have a better understanding of how fatal Tristan's presence is to your heart, we have decided it's in everyone's best interest if you and he are separated in this life."

"I decided no such thing." Scarlet's eyes stayed on Tristan, hoping to break down his icy stare with the anger she knew he could feel swirling inside her chest.

Gabriel cleared his throat. "It's only until we find a cure for you."

Scarlet slowly turned her eyes to Gabriel, staring at him with a harshness he didn't deserve. "The cure you've been seeking for a hundred years without success?"

A pained expression crossed his face.

She turned back to Tristan. "And you? What are your thoughts on this?" She started to walk toward him, but Gabriel's soft grip tightened.

Scarlet snapped her eyes to him. "Let go of me."

"You can't touch him, Scarlet," he said softly, sincere regret on his face.

"I will not touch him. I only wish to speak to him."

And maybe touch him.

With a warning glare, Gabriel slowly released her arm and Scarlet took a few steps deeper into the room until she was halfway to Tristan.

"What are your thoughts on this plan?" she asked again.

Tristan was silent for a moment. "It was my idea."

He had the funny accent too. What was happening? Everything had changed. Everything was different.

"Your idea?" She stared at him in disbelief then turned to Nathaniel. "Isn't Tristan in pain when he is away from me? Surely we can formulate a less severe arrangement. Why should he subject himself to discomfort on my behalf?"

"Because I've already lived for hundreds of years, Scarlet." Tristan's weary voice matched the look in his eyes. "And pain is nothing when compared to death, so I am leaving. Today." He kept his eyes carefully mounted to her face. Blank. Empty of feeling.

Scarlet blinked.

Today? He was leaving today?

But she'd barely come back to life!

Her heart started to pound and her throat constricted. For a brief moment, the emptiness in Tristan's eyes disappeared, replaced by something sorrowful.

Good.

She wanted him to feel her pain. To hate it. To want to soothe it.

But then he was back to standing stoic, staring at her like she was a stubborn child.

After a few deep breaths, and an inner monologue made up of several curse words, Scarlet kept her voice perfectly even. "Very well."

Without another word or look in Tristan's direction, she turned and walked from the room. She had no idea what doors led to what rooms, but she needed to get away from Tristan before she screamed. Or heaven forbid, cried. She went into the hallway, randomly chose a door, and found herself in a parlor of sorts.

Frustrated and unbelievably sad, she made her way to a large, velvet chair in the corner. Sitting down, she knotted her hands together and stared out the large parlor window. Tristan was going to leave her?

A new century she could handle. Losing Tristan, she could not.

A quiet click sounded from the door and Tristan entered the room.

"Have you come to say farewell?" she asked with all the bitterness her tongue could muster.

He nodded once, shutting the door behind him. "I am leaving in just a few minutes."

A few minutes. Her eyes stung.

She straightened her shoulders. She would not cry. "So you shall leave and then what? What will become of us?"

Tristan rubbed a hand across his mouth. "I don't know."

He had slipped back into his native accent and the gesture was so thoughtful it hurt.

She hated him. "And if we never find a cure, what then?"

"I don't know."

She hated him. "Will you leave me in every life?"

His eyes glinted. "I don't know, Scar."

Anger pricked her insides. "So because you cannot touch me, you will abandon me."

"That is not the reason—"

"Isn't it? You can't have my body so you've decided not to—"

"This isn't about touching you, Scarlet!" *Frustration laced his voice.*

"Do not be angry with me!"

"I'm not angry." *He exhaled.* "I'm terrified. I could kill you. Kill you. Again."

A moment of silence passed as they stared at each other, heartbreak colliding in the space between them.

"I watched you die, Scar. I watched my blood tear your heart in half. That is not something I can do again."

"But I came back to life." *A sliver of hope splintered her chest.* "I shall always come back to life—"

"And what of all the years in-between?" *he said.* "What of the years where I live with the memories of watching you in pain, living in guilt of your agony? The years I am completely alone and inconsolable? Shall I just forget those years?"

Her heart broke apart at his words.

"I will not kill you, Scar." *His eyes were bleak, sucking the sliver of hope from her heart.*

He looked at the floor. "*I put away some money for you. It should be plenty for whatever you choose to do with your life. Nathaniel will make sure you can access it.*"

"*I don't want your money. I want you to stay.*"

He looked at her. "*I am going to leave so you may have a life, Scar.*"

She shook her head. "*If you leave me, I will hate you forever.*"

It was a lie. It was a terrible, painful, desperate lie and Tristan knew it.

He dropped his eyes to the floor and nodded his head. "*Your hate would never change my love.*"

And then he left.

Alone in the parlor, Scarlet let centuries of tears spill down her face.

16

Scarlet exhaled through her nostrils, slowly and with a low grunt, as Nathaniel checked her eyes for the fourth time that month.

He smiled at her. "You are not a very patient thing, are you?"

"It is not a matter of patience, but a matter of I'm-fine-go-away."

Nathaniel chuckled as he dropped his hands from her face. "You do, indeed, look healthy." He listened to her chest with the odd device he'd been carrying around his neck lately. "And your heart sounds fine. I think my biggest health concern with you is your mood. It is dreadful."

"Is it?" she asked dryly.

He nodded. "Yes. And you look awful."

"You flatter me."

He looked at her sympathetically. "Too bad medicine cannot fix a sad heart."

"Too bad, indeed." Scarlet sighed, not even pretending to hide her brokenness. Nathaniel knew she missed Tristan.

Gabriel knew. The birds and the flowers knew. It was no secret.

She watched him take her pulse. "Have you ever been in love, Nathaniel?"

"I have loved before, yes. But I do not believe I have ever been in love. Not in the way you are suggesting, I suppose." He smiled. "Someday, though."

A moment passed and he cleared his throat. "I have obtained some new information about your condition."

"Oh? Is it good news?"

"Not exactly." He shifted. "It seems the connection you and Tristan share is stronger than it is supposed to be. Glowing eyes mean that the immortal blood in your body has taken on a greater power than it should—and they only glow when you are close to dying or incredibly frightened. The problem is that there is not a way to undo the strength of your connection once it has intensified. Had you and Tristan kept from touching in your last life, you potentially could have lived out a full lifetime, died, and then returned again. But because your connection became...stronger, you are permanently more vulnerable to death. So touching Tristan, even in the slightest, will strengthen the bond even more and make you more susceptible to your semi-immortal state. Which is why it is critical that you take your distance from him seriously. I know you are sad, but it truly is to protect you."

Scarlet nodded. So their excessive touching in her last life had turned her into a fragile semi-immortal? Brilliant.

Just one more reason to be angry with the world.

Scarlet managed not to grumble throughout the rest of Nathaniel's examination and, once it was over, bustled into her room. She essentially had the entire left wing of Gabriel's house to herself. Well, herself and Beatrice—the jolly woman Gabriel had hired to tie Scarlet into dresses and force her out of bed in the morning.

"What is the doctor's word, Miss Scarlet?" Beatrice asked, laying skirts on the bed as Scarlet entered the room.

"He says I'm healthy, but I look awful. Why is everyone so concerned about my mood?"

"Because Mr. Archer says you are a beautiful thing when you are happy and we would all wish to see that." Beatrice smiled.

By "Mr. Archer" she meant Gabriel—since Tristan had disappeared completely—and by "we" she meant the household driver, Jensen, and herself.

"Happiness is overrated." Scarlet stared the layers of material Beatrice was fluffing. "What is all that?"

"It is your dress for the day."

Scarlet tried to look as horrified as possible. "And why, exactly, do I need to wear a dress?"

Beatrice smiled. "Because Mr. Archer wants to take you out and I refuse to let you go wandering around in that dirty mop skirt you're so insistent on wearing every day."

"This mop skirt." Scarlet gripped at the linen around her waist, "is comfortable. This," she plucked up the light blue bodice on the bed and wrinkled her nose, "is misery. Will these blasted corsets ever go out of fashion?"

"Probably not. Now, quit arguing and come get dressed."

Scarlet sighed and made herself available as Beatrice bustled about, yanking fabric over her head and around her body. "If I didn't love you so much, Beatrice, I swear I would throw you out the window."

Beatrice laughed. "Then it is a good thing you love me."

****

An hour later, Gabriel smiled as he watched Scarlet shift around in her dress in the front room, cursing under her breath in a very unladylike—yet entirely entertaining—way.

"Are you ready?" he asked.

"Yes. Yes." She flipped a hand at him. "Let's get on with your foolproof plan to cheer me up."

He laughed. "Why are you so determined to be miserable? Not everything in your life is dreary. Just this morning I saw you smile at breakfast."

"That is because you served me chocolate."

"Then I'll be sure to keep extra chocolate around for future bouts of depression."

Scarlet put her hands on her hips. "I am not depressed."

Had he not understood how sad she was with Tristan gone, Gabriel would have laughed at her. But instead, he kissed her cheek.

"Yes, you are," he said quietly. "But that is what I'm here for." He gave her his arm. "Come along. I want to show you something."

As they headed out the front of the house, Jensen, the driver Gabriel and Tristan shared, tipped his hat at them.

"Where to, Mr. Archer?" Jensen opened the carriage door and helped Scarlet inside. Gabriel heard her growl as her skirts caught in the door latch, causing her to stumble against the seat inside.

"I hope in my next life, all women dress like boys. I'm never wearing a skirt again."

Gabriel smiled. "Well, that would be a shame. You look so good in a skirt."

"Shut up." She gathered her dress around her and sat down, facing forward with her frown back in place.

Jensen, taking in this scene with his respectful lack of interest in Scarlet's claiming to have a 'next life,' waited patiently on Gabriel's instructions.

"First we shall go to town, where I'm very much hoping there will be something to temper the cat we've just herded into the carriage—"

"I am not a cat."

"And then," Gabriel went on, "I would like to take Miss Jacobs to the back of the property."

Jensen nodded. "Very well, sir."

Gabriel crammed into the carriage with Scarlet and soon they were on their way to town. He leaned back in his seat and shook his head with a smile.

Since her return, Gabriel's life had felt full. He had not gambled, or gone drinking, or shared time in the company of less desirables one time and, oddly enough, he did not miss these activities.

Scarlet was alive. His hope was alive.

And dammit if he didn't want to make the source of his hope happy.

"What?" Scarlet said with a glare as he smiled at her.

"If you continue to contort your face into that hideous scowl you will soon look like an old witch."

"I am not scowling."

"You are. And it's adorable. But only in small doses."

"Well, we cannot all be ridiculously jolly like you."

"Ah, but we should." He leaned over and became serious for a moment. "You are alive, Scarlet. Right here, in this moment, you are living. Stop being ungrateful for the breath you have. Smile for once."

She stared at him.

Gabriel looked out the window. He fiddled with the sleeve of his shirt. He whistled. But he would not apologize *for his words.* She'd been holding onto her misery for too long.

"You're right," she said. "I will try to be better company."

He smiled.

They went to town where he showed her new inventions and made her try new foods and afterward, Jensen drove them to the edge of Gabriel's property.

Gabriel took Scarlet by the hand and led her through the wooded area behind his home.

"Where are we going?"

"I want to show you why I bought this particular property." He squeezed her hand as they arrived at their destination.

Scarlet gasped. "It's beautiful."

They stood on a grassy knoll at the edge of a large, serene lake. Lowering himself to the ground, Gabriel laid flat on his back and gestured for Scarlet to do the same. She laid down beside him, her dark hair fanning out along the grass in-between them, as they stared up at the happy sky.

Wind rustled through nearby tress and the peaceful sound matched the easy breaths in Gabriel's chest.

"Thank you," she said after a few minutes of silence.

"For what?"

"For bringing me here. Letting me see this."

"Yes. Well, I ran out of chocolate, so..."

She smiled.

"I saw this lake on the property and knew I had to build a home here. It reminds me of home."

He saw Scarlet nod from the corner of his eye. "Home seems like a long time ago."

Birds chirped and the fluffy afternoon clouds began to thin as the sun lowered in the sky.

Scarlet let out a sigh.

"I wish I could take it from you," Gabriel said, hating that her heart was so heavy. "The hurt. The loss."

Scarlet stared at the sky. "Why must he stay hidden from me? I find the entire notion preposterous."

"He is trying to protect you."

"He is breaking my heart."

Gabriel nodded. "Sometimes love makes hard decisions for the sake of what needs protecting."

"But love should fight."

He nodded slowly. "Yes, love should fight. But there is a difference between a valiant fight and a selfish fight. And love is not selfish."

She turned to look at him across the grass. "For someone who is cursed to be without love you are quite wise on matters of the heart." Sorrow filled her eyes. "I'm sorry for your curse."

He shrugged. "It could be worse. I could be cursed to an eternity of pain or a life without chocolate."

She didn't laugh.

"It's different when you're alive," he said softly, wishing to undo the distress on her face. He looked back at the clouds. "When you're alive there is almost no emptiness inside me and I'm inexplicably happy at all times." He smiled. "That sounds ridiculous, I'm sure."

"Not at all."

He could tell she was still looking at him but Gabriel kept his eyes above. "When you are alive, I am not cursed at all."

She stared at him until he turned to look at her. "I've missed you," she said.

His heart contracted as he stared at the girl who'd become his closest friend in his darkest times and his only cure to a hopeless heart.

He smiled. "I've missed you, too."

Avow

****

Charleston 1791

Scarlet laughed into the sky as she leaned out of the window of Gabriel's carriage. "These carriages are amazing!"

She heard the smile in Gabriel's voice. "Why are you hanging out of the window, woman?"

She looked back at him, her entire torso stretched out across the dirt road as it sped beneath them. "Because when the horse goes fast like this it feels like I'm flying."

Gabriel laughed. "You wish to fly, do you?"

"Fly. Swim. Dance. I wish for it all." A stinging pang shot through her heart at the thought of any of those things without Tristan and Scarlet hurried to rectify the sorrow closing in on her happy mood.

Tristan was gone and he was not coming back—a fact she was slowly beginning to accept. With gritted teeth and clenched fists, perhaps, but accepting all the same.

He had not returned for her as she had hoped. Perhaps he did not miss her, or perhaps his life was better without her. Either way, she no longer had her Hunter.

So she tried to live her life as though he did not exist. It was easier that way. Less painful.

She climbed back into the carriage and smiled at Gabriel.

He made it impossible for her to feel anything other than contentment and joy in his presence and she was increasingly grateful for his company each day. She hadn't wanted to cry or break anything in ages and she had actually quit complaining about getting dressed every morning.

"So what shall we do today?" she said.

"*Fly, of course,*" Gabriel responded. *He leaned his body out of his own window and called, "Faster, Jensen!"*

The carriage picked up speed as they both extended their bodies from the carriage windows and let the air sweep around them. As the wind whipped her hair, Scarlet looked across the carriage at the boy who had become her very best friend and—as she so often did in his company—forgot she had a broken heart.

****

Through the constant ache he hated but was still thankful for, Tristan pulled back and aimed his arrow at his target board in the distance. He released the arrow and watched it sail to the center of the target.

Archery was the only comfort he'd been able to find over the past year. Something about the forest, the trees, the weapons in his hand...something made him feel centered. And with the scoring pain that lived in his body in Scarlet's absence, being centered was what Tristan sought.

Unfortunately, the trees and bow he held brought memories along with their stability, and memories were something he'd not yet learned to cope with. He missed Scarlet with an ache that cut deeper than any cursed pain ever could.

Retrieving another arrow, he lined up and aimed again.

Jensen, God bless the nosey driver, reported to Tristan of Scarlet's good health and Gabriel reported she was happy. It seemed the distance Tristan kept from her was working and, for that, he would endure however many more painful days and sleepless nights her life had to offer him.

From Nathaniel's books, Tristan knew immortals could die if cut through the heart with the right weapon. And if Tristan could find a way to die while Scarlet was still alive, the immortal blood inside her chest would die as well, leaving her mortal.

So that was his new purpose: finding a way to die so Scarlet might live. He had dedicated most of his days to finding the right weapon, but seeing that he had no clue what type of weapon he needed, his hunt was tedious and long.

But time was something he had an abundance of so his new hobby was accumulating as many weapons as possible and eliminating them one by one.

He would find the right weapon and when he did, he would make sure his blood never stole life from Scarlet again.

He let another arrow fly and watched it split through the board far away as a tremor of agony raked down his spine.

17

Charleston 1792

Scarlet stared at the flames in the fireplace; her mind wandering a thousand places that no longer existed as midnight drew near.

She was adjusting to her new life.

Nathaniel and his quirky ways were quickly becoming a piece of her heart and Gabriel had dedicated most of his days to making her laugh and showing her new things. The only person missing from her life was Tristan.

From the conversation pieces she stole while listening to Gabriel and Nathaniel—and she did, indeed, have to steal them—she knew he lived a good distance away, but aside from that she knew nothing about him. That was the point, she supposed.

She spent many cold nights in front of the fireplace, entranced by the blaze within. Something about the flames reminded her of Tristan, and something about the sparks reminded her of herself.

Sometimes Gabriel would join her, his easiness wrapping around her as he sat beside her in the firelight. She would sink into the warm calm he provided and be wonderfully distracted from any sorrowful thoughts. They would breathe, they would talk, and they would sit in silence. It was wonderful. Easy.

If Tristan was her fire, then Gabriel was her serenity; waiting her out, lighting her face, filling her heart in the slow, patient way only peace could.

He had told her to live, and so she did. She stopped wallowing. She made friends. She laughed at dinners. She even tied herself into corsets for special occasions.

And with every passing day, she felt less fire and more peace, until her heart no longer stung. Where once her chest would ache at the thought of Tristan, it now only echoed like a canyon filled with wind.

She had not fallen apart without her green-eyed Hunter—a realization that comforted her heart almost as much as it broke it—but she had become someone else in his absence.

She bit her tongue, she reigned in her temper, and she behaved like a lady. But more importantly, she was pleasant. Gabriel deserved a pleasant companion.

"I knew I'd find you here." Gabriel's voice held a smile as it met her ears.

She turned to look at the brown-eyed boy with Tristan's face leaning against the archway into the study and smiled. "Fires are both destructive and beautiful. I find them terribly intriguing."

"Of course, you do." He smirked, and came to sit beside her on the sofa.

"How goes the state of your heart?" Scarlet constantly asked about his heart and his curse, always getting the same answer from him.

"Happy." He grinned and his dimples pulled a grin from her face as well. *"How about yours?"*

She tilted her head. "Content."

His grin softened as he reached for her hand and pulled it to his mouth, kissing her open palm. "I am glad. Now I can die a happy man."

With Gabriel's lips on her palm, Scarlet felt her heart flutter and the sensation surprised her. "You cannot die at all."

He lowered her hand from his mouth but held it in his palm. "Then I can live a happy man."

Scarlet rolled her eyes. "You are always a happy man."

"Not always." His tone was jesting, but a deep pain coursed through Scarlet's veins as she thought of Gabriel's life without her and the curse he bore.

"I do not want to die again," she said. *"I do not want you to be empty."*

He looked her over carefully, his pained eyes falling along the lines of her face as firelight flickered across his own. "You fear death for my sake?"

She nodded, realizing it was true. She was incredibly healthy and had not fallen ill in the three years she'd been alive, but death would surely come for her eventually. And the thought made her ache for Gabriel. He was full of good and her death would leave him empty.

"You are a silly woman to care so much for me. I do not deserve it."

"You do." She nodded. *"Very much."*

He leaned over and kissed her cheek. "I love you."

Scarlet's eyes fell closed with the touch, remembering a time when she thought Tristan was gone and Gabriel had loved her fully and held her in his arms with great pride.

Scarlet opened her eyes. "I love you, too. Do you know that?"

He smiled. "I do." He tilted his head to the side and sighed. "Come here." He pulled her into him and leaned back on the sofa. Scarlet willingly tucked her head into the soft place between his shoulder and chest and inhaled deeply.

He smelled good. He was safe and careful, and everything about him was familiar and warm. She nestled in further and Gabriel wrapped his arms around her completely, setting his face against the top of her head as they watched the fire.

"Stay with me," Scarlet said.

He ran his fingers down her arm and caught a strand of her long hair, wrapping it round his fingers. "I would not wish to be anywhere else."

Scarlet suddenly wanted to cry. Not for her lack of Tristan. Not for her broken heart. But for Gabriel and his dedicated patience and unconditional love for her.

Like a weary warrior after battle, Scarlet let herself relax into the arms of the man who had loved her deeply in her darkest times and cherished her heart. Not just the parts that were undamaged and beautiful, but the entire mess.

And slowly, like it had never left, love seeped in.

18

Charleston 1793

Scarlet was happy, her heart was full and life was pleasant. She and Gabriel spent nearly every day together. Nathnaiel was pleased with her health and rarely stopped over to check on her anymore. And the only socially-unacceptable thing Scarlet was guilty of was her fighting lessons with a Frenchman named Pierre.

She hired Pierre in secret, insisted they train in the forest where no one would see her, and had slowly begun collecting weapons for these occasions.

Gabriel never questioned her fascination with blades and bows, but he did raise a suspicious eyebrow every now and then when Scarlet returned home claiming to have enjoyed a brisk walk through the property. For three hours.

She refused to give her secret away. She wanted something that was just hers, and fighting in the trees suited that purpose.

Other than the fighting, Scarlet had become a true lady; curtsying, taking tea, and managing not to spew sarcastic comments at pompous men who annoyed her at parties.

The fiery girl she used to be was dead, replaced by a polished lookalike. She barely recognized herself, but perhaps this was a good thing.

She loved her life, she loved Gabriel, and she had almost completely rid her heart of Tristan.

But then she misplaced her dagger.

This was not such a grave dilemma, for she had several other weapons and could easily replace the dagger if she chose to, but this was her lucky dagger. Its handle was unique and heavier than most and it fit her hand perfectly when she was sparring with Pierre.

It was because of this that Scarlet found herself prowling on hands and knees behind the sofa in the front room—where she had last remembered sheathing the knife—and heard Nathaniel's voice in the adjacent dining room.

"Tristan is not well," was all it took for Scarlet's ears to perk up and her thief-like senses to keep her on her knees and hidden.

Nathaniel's voice came again. "He is in a great deal of pain and, might I add, dreadful company."

Scarlet crept along the sofa and crawled through shadows to stand behind a tall cabinet, where she could see Gabriel and Nathaniel seated at the dining table.

"Yes, well. Nonstop pain does that to a person," Gabriel said.

Scarlet's heart started to pound.

Nonstop pain? Tristan was hurting without reprieve because of her?

Well, that was unacceptable.

"He hasn't been able to sleep for months."

Gabriel scratched his chin. "Should we take Scarlet to him, just to give him a break?"

Yes. Yes, they should take Scarlet to them.

"No," *Nathaniel said.*

Damn him.

Gabriel nodded. "You're right. We shouldn't risk Scarlet getting sick. She's lived for so long this time."

"Yes, that. And also Tristan would kill us if we brought Scarlet to Hilldoor. He would actually kill us," *Nathaniel said.*

Hilldoor.

Just like that, the fiery girl rose from the dead.

"He would not kill us," *Gabriel scoffed.*

"He would try to."

"I doubt that."

Nathaniel said, "You didn't just spend a fortnight in his manor filled with weapons and his tendency to punch things."

"True. What shall we do with him?"

"I think," *Nathaniel sighed,* "that you should suggest he move closer to us. Not anywhere Scarlet would know, but just close enough to keep them both healthy."

"And why should I suggest this and not you?"

"Because it's your turn to suffer his miserable mood."

"My turn? I went to him last week."

"Yes, but you're his brother. He is less likely to hit you."

"You're his doctor and he actually likes you. You go."

"No. You go."

No, I'll go, Scarlet *thought, already planning a trip to Hilldoor Manor, wherever that was. And all because she had misplaced her dagger.*

It was her lucky dagger after all.

****

The next night, Scarlet bustled out the front door and tried to act like she had pertinent and very-much-approved business to tend to as she approached Jensen.

"Good evening, Miss Scarlet." Jensen tipped his hat in the moonlight as he stood beside the carriage.

She gave him her best smile. "Good evening, Jensen. Lovely night, is it not?"

"Lovelier with you under the stars." Jensen was always good for a compliment. "Where can I take you this evening, Miss?"

Gabriel and Nathaniel had been invited to a gentleman's dinner, leaving Scarlet under the scrutiny of only the household staff. Which, based on the interrogation she'd just endured by Beatrice, was almost as detouring as Gabriel himself.

"I need to get to Hilldoor Manor." Scarlet kept her smile in place, knowing this was the critical moment.

Jensen rubbed at his chin. "I seem to recall Mr. Archer insisting on you never traveling alone. I believe my job—and quite possibly my life—was threatened at the thought."

Scarlet waved a hand. "Gabriel would never harm you, Jensen. I know he adores you and he really is nothing but soft."

Jensen looked at the ground with a knowing smile. "Gabriel was not the Mr. Archer I was referring to."

Scarlet dropped her flirty act and scoffed. "Well, that Mr. Archer is a pain."

"That Mr. Archer insists that your presence is unwanted at Hilldoor and I have no intention of angering him."

Scarlet rolled her eyes. "Why does everyone fear Tristan so? He is more harmless than Gabriel, I swear. Take me to him."

"I'm afraid that will not be possible, Miss Scarlet."

"Jensen." She set her mouth straight. "Tristan is in severe pain, is he not?"

"I am not supposed to know about any such pain."

"And I am not supposed to know where Tristan is." She smiled. "But sometimes we know things we shouldn't."

The driver looked unmoved.

"Jensen," Scarlet complained. "Tristan is hurting. Do you wish for him to continue to live in agony?"

"My wishes are not important. Mr. Archer's wishes, however—"

"I have his cure." She was desperate now. "I can take away his pain."

Jensen said nothing, but Scarlet saw the indecision in his eyes and knew she had won.

With full lips and all the charm she possessed, she said, "Take me to Hilldoor, Jensen."

He sighed. "Very well."

She tipped down the edge of his hat in a friendly gesture of camaraderie before climbing into the carriage.

Then into the night they rode away. Farther from Gabriel and Nathaniel. Closer to Tristan.

****

Scarlet watched a large mansion grow up from dark hills silhouetted by the full moon above. The house was vast and elaborate, but nearly hidden in the many vines and thick foliage around the property. It looked somewhat sad.

When Jensen pulled the carriage to a stop, Scarlet took a deep breath—well, as deep as she could manage with the blasted corset top she wore—and took Jensen's hand as he helped her from the carriage.

At the front door, she did not knock. Knocking would have been polite and well-mannered, but so would have *announcing her presence. Fiery Scarlet didn't possess good manners.*

Finding the front door already open, she stepped inside and found Tristan standing there, with his arms crossed, as if he'd been waiting for her.

The open front door made more sense now.

She braced for the yelling that was sure to pour from his throat, trying to memorize his features before things got ugly.

Although it was evening and rather cool outside, Tristan was shirtless.

Of course.

The tattoo of her drawing laid against his muscles and Scarlet's heart squeezed. She had almost forgotten about the permanent design he'd put on his body and the sight of it did funny things to her stomach. Hopeful things. Warm things.

Sad things.

His dark hair was longer, almost to his shoulders, and hung about his head in disarray. Dark stubble marked his face, his eyes had dark circles around them, and his jaw was set hard and firm.

He was not a happy sight, but he was the best thing Scarlet had seen in years.

"What are you doing here?" he said.

Scarlet shut the door behind her, leaning against it as she responded. "I came because you have been in great pain."

"Yes. And because of my great pain you still live. It seems my isolation is good for your wellbeing."

"The strength of my pulse has little to do with the health of my heart."

He continued to stare at her with a scolding silence, so Scarlet casually glanced around the rather-empty house. "So...this is the dark dungeon where the very angry Tristan sleeps?"

"No. This is the dark dungeon where the very dangerous Tristan keeps himself away from a very careless young woman."

Clearly, he was in no mood for small talk.

Scarlet raised her chin. "I am not so young anymore."

"I can see that." His eyes darkened as they drifted along her face and body and Scarlet reveled in the hot look. He snapped his eyes back to hers, anger and desire in their green depths.

"You need to leave, Scar."

Yes. She should probably leave.

She didn't.

"Tristan, this is ridiculous. You are in too much pain and I miss you deeply. Come home."

"I am home."

"No, you're not. You're hiding."

"Not very well, it seems." A muscle in his jaw ticked. "How did you find me?"

"I do not recall, but it had absolutely nothing to do with Jensen."

A ghost of a smile flashed across his face, and Scarlet would have given her very heart to see the real thing.

She took a step forward. "You should not have allowed yourself to suffer for so long."

He took a step back. "My pain is not your concern."

"Everything about you is my concern. You cannot just keep yourself in pain," she said, filling up with all the fear and love she felt for him as she stepped forward again. "You are a foolish man."

He stood still. "And you are a reckless woman."

She smiled. "We are quite the messy pair."

"That we are." He searched her face then softened his voice. "You know you cannot stay here."

"Then tell me to leave." She stepped closer.

"Leave."

"No."

"Curse you woman," he said. "You are a terrible pain."

Another step closer and she was standing right in front of him, looking up into green heat.

"Yes, I am." She kissed his chest, letting her lips brush against his skin a moment longer than necessary, and felt his body sigh with the pleasure her touch brought him. "And you love me for it."

She traced her fingertips over his tattoo, following the dark lines around his skin.

"I do," he said, gently catching her hand in his. "And that is why this will never happen again."

Scarlet looked up at him. "Do not make such threats, Hunter."

"It is not a threat." He looked sad. "You need to leave."

Scarlet straightened her shoulders. "Not until you're better. Not until you've had a decent night's sleep in my nearness."

He released her hand. "Leave before I carry you out."

Scarlet narrowed her eyes. "No."

They were in a standoff for a moment, staring at each other, pulses high for more than one reason. But then Scarlet's feet were no longer on the floor as Tristan easily threw her over his shoulder, marched to the front door, and flung it open.

"Open the carriage, Jensen!" His voice was so angry Scarlet could feel it vibrate against her body.

Trying to wriggle free, she slapped his bare back, her waist and legs completely imprisoned by his arm.

"You," she saw Tristan's free arm point at Jensen, "I will speak to later."

Then Scarlet was being wrestled into the carriage by Tristan's rock solid arms until she was seated inside, his big body shadowing the carriage door in dark madness.

"Do not come back here." His green eyes cut pieces of her soul to shreds. "Not ever."

Despite his temper, or his fear, or whatever was putting that black look in his eyes, she had come for a reason and she didn't want her trip to be in vain. Reaching her hands out, she held his face, desperate to relieve him of all pain one last time.

He grasped her wrists to pull her hands off, but froze as her touch sank into him.

She watched his eyes fall closed in peace and his chest exhale in comfort. She wanted to touch him forever and always bring him this much relief.

"Do not make me leave you," she whispered.

His eyelids lifted in a heavy, sated way as he looked at her. For a moment, his resolve was gone and his hands, wrapped tightly around her wrists, loosened their grip and slowly eased up her forearms, his caress becoming more gentle the farther up her arms he felt.

Soon it was only his fingers trailing up the inside of her arms...across her shoulders...along her collarbone...and then barely stroking the sides of her neck.

Scarlet wanted to cry for how wonderful it felt to be near him—to be something other than rejected by him.

But then her eyes burned and a soft blue glowed into the night.

Tristan pulled his hands and eyes away from her. Shutting Scarlet inside the carriage, he barked, "Take her home, Jensen," before walking back into his house without a second glance.

Scarlet stared out the window, knowing Tristan was trying to keep her safe. Knowing he did the things he did out of fear and love.

But all the knowledge in the world couldn't keep the pain from her soul.

19

Charleston 1798

Tristan was a different man.

The day after Scarlet had hunted him down, he had moved to a different location and kept a safer distance from her, but she'd became ill anyway and slowly started to die. For eight months, her eyes flashed on and off. Then the nosebleeds started.

When he had felt her die inside of him, something snapped in his soul.

He had not been able to save her. He had searched for weapons and resolved himself to death, but it hadn't mattered. She had still died.

After throwing knives into walls and slamming doors around his empty house, Tristan had finally surrendered to grief. And the guilt and sorrow he carried festered low in his chest, keeping him from any real sleep. It was a blackness that thickened with time, slowly inching its way around his soul, filling him with darkness.

Drowning in darkness seemed a merciful fate.

Tonight, he was walking in the seedier part of town where most men didn't travel after dark. But most men were not immortal men and Tristan didn't really give a damn anyway as he walked in the shadows of dangerous alleyways and buildings.

"Gabriel." *A suspicious-looking fellow with a few missing teeth gripped his shoulder.* "How long has it been? Nine, ten years?"

Since there was no point in explaining to the stranger that he was, in fact, Gabriel's twin brother—no one ever believed that anyway—Tristan said, "I'm not sure. A long time."

The stranger nodded. "You still betting high stakes in the lower games?"

What the hell were lower games?

"You know me," *Tristan said dryly, wishing the man would release his shoulder.*

"Then I have a tip for ya." *He leaned in, his breath horrid as he said,* "There's a new kind of fight under the Nine Club tonight. Password is "knuckles." Tell 'em Hank sent ya. I get a cut if you win." *He winked.* "Nice seeing ya, ol' pal."

And with that, the stranger was gone.

Tristan knew he should ignore the man's words and carry on with his mindless walking, but curiosity was a relentless bastard and Tristan's feet took him to the Nine Club, where he told the man at the backdoor the password.

He was led downstairs into a well-lit cellar where people were crowded around a dirt ring. Peering above the heads of the townsfolk, his eyes fell on two large men beating each other bloody in the center of the crowd.

The spectators cheered and booed, held money up for a passing bookie, and drank themselves happy as they watched blood pour from the wounds of the fighters.

He had heard of prizefighting in England but, being that it was illegal, had never seen a fight before. And he found the sport...fascinating.

He watched with new eyes as the fighters hit, threw, and knocked one another around in the dirt circle. Blood, spit and sweat coated both bodies and the ground as the calls of the entertained crowd floated to the ceiling.

Fighting for sport. Slamming fists and body parts. Pounding out aggression with a willing opponent. The darkness in his chest expanded and Tristan raised the corner of his mouth.

Being beaten bloody sounded heavenly.

20

Charleston 1801

Gabriel sat in the dark, leaning back in a large chair with his feet propped up on the desk before him. He tapped his fingers and waited.

Tristan appeared in the hallway and headed for the front door.

"Where are you off to?" Gabriel stopped tapping his fingers.

Tristan eyed Gabriel. "Why are you sitting in the dark?" He cocked his head to the side. "Very odd behavior for a...what is it you call yourself now? A gentleman?"

Gabriel smiled. "Interesting how you always change the subject when I ask about your nightly whereabouts."

"Why do you care, brother? Have you no whores to play with tonight?"

"Is that where you spend your time? Brothels?" Gabriel dropped his feet to the ground and leaned forward with a sharp smile. "No, of course not. Not Tristan. My righteous brother does not mar his time with the company of sinners."

"Except for you."

"Will you not tell me where it is you go dressed as," Gabriel glanced Tristan over, taking in his loose, cut off pants and wider-than-fashionable shirt, "a pirate?"

"Trust me, brother." Tristan glanced at him with mischief in his eyes. "A pirate would not bode well where I go." Without another word, he exited the house, leaving Gabriel in the dark.

Rolling his eyes, Gabriel stood from the chair and grudgingly gathered his coat from the hallway.

Lofty Tristan, he could deal with.

Soft-hearted Tristan, he could tolerate.

But dark, mysterious Tristan?

Gabriel would have none of that.

There was room for only one irreverent soul in the Archer family, and Gabriel had staked that claim long ago.

He left out the front door, keeping to the shadows as he followed his brother.

Through darkened streets, questionable alleyways, and a part of town Gabriel used to frequent but never thought Tristan would set foot in, he followed his brother until they reached an abandoned building.

At least, it looked abandoned.

Tristan slinked his way down an almost hidden set of stairs and Gabriel hovered nearby, watching as Tristan nodded to a doorman—who looked just as questionable, if not more so, than the alleyways they'd just walked through—and entered a door that opened to the sound of a crowd, light spilling onto the doorman before the door fell shut.

What...the...hell?

Gabriel debated for several minutes, not sure if he should follow after Tristan or let his brother be. Curiosity was the victor, as always.

Slinking down the stairs as Tristan had, Gabriel approached the questionable doorman and kept his face as expressionless as possible.

The doorman looked confused. "Archer?"

Gabriel nodded. Sometimes, being a twin had its advantages.

"But I just…you just…how…?"

"I left out the back." Gabriel hoped this was explanation enough and that there was, indeed, a "back" to whatever this place was.

The doorman shrugged. "Alright. Best of luck tonight. I always put my money on you."

Gabriel nodded again as the doorman let him into a bright room filled with people, bookies, the smell of sweat, and the sound of breaking bones.

Well, damn.

Walking along the outskirts of the crowd and keeping in the shadows as much as possible, Gabriel moved toward the spectacle in the center of the room.

A shirtless Tristan, blood running down his face and body, had his bare-knuckled fists raised before a much larger man who was throwing punches in his direction. The larger man was far more beat up than Tristan and he was stumbling with injury and disorientation. Tristan blocked every blow the man served and, after a few minutes of watching the large man stomp unevenly from side to side, Tristan clocked him in the face.

The man fell to the blood-splattered floor and the crowd cheered. Somewhere a bell chimed and Gabriel finally understood what he was watching. He didn't believe it, but he understood it.

He waited four more matches until the crowd thinned and people began to disperse, then he stood outside the stairwell, hidden in shadows, until a bloody Tristan emerged.

Grabbing him by the nape, Gabriel threw his brother against the wall of the building. "Prizefighting? Are you crazy?"

Caught off guard, Tristan swung at Gabriel's face, pausing just before making contact as recognition set in.

God, he was a mess. Blood everywhere. A swollen eye. Sweat matting his hair and chest.

"Hello, Gabe." *Tristan smacked Gabriel's hand off him and spit on the ground.* "What brings you back to your old stomping grounds? I thought you were a changed man."

Gabriel ignored the comment, though it was true. Since Scarlet's death, he had no desire to be the slobbering, self-hating, drunken gambler he'd been before. She had loved him. He now had something to live for.

"I'll ask again," *Gabriel said.* "Are you insane?"

"No. I'm well." *He smiled. Like a crazy person, he smiled.* "I'm excellent, in fact. I've not lost a fight in many weeks."

"You are immortal. These are not fair fights, not real victories."

Tristan examined his knuckles, torn flesh slowly mending itself, then looked back up. "Now, don't go spewing morality at me brother. You have a reputation to uphold. Whatever would the townspeople do if you were to become the 'good' brother? I'm sure chaos would ensue. You must hurry and find yourself some brandy and a painted woman and fix this morality nonsense so the world may be right again."

"I'm serious, Tristan. Prizefighting is illegal." *Gabriel suddenly felt like the grown-up between them and was not comfortable with his new role.*

"I know." *Tristan's crazy smile was back.*

Who was this person?

Tristan spit again. "Since when do you care about the law?"

Since my brother went rogue, apparently.

Gabriel shook his head. "It's wrong to fight when you have an obvious advantage over your opponents—

"My advantage is not all that great. Did you know," *Tristan looked at Gabriel with something akin to glee in his eyes,* "that the more wounded immortals are, the slower they heal? All I have to do is break a few bones or cut myself up before a fight and I am almost as mortal as any opponent. I learned that from one of Nathaniel's books. Helpful information in those wizarding bibles."

Gabriel blinked. "What's the matter with you?"

"What's the matter with *you*?"

Gabriel rubbed his face, completely dumbfounded. "Explain this to me. Why are you participating in these fights?"

"Because it feels good to hit something. It feels good to be hit."

Ah.

This was punishment for Tristan. This was a way to hurt, and be hurt, in-between Scarlet's lives.

"Don't worry, Gabe." *Tristan spit again.* "The fights are more equally matched than you think. I'm not cheating. I feel the same pressure, the same pain, the same—"

"Guilt?" *he challenged.* "Sadness?"

Tristan's cocky face sobered.

Gabriel shook his head. "This doesn't bring her back any faster. Or change what will happen when she returns."

Dangerous anger filled Tristan's eyes as he lowered his voice. "Do not speak to me about Scarlet."

And then he was gone. Disappearing into the night with blood on his skin.

21

Boston 1891

Nathaniel clapped his hands together, the sound popping into the large townhouse he owned. "I call this meeting to session."

"There are only three of us, Nathaniel." Gabriel sighed as he leaned back on the couch. "This is a discussion. Not a 'meeting'."

After a century without luck in the South, they had decided to move to Boston, where Nathaniel could pursue a different cure. A medical cure.

Tristan hated the crowds and noise, but he tolerated it, Gabriel assumed, because there were big fights in the city. Underground gambling ran rampant after dark and Tristan was always at the center of the mess. He was known to his audiences as Archer. He was known to Gabriel as dumbass.

"Well, based on our last three-person discussion—the one where you two punched each other, broke my coffee table, and managed to put a hole in my wall," Nathaniel pointed to the gaping hole in the drywall of his otherwise flawless room, "I'd say our 'discussions' need some order. So I'm calling it a meeting and this time we will all take turns speaking. Understand?"

Their last discussion had been about how to take care of Scarlet when she came back to life, but had ended up being a throw down between Gabriel and Tristan because Tristan, bloody hell, Tristan was going off the deep end.

He was prizefighting. Fine.

He was collecting weapons like they were stamps. Also fine.

But it was who Tristan had become on the inside that Gabriel couldn't stand. Tristan was just plain surly; a dark man without a pinch of light inside him.

Gabriel had let him stew and wallow and slowly spiral downward for a hundred years, and now it was time for Tristan to get it together and start helping.

Tristan had announced he no longer believed the fountain existed, which was understandable based on their lack of locating the thing for hundreds of years, but to give up on saving Scarlet altogether? That was ludicrous.

"So," Nathaniel began. "When Scarlet comes back to life, we need to handle it differently. I don't think it's healthy for Tristan to remain far away from her for extended periods of time."

"It's just pain," Tristan said.

"I don't think it's healthy." Nathaniel over-enunciated each word. "So we need a new plan. Suggestions?"

Gabriel said, "She can live with me like before and we'll just keep her away from Tristan. Maybe he could live in my building so he's not too close to her."

Tristan said, "Yes, except living that close to her means I'll feel her."

Gabriel made a face. "So get over it."

Tristan scoffed. "Right."

He was such a baby about the whole feeling thing.

Nathaniel looked at Tristan. "If you have to, move further away."

"It won't work." *Tristan shook his head.* "She could still find me."

"So then we'll rationally explain to her to leave you alone." *Nathaniel shrugged.*

Tristan set his jaw. "I can assure you that won't work. So I have a plan."

"Really." *Gabriel leaned forward on the couch and rested his elbows on his knees.* "Enlighten us. Please."

"I'm going to be in Scarlet's life this time. She'll know where I am. She'll see me."

Already, this was the worst plan ever.

Tristan hesitated. "But my plan will keep her from touching me."

"So what is *your* plan?" *Gabriel asked impatiently.*

"It's a drastic plan that you don't need the details to."

Gabriel said, "I'm against this plan."

"How can you guarantee she won't touch you?" *Nathaniel did not seem bothered by Tristan's lack of information.*

Tristan pushed back from the wall. "Trust me. In her next life, Scarlet won't want me at all."

Gabriel's stomach churned at the tone of Tristan's voice and, given Tristan's dark attitude lately, the last thing he wanted to do was "trust" him.

"Yeah. I don't think so. Why don't we just go with my plan, where she lives with me and you stay the hell away from her?"

"Because your plan has a million holes in it."

"And your plan isn't a plan at all. It's a vague almost-idea and I don't trust you."

"Nathaniel." Tristan looked at their silent friend. "Do you trust me?"

Gabriel rolled his eyes. Sometime over the last hundred years, Tristan and Nathaniel had become the best of pals and, despite Tristan's unfriendliness and nonstop sour moods, Nathaniel still liked the guy.

Traitor.

Nathaniel took a deep breath. "I trust you. But I also care about Scarlet so—"

"She won't die. At least, not because of me. I promise."

"Hell, no." Gabriel started shaking his head.

Tristan exhaled. "Don't be an ass, Gabe. Just let me try my plan."

Gabriel hesitated. "Fine. What do you want us to do?"

Tristan cracked his knuckles—knuckles that spent most every night swollen and split open in a bloody ring—and said, "I'll let you know when she comes back to life."

****

That night, Tristan slowly unwrapped his hands, his heart still racing from his fights earlier. All wins.

It was in moments like these, where his adrenaline was high and his wounds were healing, that the guilt couldn't find him. Something about the pounding of flesh, the ache of physical pain being inflicted by another man, made him feel redeemed.

He stood in the alley, healing in the darkness so his opponents and fight conductors would not see. His immortal body was inconvenient in this sport—and in his life. He had yet to find a weapon that could permanently scar his skin, so he was no closer to saving Scarlet.

He turned his head and spit out the blood that had accumulated in his mouth from the last chin jab he'd taken. That's when he saw Alexandria sauntering over to him.

He bit back a groan and returned to unwrapping his hands.

"You did well tonight." She came up beside him under the dim light of the moon.

"What do you want, Alex?"

She looked up at him through her thick lashes, her sharp eyes heavy with intent. She was beautiful and the epitome of sexuality. Most men would want nothing more than her attention after a night of fighting. Tristan was not most men.

"Why must I want something? Have you considered I may, perhaps, just enjoy your company?"

"I have considered that."

Her fingertips touched his stomach and ran up his bare chest, sending a cool shiver over his sweat-glistened body.

"But then your hands find their way around my skin," Tristan said, "and I begin to question the companionship you seek."

She lifted her chin and brought her mouth near his, her lips so close he could smell the strawberries he'd seen her eating earlier. "We all need companionship, Tristan." Her hands slid back down his body and traced the waistband of his fighting pants. "Even you, with your lonely soul."

Tristan stared at the beautiful woman whose hands were doing dangerous things to his body. She had heat and vibrancy and a body that could probably do wonders for any man.

But she did not have fight or passion. And she did not have blue eyes that knew his secrets.

"I have no heart to give you," he said.

Alex moved her hands across his chest. "I'm not after your heart."

"Clearly." Tristan kept his eyes steady on hers. "But I'm not interested."

She smiled wickedly. "Not tonight, maybe."

"*Not ever.*"

She kept her smile in place, but removed her hands from his body as she stepped back. "Very well, fighter." *She looked him up and down.* "Let me know if you change your mind."

22

Boston 1892

Scarlet had been alive for exactly two days when Tristan suggested that Gabriel and Nathaniel—who now insisted on being called 'Nate'—bring her to watch one of his matches.

He was boxing now? It was hard for Scarlet to wrap her head around her gentle, peaceful Hunter slamming his fists into another man's flesh for sport and she had told him as much.

But Tristan had merely shrugged. He hadn't spoken more than ten words to her since she'd come back to life and he'd treated her coldly every time they'd been in the same room together.

No hot glances. No acknowledgement of her feelings. Nothing.

She wasn't sure what to make of his rude behavior, but she didn't push him. Not because she didn't plan to, but because she'd been gone for a hundred years and a lot could happen in a century.

Nate had warned her that Tristan had changed and, while Scarlet was sure that was true, she refused to believe he was a different person all together.

After agreeing to attend one of Tristan's fights, she retreated to her bedroom in Gabriel's house to dress. Things between her and Gabriel were a bit tense.

They'd had such a happy companionship in her last life, until she'd run off to heal Tristan like a love-sick puppy and returned to Gabriel with flashing eyes.

He hadn't been mad at her, but he'd been disappointed. And maybe even a little heart-broken. So in this new life of hers, she didn't know what to think about Gabriel. Especially with Tristan being as standoffish as he was.

She dressed herself—she was becoming rather good at the whole corset thing—and made her way back downstairs where Nate and Gabriel waited to take her to Tristan's fight.

Her stomach filled with butterflies. And not the pretty kind.

****

"Alex." Tristan shut the door behind them so it was just she and him in the small back room of the fighting hall. "I need a favor."

She turned to him, eagerness in her eyes. "A favor for Tristan? Yes, please."

"Cut it out. I'm being serious."

"You are always serious." She pouted her lips.

Tristan turned to leave. This was a mistake.

"No, no. I'm just kidding." Alex reached for his arm and turned him back around, desperation in her voice. "I will behave. I promise. What is it you need?"

He sighed. "I need a woman."

A hungry look came over her face. "Then consider me yours. Shall I undress right here?"

His jaw flexed. "Could you, for one moment, cease to be obvious? I do not need your body, Alex. I need your assistance."

"That sounds like the same thing."

Tristan glared at her.

"Fine." *Her sex-laced voice disappeared.* "What do you need?"

"I need you to put on a convincing show of your affections for me in front of a particular person."

She narrowed her eyes. "A person? Or a girl?"

"A girl."

"Ah." *Alex smiled.* "This would be the girl that has your heart all to herself, no?"

Tristan didn't answer.

"I will be happy to fawn over you," *Alex said.* "And who knows? You might even enjoy it." *She winked.*

He clenched his jaw at the thought of breaking Scarlet's heart.

"I will hate every second of it," *he said, sinking deeper into his self-loathing as he explained to Alex what he wanted her to do.*

****

Scarlet watched the fight and the butterflies in her stomach grew uglier.

While she understood there was something liberating about fighting—she had invested good time and money into learning to fight—she hated every fist that crashed into Tristan's body and drew blood from his torn skin.

Her eyes skimmed him over, lingering on his bare chest. At the sight of his tattoo—his piece of Scarlet forever inked into his skin—the butterflies in her belly fluttered wildly. The tattoo was very faded and Scarlet figured immortal bodies could only hold a tattoo for so long before healing it away. She wondered how long it would be before her drawing disappeared completely from Tristan's body.

Gabriel and Nate sat on either side of her. Apparently, not many women came to these fights and Gabriel was being extra protective of her. She reached for Gabriel's hand and held it with her own, squeezing it gently. He turned and smiled at her as the bell rang to signal the end of the last fight.

Thank God. She didn't think she could handle watching more of Tristan's blood spill.

She watched Tristan, covered in sweat and blood, walk to the outer ring to where a short man with a cigar was making broad hand gestures and visibly spitting as he spoke.

Tristan turned around, as if he were looking for someone, and soon his eyes landed on his target.

A beautiful redhead stood off to the side, watching the ring from the contestant's area as if she were an organizer of some sort. The redhead saw Tristan and desire lit up her eyes.

Scarlet had been watching women react to Tristan for centuries, so the women's interest in the green-eyed fighter was not surprising. Tristan's reaction to her, however, was shocking.

He smiled and the redhead came up to him without any hesitation, slowly wrapping her sexually sculpted body around Tristan's hard muscles and tight skin.

Scarlet blinked.

Tristan did not refuse the woman, but embraced her back, his mouth coming down to the woman's neck as he murmured something below her ear while the woman ran her hands up his back and into his hair.

That was Scarlet's Hunter. That was hair only Scarlet could run her hands through. Those were green eyes only Scarlet could look at with such lust and want.

Scarlet's heart began to pound as she watched in horror as the woman turned her outrageously beautiful head to the side and caught Tristan's mouth in a kiss. An intimate, wet kiss that spoke volumes of how very comfortable the two of them were with each other and Scarlet stopped breathing.

Beside her, a muttered curse fell from Gabriel's' mouth and Scarlet tried to get control of her emotions. Every single piece of her wanted to jump from her seat, charge over to the woman whose hands were laced around Tristan, and rip her lips from her face.

Gabriel's mouth was suddenly at Scarlet's ear. "Let's go."

Scarlet blinked again and realized she'd been squeezing the blood from Gabriel's hand as she watched the exchange between Tristan and the redhead.

"Why would we leave?" Her voice cracked.

Gabriel looked at Scarlet with a pained expression, searching her eyes for the truth. "Scarlet..." He looked her over like he wasn't sure what to do with her.

"Why would we leave?" she repeated, feeling hot tears behind her eyes.

Gabriel stroked a strand of hair from her cheek and she could tell he was trying to come up with something to say.

"Why would we..." Scarlet tried to finish her repeated question, but a tear fell from her eye and her throat closed off.

Gabriel cursed again and, rising from his seat, gathered Scarlet up beside him and shuffled her through the crowd and to the back door, Nate right behind them.

Everything was blurry and hot and suffocating as Scarlet blindly let Gabriel usher her outside and into the carriage that awaited them. No one said a word as the three of them rode in silence back to Gabriel's home.

Scarlet bit the inside of her cheek, dug her nails into her arms, curled her toes...anything she could think of to keep her tears at bay. But soon the pressure was just too much and she no longer wanted to fight.

She had lost Tristan.

Scarlet began to openly cry. Because, before this night, there had never been a doubt in her mind that Tristan loved her. But now....

Scarlet hide her face in her hands as more tears fell and felt warm arms come around her.

Gabriel lifted her into his lap and turned her into him so her face was against his jacket, hot tears streaming down her cheeks.

Forget the curse and the immortal blood that pulsed in her chest.

This—this searing ache cutting through her core—this was a broken heart.

****

With Alex still in his arms, Tristan yanked his mouth away from her and gripped the back of her neck. Hard.

"Ow," Alex complained. "Tristan, what are you—"

"What the hell was that?" he asked darkly, murder in his veins.

Alex batted her lashes. "You wanted me to be convincing, didn't you?"

Tristan thrust his hand away from her neck and stepped back. Scarlet's heartbreak and deep pain was rushing into him and it made him want to vomit. "Not that *convincing."*

Alex rubbed the back of her neck, then smiled at him. "Oh, don't act like you didn't enjoy it."

"I didn't."

"You did." She stepped back over to him. "And so did I."

"You could rub your naked body against an elephant and enjoy it."

Alex cocked her head. "I've never seen you so angry before." She smirked. "Who is this girl you so deeply wanted to wound tonight?"

"I did not want to wound her. I wanted to send her a message."

Throwing her head back, Alex laughed. "Oh, message received, I'm sure."

Tristan pushed past Alex and made his way into the back room. The redhead trailed after him.

Scarlet was hurting so much—it was all he could do not to chase after her and drop to his knees in apology and beg her to forgive him. His chest began to tighten. His hands were shaking. Dammit.

He stopped at his locker and gathered his things to leave for the night.

Alex leaned against the locker beside his, making sure her body brushed against him with the motion. Tristan slammed his locker closed and refused to look at her. He was suffocating. Scarlet was suffocating. What had he done?

His heart pounded and shriveled at the same time. He cursed.

Alex clucked her tongue at him in pity. "Whoever this girl is, she has you completely imprisoned."

Tristan shrugged away from the despicable woman and headed out the back door. "You have no idea."

He had broken the most precious thing he'd ever known and there was no turning back.

23

First thing the next morning, Gabriel marched into Tristan's house, barreling into the back room where Tristan spent every waking hour beating the crap out of a punching bag.

"What. The. Hell." Gabriel was seething. He slammed the workout room door closed so it was just he and his brother surrounded by mats, boxing gloves, and the smell of sweat, as Tristan glanced at him and then went back to punching.

Gabriel had never felt his jaw pull so tight. "That was your plan? That was your plan?!"

How could he do that to Scarlet?

He wanted to roar. "I understand that you needed to keep Scarlet from touching you, but don't you think that was a bit cruel last night?"

"Yep." Tristan threw another punch into his hanging target, dark bags under his eyes like he hadn't slept in years.

"Scarlet's a person, Tristan! You can't hurt her like that. You can't—you can't—"

"I can't what?" Tristan caught the swinging bag. "Break her heart?"

Gabriel pursed his lips.

Tristan steadied the bag and rolled his shoulders. "It was the only way." He punched again.

"No." Gabriel shook his head, fury and protectiveness making his muscles jump. "It wasn't fair. Go tell her the truth."

"What truth would that be?"

"I don't know, but you let her believe something that's not honest."

"No. I let her see something. She chooses to believe whatever she wants."

"She cried, Tristan!"

Tristan's fists froze, the only sound in the room the creak of the chain the punching bag swung from.

He swallowed. "She'll be fine." He went back to punching.

"No, she won't."

"You don't give her enough credit, Gabe. She's brave and stubborn and tough as hell. She's not the breakable doll you want her to be."

"I don't care if she's made of steel, Tristan. Because of you, she's in pain."

"Yes, well, I'm sure it's less pain than the pain she suffers when she's dying."

"You're an ass."

Tristan nodded. "Yep." Then an odd glint entered his eyes as he stopped and stared at Gabriel. He cocked his head. "You love her."

"Of course, I love her."

"No." Tristan wiped a hand across his forehead. "You love her more than you used to. You want to protect her." He said this like it was a revelation.

"Quit changing the subject." Gabriel pointed to the door. "Go fix this."

"No." Tristan threw another punch into the bag. Then another.

"You need to apologize to her. She loves you!"

"And that's the problem, isn't it?" Tristan quit punching and faced Gabriel, breathing heavily from his exertion. "Her love for me is like poison and you just enable it. You just keep letting her love me." He shook his head. "I asked you to take her away and what are you doing? Telling me to apologize to her? To tell her the truth? You're just as destructive as she is! Don't you see? If I don't do this—if I don't break her heart—the cycle will never end! She'll die and die and die. And you're just chicken shit enough to let her." Tristan's eyes were wild and reckless. "So she cries. So what? Take care of her, dammit! Don't come to me with your bullshit wants and needs like I just made your life hell. I'm in hell. I'm in hell." He jabbed at his sweaty chest with a finger. "But I'm also the only one unafraid to make hard decisions around here. So, don't tell me what to do." He started unwrapping the bindings from his hands, his green eyes cold as they focused on the task.

Gabriel was enraged, but more than that, he was flooded with disappointment. "I hate you."

"Yeah, well," Tristan threw his undone wrappings to the floor, "I hate you too." He pushed past Gabriel, the door to the room swinging open and closed with a heavy thud.

24

There is a difference between a heart that no longer aches and a heart that no longer feels. And Scarlet's heart no longer felt anything.

Not joy. Not pain. Not love. Not hate.

Nothing.

She didn't know if Tristan cared for the redhead he'd kissed, or if he'd just wanted Scarlet to assume he cared. But either way, Tristan had wanted to hurt her. And the revelation had changed her.

A switch had gone off inside Scarlet, extinguishing the light of Tristan and leaving her dark and numb. Safe from pain.

She no longer loved Tristan because she no longer loved anything.

That is the beauty of a heart that no longer feels.

25

Boston 1895

"You know," Gabriel mused as Scarlet lined up another arrow, aimed, and released. "Most women pass their time walking with parasols and visiting dance halls."

She pulled another arrow. "Most women are boring."

Drawing back on her bow, she released the arrow into the long hall before her and watched as it pierced the target ahead.

"Very true. There is nothing boring about an armed woman. Alarming, perhaps. But certainly never boring."

Scarlet lowered her bow. "What are you doing here, Gabriel?"

"Watching you shoot arrows."

After the Tristan Incident—that's what she was calling it, the Tristan Incident—Scarlet refused to be codependent ever again. She had precious few years to live and she wanted to make the best of it—without the assistance of over-protective immortals.

So she'd bought her own home and made her own friends. She made a life for herself and for the first time in all her centuries, Scarlet felt like an adult. She needed no one, so she never sought out Nate or Gabriel.

Though that didn't stop them from coming to her.

Nate visited once a week to draw her blood. He was working on a vaccine, hoping to cure Scarlet through medicine. She had no such hopes, but she let him draw her blood anyway.

But Gabriel visited her every other day and almost always commented on how odd it was for a woman to convert her home's hallway into an archery range. It was dreadfully annoying.

But it was also the only thing Scarlet looked forward to each week.

She didn't want him in her life, yet she felt empty when he was not there. Something about his patience and crooked smile made Scarlet feel loved and undamaged. And dammit if those weren't two things she wanted more than anything.

Not that she'd ever let Gabriel know that. This life—her life—*was for her alone. No broken hearts. No maddening curses. No gray love. She just wanted...simple. And so she had built herself a simple little life and pretended to be annoyed with Gabriel's incessant drop-ins.*

"Don't you have better things to do than loiter in my home?" Scarlet asked.

He smiled. "Would you like me to leave?"

No!

Scarlet hurried to shut off her ridiculously needy heart.

Numb. I want to be numb.

"You may stay if you wish, but do not expect me to entertain you."

"Too late." His smile grew. "I miss you, Scarlet."

She wished he would not say such things to her when she was trying to be numb. Words had a way of making her heart stir and Scarlet didn't want to feel her heart. Not now. Not ever again.

She said nothing, mostly because she could not trust her traitorous heart to speak coldly to the loving man who so wished to make her life beautiful and was so desperate for love himself.

"So," *he continued, unfazed by her lack of response.* "I was thinking we could travel somewhere. Would you like to see Paris?"

"No."

"Would you like to go to a play with me?"

"No."

"Would you like to shut yourself up in your house and pretend as though you are someone else? Or at least no longer you?" *He smiled.*

Yes. Exactly.

How did he know that?

"Scarlet." *He walked up to her.* "You can shut me out forever. That's fine. But I will always be here. Not because I think you need me, but because I love you." *He leaned in and kissed her cheek, and Scarlet's eyes fell shut at the contact.*

She missed him. She loved him.

But she wasn't ready to feel again.

Was she?

She opened her eyes but Gabriel was already gone.

26

Boston 1896

Scarlet stood on Gabriel's doorstep. She didn't know why she was here. She knew why she wasn't at home, but she still wasn't sure why her feet had brought her to Gabriel's.

She had not seen or heard from Tristan since the night of his fight and had not shed a tear since the same night. Her numb heart kept away the pain, setting her free of love.

But freedom felt a lot like death.

Empty. Numb.

Scarlet bit her lip as she looked at Gabriel's door. She should knock. She should go back home.

He wanted to care for her. Heal her. Love her.

Even when Scarlet would push away his patient heart, his patient heart would come right back. The nothingness she felt was safe, but it was also empty. She was empty. Just like Gabriel.

She knocked on the door.

He answered and a pleasant smile spread across his face as he ushered her inside and closed the door. "Hey."

"Hey." She fidgeted for a moment, shifting her weight from side to side as they stood in silence.

Gabriel waited patiently, smile still in place.

"I don't need anyone," she blurted.

"I know."

"But I miss you."

"I miss you too." He looked at her with his loving brown eyes.

He wanted love and she no longer wanted to be numb.

It was gray. It was completely gray.

But gray was better than empty.

So she kissed him.

Because this was not a time for safety or confusion. This was a time for healing. And they were both so broken.

He hesitated for a moment, then kissed her back. Fully, completely, honestly. Wrapping his arms around her, he pulled her up against him and Scarlet no longer felt numb.

27

Boston 1897

Tristan was back to shooting arrows at trees to ease his restless heart. The night after his kiss with Alex, he'd lost his first fight in decades.

He didn't want to fight back. He didn't want to fight at all.

So he went blind in agony, felt muscles burn, heard bones break.

And then he healed.

Because his immortal flesh never failed to come away from a beating unscathed. His heart, however, had no such luck.

Fighting had fed the darkness inside him for a long time, but after crushing Scarlet, fighting no longer helped him escape the pain that haunted him. He retired the sport and moved outside of town, where his limbs ached with Scarlet's distance but his mind had room to breathe.

He never saw Scarlet, but Nate—who visited frequently, though Tristan insisted he did not need company—had kept him informed of Gabriel and Scarlet's relationship.

It seemed they were growing closer. A fact that almost made Tristan want to go back to fighting. But isn't this what he had wanted all along? Scarlet safe. Scarlet happy. Scarlet loved.

Yes. This was what he wanted.

A crunch of dead leaves alerted Tristan to someone nearing him in the trees. He turned to see Gabriel approach from the side and then went back to shooting without a word.

Gabriel pursed his lips. "We need to talk about Scarlet."

Tristan lowered the bow as a ripple of tension rolled through his body.

"I love her," Gabriel said.

Something twisted in Tristan's chest. "Good."

Gabriel paused. "If you want her, you need to come home and make things right with her. Now."

Tristan stared at him. Was this a threat? Or an opportunity?

Did it matter?

When Tristan didn't speak, Gabriel scratched his chin. "I've watched her heart break over you too many times. I won't let it happen again. If you don't fix things with her now, I won't give her back."

Tristan rubbed the back of his neck, hating his life. But what could he do? What could he possibly do?

Not a damn thing.

He shook his head. "There's nothing to fix."

Gabriel looked sad—the bastard actually looked sad. As if Tristan's surrender of Scarlet had somehow wounded him.

With his eyes on the ground, Gabriel nodded. "I'll make sure she's happy."

And then Gabriel, who had somehow become the better man between them, turned and walked away.

28

New York 1983

From the moment Scarlet awoke in a park, staring across blades of grass at Tristan's green eyes telling her she was safe, she knew something was wrong.

But it wasn't until an hour later, when everyone gathered in Nate's house for a Welcome Back To Life meeting, that Scarlet realized what it was.

"I'm making progress on a vaccine, but I'd like to do some more experiments with your blood."

Scarlet said, "Of course."

Nate nodded. "I will begin performing a sequence of tests in an effort to..."

Her thoughts drifted away from Nate as she thought about being cured. A cure would mean no more dying. It would mean Gabriel could love whomever he wanted. It would mean she and Tristan could—

Tristan shifted uncomfortably in his seat across from her.

Scarlet wrinkled her nose. She'd only been alive for an hour and already she was annoyed with their connection. With Tristan.

He'd looked at her. He'd felt her. But he hadn't spoken a word to her since they'd left the park. If he was going to continue reading her emotions like an open book, the least he could do was exchange a word or two with her in return. But what had she expected? A plea for forgiveness? A confession of true love?

An image of him kissing the sexy redhead snaked into her head and unsolicited jealousy stirred low in her belly. She clamped down on that emotion for fear of Tristan reading her again and getting the wrong idea.

She no longer had any interest in the green-eyed Archer. Shaking him out of her head, Scarlet looked around Nate's large living room, taking in the tall windows, giant rugs, and leather furniture. Huh. Nate never used to be so...coordinated. She ran her hand along the soft, leather armrest of the couch she sat on and, once again, felt like something was wrong.

There was a different vibe in the air, a tension of sorts, that hadn't existed in her prior lives. What was it?

She looked at Gabriel, who gave her an easy smile. She smiled back. She had tried—truly tried—to give her heart to him completely in her last life, but thoughts of Tristan snuck into her soul as she was dying, leaving no doubt that her heart had never been, and never would be, completely Gabriel's. So she and Gabriel had some issues to work out.

But that was not what felt wrong.

Tristan slanted his green eyes to her.

Why was he even here? Wasn't he supposed to flee from her presence the moment she came back to life?

"...so we'll start next week," Nate's emotionless voice said. "One of the tests will require both of you to come in at

the same time, but it should only be for a day. Maybe then we'll be on our way to a possible cure."

Scarlet blinked her attention back to Nate. "Wait—what?"

Nate looked like he hadn't slept in weeks. "I need both you and Tristan to spend a day in my lab."

"Together?" she squawked. She actually squawked. Very embarrassing.

Nate nodded.

Scarlet opened her mouth to explain rationally and maturely—without squawking—how she didn't feel like hanging out with Tristan for an hour, let alone a whole day. But Tristan cut her off.

"Yeah. That's not happening."

She blinked. It was one thing for Scarlet to reject Tristan's company. It was another thing entirely for Tristan to reject hers.

"Why is he still here?" she asked, pointing to Tristan.

A muscle flexed in his scruffy jaw. Why did he always have sexy scruff? Did the man not own a razor?

His hard eyes shifted and a look of, well...Scarlet wasn't sure. Contempt, maybe? Hot lust? A look of something passed between them, making Scarlet's throat go dry.

"Tristan is here." Nate crossed his arms, "to help with my experiments to find you a cure. I've insisted that Tristan live relatively close to you this time, both for his sake and yours. I need Tristan's blood to be strong while I'm running these tests and distance from you weakens him. And I'll need your blood to be somewhat weak so I can create a vaccine based on your most vulnerable state. Limited interaction between the two of you will be safe as long as you don't touch one another, and it will only be for a few weeks."

Scarlet swallowed, trying to get the dryness out of her mouth.

Nate continued. "I'll be monitoring you very carefully and, if your eyes begin to glow, we'll make a new plan. In the meantime, I need to take daily blood samples. Where will you be living? With Gabriel?"

Scarlet felt trapped.

If she moved in with Gabriel, he would expect their relationship to pick back up, and Scarlet couldn't do that. She couldn't give him an incomplete heart. She needed to end things with him and living with him would certainly make that difficult, if not impossible.

Tristan was eyeing her sharply and suddenly Scarlet's palms were sweaty and her heart was racing and all she wanted to do was leave the room.

Gabriel looked at her with his kind eyes and calm presence. Why did he always have to be kind and calm? She couldn't crush him. She didn't want to hurt him.

Nate furrowed his brow, waiting for her answer.

"I don't think Scarlet should live with Gabriel," *Tristan said easily, but his body seemed tense as he flicked his eyes back to her.*

Scarlet blinked.

He was saving her.

Cold, distant Tristan was coming to her rescue.

Gabriel made a face at him. "Why are you even talking right now?"

"It makes more sense for Scarlet to live with Nate," *he said.*

Ooh, Scarlet hadn't thought of that.

Gabriel said, "How does Nate make more sense?"

He shrugged. "Nate needs to take her blood daily and do tests on her and that will all be easier if she lives with him."

Scarlet loved Tristan.

She still hated him for all the hurt and pain he'd caused her, but she loved him for this.

Nate rubbed his cheek. "Tristan has a point."

"I think me living with Nate is a good idea," Scarlet said.

Confusion crossed Gabriel's eyes. "Are you sure?"

Scarlet nodded and looked at Nate. "But only if you're okay with it."

"Of course." Nate ran a hand through his disheveled hair.

It was then that Scarlet realized what was wrong.

Nate.

She waited until their meeting had ended and Nate and Tristan disappeared down the hall, then turned to Gabriel.

"What's wrong with Nate—"

"What was all that about—"

"You go first," Gabriel said.

"What's wrong with Nate?"

Gabriel looked at the hallway and sighed. "While you were...gone, Nate fell in love with a girl named Molly and they got married—"

"That's wonderful." Scarlet smiled.

Marriage seemed like a fairy tale to Scarlet. Like it was some great reward she would never achieve. Because what place does marriage have in a life that comes and goes?

Gabriel cleared his throat. "But Molly wasn't immortal, so she...."

Scarlet covered her mouth, instant sorrow filling her chest at the realization that Molly had passed away.

Gabriel nodded solemnly.

"Oh, poor Nate," Scarlet whispered, her heart heavy for his loss. "When did...how...is he...is he okay?"

Nate had found someone worth loving only to lose her. Was there no justice in the world at all?

Gabriel shook his head. "He hasn't been the same since. For a week after Molly's death, he locked himself in his lab and wouldn't come out. When he finally emerged, he just sort of threw himself into all kinds of medical research and hasn't quit."

Scarlet shook her head, unable to speak.

"He's been a bit of a mess, but Tristan and I don't know what to do. It's like he's...gone. You know?"

"Do you think me living with him is too much? Should I let him be alone?"

"No. I'm sure company will be good for him." Gabriel scratched his chin. "What was all that about anyway? Why don't you want to live with me?"

Her shoulders sank. She didn't want to discuss this now. She didn't want to discuss this ever. But she also didn't want feel guilty anymore. Guilty for falling short of what Gabriel needed. Guilty for loving him, but not enough to take away his emptiness.

Scarlet took a deep breath. "We need to talk."

****

Later that night, Tristan stood in the doorway of Nate's home laboratory and hung his head to the side. "Dude. What are you doing to me?"

Nate was typing like mad on the giant computer he'd been talking nonstop about since he'd bought it a month ago. Computers were bulky and loud and Tristan had no idea what Nate hoped to achieve by using one. "I'm not doing anything to you."

"I agreed to stick around and attend your little team meetings, but that was all. You can't lock Scarlet in a room with me all day."

"I can and I will. Stop being a baby." Nate left the computer and slid a Petri dish under one of his microscopes.

He never stopped working. He never took breaks, never ate, never slept.

Tristan watched him bustle about for a few minutes. "Nate."

"What?" He sounded annoyed as he pressed his eye to a second microscope.

"You have to stop killing yourself in pursuit of this cure. I know Scarlet's alive again and that puts a clock on the whole thing, but this," Tristan gestured at Nate's haggard appearance, "is not healthy."

Nate lifted his head. "When Molly was dying; when she was fading away and I was a useless, empty soul jealous of her mortality, do you know what she said to me?"

Tristan had never seen such a hopeless expression on Nate's face before.

"She said, 'Nate, you have no way to die, so you need to find a reason to live.'"

Tristan pressed a fist to his mouth, not sure what to say to that.

"So that's what I did. I found a reason to live." Nate swallowed and went back to his microscope. "My reason used to be Molly. Now, it's this cure."

Tristan watched Nate work for a moment.

"It's more like a curse sometimes, isn't it? Our immortality?" Tristan said.

Nate didn't look up.

"It's hard to live without Molly," Tristan continued. "It's hard to imagine living not just one lifetime, but an eternity of lifetimes, without her." His chest began to ache with his own memories.

Nate paused. "Part of me wants to die every day."

Tristan nodded. He understood that all too well.

Knowing Nate would continue working through the night, Tristan turned to let himself out of the house, but changed his mind and headed up the stairs to Scarlet's new room.

Her door was open and, for a moment, he stood in the dark hallway and watched her run her hands down a large wardrobe against the back wall.

Stepping forward, he cleared his throat. "Hey."

She blinked at him, a hand still running down the grand piece of furniture in reverence. "Hey."

"It's a nice wardrobe." He nodded at the cabinet. Why was he making small talk?

She looked back at the wardrobe with softness in her eyes. "My father used to have one just like this when I was a little girl. His wasn't as crafted or smooth, but it looked similar. I used to make beds for my dolls in the drawers." She touched a finger to a drawer handle then cleared her throat and looked back at Tristan.

"Thanks for...earlier. With the living situation."

Tristan nodded and slowly said, "Was there a reason you didn't want to—"

"No." She shook her head. "No. I just—I just tried to be with Gabriel like that last time and it wasn't..."

Tristan held his breath, nervous and eager and scared as hell to hear whatever words she came up with.

"It wasn't...right."

His whole body relaxed. Not in relief, but in selfish, selfish love.

"So, what's up?" she asked.

"Oh, uh..." He pulled her mother's brooch from the pocket of his jeans and carefully set it on the dresser by the door, turning to leave before Scarlet could say anything. Or worse, feel anything.

****

Scarlet stared at the brooch and her heart clenched. All these years, all the hurt, and Tristan had kept this token of family for her. What did that mean? Did that mean he still cared for her?

Scarlet closed her bedroom door as she gingerly picked up her mother's brooch and absently rubbed at the design on the side of the circle.

Click.

The brooch in her hand broke apart and Scarlet's heart fell.

The beautiful etching had snapped and was barely hanging onto the band. Scarlet scowled as she looked down at the only remaining piece of her family and hated herself for being so careless.

She gently touched a finger to the design, hoping to repair her damage, and watched as it swung back into place—as if it had never been broken at all.

Odd.

With careful movement, she ran a soft finger over the design again and it swung back out.

What the...? Turning the ring over in her hand, Scarlet realized the brooch was hollowed out and the markings she had dislodged were acting as a latch.

Her heart began to pound as she peered inside the hollowed ring and saw a piece of parchment rolled up inside.

Sliding it out, she realized the parchment must have been trapped inside the brooch for hundreds of years. Had her mother known about it? Had her mother planned for Scarlet to find it?

She slowly unrolled the ancient paper.

Okay. Okay, okay, okay. What was she looking at here? A tree that said Avalon. Some weird lines running through *the tree. And the Spanish words for eternal water.* Her heart leapt in her chest.

Eternal water! Eternal water!

Scarlet started to shake and a smile stretched out her mouth, filling her with hope.

Her mother had purposely hidden this parchment and it had the words Eternal Water on it—that couldn't be a coincidence. It had to have something to do with the Fountain of Youth!

She looked over the parchment again. It looked like the eternal water had something to do with a place called Avalon. How many Avalons could there be in the world?

Scarlet laughed out loud, delirious with joy and had just jumped from her bed to go show Nate when she noticed dark lettering on the edge of the map.

Sitting back down, Scarlet read:

Through Bluestone you shall find the Fountain of Youth, but even immortality cannot withstand the caves. A sacrifice must be made, for while bringing life, The Fountain of Youth is true death for all.

Her head started spinning.

Immortality cannot withstand the caves? Sacrifice?

Her joy was quickly turning to fear. The fountain was true death for all?

Even immortals?

She needed to tell Nate and have him examine the drawing. Yes. That's what she would do. She stood and started for her bedroom door, then paused.

If she told Nate that the fountain was dangerous, would that stop him from searching for it? Would it stop Gabriel? Tristan?

Probably not.

She could beg them not to hunt for the fountain, but if they knew it would cure her they would probably walk right into death to find it. With careful hands, Scarlet rolled the tiny scroll up and tucked it back into the ancient brooch. She would not risk sharing this clue with anyone until she knew just how deadly the Fountain of Youth really was.

29

Scarlet had spent the past five days at the library searching for information on the Fountain of Youth and the word Avalon and found only one promising lead: a town in Georgia called Avalon.

Not only was the town closely located to where Scarlet's uncle claimed to have found the fountain, but it was also the only place in the world one could find Bluestone—the rarest rock on earth.

Coincidence? Scarlet didn't think so.

But she needed more details, which was why she was headed out to meet with someone who might have more answers for her.

She tiptoed down the stairs and hoped her roommate was too consumed with his research to notice her leaving the house so late.

She liked living with Nate. He was quirky and quiet but he kept out of her business. He didn't pander after her like Gabriel or shy away from her like Tristan. He was just...normal. Normal and sad.

The last thing she wanted to do was add an additional worry to his heavy shoulders. Quietly, Scarlet strode to the front door and opened it without a sound. She was basically a ninja. Stealthy. Silent. Blending into the night—

"Good evening," Nate said.

Scarlet jumped and spun around to face him with a loud exhale. "Don't sneak up on me like that."

"Okay. Then don't sneak out on me like that."

"I'm not sneaking out."

He squinted. "You were tiptoeing through the hall, hunched over like the Pink Panther."

"The who?"

"Never mind. Where are you going?"

"I'm meeting someone. A friend."

Nate waited.

"A guy named Kirk," Scarlet said. "Happy?"

Nate shrugged. "I'll come with you to see Kirk."

"No, you won't."

He narrowed his eyes. "What's going on, Scarlet?"

She ran a hand through her hair. "There's just some stuff I have to do, and I need to do it on my own. Trust me."

"I do trust you. But you can trust me too, you know. You don't have to keep secrets."

Scarlet shifted, guilt making her uncomfortable in the doorway. "I know."

After a long pause, Nate exhaled and moved to leave. "Don't stay out too late. Tomorrow is testing day with you and Tristan."

Scarlet's stomach filled with dread. "Yay."

She left out the front door and headed for New York University. Once there, she entered a stairwell door and climbed her way to the third floor of the building.

She stopped outside an office with a sign in the window that read GENEOLOGY and softly rapped her knuckles *against the open door.* A middle-aged man wearing the world's worst toupee looked up at her and smiled.

"Are you Miss Jacobs?"

"Yes." She stepped into the office. "You must be Professor Baker."

"Yes, but you can call me Kirk. You're here about researching your family history for a school assignment, correct?"

Scarlet nodded. So she'd lied a little on the phone.

"Then you've come to the right place. I help students retrace their family trees all the time. Please, sit."

Scarlet sat in the chair across from Kirk's desk as he scratched the top of his head, his toupee moving back and forth with the motion.

He pulled a form from a desk drawer. "Do you have a list of surnames we might begin with?"

"Yes." Scarlet pulled a piece of paper from her pocket with the names of her mother, father, and uncle written down. "I want to look for anything related to these names in or around the Avalon, Georgia area."

"Oh. That's a rather specific request." Kirk scanned the list and gave a single nod. "I'll see what I can do."

****

"I'm not doing this." Gabriel held up the joystick in his hand. "It's weird."

"It's not weird," Tristan said. "It's Atari."

Nate made a face. "Isn't Atari a video game for kids?"

"Yeah. It'll be fun."

"I don't really feel like having fun."

"And that's the problem." Tristan shoved the other joystick into Nate's hand. "You're miserable. You need a distraction, so suck it up and play the damn game."

Tristan started hooking the cables to the TV.

Gabriel looked around. "Is Scarlet here?"

Nate frowned. "Nope. She snuck out an hour ago."

"She snuck out?" *Gabriel asked.* "Where did she go?"

"I don't know." *Nate shrugged.* "But she's been secretive lately, sneaking off every day to go to the 'library'. So who knows?"

Tristan felt his chest twist up. Scarlet's emotions had been all over the place lately. Scared, excited, worried, afraid. And now she was sneaking out?

What was she up to?

30

"It's so early." Scarlet stretched her arms above her head.

Tristan shifted in his seat across from her at the table in Nate's lab. His dark hair was tousled and long enough to hang in his eyes and the black T-shirt he wore stretched across his shoulders in a way that made the butterflies in her stomach want to dance.

Dropping her arms, she looked away from him and yawned. The professor had loaded her up with ancestry books before she left his office last night and Scarlet had stayed up until the early hours of dawn searching through their pages for any sign of her relatives. She found nothing. Kirk was going to make a call to someone in Avalon to see about family documents so maybe they'd have better luck there.

Tristan stretched his neck, his trap muscles moving as he did so, and Scarlet's butterflies started to waltz. Damn him and all his muscles.

He shifted again, scooting his chair back even farther than he had the last three times he'd moved since they'd sat down. The good doctor was only ten minutes late and Tristan was already halfway to the door in his chair.

Even though they'd seen each other at Nate's house a few times—apparently, Tristan and Nate were best friends now—she and Tristan barely spoke. Half of her was fine with that, but the other half—the stupid half—wanted to climb into his arms and beg him to love her and kiss her and touch her until she died.

He shifted again.

"Really?" Scarlet blinked. "What's your plan here? Are you going to scoot your way out of the lab?"

He rubbed the back of his neck. "I just don't want to be here."

"Neither do I, but you don't see me squeaking my way to the door with my grumpy face on." She leaned back in her chair. "Are you really that uncomfortable around me?"

"Yes."

"Why? We're not touching. There's an entire lab table between us and if anyone should be freaking out about us hanging out in the same room, it should be me, remember? The girl who keeps dying? Unless you're planning on accidentally falling on top of me, I'm pretty sure you can relax."

He flexed his jaw. "I'm not stressed about touching you, Scar."

Scar.

"Then what is your deal?"

He stared at her. "I can feel you."

"Oh." Oh.

Note to self: no more touching Tristan thoughts.

She tried to act casual. "Well, get over it."

He scoffed and tipped his head back. "Right."

She watched his Adam's apple move as he swallowed.

"See?" He brought his face down. "Like that. What the hell was that?"

"What are you talking about?"

"Good morning!" Nate grinned as he entered the lab. He shuffled around the table between them and picked up a needle. *"So,"* *he lifted the needle in the air, "who wants to give blood first?"*

****

Four hours later, Tristan sighed into the strained silence and kept his eyes fixed on the ceiling. He and Scarlet hadn't spoken since Nate entered the lab and started drawing their blood and monitoring their vitals.

"So," Nate attempted conversation for the third time. He seemed to be in a better mood lately. "Do you guys maybe want to talk about how very uncomfortable this is?" He smiled tightly, looking first at Tristan, then at Scarlet. "Because I don't know about you, but I feel awk-ward. Let's hash it out, shall we? Tristan," Nate said brightly. "We'll start with you. How are you feeling?"

"Annoyed."

"I like your honesty and openness." Nate turned to Scarlet. "What about you? How are you feeling?"

"Tired," she said. "Nine in the morning is too early for needles."

Tristan said, "Maybe if you hadn't stayed out so late, you wouldn't be so tired."

Scarlet said, "Look who's decided to speak again. Suddenly, the silent and dark Tristan has an opinion on my life."

"Oh, I have many opinions."

"See?" Nate said, his smile tighter than before. "Isn't all this openness refreshing?"

"Like what?" Scarlet glared at Tristan.

"For one," he said, not sure why he was provoking her. "I don't like how you snuck off to a secret meeting last night."

She curled her lip. "How do you know about that?"

Nate swallowed audibly and Scarlet turned her eyes to him. "You tattled on me?"

"I was not tattling. I was making small talk. You're the one being all secretive about guys named Kirk—"

"Kirk?" Tristan's veins were on fire. "You're sneaking off in the middle of the night to hang out with a guy?"

Who the hell was Kirk?

She made a face. "Since when do you care about my life? You certainly didn't care all that much a hundred years ago."

Tristan's gut dropped.

Nate held up a hand. "Okay, maybe less openness is better."

"All I'm saying," Tristan said, leaning forward on his elbows, "is that your late night activities are suspicious. I don't know who this Kirk guy is, but—"

"Kirk is none of your business."

"Like hell. I don't want you slinking around in the middle of the night with some random guy you don't even know."

"And I don't want you making out with some slutty redhead after you just beat the crap out of someone. But we don't always get what we want, do we?"

Hurt, pain, sadness, betrayal.

Tristan felt his defenses waiver and knew he was close to caving. He couldn't stand hurting her. The pain she felt...the pain he caused her....

He needed to calm down before he did something stupid—like jump across the table and kiss her until things like curses and redheads and Kirks no longer existed.

He lowered his voice. "That was different—"

"*Different how? Do you usually go for blondes?*"

"*And...openness time is over.*" Nate started undoing tubes and wires from both Tristan and Scarlet.

Tristan stared at Scarlet. "*Stop it.*"

"*Stop what? Stop bringing up the past?*" She waved her hands in a spooky way. "*God forbid we talk about something real. Like how you made me watch you stick your tongue in someone else's mouth.*"

"*And on that note,*" Nate smiled at them, "*I'm leaving. I think I've got everything I need from you two. Good luck with all your relationship drama. Glad to see you kids are finally working things out. And by 'working things out', I mean bickering like an old divorced couple. So fun.*" He gave a curt nod. "*See you later.*"

Sharp hurt rose up inside Scarlet and Tristan hated himself.

"*First of all,*" he lowered his voice and pointed at her, wishing he could grab the pain inside her and stomp it into the ground, "*my tongue stayed in* my *mouth. Second, I had no choice.*"

"*Funny. I didn't see a gun pointed at your head.*"

"*I did it to keep you safe.*"

"*What?*" Her eyes were incredulous.

"*You came after me even when you knew you would die.*" He thrust his hands out, his heart pounding in fear thinking about how careless she'd been.

"*Because you were in pain.*"

"*So you risked your life?*"

"*Of course!*" Love exploded in her chest and he wanted to scream.

"*And that,* that right there, *is why I did what I did in your last life. To keep you safe from me—from yourself. You reckless woman.*"

"You thought kissing another girl in front of me would keep me safe? Safe?!" Scarlet's mouth dropped open. "You crushed me."

"I was trying to keep you alive."

"And I still died, Tristan!" Her face was flushed. "The only difference was I died with a broken heart!"

"And I've hated myself for it every day since." He inhaled, his eyes wild and hot. "But I don't regret it."

He was so worked up he didn't know if the pain and hurt and love he felt was his or Scarlet's.

Her lips parted as she stared at him, defeat and sadness taking over all the emotions in the room. "Well, that makes one of us."

And then she left, her heart breaking in her chest and falling to pieces in his.

31

After knocking, Scarlet stood outside Tristan's door and waited for him to answer as the wind picked up, blowing leaves and small purple flowers from a nearby tree into her face.

Unlike the rest of them, Tristan lived outside the city on a small piece of land with a single home in the center. Like a Tristan island.

Her stomach did flips as she heard the knob turn from the other side. Tristan opened the door. She and Tristan hadn't spoken since the last time they'd run into each other at Nate's. Tristan had played video games with Nate all night and afterward the three of them had eaten pancakes together. It had been a perfectly pleasant evening, but then she and Tristan had argued and he'd left. So the moment of silence they were standing in now was very awkward.

"What, uh...what are you doing here?" he asked.

His jaw was dusted with more sexy scruff. She was so getting him a razor for Christmas.

Who was she kidding? She liked the scruff.

Scarlet said, "Nate sent me here to pick up some Atari game you have?"

"Why didn't he just come himself?"

"Because he's in his 'cave of concentration' or something like that and refuses to leave the TV."

Tristan shook his head and muttered, "I've created a monster." He gestured for Scarlet to come in and she moved past him, careful not to touch.

"I meant to thank you before, for saving my mother's brooch for me. You kept it and..." Her throat constricted with emotion. She cleared it. "And I'm very grateful for that piece of my past."

And the drawing that was inside, whatever it was.

Tristan nodded and his eyes caught on something beside her head. "You have a..." He motioned to her head and Scarlet put a hand up to her hair.

"What?"

"There's a flower..."

She started patting at her hair and running her hand down the strands, trying to capture said flower. "Where...?"

Stepping forward, he reached to her hair and Scarlet held her breath. She stared at his chest, now just inches from her face, as he withdrew the flower from her hair. He smelled like leather and his body heat warmed her skin and everything beneath it.

Pulling his hand back with a small purple flower trapped between his fingers, he looked down at her. Their faces hadn't been this close in a hundred years, their breaths colliding into one another as lips parted to make passage for oxygen.

His green eyes dove into hers and her heart started to pound.

No, she thought. Don't look at me like that. Don't love me with your eyes. Don't search me like I'm something you've lost but desperately need. Don't love me like that. It's not fair and it hurts.

Tristan tilted his head and for a moment, for a crazy, wonderful moment, Scarlet though he was going to kiss her and the pounding in her chest became more demanding. But then his eyes, which had fallen soft and hazy, sharpened and he stepped back, clearing his throat.

"The game is over here." *He led her into his living room, where he shuffled through a cabinet.*

"I like your house," *Scarlet said, desperate to cool the heat in the air as she moved into the hallway.*

"Thanks." *Finding the game, Tristan held it out to her as they started walking back for the front door. Her eyes caught on a room to her left—the contents inside making her jaw drop in appreciation.*

Weapons were everywhere. Lining the walls, covering a desk, piled on the floor. Old weapons, new weapons, shiny ones, tarnished ones. Scarlet instinctively smiled at the idea of Tristan still wielding daggers.

"Look at all these," *she murmured, stepping into the room to admire the weapons on the wall. She glanced back at him.* "Can I touch them?"

Was that a glint of happiness in his eyes?

He nodded, but stayed in the doorway.

Smiling, Scarlet carefully lifted a bow from the wall, examining it with a look of wonder. "This is incredible. How does it work?" *she asked, running a fingertip along the bowstring.*

"It's called a compound bow. It gives you more control. That one is my personal favorite," *he said. And then he smiled—dimples and everything—and Scarlet's heart jumped.*

She placed the bow back on the wall and walked past a desk covered in weapons. An assortment of arrows was strewn about the desktop. A silver arrow, a blue-tipped arrow, an arrow with a dramatic fletch, an arrow made of bamboo. They were spilling out of a long, rectangular cardboard box.

"What's with the sample arrows?" Scarlet asked.

He hesitated. "I'm looking for a specific kind of arrow."

"What for?"

Certainly not to hunt.

"For my collection." He stretched his arms over his head in a nervous act of impatience and the hem of his T-shirt came up, showing off the patch of skin where his tattoo was inked.

Scarlet's heart stopped.

The tattoo was darker. Much darker.

Following her gaze, Tristan dropped his arms. "You should probably get back home."

Scarlet marched up to Tristan and yanked his shirt up—curse be damned. Ripped abs, tan skin, and the dark lines of a familiar tattoo met her eyes.

He shoved his shirt down, stepping away from her with a hard expression.

"You darkened your tattoo." She looked up at him. "The last time I saw your tattoo, it was faded. How did it get darker?" Scarlet already knew the answer.

He jutted his jaw. "You need to go."

She meant to yell at him, but instead her voice came out in a near-whisper, "You had it redone."

He pursed his lips.

"My design was fading, so you had it redone," she said and the space between them became electric.

He stepped back, but it was too late. Scarlet had already seen the truth in his eyes and her heart caught fire.

He loved her. He missed her. She was still a part of him. The centuries that pushed them apart had not changed anything. She covered her mouth, trying to hide her face, though it was useless because everything within her burned with love and desire and hope for Tristan.

And he felt every single sensation.

"Stop it, Scar," he said hoarsely.

She shook her head. "I can't stop."

"Please stop," he begged.

"Don't tell me to stop. I'm not an emotionless robot, Tristan. If you don't like how I feel, then stop feeling me."

He rubbed a hand over his head. "I can't turn it off and you know it."

"Then deal with it."

He shook his head and muttered, "You have no idea how burdensome it is to feel you."

"Burdensome?" All her warm feelings of love and hope turned to ice.

"Yes, Scar. Burdensome. I can never relax around you. I can never turn you off. You're always right there, inside me, and I'm always one breath away from killing you. I have to be careful every single second of every single day. So yeah. It's burdensome."

Scarlet's whole being resonated with hurt and anger and grief. She gave him a hard look. "Well, allow me to alleviate some of that miserable weight for you."

She walked out of Tristan's house and drove away, but she didn't head home. She just drove and drove until the sun set.

And then she realized Tristan had done it again. He had pushed her away, and she had left.

And wasn't that the cycle of sadness in her life?

He didn't push her away because he didn't want her. He pushed her away because he didn't want to be careful.

She turned the car around and headed back to Tristan's house.

He had been careful long enough.

****

Tristan felt Scarlet before he saw her. Half of him was excited. The other half was terrified. Story of his life.

He walked into the front room where Scarlet had let herself in and was standing with resolution in her soul—the most dangerous of all her emotions.

He leaned his shirtless body against the doorjamb of his bedroom and their eyes met. Love and want coursed through her, echoed in him, and made him feel like a caged animal. Pacing behind bars. Waiting.

He tried not to look at her lips. "What are you doing here?"

She moved forward, her heart pulsing against his, until she stood right in front of him. So close, if he inhaled deeply their chests would rub together.

Her eyes traveled along his face, his jaw, his throat, until they landed on the skin above his heart and, soon, her heart began to beat in time with his.

"Scar," he said, his voice dry and gravelly. "What are you doing?"

And then a wave of all the emotions he didn't know how to ignore blew into him.

Love, want, passion, need, hope, faith, desire, love, want, want, want...

The caged animal continued to pace.

"You are so careful." She tilted her head. "You have always been so careful. But what if I don't want you to be careful?"

Then I will be reckless and dangerous.

She put her palm against his chest and the caged animal wanted to cry out in ecstasy. She hadn't touched him for two hundred years and now, with her small hand on him, she had him on the verge of howling.

He closed his eyes and tried to focus on something—anything—other than the bliss of her touch. And how wonderful she smelled. And how if he just leaned in...ever so slightly...he could taste her...

He swallowed. "Scar." He opened his eyes. "You need to leave." Against every desire the animal within him had, he wrapped his fingers around her wrist and gently pulled her hand from his chest.

The animal roared in protest.

She shook her head. "No."

He could feel his resolve crumbling and panic began to overtake him. He exhaled, wishing for a miracle to save him from touching her, killing her. "Don't be difficult."

He paced to the other side of the room.

"Why do you keep pushing me away?" she asked, like she didn't already know the answer. Like she didn't understand in great detail what his motivations were.

He strode to the door, frustrated and impatient and turned on. "I'm not having this conversation with you again."

"Do you think pushing me away will make me stop caring about you?"

God, I hope not.

He opened the door. "You need to leave."

"Maybe you've stopped loving me, but my feelings for you haven't changed."

Stopped loving her? She thought he'd stopped loving her?

He slammed the door, the animal clawing through the bars of his cage with delirious anger. "First of all, I couldn't stop loving you even if I tried. And I've tried." He laughed without humor, wishing his life wasn't so screwed up. "God, how I've tried. But I am completely lost to you. I am lost and empty and broken—"

"My heart is broken, too—"

"My heart is not broken Scar. My heart is dead!" He didn't mean to scream it, but he had. And the bars were breaking and his claws were bleeding and he needed her to get the hell away from him immediately. "It is a hollow black object that sits in my chest without purpose, haunting me with memories."

He'd never said a more honest thing in his life and now, now that the words were free, he felt the sorrow he'd always tried so hard to keep at bay slam into him and wrestle with the desire that spurred on the animal. "It's dead," he repeated.

And then she said it. She said the thing he could not let himself hear.

"I love you." Her eyes were big and full and he wanted to kiss the flashing blue from their depths and fall into black oblivion with her like a crazy person.

He tightened his jaw. "Loving me is reckless."

"It's honest."

"It's dangerous, Scar!"

I'm dangerous! Run away. Run away.

"So?" She threw her hands up. "Loving anyone is dangerous! There's always going to be something at stake."

"Your life is not just 'something,' Scarlet." He emphasized the 'let' in her name. "It's everything." His voice cracked.

The animal clawed and moaned and whimpered and roared.

Good God, he needed her to leave.

"So, what then? You're just going to keep pushing me away because you're scared?"

"I push you away to keep you safe."

"You push me away because it's easier!"

"Easy? Easy? Are you insane?" His heart was as restless as the feral creature inside him. "Nothing about this is easy! Do you think it's easy to see you with Gabriel? Do you think it's easy to watch you die over and over again?"

"I don't know what to think, Tristan!" She fisted her hands. "You treat me like I'm a disease. You don't talk to me. You don't touch me—"

"Because you could die!" Now it was he who roared.

"I'll die anyway!"

Tristan's heart skipped a beat because he knew it was true. She would die. She would die and he hadn't yet found a way to save her. He wanted to cry. To howl. To break free of the cage and cling to her for the remainder of her heartbeats.

She continued, "We have no cure, no fountain. I'm as good as dead no matter what. But you still barely look at me—"

"Is that what you want?" He was feverish now. No longer in control of his temper or his body. "You want me to look at you?" He marched up to her face, staring at her with angry, terrified eyes. "Well, here you go, Scar. Me looking at you. How's this? Better? Easier?" He exhaled and felt the tremor of desire run through her and instantly knew he'd made a mistake.

He was too close. Too close.

Pain. Heartbreak. Sorrow.

"No, it's not easier!" She yelled, lifting her chin to look up at him more fully, her lips almost brushing his. And all he saw was Scarlet in the trees. Scarlet in the forest. The sharp-tongued thief who had captured his heart and wound herself around his soul for half a millennium. He was lost. He was so lost.

"It hurts like hell," she said, her eyes brimming with tears at all she wanted from him. Everything he'd kept from her for so long. "But it's better than feeling like you don't want me."

"I do want you!" he growled, bars coming down. "I want you more than my next breath."

"Then stop pushing me away!"

Defeat. Pressure. Love. Want. Want. Want.

"I can't have you, Scar!"

"Too bad!" A tear fell down her face and Tristan couldn't breathe. "I'm already yours! I was yours in the forest and I'm yours right here—"

And the caged animal broke free.

Crushing his mouth to hers, Tristan pulled her up against him and kissed her like he'd wanted to for so many years.

And she kissed him back, her emotions spilling out of her heart and falling into his soul and making him feel content and unbroken for the first time in centuries.

She was small in his arms, melting into him and letting him hold her. He'd missed this. Her body by his, her mouth in surrender, her heart pressed against his chest like it should have been their entire existence.

He kissed and kissed and demanded and kissed some more. Scarlet clawed at his shoulders as he grabbed her hips and pressed her into the wall, pushing up against her to trap her there, in his arms, where no one could take her away from him.

She had her hands in his hair and he had his hands under her shirt, feeling the soft skin of her stomach.

Scarlet exhaled as he moved his mouth to her ear, pulling shivers from her body. His mouth moved to her jaw, her throat. He couldn't get enough of her.

He held steady to her hips, locking her in place against his body as his lips went back to hers. She was completely intoxicating.

Her hands tucked into the waist of his jeans, tracing the line of her drawing on his hip as Tristan sank his mouth into hers.

And then he felt ice-cold pain cut through Scarlet's chest, sucking the air from her lungs as her body recoiled within.

He immediately released her, the warm haze of love and need disappearing instantaneously the moment he felt her pain.

Scarlet's eyes were closed for a moment as the pain subsided from her chest. Tristan wanted to die.

He wanted to die a slow and painful death right that instant.

Scarlet opened her eyes and looked nervous. "Tristan, I—"

"*I hurt you.*" *He rubbed a hand over his mouth.* "*I hurt you,*" *he repeated.*

"*No,*" *Scarlet lied, shaking her head vehemently.*

He nodded. He'd felt the pain, he'd felt what he'd done to her. And all because he couldn't resist.

He needed to die.

32

The next day, Scarlet let out a frustrated moan, her thoughts stuck in a tailspin over her kiss last night with Tristan.

What a disaster.

A hot, wet, sexy disaster—but a disaster no less.

He was never going to touch her again. She knew it. Why did her eyes have to burn? Why couldn't they have just been normal eyes for one freaking night so she could kiss Tristan freely?

And the horrified look on his face? The face that made her feel like she'd just stabbed his heart with a fork and flung it into the garbage can or something—it was enough to make her scream.

So unfair.

Scarlet entered Kirk's office and sat down with a heavy sigh.

"Good afternoon, Scarlet." Kirk smiled. "Rough day?"

Rough century. "Something like that."

"Well I might have some news that will cheer you up."

I doubt it.

He continued, "My contact in Avalon sent me a journal that belonged to a William Jacobs. But the name William Jacobs was very common back then, so there is a chance this is not the William you were looking for."

Scarlet's thoughts immediately left Tristan and focused on the professor as he held out an old, leather-bound book.

"Yes, it is," Scarlet whispered as she took the journal from the professor's hands. Scarlet could barely breathe. On the front cover was a beautiful drawing of a dark-haired woman wearing a circular brooch. Scarlet's mother. Her father had drawn a picture of her mother on his journal and somehow that journal had ended up in Scarlet's hands.

Hands that were now shaking.

"Are you okay?" he asked.

Scarlet looked up at him. "Can I borrow this for a few days so I can read through it?"

"I'm afraid I told Mr. Brooks I'd keep it here at the University."

"Mr. Brooks?"

"Yes. George Brooks is my contact in Avalon. His family founded the town centuries ago and he keeps a private collection of historic journals and ancient maps and some kind of blue weapons he's very proud of. He seems fascinated with all things Avalon, so if this journal doesn't help you find what you're looking for he may have something else for you. But the journal will have to stay on campus. There's a reading area downstairs, if you'd like to start now."

Scarlet blinked.

This was her father's journal? And she couldn't take it home with her because some random Mr. Brooks guys said so?

Ha.

"I think I'll do just that," Scarlet said, taking the journal with her as she left the office. She had no intention of keeping the journal at the school and the thief inside her wouldn't let her do so anyway.

Scarlet left the university building and headed home with the journal.

As soon as she got to her room, Scarlet shut herself inside and sat on her bed. Opening the journal, she found most of the pages damaged with water, but those that were still legible she read with hungry eyes.

Turning a page, Scarlet sucked in a breath at what she saw. It was an exact drawing of the tree picture Scarlet found in the brooch and on the adjoining page was an entry that told Scarlet what the drawing was.

A map to the Fountain of Youth.

She wanted to squeal. She could cure her heart and release Gabriel from his curse and relieve Tristan from pain.

She eagerly read the passage.

Natives say… The only way to the fountain is through a labyrinth of Bluestone caves deadly to immortals. Poisonous vines guard the caves and can only be cut with immortal blood, for immortal blood kills that which is made of magic. The caves lead to a chamber where a single tree grows.

This is the Avalon.

From the Avalon comes the Fountain of Youth, but the water that gives birth to immortality demands death in return. Touching the Avalon is fatal, but from the sacrifice comes eternal water and the Avalon fruit, which heals all who are addicted.

Scarlet's face fell. Deadly to immortals? This was what they'd all been looking for. But would she risk the lives of her loved ones to break the curse?

She read on in the journal, absently turning pages until her eyes lit on a detailed picture of an arrow and she paused.

The drawing was described as an arrow made of Bluestone and that Bluestone weapons had the ability to kill immortals.

Scarlet eyes snapped back to the picture. She'd seen that very arrow before—in the assorted collection on Tristan's desk. She needed to warn him immediately—just in case he fell on top of the Bluestone arrow he had and accidentally sliced his heart in half.

Closing the journal, Scarlet picked up the phone receiver by her bed, but froze when she heard Tristan's voice already on the other line.

"...can't do this anymore."

"Yes, yes." Nate sounded exasperated. "We're working on it, Tristan. I'm making progress with your blood and I'm still looking into possible fountain locations."

If Scarlet had any manners, she would hang up her phone and let them carry on their conversation in private. But Scarlet was fresh out of manners.

"I'm not talking about the fountain." Tristan was using his serious voice. "I'm talking about finding a way for me to die."

Scarlet sucked in a breath and waited for her heart to start beating again.

"Are you crazy?" Nate said.

"Yes. I'm insane and I'm crazy and I'm in love with someone who dies when I touch her. Help me die."

Scarlet tried to swallow, but her throat was too dry.

Nate lowered his voice. "I don't know what happened last night, but death won't fix it."

"Yes, it will. You even said yourself that if my blood were to die while Scarlet was alive, then the immortal blood in her heart would die too. She would be healthy again."

There was a long pause and Scarlet could just imagine the baffled look on Nate's face. "But you would be dead."

"Yes. And Scarlet would have a real life, Nate. A real chance at living."

Scarlet's heart puckered in disbelief.

What was he saying?

"Let's put aside, for a moment, the fact that you're crazy and stupid. You're still immortal, Tristan. You can't die."

"Your books said there was a weapon that could kill any immortal being. It's possible, Nate."

Scarlet put a hand over her mouth. There was actually hope in Tristan's voice. Genuine, beautiful, little boy hope and it was tearing her down the middle.

"If I can find a weapon that will cut my heart in half," Tristan continued. "then Scarlet will be free, correct?"

Like a shock of cold water, reality slapped Scarlet in the face as she realized Tristan wasn't crazy. There were weapons that could kill immortals—and one of them was an arrow already in Tristan's possession!

Oh God. Oh God.

Nate sighed and his voice was strained. "Freedom without love is not freedom at all. If you die, Scarlet will hate you forever."

Tristan hesitated. "If I live, Scarlet will suffer forever."

A long minute passed and Scarlet considered screaming at Tristan through the phone. There was absolutely no way she was going to tell any of them about the immortal-killing weapons now that Tristan wanted to die.

Her hands went numb and her heart pounded.

Tristan said, "What would you do if it was Molly?"

"That's not fair."

"Exactly. It's not fair."

Another long pause.

"I'm not going to help you kill yourself, Tristan." He sounded stern and Scarlet suddenly loved Nate more than she ever had before.

Tristan made a huffing sound. "Maybe not right now, but there will come a time when all the death and brokenness has to end. Scarlet might not be selfish enough to admit it, but she needs it to end."

Feeling her throat start to close up, Scarlet silently hung up the phone before she gasped or choked and gave herself away.

Sweat began to form along her brow.

She stared at the journal on her bed for a moment.

Nate and Gabriel had worked for centuries trying to keep Scarlet healthy, trying to preserve her life. They had protected her in every way they could and she loved them deeply for it. They were her best friends and they would risk their lives in a heartbeat for her.

And Tristan was her very soul and there was no way in hell she was going to lead him to death—a death he would probably welcome, damn him. And there was an entire collection of immortal-killing weapons in Georgia right now that Tristan might stumble upon in his suicide mission.

Scarlet stood in her room for several minutes, trying to think through every possible scenario that would keep everyone safe. Taking several deep breaths, she came to a decision.

She would go to the fountain by herself. If she died, Tristan's blood would bring her back to life and she could try again in her next life. But if Tristan, Gabriel, or Nate died, they would never return.

She would find Mr. Brooks and buy up his collection and keep it from Tristan. And she would find the fountain

and try to cure herself with the blue water without endangering anyone else.
It was a stupid plan. It was reckless and crazy.
And it was absolutely what Scarlet was going to do.

****

It took all of Scarlet's will power not to sprint to Tristan's house the second she'd hung up the phone. But that would have been rash. Instead, she spent a few hours thinking through her plan, coming to only one conclusion: there was a good chance she was going to die.
Not a happy thought, but meh.
She was used to dying.
Arriving at Tristan's, Scarlet parked her car in the shadows and sat for a moment, going over her options. She needed to get that arrow away from him and his suicidal stupidity.
She could ring his doorbell, wake him up, and approach him maturely.
Hey, Tristan. You know how you're looking for a special weapon to kill yourself? Guess what? You already have it! So, if you don't mind, I'm just going to take it off your hands.
Yeah, no.
She could try threatening him.
Give me the arrow or I will climb onto your body and stay there until I die.
Tempting, but not very mature.
Or...
She could sneak into his house and steal it.
Journals. Weapons. She was on a stealing streak today.
She crept quietly through the shadows, hoping Tristan was fast asleep and not able to sense her presence as she tried the front door. Locked.

Bummer. That would have made things easy.

She went around the side of the house to the weapons room and was pleased to find the window unlocked. Opening it, she slid inside, feeling confident she would be able to pull this plan off after all.

Squinting, she tried to make out weapons in the dark. Had she been smarter, she would have thought to dress in all black and bring a freaking flashlight with her, but no.

At least Tristan was a deep sleeper.

She studied the arrows on the desk until she found the one with the blue tip and picked it up, letting out a silent exhale as she tucked it into her back pocket.

Looking around, another idea struck. She was going to need immortal blood and weapons—lots of them—if she hoped to cut through deadly vines.

She hurriedly started plucking knives off the walls and tossing them out the window. She grabbed a few bows, a few dozen arrows, and threw those out the window too, just in case.

Jumping back outside, she loaded up her arms and carried Tristan's weapons back to her car. It took her three trips to get them all loaded and, just when she was about to close her trunk, Scarlet started to feel nervous.

Why was she nervous?

Then curious.

What the...?

She heard a sound behind her and spun around to see a very upset Tristan glaring at her.

Oh crap.

"Scarlet," he said, not surprised to see her. The whole connection thing was inconvenient on all sorts of levels.

"Hi." She waved at him awkwardly as she leaned a hip against her trunk like it was perfectly normal for her to be

packing up weapons in the middle of the night and acting super creepy in his front yard.
She felt relieved.
Wait, what? Why did she feel relieved?
"Are you okay?" he asked. His eyes fell to her trunk. "Are those my weapons?"
Confusion.
"Yeah. I know it seems weird," she said. "And I'd really love to explain myself, but honestly, you came up out of nowhere and I haven't had time to put together a good lie."
"You snuck into my house," he said.
"Yes."
"And stole a bunch of my weapons," he looked at her trunk again.
"Yes."
"Why?"
Confusion.
Fear. Desire. Fear. Love.
What was going on?
Scarlet made a face. "Because I need...them?"
"So do I."
She made a face. "You don't need them."
Fear. Love.
Why were her emotions all out of whack—
Scarlet gasped and covered her mouth.
"What? What is it?" Tristan looked around in alarm.
She dropped her hand, her mouth falling open. "I can feel you."
He stared at her, his eyes growing huge. "You can feel me?"
She nodded.
Oh no. This was bad.
Well, it was awesome because it meant that Scarlet now had an inside track on all things Tristan. But it was still bad.

"No." He started shaking his head, stress jumping out of his core. "No, no, no. That means the connection is stronger. I shouldn't have touched you."

"It's amazing." Scarlet set a hand to Tristan's chest, wanting to feel more of him. "Our connection must be both ways now. Wow." Warm, wonderful bliss slid into her hand and up her arm as she touched him.

He pulled her hand off him. "This is bad." He cursed, rubbing his head. "We shouldn't have touched."

Scarlet tapped into Tristan's feelings and was overwhelmed by love and passion and loyalty. He loved her—deeply. Everything pulsing out of him was laced in love and protection.

"Why are you smiling?" He asked.

"Because you love me. And I love you. And it's the most powerful thing I've ever felt."

He slowly nodded. "We have a very powerful love, indeed."

They stood in his front yard, under the stars, staring at one another like they had when they were Scar and Hunter in the woods. Carefree. Hopeful.

He exhaled as a sliver of fear ran through him. "Which is why I'm concerned about you sneaking into my house and stealing my things—"

"Borrowing. Oh!" She thought of something else. "And I need money. Can I borrow some money?"

He narrowed his eyes. "Why do you need weapons?"

"Is that a yes on the money thing?"

He crossed his arms. "Tell me what's going on and you can have whatever you want."

"I can't."

He scowled.

"Listen," she said. "I have to do something. And I know you'll be tempted to track me down or whatever, but you can't. I have to do this alone."

"What do you have to do?"

"Can't you just trust me?" She pleaded. "I have to go kind of far away, but I don't want you to be in pain. Follow me if you have to, but don't find me. Okay?"

"Not okay."

"You are such a pain." She growled. "Just let me do this without asking questions. Please?"

"Are you insane? You have a trunk filled with weapons, you're asking for money, and our connection is now both ways, which makes you more vulnerable than ever before. And you don't want me to ask questions?" His jaw tightened.

Fear, anxiety, faith, fear, love, confusion, love...

"I know you're worried. I can feel that you're worried. But give me one week. That's all I'm asking." With pleading eyes, Scarlet looked at the boy whose heartbeat was now echoing in her chest. "Trust me, Hunter."

****

Racing back to Nate's house, Scarlet ran inside with the Bluestone arrow, desperate to hide it somewhere apart from her in case Tristan ended up coming after her and riffling through his weapons on his I-must-die mission.

Upstairs in her room, she dropped to her knees in front of the wardrobe and pulled out the bottom drawer. Remembering her dolls from when she was young she searched for...aha! A false bottom—just like her father's wardrobe. Once upon a time, Scarlet had stored doll shoes and ribbons in a secret compartment such as this. And now she was hiding the most dangerous thing she'd ever held.

She placed the arrow into the secret compartment, replaced the false bottom, and pushed the drawer closed. Satisfied that the arrow—and therefore Tristan—was safe, she hurriedly started packing, running around her room like a crazy person.

Throwing her duffle bag over her shoulder, Scarlet retrieved her mother's brooch and walked downstairs, quietly slipping into Nate's lab.

She searched through the blood samples he had stored and grabbed everything labeled TRISTAN. She was crawling with nervousness. She would be traveling by herself for the first time, hiking around in a bug-infested forest while searching for a mythical fountain, and battling magical vines with immortal blood-stained weapons.

It was a lot to think about and she was scared. But she was also determined.

Finishing in the lab, she went down the hall and knocked on Nate's bedroom door. She heard the Atari game playing within and smiled to herself at his newfound hobby.

He opened the door. "Hey, Scarlet. What's up?"

She took a deep breath. "I have to go somewhere for a little while. And I can't explain. But I need a favor."

He narrowed his eyes. "What's going on?"

Scarlet held out the brooch. Since she had the journal, she already had a copy of the map and no longer needed the original, but she didn't feel comfortable traveling with both copies at the same time. "Will you keep this for me, please? It's very special and I need you to take care of it."

He looked alarmed. "Are you planning on dying? Are you—"

"No. No, of course not." She was just full of lies. "I just don't want to take any chances. Oh," a thought struck her, "and, you know, if anything should happen to me—which it won't, by the way—could you keep my bedroom wardrobe, too? I really like it and I'd hate to lose it."

Nate took the ring from her hand without breaking eye contact. "You're scaring me, Scarlet. Tell me what's going on."

She smiled sadly. "I'll tell you someday, I promise." She kissed his cheek, her chest tightening as she did so. "Trust me."

Turning in the hallway, Scarlet left the house with shaking hands and a hammering heart. There was no turning back.

Jumping into her car, Scarlet headed to Avalon. Ready for life. Ready for death. Ready for anything.

33

There were no cabins or hotels near the forest where the Bluestone caves were located, so Scarlet had to find a place to stay in the town of Avalon instead. She settled on a tiny cabin in the woods. It was dark and a bit dirty, but it had a boarded up cellar with an old workbench and a pegboard.
Perfect.
After settling in, Scarlet wasted no time lifting the floorboards in the cabin's kitchen and making herself a workspace in the cellar where she coated a few of Tristan's weapons in blood.
Then she grabbed her father's journal and headed out the front door. She was off to see a man about some Bluestone weapons.

****

Scarlet hiked through the dense forest of Avalon.
Her visit with Mr. Brooks yesterday had been disappointing. He had refused to sell her his weapons. Not

even when she'd offered to trade him a map to the Fountain of Youth had he conceded. Realizing there was no swaying him, Scarlet returned her father's journal to Mr. Brooks—with a few key pages ripped out, of course—and left.

She would just have to be successful in finding the fountain so Tristan had no reason to try and kill himself.

A twig snapped behind her and Scarlet spun around.

Nothing.

She shook her head. After leaving Mr. Brooks yesterday, Scarlet had visited the old Avalon cemetery in the hopes of finding her father's grave. She hadn't found any tombstones marked William Jacobs, but she had gotten the chills several times while she was there, like ghosts were watching her or something, and the eerie sensation had stayed with her ever since.

And now here she was, in broad daylight, spooked at the sounds of nature.

She slowed her hike and pulled out the forest map she'd brought.

Knowing she planned to return the journal to Mr. Brooks—where it was much safer than in the hands of, say, an immortal friend of hers who might to try to survive the caves of death—Scarlet had memorized the map.

The tree branches were filled with lines running off in different directions and those lines were the cave tunnels. There were a few tunnels that would take Scarlet to the Avalon chamber, but first she needed to find the caves themselves.

She studied her location on the forest map with a frown. She still had a long way to go and it was already noon. According to her research, the Bluestone caves were notoriously hard to find and Scarlet didn't want to hunt for them in the dark. She needed to hurry.

Something rustled to her left and she froze, her eyes shooting in that direction before she mentally scolded herself for being so paranoid.

Scarlet resumed her hike. Stupid, creepy graveyards and their hitchhiking ghost vibes—

Stiff hands grabbed her from behind and threw her to the ground.

Stunned for a moment, Scarlet could do nothing more than stare at the man looming over her. His eyes and teeth were yellow, his skin ash-gray, and his jerky movements made him seem more like an animated monster than a crazy man in the woods.

Scarlet snapped out of her shocked state just as the odd being grabbed at her bag. Snatching her bag from his grasp, Scarlet jumped up and raised a hand to block the blow her attacker threw at her.

Instinct kicked in and Scarlet kicked at the man—who she now decided was not much more than a decrepit creature—and made contact with his hip, kicking him to the ground. He grunted and spittle came from his mouth as he fell.

Reaching into her bag with deft precision, Scarlet pulled out her hunting knife and flung it into the man's chest just as he rose and came at her again.

Her adrenaline pumping, Scarlet watched the blade sink into the odd-colored skin of her attacker and waited for him to drop to his knees. But he simply looked down at the knife in his chest, pulled it out, and charged her again.

Stunned, Scarlet pulled out one of the bloodstained daggers and desperately thrust it into the abdomen of the creature that was nearly on top of her. The being stumbled back and collapsed onto the forest floor, its body crumbling into a pile of ash, leaving only the dagger behind. Scarlet froze in place at what she had just witnessed.

Hearing a sound behind her, she whipped around to see another creature charging her. Without a weapon to defend herself, Scarlet threw a punch into his jaw—which felt as though it was made of stone—and a heavy kick to his groin. He wobbled for a moment and Scarlet felt her eyes start to burn as a blue light lit up the trees around her. When the burning subsided, Scarlet saw the being had recovered and was coming at her again. Quickly, she lunged for the bloodstained dagger lying on the forest floor. She grabbed it and flung it at him. He, too, fell to the ground and disintegrated.

She took a moment to look around. Three more manlike creatures were charging toward her. Fear spiked her veins as she realized she was outnumbered and sorely unprepared for a fight of such caliber. Turning around, Scarlet ran through the trees blindly, her lungs burning and her legs going numb. Her eyes felt hot and flashes of blue bounced off the forest around her. She saw a few spots of blood fall from her face and realized her nose was bleeding as well.

What? No. Not yet! She couldn't be sick yet.

Faster and faster she ran, blood running down her face, until she was certain she had lost her attackers. Doubling over, she caught her breath and wiped her nose.

The creatures had not been normal humans. They had not been human at all.

What were they?

She straightened up and caught her breath. It didn't matter what they were. What mattered was that they stood between her and the fountain and it seemed they could be defeated with immortal blood—something Scarlet happened to have on hand.

She was going to need more weapons.

Another drop of blood fell from her nose.

And she was running out of time.

When she got back to the cabin, Scarlet carried the remainder of the Tristan's weapons—thank you Tristan for treating me like an equal partner in war at all times— *to the cellar and carefully coated them with Tristan's blood.*

She spent the rest of the day practicing the feel and weight of each weapon before hanging them up on the wall. When she was finished, she had a wall of bloody weapons that closely resembled the wall in Tristan's house.

She smiled to herself.

He would be proud.

Well, no, actually. He would be pissed. Tristan would hate the idea of Scarlet taking on a troop of nonhuman creatures by herself, but whatever.

Another warm trickle fell from her nose and she cursed as she brought her hand to her face. This was bad.

Walking back upstairs, Scarlet headed for the cabin's only room and cleaned her nose before heading to the kitchen.

She looked out the window, concerned by her rapidly accelerating illness and nervous for the battle that lay ahead of her.

But then she thought of Tristan and she wasn't afraid.

Staring out into the twilight forest, she whispered, "There is no victory without a battle."

34

The next morning, Scarlet crouched high in a tree in the Avalon forest and watched the creepy beings from the day before mill around the clearing below. She counted eight of them.

Scarlet pulled back on her bow and set a bloodstained arrow in line with the nearest creature. Silently cutting the air, her arrow struck her target's heart and he fell to the ground with a grunt, his body breaking apart into ash.

Scarlet's heart raced in excitement. Without hesitating, she pulled out seven more arrows and shot down the remaining beings without batting an eye, all of them falling to ash as their little weird buddy had.

If Scarlet hadn't been trying to be so sneaky, she probably would have laughed in victory as she carefully climbed down the tree.

An ash being charged at her from the bushes in front of her and Scarlet yanked a dagger off her back and thrust it into his stomach.

Ash guy down.

She heard rustling from the trees behind her and turned to see two more attackers coming at her. Pulling out another knife, she cut into the creaturemen until they were ash as well.

Out of breath and eyes burning, Scarlet turned and saw three more coming at her from the large boulders in the clearing.

Really? This didn't seem fair.

With a sigh, she dropped her bag and loosened her arms as the men of ash neared. One by one, she stabbed and sliced. She took blows to the face, she was kicked and bloodied, and she was choked and slammed against trees.

But in the end, she prevailed and found herself standing amidst several heaps of ash with no more creatures charging her.

Her nose was bleeding and her eyes were burning nonstop. She had an hour, if that, to live. Scarlet looked around and her heart fell. The fountain was too far away. Even if she sprinted she wouldn't be able to make it before her body gave out.

She had failed. All her plans, all her best intentions, were for nothing. She wanted to scream in frustration. She had been so close. So close.

She heard the sound of a gun cock behind her.

Slowly turning around, Scarlet's mouth fell open when she saw who was standing on the other side of the gun barrel that was pointed right at her head.

Raven.

How was she still alive?

"Hello, Scarlet," Raven said. "Give me the map and I might not shoot you in the face."

Scarlet blinked. "The...what? What are you...? Why—"

"The map to the Fountain of Youth, Scarlet. I need it."

"I don't have the map."

"Yes you do. That man you spoke with yesterday, Mr. Brooks? What a nice gentleman he is. I struck up a lovely conversation with him after you left and he told me how you offered to trade him a map to the Fountain of Youth for some of his valuables."

"I don't have—"

"Don't lie to me." She nodded to something behind Scarlet and suddenly Scarlet found herself being wrestled into the arms of two ash creatures she hadn't seen coming.

She kicked and struggled, but the decrepit beings quickly disarmed her and held her fast. A third being yanked her backpack off and handed it to Raven, who riffled through it before throwing it to the ground with a frustrated noise.

"Where's the map?"

Scarlet spit out the blood that was trickling into her mouth from her nose. "I told you, I don't have it."

Raven cocked her head. "You don't look well. Perhaps I'll wait until you fall dead and then I'll just riffle your pockets and that little cabin of yours."

"You'll find nothing useful." Scarlet's eyes burned as she smiled in triumph. Maybe she hadn't reached the fountain, but she'd kept the map safe.

Raven looked livid. "Take me to the fountain."

"No."

"Very well. I guess you'll be coming home with me until you change your mind."

The ashy creatures pushed Scarlet forward and she didn't fight. She needed to buy herself time to figure out a way out of this.

"What are these things?" Scarlet asked, wriggling in the hands of one of the man beings.

"I call them my dead helpers. They're corpses from the Avalon graveyard that I brought back from the dead."

"That's disgusting."

"It's effective." Raven pushed her forward. "I'm actually quite glad things worked out this way. Now I'll have a map and a sacrifice."

"What?"

"Certainly you know about the sacrifice that the fountain demands."

Scarlet tried to remember what the journal said.

Touching the Avalon is fatal, but from the sacrifice comes eternal water and the Avalon fruit which heals all who are addicted.

Raven laughed. "You're out here searching for the fountain and you don't even know about the sacrifice? The fountain requires a heart and therefore death, before it will release its water or its fruit. One touch of the Avalon tree will drain your heart of life and give me that fruit."

Scarlet blinked. She'd been so concerned about the caves that threatened immortals, she hadn't stopped to consider what the passage had meant about a sacrifice.

Someone would have to die in order for the fountain water to be accessed?

Scarlet would never be cured.

All this—all this time and effort and hope was for nothing. Scarlet was dying, and she would always be dying.

Now she was pissed.

Whipping to the side, Scarlet kicked the gut of the creature on her right and then wrestled herself out of the arms of the other being until she was loose enough to kick Raven's gun from her hand. Scarlet dodged the creaturemen and snatched a bloodstained knife from her pack—now lying on the ground abandoned—before slicing into the ashy beings until they crumbled.

Raven caught her by the hair and yanked Scarlet's head back, pressing a very sharp, very mean looking knife against her throat.

"Tell me where the map is or I'll slit your throat."

Scarlet started laughing wildly, blood from her nose streaming down her cheek. "You are so stupid."

Raven gripped her tighter, but Scarlet only laughed harder.

"Shut up!" Raven yelled into Scarlet's ear.

Her laughter dead in her throat, Scarlet whipped around and reversed their position, holding the knife to Raven's throat with one hand as she pulled Raven's head back by the hair with the other.

"You can't kill me, you know. I have fountain water in my body." Raven sneered.

Scarlet hit Raven as hard as she could with the handle of the knife, dropping the unconscious witch to the ground.

For a moment, adrenaline kept Scarlet feeling strong. But then the world started spinning and things went fuzzy. Her heart was pounding so hard her chest felt like it was tearing in half.

Blood filled her mouth, her hands went numb, and hot pain shot through her limbs. She tried to move, but her feet were made of lead and carried her only to the ground, where she dropped on her knees. Her eyes were seeing white and she knew this was it. This was the end.

She let her body fall to a heap on the earth beside her enemy, wanting to cry and scream for everything that was unfair and everything she couldn't fix.

But instead, she whispered, "Tristan."

Because somewhere inside her, Tristan was there, coming for her, feeling her, scared for her. He was sad. He was scared. And he was so in love.

He was getting closer, making her pain more acute, but her death more bearable. He loved her so much, it filled up more than the air in his lungs and the blood in his veins.

He was powerful. He was mad. He was everything she wanted forever.

And she was losing him.

She felt his gripping love for her wrap around her soul and tuck her in, rocking her to sleep through the blinding pain that took the light from her burning eyes and stole her away, once again, into death.

35

The worst way to wake up, Heather decided, was tied to a freezing cold pillar with rope burns on her wrists and a half-naked immortal guy hanging across from her.

Gabriel shifted his body and his stomach muscles flexed with the movement.

Okay, so maybe the half-naked immortal guy part wasn't all that bad.

"So…" Heather nodded slowly. "We're still here."

"Yep. I think your team of SWAT guys got lost. Probably looking for their shirts."

She made a face at him. "You're effing hilarious."

"I try."

Heather wiggled her freezing toes. She could really go for a blankie or some long underwear. She closed her eyes and dropped her head back against the pillar. "I want to go home."

"You will," Gabriel said. "Soon."

"Is that right?" she said dryly.

He nodded. "Tristan won't stop until he finds us. Well, until he finds *me*. He'll find *you* by default."

"How are you so sure Tristan will track you down?"

"Because if Tristan had been kidnapped, I wouldn't stop until I found him and got him the hell out of wherever he was. He'll find us."

"I hope you're right." A shiver went through her as she shifted against the pillar. "It's so cold."

Gabriel scoffed. "Try hanging out without a shirt on."

Their eyes met.

Awkward.

He cleared his throat and looked at the ground while Heather tried not to think about being tied up and topless with Gabriel.

Another shiver went through her. "Do you think the Hostage Hotel serves food? A bagel sounds good—Ooh, or a cappuccino. A cappuccino sounds delicious."

"Yeah, I'm sure Raven's whipping up a five-star breakfast for us in her Millhouse apron right now."

"Wow. You're king of sarcasm today."

"*Maybe sarcasm is how I cope*," he mocked.

"Ha. Ha." Heather shifted again and winced as the ties around her wrists cut into her raw skin. She frowned at the crappy rope. "Your ex-girlfriend sucks, Gabriel."

"Yeah, yeah. I have terrible taste in women." He jiggled his own ties, staring up at them like maybe he'd overlooked a secret trap door out of the bindings.

"Not entirely. I thought Scarlet was a good choice."

Heather watched as the skin around his wrists tore open against the rope, only to immediately close back up.

"Yeah." He twisted his arms. "But Scarlet wasn't really a choice."

Heather blinked. "Wait, what?"

"Tristan was with her first, but he asked me to marry her when he was sent off to war," he said casually.

Like this wasn't a giant bombshell that changed everything in the whole freaking world.

"Whoa, whoa, whoa. Back up, Romeo." Heather was fully awake now. "Start at the beginning."

Gabriel stopped wiggling his ties and briefly recounted how Scarlet and Tristan had been engaged, but Tristan had been sent away and asked Gabriel to marry Scarlet in his place so she would be taken care of. And then how Gabriel and Scarlet had grown close, only to have Raven shoot Scarlet through the heart with an arrow on their wedding day.

Heather's mouth hung open as Gabriel finished his story. "Well, that explains it."

"Explains what?" he said.

She shrugged—or at least tried to shrug. Shrugging while tied to a block of ice was difficult. "Why you and Scarlet don't have chemistry. I always thought it was strange—like how can two people who so obviously care about one another not have chemistry? But now it makes sense."

He frowned. "Scarlet and I have chemistry."

Heather rolled her eyes. "Oh please. Don't get me wrong. You're both hot and you look great together, but there's no passion between you guys. Like at all. And you *never* fight. It's super strange."

"We've fought," he said.

"Really? Over what?" she challenged.

He furrowed his brow.

"Wow. If it's that hard to remember a fight, then you've never had any fights worth remembering." Heather shook her head.

"Who wants to have memorable fights?"

"People who are passionate about each other!" she said. "Geez, Gabriel. Haven't you ever wanted to kiss someone and kill them at the same time?"

"No."

Heather opened her mouth, but no words came.

O-M-G.

Gabriel had never had chemistry with someone. He'd never had *love*.

Even though Heather knew that's what the curse was, she'd never really believed it.

But now...

Heather swallowed. "Well, even if you've never experienced it, surely you've seen what it looks like when two people are in love. Not just loving each other—like you and Scarlet—but *in* love with each other. It looks...I don't know. It just looks like chemistry."

"I know what chemistry looks like." His eyes fell to the floor for a moment. "Tristan," he said, lifting his eyes back to hers. "Scarlet and I have fought before. About Tristan."

Of course.

The door to the warehouse creaked open and Raven walked into the room.

Wearing bunny slippers.

Uh...

Heather blinked and the bunny slippers morphed into a pair of evil-looking heels—which made more sense.

She was hallucinating again. Awesome.

Lack of food and sleep was clearly taking its toll.

But bunny slippers didn't sound half bad.

"Ransom day," Raven announced as she walked to the table and started preparing to take more of Gabriel's blood. "Who's excited?"

Gabriel looked bored while Raven drained another pint from him and sealed it in another vampire baggie.

Heather cleared her throat. "Um, Raven?"

"What?" she snapped, withdrawing the needle and tubing from Gabriel's neck.

Heather licked her lips. "Could I maybe get some coffee?"

Gabriel made a face. "You have a problem."

Cocking her head to the side, Raven smiled at her. "You've become quite the fan of my coffee. I bet you're just *dying* to get more."

"Uh..." Heather wasn't sure what to say to that.

"Ah, hell," Gabriel muttered as he glowered at Raven. "What did you do?"

Raven shrugged as she set the baggie of Gabriel's blood on the table next to the scissors. "I needed insurance, so I've been tainting Heather's coffee for the past few weeks with fountain water."

Heather's throat constricted in fear.

Gabriel said, "You've been poisoning Heather?"

Raven sighed. "Yes. The girl just couldn't get enough of my coffee. I had to cut her off from the good stuff a few days ago."

"So I'm like a...like a drug addict now?" Heather squeaked the words out.

"Yep," Raven said.

No. This couldn't be happening.

Heather didn't do drugs. Not ever.

Raven looked at Gabriel. "This way, if Scarlet doesn't come through with the map, she'll have to find the fountain to save Heather. At which point, you and I," she ran a purple fingernail down the center of his bare chest, "will just follow her there. But until then, Heather over here is going to be pretty thirsty."

Raven turned to Heather. "I'd offer to give you more, but I took my final dose last night. And since the only cure is the one Avalon fruit by the fountain, you might be screwed."

Heather couldn't think. Or breathe.

"What's the matter? Not feeling well?" Raven eyed her carefully. "I'm sure the withdrawals will start kicking in soon. It shouldn't be long before the hallucinations begin. And then comes the madness."

"I'm going to go crazy?"

"Only if you don't get more fountain water. First you'll go crazy," Raven shrugged, "and then you'll die."

****

Scarlet woke with stiff arms and legs and her head hurt. Semi-painful sleep wasn't very satisfying. Still wrapped in the scent of Tristan, she rolled out of the big, white bed and padded across the floor. Opening the door, she stepped into the hallway and tripped over something that grunted on the floor.

Looking down, she saw Tristan sprawled on his back outside her door, an arm behind his head as if he was perfectly comfortable snoozing on the hard basement floor. He stared up at her with sleepy green eyes.

"What are you doing?" She put her hands on her hips.

He yawned. "Sleeping as close to your stubborn ass as possible so you don't toss and turn on that noisy bed," he looked at her pointedly, "in *pain*."

Crap. The stupid bed had given her away.

He stood up and stretched his arms above his head, his shirt lifting just enough for her to see his tattoo and her insides got all soft and warm.

Moving her eyes back to his, she tried to glare at him through all the fluttering in her stomach. "You slept in the hallway all night?"

He dropped his arms and gave her a crooked smile. "You've been awake for thirty seconds and you're already angry with me?"

"Yes, Tristan," she said. "You can't just sleep in the hallway because I'm tossing and turning."

"I can." He stretched out a kink in his neck. "And I will. Come on. Let's go have breakfast." He held out his hand.

Scarlet stared at it.

Like she was going to latch onto him with her touch of death.

"No?" He shrugged and let his hand drop as he headed up the stairs. "It was worth a try."

"Unbelievable," she muttered, following after him, completely confused by his chipper mood.

"By the way," he looked over his shoulder and ran his eyes up and down her body. "I like you in my clothes."

He smiled—truly smiled—dimples and everything. She eyed him suspiciously as he walked up the stairs and tried to tap into his feelings.

Happiness. Relief. Hope. Love.

Realization struck her. He was happy because he no longer hurt her.

Tristan stopped at the top of the stairs and stared down at her, still smiling. "You coming, or what?"

This wasn't the dark, tormented Tristan from her previous lives looking at her with his little boy grin.

This was Hunter.

Which was wonderful and terrible at the same time.

Bossy, dark Tristan Scarlet could avoid.

But charming, sweet Tristan?

Scarlet was going to be putty in his hands.

No. I will not be putty. I will be hard as a rock. Like Play-Doh left in the backyard on a hot summer day.

Tristan stared down at her with his patient dimples.

I am dried Play-Doh.

Scarlet hardened her face and walked up the steps, trying to focus on something other than his sleepy warm body and mussed up hair.

She cleared her throat as she ascended. "I was thinking maybe Nate could track Heather and Gabriel's cell phones. There's always the possibility their phones are nearby wherever they are. Maybe he could get a GPS location from that."

She reached the main floor and stood before Tristan, who wasn't moving.

She waited.

He smiled.

With rolling eyes, she brushed past him, their chests rubbing together as she moved into the main hallway. Bliss skittered through her veins and her knees weakened for the briefest of moments. Tristan smiled.

Damn him.

Scarlet walked to the kitchen and watched him open the pantry and grab various things.

"An-y-way," she said. "I thought the cell phones might be a good place to start."

"Uh-huh." He grabbed things from the fridge.

Scarlet sat down at the bar counter. "And then maybe we could go back to the graveyard and see if there are any Ashmen roaming about that we could follow back to Raven's hiding place."

Tristan retrieved a frying pan. "Uh-huh."

"Or maybe go to the Millhouse and talk with Clare's other employees." She cocked her head to the side in annoyance. "Are you even listening to me?"

"Yes." He started mixing things in a bowl.

"And if that doesn't work, maybe we can—what are you doing?"

"Making pancakes."

"Why?"

"Because you like pancakes."

"Oh my—" Scarlet rolled her eyes again. "We do not have time for pancakes, Tristan. Heather and Gabriel are probably lying in a ditch somewhere—"

"They're not lying in a ditch."

"Or bleeding to death—"

"They're not bleeding. Do you want chocolate chip or blueberry?"

Scarlet blinked. "Heather isn't immortal. She's probably scared out of her mind and screaming at the top of her lungs—"

"Blueberry it is."

"Tristan! I'm being serious."

He turned to look at her with a spatula in his hand. "I know you are. But you need to calm down."

"Don't tell me what to do."

Putting the spatula down, Tristan stepped up to the counter and leaned over so their faces were just inches apart. "Gabriel and Heather are safe. Raven doesn't want them dead, she wants them as leverage. We don't know where they are and until we do, there is nothing we can do to bring them back any faster. So please calm down and eat some pancakes."

Scarlet narrowed her eyes. "I don't want pancakes."

The corners of his mouth turned up. "Yes you do. You want blueberry pancakes."

"No. I want chocolate chip."

They stared at each other, his emerald eyes bright and amused.

"Good morning, cursed ones." Nate entered the kitchen.

Tristan went back to pancake-making.

"Morning," Scarlet said. She glanced Nate up and down. "What are you wearing?"

He looked down at himself. "This is my bathrobe."

Scarlet said, "It looks like a fur coat."

Tristan pointed at Nate with the spatula. "Told you."

Nate made a face. "For the last time, this is not a fur coat. It's just a very thick and warm bathrobe."

"With fur," Tristan added.

"There is no fur—never mind. I need breakfast." He padded to the pantry and grabbed a box of Lucky Charms. "So...how did everyone sleep? Far apart from one another and in no pain, hopefully?" He smiled at Scarlet as he made himself a bowl of cereal and grabbed a spoon.

"Yes," she said.

"No," Tristan said at the same time. He flipped a pancake before turning around. "Scarlet was in pain all night because she wouldn't let me sleep with her."

Nate coughed on a bite of Lucky Charms.

Scarlet pursed her lips. "And *Tristan* slept outside my door because he's trying to die."

Nate struggled to swallow his bite. "Sounds like you both need a time out. Or maybe a twenty-four hour chaperone."

"No. Tristan just needs to get over the fact that distance from him causes me pain," Scarlet snapped.

"Yeah. That's not going to happen." Tristan whistled as he flipped a few more pancakes.

Scarlet looked at Nate and sighed. "Would you talk some sense into him? Please?"

Nate stopped chewing and watched Tristan set a plate of chocolate chip pancakes in front of Scarlet with a fork.

"What are you doing?"

Tristan smiled at him. "Want some pancakes?"

"See?" Scarlet said to Nate, exasperated. "We have a serious situation at hand and Tristan's over here whipping up breakfast pastries like our friends' lives aren't at stake." She took a bite—um, delicious.

Tristan rolled his eyes. "Don't act like you're mad I'm feeding you."

Scarlet swallowed her bite and glared at him. "I'm totally mad."

Tristan grinned as he sat down beside her and started eating his own pancakes. "You're a terrible liar."

Nate looked at Tristan. "Are you—are you smiling?"

"Yes, he is," Scarlet said incredulously. "And he's sitting next to me—right next to me—like I'm not death with a fork." She lifted said fork and pointed at his pancakes. "Are those blueberry?"

"Never fails," Tristan muttered, sliding his plate toward her. "You always want blueberry."

"No, I don't." She shoved his plate back and took a purposeful bite of her chocolate chip pancakes.

"I'm so confused." Nate shook his head. "What's happening here?" He waved his spoon around at Tristan. "Why are you whistling and making breakfast? Why are you doing happy person things? This is very unsettling. "

Tristan shrugged.

Scarlet said, "He's happy because his touch no longer hurts me—even though *my* touch can now hurt *him*," she looked at Tristan before reaching over and taking a bite of his blueberry pancakes. "Could you try not to be so jolly that our roles are reversed?"

"Nope." Tristan smiled.

Nate kept blinking.

"So we'll leave for Laura's soon?" Scarlet took another blueberry bite from Tristan's plate. "Hopefully we'll find a clue as to where Raven would keep prisoners."

Tristan scooted his chair closer to Scarlet's and she glowered at him.

"Yes. Hopefully," Nate said slowly. He'd stopped eating his cereal and watched Tristan in bewilderment. "There were a few things I wanted to check online, but after that we'll leave."

Scarlet reached for another blueberry bite and Tristan wordlessly switched their plates so Scarlet had the blueberry pancakes in front of her.

"We should probably go back to the shack and grab a few more bloodstained weapons as well." Tristan took a bite of the chocolate chip pancakes that were now his property.

Nate shook his head. "Ah, yes. I almost forgot about Scarlet's creepy wall of bloody weapons." He glanced at Scarlet and took another bite. "Is there any explanation for that?"

"Yep." She finished the rest of the pancakes formally known as Tristan's and stood from her seat. "But we can talk about that later. Right now, I want to focus on Gabriel and Heather. So can you please hurry with your internet searches so we can get going?"

Nate shrugged. "Sure, let me just slip out of my *bathrobe*," he gave them a pointed look, "and we'll be on our way."

As Nate left the kitchen, stress seeped into Scarlet's limbs. She was worried about Heather and Gabriel and there was absolutely nothing she could do about it. Except wait.

She needed a distraction.

Looking around the cabin, Scarlet got an idea and headed out the backdoor.

Finding Tristan's array of bows set up against the side of the cabin, Scarlet chose one of the compound bows leaning in the shadows and grabbed a quiver of arrows from a hook a few feet above.

God love Tristan and his arrow organization.

Walking to the post she'd shot from before—back when she was Amnesia Scarlet and didn't think she knew what she was doing—she strapped the quiver to her back and took out a single arrow.

Pulling back on the powerful bow in her hands, she aimed and let loose, watching the arrow cut through the air and find a faraway bull's-eye.

She could already feel the stress leave her body.

She shot for a few more minutes in silence.

The back door opened and Tristan stood on the porch, watching her.

"Did you come to smile and be cheerful?" she asked him.

"Maybe." He took a seat on the porch steps and rested his forearms on his knees. "Or maybe I just like watching you shoot things."

She smirked at him and let another arrow fly.

He cleared his throat. "Are you going to be okay going back to Laura's house—your house—today?"

Scarlet paused for a moment, the bowstring pulled back against her taut muscles. *Would* she be okay?

She let the arrow fly. "I don't know. I haven't really had time to process the whole my-guardian-was-a-semi-bad-guy thing. I still don't know how I feel about her death. Laura took good care of me, but she was also working for Raven, so…I don't know what to think. Do I miss her? Do I hate her?"

Do I care either way?

Scarlet swallowed and pulled another arrow from the quiver. Tristan's eyes followed the arrow as she shot.

"It's okay to do both, you know," he said. "To miss Laura and hate her at the same time."

Scarlet looked at Tristan for a long time and every fiber of her being wanted to climb into his arms and cry and yell and mourn and cuss.

She was so not summertime Play-Doh.

"Hey guys?" Nate called from the back door, walking out onto the porch with a horrified-slash-perplexed expression. "You might want to come see this."

Putting the bow and arrows away, Scarlet followed Tristan inside the cabin as Nate led them to the front door.

There, on the front porch, stood an Ashman.

But instead of a Bluestone weapon in his hand, he held a piece of paper.

Uh...?

"He just rang the doorbell. Like a dead mailman," Nate said.

Tristan made a face. "And you answered it?"

"Well, yeah. How was I supposed to know it was an Ashman?"

"I don't know, the peephole maybe? What's on the paper?"

Nate chewed on his lip. "I'm half afraid he's going to start singing and do a jig if we take it from him. Like a really creepy singing telegram."

Tristan snatched the paper from the Ashman's rigid hands and looked it over. "It's a ransom note from Raven. Addressed to Scarlet." He handed the note to Scarlet and they all peered over her shoulder as she read.

The fountain for your friend. Meet me where you died in your last life. Sunset tonight.

Nate reread the note. "The fountain for your friend...does Raven mean Heather? What about Gabriel?"

Scarlet's palms started to sweat and her heart pounded. Gabriel. She had to save Gabriel.

Ohmygoodness, ohmygoodness.

"And how did you know Raven in your last life?"

"And why does she know where you died?" Tristan looked like he wanted to break something.

Scarlet bit her lip. She knew she couldn't avoid these questions forever. After all, if she wanted Tristan to live, she needed to find the fountain, so keeping the fountain's location a secret was no longer an option.

Taking a breath, Scarlet briefly recounted the details of her last life, leaving out the part about how someone has to die in order to gain access to the water. No one needed to know that but her. Because no one was going to die, but her.

"So let me get this straight," Nate held up a hand after she finished. "The Fountain of Youth is in an underground cave?"

"Yes." Scarlet nodded once.

"And to get to this cave, we have to go through a series of other caves that are basically kryptonite for immortals."

"Yes."

"And you didn't tell us about any of this in your last life because you were afraid we'd try to track down the Fountain of Youth with you and die in the process?"

"Yes."

Tristan slid his eyes to her.

Look convincing, Scarlet. Look awesome and believable.

His eyes stayed on her.

Nate said, "But Raven found out and came after the map and then you died?"

Scarlet nodded.

"That still doesn't explain why Raven would want to keep Gabriel," Tristan said.

"She's obsessed with him," Scarlet lied. She shrugged, just to add icing to the cake of deceit she was throwing together here. "I'm sure Raven's just screwing with him or whatever."

Nate ate the cake. "Sucks to be Gabriel."

Tristan did not. "Huh." His eyes bored into her like tiny, cake-destroying lasers.

Nate exhaled. "Okay. Well, now we know what we're up against. And we have," he looked at his watch, "five hours to get to—where is this place we're meeting Raven?"

"It's called the Avalon forest, but it's actually about a hundred miles outside of Avalon. Once we get there, we'll have to park and hike a mile or so in."

"Hiking. Oh goodie." Nate said. "Why does Raven want to meet in the middle of the forest?"

Scarlet took a deep breath. "Because from there, it's only a two day hike to the Fountain of Youth."

Nate grinned. "Then let's get packing."

"No, no." Scarlet sounded more panicked than she'd meant to. "Tristan and I will go. We'll send Heather and Gabriel back here and then go to the Fountain of Youth, grab some water, and come back."

"What?" Nate said. "That's a crazy plan."

"Is it? Why put yourself in danger? You don't need the fountain for any reason."

"But I *want* the fountain," he said. "I'm over being immortal. Sure, it was fun for a few centuries, but I'm ready for something else. So when we get there, I'm so drinking the fountain water so I can be mortal."

"Seriously?"

"Yep." He grinned.

Scarlet frowned. This was not part of her plan.

"Are you sure you don't want to stay here where it's nice and safe and guard the cabin?" She smiled.

Did her smile look forced? It felt forced.

Tristan shifted and his arm brushed against hers, and Scarlet stood frozen for a moment while the pleasure swirled around inside her.

"I'm sure. And besides," Nate lifted a brow, "do you *really* think you can survive a booby-trapped cave, a crazy-ass witch, and Tristan's freakishly happy mood without me?" He shook his head. "I don't think so. At the very least I need to be there so you guys don't accidentally get naked with one another."

Okay, wow. Super awkward.

"Really?" Tristan said.

"Yes," Nate said emphatically. "In fact," he shoved Tristan and Scarlet away from one another, disconnecting the stream of bliss Tristan's arms had been sending into her veins. "Is ten feet really so hard? It's like you're both trying to die. I'm so coming along."

"Fine. Come," Scarlet conceded, hating that this was turning into a group trip.

"Excellent!" Nate grinned. "I'll go get my Thor hammer."

36

Gabriel watched Heather's pink toes wiggle as they hung in silence.

She was obviously freaked out, and why wouldn't she be? Raven had drugged her and basically sentenced her to death.

He tried to cheer her up. "Don't worry. We'll get out of here and we'll find the fountain and everything will be fine."

"Except my brain since I'm going to go crazy. And then, you know, I might just die. So yeah. Everything's totally going to be fine."

Gabriel's lips twitched. At least Heather was approaching her imminent death with a sarcastic attitude. Sarcasm he could do. Tears, he could not.

From the warehouse hallway, he heard Raven's voice ring down the hall. "We're moving them in just a minute, but keep them bound during transport!"

Gabriel's spirits lifted.

"Hey," he whispered to Heather's downcast face. "We're being moved."

"Ooh, yippee. I can die while being transported."

"No," he lowered his voice even more, "we can escape."

Heather blinked and her eyes lit up. "Oh yes! Let's do that. Yes, yes, yes. How?"

"I don't know."

Her face fell. "Way to get my hopes up, Mr. Useless Immortal Guy."

"Wait. I might have a plan."

Gabriel explained his idea to Heather and, after arguing with him and throwing her two cents in about everything—she was so annoying—they finally agreed on an escape strategy.

So when the Ashmen entered to free them, Gabriel was feeling optimistic.

Two Ashman untied Heather first, as expected, and kept her hands bound in front of her as they stood her up and cut the ties around her ankles so she could walk.

The remaining three Ashmen did the same with Gabriel, keeping surprisingly tight grips on his arms as they pushed him toward the warehouse door.

Right before they reached the door, Heather started to cry.

She flopped to the floor and threw an all-out temper tantrum, kicking her legs and screaming bloody murder like an overgrown toddler.

Brilliant.

While the Ashmen were busy looking at Heather in confusion, Gabriel threw his elbow into the Ashman on his left, then the one on his right, before wrapping his bound wrists around the third Ashman's neck.

Using the Ashmen caught in his hands as a shield, Gabriel spun around and shoved into the two Ashmen he'd just elbowed, knocking them both to the floor.

Seeing their comrades under attack, Heather's guards came after Gabriel, leaving an incredibly loud Heather unguarded on the floor. As Gabriel struggled to avoid the Bluestone knives coming at his body and keep the struggling Ashman in his grip from slipping away, Heather rolled over and stuck her bare feet to the table.

Gabriel created more of a diversion by lifting the Ashman in his arms by the neck and tossing him into the two Ashmen to Gabriel's right. A sharp pain cut through Gabriel's forearm and he spun around just in time to block a second jab of Bluestone coming down at him from one of Heather's Ashmen.

Gabriel led the fighting away from the table as Heather used the scissors Raven had left to cut her ties off before grabbing one of the blood bags from the bin.

Heather cut open the bag and dipped the scissors into Gabriel's blood, coating them in the only substance they knew that could destroy an Ashman.

Gabriel was losing ground against his opponents and another sharp pain tore through his back as he spun around and tried to defend himself with his tied hands.

From the corner of his eye, Gabriel saw Heather charge at the Ashman nearest her and stab him in the back with the bloody scissors.

And holy hell, he couldn't help but think that was a little hot.

Yanking the scissors from the crumbling body of ash before her, Heather threw them to Gabriel and he snatched them out of the air. Holding them in his bound wrists, Gabriel swung through the remaining four Ashmen until all that was left were piles of Ash scattered about the warehouse floor.

Heather ran over to him as he was cutting off his ties and they quietly snuck from the warehouse room.

Gabriel led the way with his hand stretched out behind him as if to shield Heather from, well, he didn't know. But he just felt safer with his hand in front of her.

Outside the room was a long, narrow hallway leading to a single door.

Freedom.

Looking from side to side, Gabriel saw no other Ashmen.

He gestured to Heather and they soundlessly padded to the door. Gabriel stopped for a moment and braced himself, sure there would be a slew of Ashmen guards outside.

He slowly pushed the door open into the morning light.

He saw another warehouse. And then another.

But no Ashmen.

Looking to the left and right, he realized they were in the warehouse district of Avalon. The sun was rising in the sky and warming the ground beneath their feet as Gabriel grabbed Heather's hand behind him and pulled her out of the hostage warehouse and into the day.

Gabriel took a silent breath and tried to evaluate the best way out of there. Heather's hand was cold and small in his own as he gripped it tighter than necessary.

He crept along the side wall of the warehouse they're been trapped in until they stood in the shadows between warehouse and caught their breath. If he could just get them to the base of the nearby hill, he could hide Heather in the shadows of hill's trees and come up with an awesome and foolproof let's-get-the-hell-out-of-here plan.

But in order to do that, he'd need to turn the corner up ahead and cross the front of the warehouse. The odds of Raven having some of her foul helpers stationed out front were good and the only thing Gabriel had left for defense was the pair of scissors in his hand.

It would have to be enough.

Creeping to the edge of the corner, Gabriel glanced over his shoulder to check on Heather. She looked alert and ready and not at all like she was going to cry.

An odd sense of pride swelled in his chest as he turned and faced forward. She could do this.

"Okay," he whispered, "When we turn this corner, I want you to run for the hill and hide in the trees, got it? I'll take care of any Ashmen waiting out front and meet you at the top of the hill when it's safe. If I don't make it there, just run."

"What do you mean?" she whispered with big eyes. "I'm not leaving without you."

"That's sweet and everything, but if I bust my ass to get you to safety, you sure as hell better run for your life. Do you understand?"

She glared at him. "Yes."

He got the funny sensation that yes really meant no, but he didn't have time to argue with the tiny blond. "Ready?"

She nodded and he faced forward, still gripping her hand as he moved toward the front of the building. When he reached the corner, he took a deep breath.

It was now or never.

"Go." he whispered to Heather as he rushed around the corner to the front of the warehouse and thrust her hand in the direction of the trees.

There were only three Ashmen standing at the ready and Gabriel slashed through them easily.

Too easily.

He heard Heather squeal and turned around to see a caravan of black vans coming to a dusty stop at the base of the hill, Heather already caught in the arms of two Ashmen who'd jumped from the moving vehicles.

Raven exited the nearest black van with a tired expression on her face. "Seriously?"

She raised her arm and pointed a gun at Gabriel—was it a tranq gun? He couldn't tell—as another dozen Ashmen poured from the van behind her, armed with Bluestone weapons. "You think I'd let you escape that easily?"

The side door of another black van stood open and Gabriel's eyes darted around, trying to come up with a brilliant last-minute escape plan.

More Ashmen climbed from the vans and Gabriel realized Raven had an army of Ashmen loaded into her nondescript vehicles.

Well this sucked.

Raven sighed. "I really want to kill you right now, Gabriel. Mostly because you've just been so obnoxious for hundreds of years. But since killing you might mess up my plans..." She pointed the gun at Heather.

"No." Gabriel shouted before thinking.

Raven narrowed her eyes at him. "Protecting the damsel in distress, are we? Interesting." An evil smile spread across Raven's lips. "You know what? You're right. I shouldn't shoot Heather."

Raven walked up to Heather, who was caught in the stiff arms of two guards and punched her in the face, knocking Heather's head back. Blood immediately began to spurt from her nose.

"What the *hell,* Raven?" Blood rushed through Gabriel's ears, drowning out all other sounds as he tried to get control of his instant desire to kill something.

Raven spun to face Gabriel with angry eyes. "Try to escape again and I'll break her fingers."

****

On his way to the basement, Tristan walked past the den and stopped. Inside, Scarlet was lifting bows off his wall of weapons and testing them out, looking for one to pack.

He leaned against the doorframe. "Can I just say how hot it is to watch you riffle through my weapons?"

She smirked as she chose another bow from the wall. "Yes, well I feel like Goldie Locks over here. This one is too small, this one is too big." She frowned at the longbow in her hand before placing it back on the wall beside the others.

Tristan walked around Scarlet to the other end of the room and grabbed a smaller bow. "Try this one."

She took the bow in her hand and tested it out with a smile. "Just right."

He smiled back and for a moment the air was electric.

Dropping her eyes to the bow, Scarlet cleared her throat. "Is Nate back yet?"

Tristan shifted his weight and took a step back. Not because he wanted to, but because he knew he'd been pushing it with her all morning and he didn't want to set her off. As cute as she was when she was angry, he didn't like being the recipient of her temper. Not usually, anyway.

"No," he said. "He's still at the shack grabbing more bloodstained weapons."

Scarlet looked out the den window. "We need to hurry if we want to make it to the Avalon forest before sunset."

Tristan eyed her carefully, watching her shoulders tense as she turned from the window. "Why are you nervous?"

She narrowed her eyes at him. "I thought you couldn't feel my emotions anymore."

"I can't." He cocked his head to the side. "But I know you, Scar. And your nervousness is making me nervous. What's wrong?"

She ran a hand through her hair and let out a slow breath. "I just want to make sure we get Gabriel back."

"I won't let anything happen to Gabriel."

No question.

"I know," she said quickly. "I know. I just...we just need to make sure Raven doesn't take off with him and flee into the woods or anything. I don't want Gabriel to become an ingredient in one of her witch spells or anything."

Tristan looked her over. "Stop it."

"What?"

"Stop lying. Or pretending. Or whatever the hell it is you're doing right now. What's going on, Scar? What does Raven want with Gabriel?"

"Nothing."

"This is Gabriel we're talking about here. Stop lying to me."

She looked like she was ready to fight with him, but then her eyes went pained. "How do you do that? How do you love me so much even when you're upset with me?"

He blinked.

"Like right now, you're freaked out. You're all worried about me and scared. But I can feel that you still have so much..." she shook her head in disbelief, "*love* for me. How do you do that?"

"That's how love works, Scar. It's unconditional and constant. You were the same way. In your past lives. Even when you hated me—even when I broke your heart," his chest tightened for a moment, "I could still feel your love for me. Love is something that just...doesn't go away. It never dies."

She looked at him with pain and hurt and heartbreak in her eyes. "Promise?"

His heart cracked at the doubt in her voice . He gingerly touched her cheek.

"You could die—"

"I won't."

She let him run his fingers across her cheekbone and down to her lips. He cupped her face and looked into her eyes as his thumb ran along her lower lip. "I will love you forever," he said, desperate to chase the sadness from her eyes. "Don't ever question that."

She looked lost and scared as she stared up at him and he felt hollow inside. What wasn't she telling him?

"Touching again, I see." Nate entered the room with a large, overflowing duffle bag. "Clearly, life is not a priority for either one of you."

Tristan reluctantly pulled his hand away from Scarlet's soft lips and stepped back.. "Did you get what we needed?"

Nate set the duffle bag on a table on the center of the room and started unpacking a plethora of bloody weapons, several bags of blood—presumably from his medical stash upstairs—and the map to the Fountain of Youth.

"Yep. I made a copy of the map. You know, just in case we do decide to negotiate with the mad witch from hell."

"We're not negotiating," Scarlet snapped.

Nate raised his hands up defensively. "I know. I'm just being prepared. Like a boy scout. Or a coupon mom on Black Friday. So anyway, copy of the map? Check. I also grabbed the sturdiest weapons from the shack." He looked at Scarlet. "Real creepy, by the way, how you stole Tristan's blood in your last life and made yourself an arsenal in a haunted cellar."

"It's not haunted."

"I don't care. It's still creepy." Nate put the blood bags on the table. "Since you two are determined to use bows and arrows out there like Robin Hood's band of thieves—" he looked at Scarlet and smiled, "Thieves. How fitting—I'll let you guys start coating arrows in Tristan's blood," he pointed to the bags, "and I'll gather the rest of the camping equipment we'll need and the bear spray."

"Bear spray?"

"Yeah." Nate nodded. "To ward off any angry bears. It's a thing."

Scarlet's eyes grew huge. "Do you think there will be bears there?"

Nate shrugged. "I don't know. But I love how you're obviously more scared of bears than Ashmen and witches. It bodes well for you on this trip. Peace out, lovers. I'm off to find some long underwear. Try not to make any babies while I'm upstairs. You'd think I wouldn't even have to say that, but seeing as you two were halfway to Babytown when I walked in here—"

"Just shut up and go pack," Tristan said.

"Ooh, feisty." Nate shook his head at Scarlet. "Tristan doesn't like it when I talk about you guys having sex."

"Neither do I. Geez." Scarlet was blushing as she shooed Nate from the room.

Nate exited and Tristan and Scarlet spent the next half hour lacing arrows in blood and not making eye contact.

Nate had said "sex" and now the whole room felt like a sauna of forbidden tension. Just for that, Tristan was going to decapitate one of Nate's Star Wars figurines. It was happening.

Scarlet cleared her throat for the third time since they'd been alone.

"What's up?" Tristan dipped an arrowhead in the bowl of blood they had set up on the table between them.

She sighed "Can't you just think about sex like a normal guy?"

He blinked. "Excuse me?"

"How are you *not* thinking about sex right now?"

"You don't know what I'm thinking about."

"Yeah, but I know what you're feeling. And you're feeling…happy. Where's all the desire and want?"

He picked up another arrow. "Are you seriously mad at me right now because I'm not having lustful thoughts?"

"No. I'm just confused. I mean, *I'm* thinking about sex. But you're over there coating arrows in blood and thinking about God knows what—"

"Star Wars figurines."

"What?"

"That's what I was thinking about."

She blinked in confusion. "Star Wars figurines make you happy?"

He smiled and went back to the arrows on the table. "No. *You* make me happy. My happy feelings are because of you. My desire and want feelings—which I have plenty of—are also because of you, but I have those contained right now because I'm trying not to overwhelm you with emotions."

"Oh."

"Trust me," he grabbed another arrow. "You don't want me to think about sex when you can feel my emotions. It's very intense. I could barely handle it with you and I had five hundred years of practice."

She shot her eyes to him. "What are you trying to say? That I'm some kind of baby? I can handle it."

He shook his head and smiled. "You have no idea what you're talking about."

"Try me."

This was a dangerous game, but since only his life was at stake...

"Okay." He shrugged and started thinking about sex. With Scarlet.

He watched as she stood frozen and the color drained from her face as everything he felt rolled into her. Then bright red color returned to her face and she looked like she might catch fire. He kept his eyes on her as his feelings stayed in the hottest parts of his being.

She looked at him with hungry eyes and moved her mouth to speak but no sound came out. He watched her breathing grow heavier. She dropped the arrows she held and stared at him.

He changed his pattern of thought and tried to calm his emotions so she wouldn't do anything she regretted.

Once his thoughts were back on happy non-sexual things, he glanced at Scarlet, who was still frozen in place with red cheeks and parted lips.

"Scar?" He leaned to the side to look in her far away eyes. "You okay?"

She mouthed something and nodded, then tried again. "Yeah." Her voice cracked. She was staring at the wall with big eyes. "I'm, uh…I'm good. I'm great."

He went back to the arrows and smiled. "Told you."

Scarlet blinked a few times and looked at Tristan. "We definitely need a chaperone."

****

Heather frowned at her pink dress—now stained with blood from her busted nose—as she sat kitty-corner from Gabriel in the back of one of Raven's evil kidnapping vans.

Of course the witch had a sinister black van with taped off windows and no back seats.

Of course.

Heather didn't know where they were headed but the road they'd been traveling on for the past hour was super bumpy and whoever was driving the black van of doom—she couldn't tell since she and Gabriel were partitioned off from the front seat like this was some kind of creepy limo—wasn't making an effort to drive smoothly.

Gabriel was staring at her again.

He'd been glancing at her like a guilty puppy ever since Raven had clocked her in the face, and it was all Heather could do not to snap at him to quit looking at her like she was a broken doll.

Though that's how she felt. Broken. Dirty.

She was like the one-armed Barbie with nappy hair at the bottom of the toy box—the Barbie that always ended up in the trash by the banana peels and smelly diapers.

She looked around the van. Boxes filled with what looked like camping gear took up most of the van's back interior, leaving only a few feet of space for Heather and Gabriel to sit restrained.

Both their wrists and ankles were bound again. Raven had overseen the knot-tying herself this time, so the ninja knots were extra tight and impossible.

Gabriel leaned against the back door of the van. He was still shirtless and the Bluestone cut that marred his chest was just as split open as it had been yesterday, but no longer bleeding.

His giant body took up most of the space they shared and, even though he tried to keep himself contained against the wall, the nonstop bumps in the road kept shifting him closer to her, so every once in a while, their legs would knock into each other.

They hit another bump and she winced as her bruised face throbbed with the jolt.

Concerned eyebrows lowered over the brown eyes beside her. "Are you okay?"

"I'm fine," she snapped, not wanting his pity.

She closed her eyes as they rode along, thinking about her odds of survival. Would Raven hand Heather over to Scarlet? Or would Raven get the map and then kill Heather? Or would Raven kill Scarlet? And Gabriel? And anyone else who showed up?

The dire reality of her situation sank in and Heather felt her lip tremble. She had told her parents she was staying with Scarlet for the week, so no one would come looking for her. Her escape attempt with Gabriel had failed and now they were being hauled off into God-knows where with a posse of Ashmen who were probably going to slaughter them. And Heather would never see anyone she loved again.

A hot tear fell down her cheek as she thought of her family; her happy parents and her annoying brothers and her sweet little sister. She hadn't loved them enough. She hadn't appreciated them enough. She thought of all the things she'd never get to do; all the places she'd never get to see.

Another tear fell and Heather gave into the gloom she'd been fighting for the last twenty-four hours.

"Hey," Gabriel said softly. "Don't cry. We're going to be fine."

Hearing the plea in his voice just made her cry harder. "No, we're not."

"Yes, we are. Look at me."

She opened her eyes and stared at Gabriel's blurry face through her tears.

He smiled. "I'm Fierce Jaguar, remember? I'm not going to let anything happen to us."

She huffed out a sad laugh. "I thought you didn't have a code name."

"Well after our kickass escape attempt, I figured a code name was in order." He tilted his head, still smiling. "You were pretty amazing back there with your epic temper tantrum."

"Yes, well." She sniffed and the sharp smell of blood swirled inside her wrecked nose. "I have a little sister so I've seen my share of pouty throw downs." The thought of Emily's little face and blond curls brought tears back to Heather's eyes.

Gabriel looked panicked. "And what about your badass scissor skills? You took out that Ashman without batting an eye. You were like Lara Croft."

She sniffed again. "I would be a pretty awesome tomb raider."

"No doubt."

"But my boots would be pink."

"Of course." His crooked grin went sincere. "But seriously. You were pretty amazing today."

Heather didn't feel amazing at all. "Maybe next time we get kidnapped and try to escape, we should check for black vans first."

He nodded. "Good call."

Another bump in the road had her wincing again.

"Sorry I got you punched in the face," Gabriel said.

She shrugged. "It happens."

He was still all guilty-looking, so Heather tried to lighten the mood. "How do I look with my bloody nose and swollen lip?" She tilted her face to one side, then the other, mock posing for his appraisal. "Sexy? Drop dead gorgeous?"

"You look..." he tilted his head, "brave." He paused. "You are brave." His features hardened and Heather realized he wasn't joking.

Pride expanded in her chest.

She leaned against the van wall. "Well, hopefully my bravery can last through my new drug addiction and the consequential withdrawals I'm sure to be experiencing shortly."

He nodded. "You can handle it, Tomb Raider."

She shook her head. "You're ridiculous."

"I know."

The van went over another bump and made a sharp turn, throwing Heather into Gabriel and causing them both to topple over. Heather landed on top of his bare chest.

His hot skin burned against her tear-stained cheeks and she immediately tried to wiggle her way off of him. Her bound wrists and ankles made it difficult for her to wiggle effectively, though, and the back of the van was too cramped for either of them to rollover completely.

Just when she'd scooted down to his stomach where there was more room to move, the van turned again, shoving her right back up his chest. Gabriel had his bound arms raised above her, hanging out in the air like he didn't know where to put them.

"You've got to be kidding me," she muttered. With her hands pinned between them—and her arms accidentally brushing against several parts of his body—Heather started wiggling all over again.

"Heather?" Gabriel said, his arms still frozen in the air.

She wiggled down his chest until her face got to his stomach. Why were his abs so big? That couldn't be normal. Or healthy.

"Heather," he said again.

"What?" she started scooting again.

"Stop wiggling," he said. "Please."

She froze, tucking her lips in as she stared at the very large ab muscles right by her face.

"Okay," Gabriel said calmly. "I'm going to hold you against me and sit us both up. So try to keep your face away from my body so I don't hurt your nose, okay?"

Heather nodded at the ab muscle.

"And for the love of God," he added, "don't wiggle."

"No wiggling. Right. Got it."

Gabriel's arms came down around her, his elbows bending so he could press her against him and he pulled her back up his body so she was now staring at his oversized pec muscles. Did he moonlight as a bodybuilder?

She shifted her nose away as instructed, turning her chin up so she was now staring at his face. At close proximity.

Very close proximity.

The van went over a few more bumps and their tangled bodies knocked together. Gabriel gritted his teeth and Heather bit back a smile.

She shifted her face again and her nose brushed against his skin.

"You *smell* good?" she accused. "How is that fair? You've been beaten and stabbed and kidnapped. You should at the very least smell like misery and hopelessness. Not," she sniffed his chest again, "mountain rain or whatever the crap this is."

His arms loosened around her. "Are you seriously smelling me right now?"

"Well maybe if you didn't smell like a meadow—"

He sniffed her hair.

"Um, W-T-F, Gabriel?" She made a face at him.

"Why do you always smell like cupcakes? Hold still." He took a deep breath and Heather's body lifted as his chest filled with oxygen. She felt his body tense beneath her for a brief moment, and then he tucked her against him, twisted slightly to the side, and pulled them both up into a sitting position with his oversized abs of steel.

His arms were still around her body as they righted themselves and shifted into a haphazard sitting position. He slowly raised his arms back over her head, careful not to brush her nose as he did so until they were no longer tangled together.

Their eyes locked for a super awkward second and they both scooted in opposite directions, going back to their respective sides of the van. Not looking at each other.

Their bumpy trip continued, but the bumps were less awkward now that no body parts were rubbing together.

****

Scarlet growled when her seatbelt wouldn't come undone. "I hate your car, Tristan."

They had just arrived at the forest and Nate was already out of the car and digging through the trunk for his gear. Because *his* seatbelt wasn't the spawn of Satan.

"Here, let me do it." Tristan reached over and brushed her hand away from the demon clasp.

A zing of pleasure skittered up her arm at his touch and she really wanted him to touch her again.

No she didn't.

Yes she did.

He easily undid the belt buckle and freed her hips.

"Thanks," she said, giving the seatbelt one last dirty look before climbing out of the car.

She and Tristan went to the trunk and started pulling out their supplies as well.

Their trip to Avalon forest had gone by swiftly. After leaving the cabin, they'd stopped by Laura's house, which was technically still Scarlet's house, but it no longer felt like home to her.

She expected to be sad and emotional when she walked inside, but instead she felt…nothing. So she ran around and packed up clothes and shoes for herself and Heather and then she left Laura's house without looking back.

"Don't you guys just love road trips?" Nate smiled as he shrugged into his backpack.

"Meh," Scarlet said.

Tristan shrugged.

"Well, I love road trips. Molly and I used to go on road trips all the time. We would pack up the car and just drive—without a plan. We'd just go and go wherever the roads took us." Nate kept smiling. "It was awesome. Freeing, you know? And we'd listen to music and sing off key and talk until all hours of the night." He nodded. "I love road trips."

Scarlet smiled. She liked it when Nate talked about Molly. It made her feel hopeful. Like maybe Nate wasn't permanently broken. Maybe he would find love again. Did he *want* to find love again?

Scarlet secured her backpack to her shoulders and strapped a quiver to her back as Tristan armed himself with more weapons than she knew a person could carry at one time.

Grabbing her compound bow and throwing it over her shoulder, she then tucked two knives into her waistband.

Tristan was wearing jeans and a black T-shirt—which was like his uniform, apparently—as he threw his own backpack on and started clipping things into place.

Tristan shut the trunk and looked at Scarlet. "So what's the plan?"

"We'll hike about a mile in to the cluster of large boulders where Raven and I met in my last life. Hopefully, that's where Heather will be." *And Gabriel.*

Scarlet's palms started to sweat. "If we come up from behind the rocks, I think we'll have a better chance of viewing the meeting place without being seen. We can scope it out and see what our chances are of rescuing Heather without negotiating the map."

"Awesome." Nate grinned. "This is like epic camping. With bad guys."

"And potential death," Tristan added.

"I know." Nate nodded, still grinning. "Epic."

Scarlet took a deep breath and started for the trees. The last time she'd set foot in this forest, she hadn't come out alive.

Guilt pressed against her lungs as she glanced at Tristan.

History was about to repeat itself.

37

Gabriel and Heather were tethered to a handful of Ashman with leashes made of rope.

Like dogs.

The Ashmen led them through the forest with Raven as their leader.

Gabriel counted only twelve Ashmen in their immediate vicinity—all of whom had Bluestone weapons. Where were the rest of her minions?

Gabriel could probably take the nearest Ashmen out and attempt another escape, but he didn't want to invoke the wrath of Raven and risk hurting Heather again.

Raven's black hair swished across her back as she walked ahead of Gabriel and he noticed the Ashmen were loaded up with camping gear. Lots of camping gear.

How long did Raven plan on being out here?

Heather stumbled against her leash but quickly resumed her walking. He looked at her cut up bare feet and frowned.

"So Raven," Gabriel tried to sound casual and friendly. "Where are we going?"

"Why are you talking?" she snapped.

"Because you forgot to gag me." He stretched his neck.

"How much longer until we get to wherever we're headed?" Raven whipped around and marched up to Gabriel.

"Whoa..." he said, caught off-guard by her appearance.

Raven looked older. *Much* older than she had a few hours ago.

Her dark hair was graying at the roots, the skin around her eyes was crinkled and weathered, and her cheeks were a bit sunken.

She no longer looked thirty. She looked fifty.

"It's not pretty, is it?" Raven sneered. "I need that fountain *now*! And if you keep whining like a toddler I will break your neck over and over again until you beg to be mortal!" She screamed this at the top of her lungs, her voice echoing off the trees around them. "We will *get* there when we *get* there!"

Gabriel stared at the clearly-insane witch, speechless. Beside him, Heather looked terrified.

Raven started marching forward again, yelling at the Ashmen nearest her, "And why is everything on *fire*?! Put out the fires!"

Gabriel blinked. There were no fires anywhere.

Given that the witch was off her rocker and Heather was probably scared out of her mind, Gabriel decided not to talk anymore as they made their way deeper into the trees.

Heather winced as she stumbled over more sharp rocks. The Ashmen yanked on the ropes around her body, causing her to lose her balance and fall to the ground.

"What is the *problem*?!" Raven crazy-yelled, whipping around to glare at Heather. "Get up!"

With her wrists bound, it took Heather a moment to stand up and, when she did, she gingerly took a step forward on the rocks and looked like she was going to cry in pain.

Gabriel moved to help her but the leashes around his body tightened. "Faster!" Raven yelled.

"Here." Gabriel shifted to kick his shoes off. "Heather can wear my shoes."

Raven looked furious. "We do not have time for shoe switching!"

Good God. Could the woman yell any louder? And what was with her face? It was growing more wrinkled by the second.

"Heather can't walk fast with bloody feet, Raven."

She marched toward Heather with a knife in her hand. "Then I'll just have to motivate her!"

Oh hell no.

"I'll carry her!" Gabriel said, desperate. Again. He'd been desperate a lot lately. "I'll carry her the rest of the way. That way you won't have to injure your leverage and we'll get there faster."

Please dear God, let this work.

Raven huffed. "Fine." She pointed to an Ashman who picked up Heather and her bloody feet and brought her over to Gabriel.

Gabriel lifted his tied hands, making a hoop for the Ashman to move Heather's body through so she was draped over his shoulder, then lowered them back down over Heather's legs.

"Thanks," Heather whispered by his ear.

Her breath warmed his neck and a funny sensation skittered inside him.

The skirt of her poufy, pink dress rode up a little and Gabriel smoothed his bound wrists down the back of her body in an attempt to pull it back down.

No dice.

"Let's go!" Raven screamed, charging forward into the trees.

Gabriel maneuvered through the forest, feeling Heather's upper body dangle off his back with every step.

"So...this is weird," she muttered. "I bet you never thought you'd be carrying a girl over your shoulder through a forest filled with zombies."

He smiled. "Uh, no."

He looked down at her feet where blood still trickled from her many wounds and his smile faded.

She sighed. "I'm totally flashing everyone."

"I'm pretty sure the Ashmen don't give a damn."

She dangled in silence for a moment. "Raven looks crazy old, doesn't she? Like...scary old."

"Yeah," Gabriel said quietly. "The water is wearing off really fast."

He could hear Heather smile. "Hey, maybe she'll die of old age and we can get the heck out of this weird Ashman dog-walking situation we're in."

He smiled. "That would be ideal."

Raven led them down a steep hill and Gabriel shifted Heather's body so he could hold her more securely as they descended, moving his tied hands up her legs.

"Hey now. Don't try to cop a feel, Gabriel Michael."

"Cop a feel?"

"Yes, mister. Keep your hands to yourself."

He silently laughed. "I love how our lives are at risk and you're worried about me feeling you up. Like this is somehow sexy for me."

"What's not sexy about old witches and dead guys and bloody feet? You don't find this whole thing hot?"

"Not even a little," he smiled. "And my middle name isn't Michael."

"What is it then?"

"I don't have a middle name."

"Well, you do now. Michael."

He shook his head with a smile.

"Shut *up*!" Raven screamed.

They did.

Raven eventually led them to a valley of boulders and ordered the Ashmen to remove Heather from Gabriel's shoulder and tie the two of them up against a set of large rocks.

Not comfortable.

Gabriel looked at Heather. "How are you doing?"

She shook her head. "Not good. I don't feel right. I have a really bad headache and I keep seeing sparkles everywhere."

Gabriel looked around. No sparkles.

He nodded. "It's probably just the withdrawal setting in. I'm sure Tristan will get us out of here in no time. And then we'll get you to the fountain so you don't…see sparkles."

Or die.

A twinge of protectiveness and fear struck his chest and he marveled at the feeling. He'd never felt protective of anyone other than Tristan and Scarlet before—and even then, the protectiveness that shot through him when he looked at Heather was…different.

Raven appeared before them with her hair more gray than it had been twenty minutes ago. "Get the girl and bring her with us," she commanded a nearby Ashman.

Heather was quickly untied from the rock and shoved through the boulders on her bloody bare feet as Raven walked behind her. They disappeared around a large rock and the unfamiliar pang of protectiveness coursed through him again.

****

Just as the sun began to set, Scarlet led Tristan and Nate up a hill behind the group of boulders she'd once died beside. Morbid memory, but hey. This trip was all about death anyway.

At the top of the hill, Scarlet crouched down and squinted at the rocks below, searching for any sign of Heather or Gabriel.

Tristan came up beside her and did the same, his bicep brushing her arm as he did so, sending a swirl of pleasure through her. She closed her eyes for a moment, getting a grip on her body, then stared back down at the scene as Nate crouched on her other side.

Scarlet scanned the boulders until movement caught her eye. In a small clearing far below them, twelve Ashmen were circled around a tied up Heather and an impatient-looking Raven.

But no Gabriel.

Scarlet's stomach dropped.

Of course this was the first thing Tristan noticed. "Where the hell is Gabriel?"

Nate twitched his lips. "Maybe he had to pee?"

Scarlet let out a long breath as she tried to keep from shaking.

No. This couldn't happen. Gabriel would not die just so Raven could live forever. That would just be wrong on so many levels.

Tristan was tense beside her as he stood and paced the top of the hill, gazing down on the other side, his green eyes sharp and filled with determination.

"What are you looking for?" Nate said.

Tristan shoved his backpack off and rummaged through its contents until he came up with a pair of binoculars and searched the side of the hill again. "If Raven knows the fountain is nearby, she must have set up a camp in anticipation of gaining the map and going after the fountain."

Scarlet looked back at Heather. She was alive and breathing.

How was Scarlet going to get Heather away from Raven without sacrificing the map? Because there was no way in hell she was going to hand the map over to Raven and her greedy I-have-no-problem-sacrificing-any-heart hands.

Tristan cursed and Scarlet turned her attention back to his tense jaw. He was worried. Very worried. And scared.

Gabriel was everything to him. Scarlet couldn't imagine what Tristan would do if Raven had her way with Gabriel—

Nope. No more sacrificing thoughts.

"Nothing?" Nate asked tentatively.

Tristan shook his head.

"What's that?" Nate pointed to a ripple in the sky. Tristan jammed the binoculars back up to his eyes.

Scarlet squinted and realized the ripple was actually a stream of smoke rising into the air from the forest below.

Tristan's tensed shoulders relaxed. "Found her camp," he said. "And found Gabriel too. He's just on the other side of these rocks."

Scarlet let out a breath she didn't know she had been holding as Tristan moved away from the hillside and put the binoculars back in his bag.

"Okay." He stood up with a renewed look on his face. "Let's do this."

They talked through their plan to rescue Heather and Gabriel and headed down the hill where they parted ways. Sort of.

Since Scarlet was somewhat tethered to Tristan—and the selfless hottie refused to move outside the painless boundary their little curse provided for Scarlet—the two of them had to stay somewhat close to one another. But whatever.

Ten minutes later, Scarlet was perched in a tree and hidden by the shadows of the giant boulders that surrounded them. Tristan positioned himself several yards away in a second cluster of trees, close enough for Scarlet to maneuver without grimacing, but far enough away where she felt the uncomfortable tightness of his absence wrapping around her muscles.

But pain was nothing when compared to what was at stake: Her friends.

Scarlet scanned the small clearing where Raven stood with her hostage.

Heather's blond hair had lost its perky curl and hung around her dirty cheeks in deflated waves. Dried blood marked her nose and lip and the pink dress she wore was tattered and bloodstained. Her wrists were bound and her body was tied to several Ashmen at the waist. Her feet weren't tied together, but from the bright red marks circling her ankles it looked like they had been recently.

Scarlet swallowed back a lump in her throat. She couldn't remember ever having such affection and fierce love for a girlfriend before. In all her lives, no other girl had made Scarlet feel so real and normal and *happy*.

Heather was a truly bright thing in Scarlet's otherwise murky life. And there she was, terrified and bruised, at the mercy of this mess.

Scarlet shifted her attention somewhere else—anywhere else—to keep her thoughts from distracting her from the mission at hand.

Her eyes coasted to Raven and she noticed Raven's black hair was silver at the roots and her face was more shadowed and aged than it had been in the graveyard. Which meant Raven was out of fountain water.

Suddenly, Raven dropped to the ground and started digging up the earth at her feet. Like a savage animal, she clawed at the dark dirt until she had a hole dug. Then she scooped up a fistful of dirt and shoved it in her mouth.

What the...?

Raven chewed for a moment, then spit it out. "I need that fountain!" she screamed to nobody.

O-kay. Clearly, the withdrawals were kicking in. Their Raven takedown might be easier than Scarlet originally thought.

The twelve Ashmen guarding Heather and Raven would be no match for Scarlet and Tristan—especially not when they had the advantage of a surprise attack.

She glanced over to where Tristan was perched, his figure strong and poised to kill as he waited for Scarlet's signal.

And Nate...

Scarlet glanced to the bottom of the hill she had just descended and saw a Nate waiting behind a group of tall rocks.

God love Nate.

The man was a saint. Always leaving his comfort zone to help his friends. Always with a positive attitude. She watched him nervously rub his palms on his pants.

Scarlet was nervous too, but she was not fearful which perplexed her.

What made her brave?

She looked down at Heather and her trembling lip and red ankles. She looked at Tristan and his determined face and selfless eyes. And she knew.

Love.

Love made her brave.

It made her fearless to fight and determined to win, and hopefully, when this was over and she was laying her life down, it would leave her regretful of nothing.

She glanced at Tristan again and the lump returned to her throat.

Taking a deep breath, Scarlet caught Nate's attention and nodded in his direction. He nodded back and marched into the clearing. Timidly.

Please let this go according to plan.

When Nate came into view, Raven immediately started screaming, her face still covered in dirt from her mud snack.

"Why are *you* here? Where is Scarlet? I need the map!" Her silver eyes glinted in the dying sunlight.

"I have the map," Nate said. His voice cracked.

Scarlet pulled an arrow from her back and lined it against her bow. Slowly drawing it back, she took careful aim and waited.

If Nate could just lure Raven away from her circle of Ashmen, Scarlet could pierce her heart with an arrow and Tristan could take out the Ashmen guards while Nate rescued Heather.

Raven took a step forward, but not outside her circle of safety. "Let me see it."

"Untie Heather first, then I'll show you the map."

"No!" Raven flung her arms out. "Give me the map!"

Nate took a step backwards and Raven, in turn, stepped forward.

Good job, Nate. Just keep pulling her out.

He held up an aged piece of scrap paper that was most definitely not the map, but Raven was too far away to notice. The real map was tucked into Scarlet's front pocket.

They'd left all their backpacks and gear at the base of the hill, but didn't dare leave the map unguarded with their other items.

"Here you go." Nate waved the paper, and took another step back. "Now, let Heather go."

Raven stepped forward. "Hand it over."

One more step forward and Raven would be a clear shot for Scarlet.

Nate shook his head and stepped back. "First release Heather."

Raven stepped forward…

Scarlet let her arrow sail through the air, flying to the center of Raven's heart.

An Ashman lunged at Nate to grab the map and the creature's large body moved in front of Scarlet's arrow, effectively blocking the dart to Raven's chest.

The Ashman fell to the ground in death and Raven's eyes shot to the trees where Scarlet was hidden. The remaining Ashmen broke into two halves. One side rushing Nate, the other side charging into the trees by Scarlet.

So far, not according to plan.

Arrows started flying from Tristan's tree, sinking into the Ashmen bodies charging at Nate with deadly precision as Raven fled into the trees at the south end of the clearing.

Dammit. She was getting away.

Scarlet pulled arrow after arrow from her back and shot down the Ashmen headed her way as Nate moved through falling bodies of ash toward Heather. Using a knife from his pocket, he cut her ties, and they started running to the base of the hill.

Tristan shot down the last Ashman, jumped from his tree, and gave Scarlet a nod. She nodded back, silently telling him she had the situation under control so he could go rescue Gabriel.

He hesitated, probably worried his distance from her was going to be too painful, so Scarlet urgently waved him off until he finally conceded and disappeared behind the rocks.

The tightness intensified around her muscles and Scarlet climbed from tree to tree, keeping her body as close to Tristan's, with her bow still ready as she watched Nate and Heather exiting the clearing. They were almost to the hill when, from behind the great boulders to their right, came more Ashmen.

Lots more.

Scarlet immediately found a spot to crouch in the tree she was in and pulled another arrow from her back. With Tristan gone and Nate armed with only one knife, she was on her own.

The Ashmen charged at Nate and Heather as Scarlet deftly retrieved and shot arrow after arrow into their ashy chests, taking out the Ashmen closest to them as fast as possible.

A second army of Ashmen rose up from the opposite side of the clearing, effectively trapping Heather and Nate, and Scarlet's heart started to pound.

Heather's eyes were wide in fear and Nate's hand, though steadily holding his knife, shook ever so slightly as he and Heather braved the walls of Ashmen closing in on them.

Scarlet desperately drew arrow after arrow piercing her targets, but it wasn't enough. Everyone she had ever loved was in this God-forsaken forest on the verge of death and Scarlet was running out of ammunition.

No.

No one she loved was going to die.

Pulling the last arrow from her quiver, Scarlet aimed, shot, and jumped from the tree. Pulling out the two daggers she'd stashed in her belt, she armed both hands as she started running for her friends.

Her bodily pain intensified and she had to grit her teeth to make her legs carry her into the boulder-surrounded clearing. She was immediately attacked by Ashmen on all sides. The pain coursing through her body became like the sharp talons of a vicious bird, clawing through her insides, raking against her organs.

She fought against both pain and opponent, not sure how long her body could withstand both at the same time.

She slashed through the dusk, cutting into her opponents as rapidly as possible, trying to get to Heather. Trying to get to Nate. Trying to survive.

Nate held his own against the Ashmen bearing down on him and Heather, swinging his knife with an impressive force.

Scarlet cut her way through Ashman after Ashman until she finally reached Heather. Nate moved to the side, fighting back the Ashmen as Scarlet handed Heather one of her daggers before grabbing her friend's arm and yanking her toward the hill. If she could just get Heather to the trees or a boulder or someplace she could hide.

But they were surrounded and all thoughts of pain left Scarlet's mind.

Ashmen swarmed, encroaching on the small space she stood guarding her friend. Nate had been swallowed in the mass of Ashmen coming down at him, and all Scarlet could see of him were his thrashing limbs as he fought against his attackers. Two Ashmen lunged for Heather and Scarlet hacked through them both with one swing of her knife, but a third Ashman took Scarlet by surprise and knocked the dagger from her hand, leaving her unarmed.

A fourth Ashman threw Heather to the ground and stomped on her wrist until she lost her grip on the dagger she held, and he kicked it away.

Scarlet and Heather were both unarmed.

The fourth Ashman raised his Bluestone blade above Heather. Scarlet whipped around but she wasn't fast enough. The Bluestone knife thrust toward Heather's throat—

The Ashman fell dead.

Several yards behind the crumbling creature stood Gabriel with a bow and arrow. Without hesitating, Gabriel pulled another arrow and began shooting down other the Ashmen bearing down on Heather and Scarlet.

Yanking Heather to her side, Scarlet pulled her friend away from the dangerous cluster of Ashmen, no longer feeling the agonizing claws inside her skin.

From the corner of her eye, Scarlet saw Tristan at the top of a nearby boulder, shooting arrows at warp speed like Gabriel. Ashmen everywhere began to fall and soon the clearing became more ash than Ashmen.

When only a handful of Ashmen remained standing, Gabriel hurried over to Heather and Scarlet as Tristan continued shooting.

"Let's go!" Gabriel ordered.

Tristan jumped from the rock and started walking backwards toward the hill, loosing arrows as he went.

Scarlet started to run alongside Gabriel and Heather, but froze in her tracks when she caught sight of a dark-haired figure in the shadows holding a sharp blue weapon to a body on the ground.

Nate!

Scarlet rushed into the shadows, momentarily forgetting she was unarmed.

Raven held the tip of a Bluestone knife against Nate's heart, her silver eyes crazed as she waved a piece of paper in her other hand. "This is *not* the map!" Searching around, Scarlet spied a Bluestone axe beside a pile of ash and snatched it up. A twig snapped beneath her foot and Raven turned.

"You," she sneered, dirt still smeared around her mouth. "Give me the map, Scarlet, or I'll kill my cousin without blinking."

"I don't have the map." Scarlet took a careful step forward, lifting the axe.

"I *need* that ma—" Raven's eyes caught on Scarlet's pants and her lips curved into a wicked smile. "There it is."

Scarlet looked down.

Crap.

A corner of the map was sticking out of her pocket. Well wasn't that just perfect?

Scarlet slowed to a standstill, gripping the heavy weapon in her hands. "Let Nate go."

"Negotiation time is over. You blew your chance with my good graces when you ambushed my trade off. Now, give me the *map*!"

Scarlet took a step forward and Raven jabbed the point of the Bluestone blade into Nate's chest. He winced and blood started to seep through his shirt.

"What's it going to be, Scarlet?" Raven twisted the tip of the blade and Nate's face contorted. "The map? Or your precious little friend over here?"

"You don't want to kill Nate," Scarlet said. "You might *need* him. Remember?"

Raven squared her jaw. "A heart to sacrifice is pointless without the map." She twisted the blade again and Nate groaned in agony.

Scarlet charged Raven and swung the axe at the aging witch's head. Raven blocked the blow with her knife and Scarlet used the opportunity to kick in Raven's stomach. She stumbled backward as Nate pulled himself up and moved away from the now swinging Bluestone weapons Raven and Scarlet held.

The axe was heavy and difficult to control, but its blow was powerful as Scarlet raised it above her head and brought it down on Raven. The axe sliced through Raven's chest, red blood spurting from the wound and, for a second, Scarlet felt both triumphant and guilty.

But then Raven laughed—a wicked sound against the blood escaping her large wound—and Scarlet watched in disbelief as Raven's aging body began to heal.

The fountain water was still in her system.

Scarlet was stunned for only a moment, but it was long enough for Raven to retaliate with her magic of choice: Fire.

A blast of heat went up around Scarlet, encircling her in fire as Scarlet lunged to escape the walls of flames, but a sharp pain in her arm caused her to stumble and Raven's hand was suddenly gripping Scarlet's throat through the fire, squeezing until Scarlet saw nothing but black splotches.

Her hips were shuffled from side to side, then she was released. The fire walls instantly disappeared and Scarlet saw Nate—the wound in his chest still leaking red—battling against Raven.

Scarlet joined in, swinging the axe once again at Raven's neck, but the witch disappeared behind another wall of fire. The fire disappeared almost as quickly as it had come, but Raven was nowhere in sight.

Out of breath, Scarlet turned to Nate. "We need to get you stitched up."

He shook his head. "It's shallow. You might need some stitches, though."

Scarlet looked down and frowned at the cut across the top of her left arm. She looked down further and her frown grew darker.

Raven had stolen the map.

Nate took a step forward and grimaced. "What did Raven mean about a heart to sacrifice?"

Scarlet looked up. "Nothing. Let's go."

Nate didn't move. "What sacrifice?"

Scarlet didn't have a lie ready, so instead she said nothing.

He nodded slowly. "The fountain requires a death, doesn't it? I should have known." He exhaled. "Well, you could have told us sooner. Now what are we going to do? There's no point in hiking to the fountain if we can't even access the water. It's not like we have an extra heart lying around."

Scarlet looked to the side.

Nate inhaled sharply. "Wha—Scarlet, *no*. No. Are you kidding me? Is that what you were trying to do in your last life? Sacrifice yourself?"

"No." She looked at him. "But it's sure as hell what I'm going to do in this one."

"Are you insane?"

"Yes, Nate! I'm insane and I'm in love and Tristan is dying! How else can I save him?"

He shoved his hands in his hair and stared at her with a slack jaw. "Are you hearing yourself? You sound like a crazy person."

"Scarlet!" Heather's voice called into the trees.

"Nate!" Gabriel called.

Scarlet shook her head. "Believe me, Nate. If there was any other way—"

"There must be another way." He nodded. "I will *find* another way."

The determination in his voice was both moving and tragic because Scarlet wanted to believe there was a way out, but she knew better.

****

Tristan watched the ten or so remaining Ashmen flee into the trees and cursed under his breath. Where the hell did Raven get so many dead people? It was like the zombie apocalypse out here.

He put his bow away and jogged up to where Gabriel was taking off his shoes and giving them to a very dirty, pink Heather.

"Where are Scarlet and Nate?" Tristan looked around, a sliver of panic skating up his spine. Scarlet could handle herself, he knew that. But he couldn't keep from worrying—

"Holy mackerel, did you guys see Raven? She looks *old*!" Nate said, out of breath as he ran up to them.

Scarlet was right behind him.

Not out of breath.

"Yeah," Gabriel said, steadying Heather's elbow as she slipped her feet into his shoes. "She's addicted to fountain water and her withdrawals are making her age. And go crazy."

"Drugs are bad, people." Nate shook his head. "Drugs are bad."

Gabriel and Heather exchanged an uncomfortable look.

"What?" Scarlet said.

Tristan noticed her arm was bleeding and hoped it wasn't as bad as it looked.

Gabriel hesitated. "Raven's been poisoning Heather with fountain water."

Scarlet sucked in a breath. "No."

Heather nodded. "She wanted insurance just in case you didn't come through with the map."

"Well that sucks," Nate said.

"How much time do we have?" Scarlet turned to Nate. "Before Heather gets…sick?"

Nate twitched his lips and looked at Heather. "How long have you been without fountain water?"

"A few days. Maybe longer."

He nodded. "Then you probably have a few more days."

Scarlet's mouth fell open. "*Days?*"

"Maybe a week," Nate added hurriedly. "Maybe longer. It depends on how long Raven's been poisoning Heather. The longer the water was in her body, the faster the she'll get sick."

Heather looked like she was going to cry and Gabriel shifted his weight so he was standing a bit closer to her.

Interesting.

"Raven mentioned something about the fountain having a cure," Gabriel said.

"Oh, yeah!" Scarlet said. "There *is* a cure. The Avalon fruit grows at the fountain and it's an antidote to the water. If we can reach the Avalon tree, Heather can eat the fruit and be cured.

"Seriously?" Heather's face brightened. "Seriously?"

Scarlet nodded. "But there's only one fruit, which wouldn't be so bad, except Raven just stole the map. And if she's after the Avalon fruit…well, we just need to get to the fountain before she does."

"Then let's get going," Gabriel said, straightening his shoulders.

Nate pointed a finger in the air. "Um, I'm sorry. We're just going to hike, in the dark, to a bunch of deadly caves, when there are Ashmen all over the place?" He shook his head. "No. We need to regroup and eat and rest and maybe find a pair of shoes for Gabriel." He gestured to Gabriel's feet, then to Heather's. "What's happening here?"

"We don't have time to regroup and eat and drink and be merry, Nate," Gabriel said impatiently. "We can't let Raven get that cure before Heather."

Huh. Tristan had never seen Gabriel worry about any girl other than Scarlet before. It was…odd.

"I think Nate might be right," Scarlet said, "Finding the cave entrance in the dark would be difficult and we could end up wasting time and energy searching for it. And," Scarlet and Nate glanced at one another, "Raven won't be able to get what she wants tonight, anyway. So let's find a safe place to camp for the night and start out at the first light of day."

38

Everyone sat around the campfire in silence, eating the cold sandwiches Nate had thought to pack everyone for dinner.

They'd found a hidden clearing in the center of several boulders. Raven might have the map to the fountain, but Scarlet had no doubt the witch would take any opportunity to capture one of them to use for the sacrifice. So hiding was key.

Scarlet looked at the stitches in her left arm, expertly sewn by Nate, and examined her wound. It ached a bit, but it would heal quickly.

Across the fire, Heather grasped at invisible things in the air.

Gabriel reached for her wrists and gently lowered them. "There are no sparkles."

"Oh no, was I doing it again?" Heather said. "Was I grabbing for nothing like a psycho?"

Scarlet's heart twisted.

Tristan's shoulder brushed against Scarlet and sent warm pleasure into her body.

She eyed him sideways. He was so doing it on purpose.

He gave her a devilish smile and the twist in her heart grew tighter.

Tomorrow, if things went well, Scarlet would be dead. She was not afraid of death and she would not hesitate when the moment came, but she knew it would break his heart.

He had lived so long for her and she was going to strip that away from him. She was going to do the very thing he'd been trying to do for years; end her life so he might live. But the alternative was worse. If she didn't die, they would have no access to the fountain.

Tristan would die.

Heather would die.

And if she announced her plan—which she certainly would not—someone else might try to die in her place, and Scarlet would never allow that.

She took a bite of her sandwich and tried to think on the happy things the fountain would bring everyone else. Tristan would never be in pain again and he would live a healthy life. Gabriel could fall in love with someone in a real way—God knew he deserved to. Nate could truly live, without constantly being dragged into all their cursed mess. And Heather would be cured.

Scarlet looked at her best friend. Of them all, Heather deserved life the most. She had been nothing but positive and filled with hope in all this. The curse had not tainted her, had not made her a tortured soul like Tristan, or a hopeless romantic like Gabriel, or a lonely heart like Nate. Heather still had a chance at being bright.

If for nothing else, Scarlet would absolutely die for that.

Nate put the map copy away and grinned at everyone. "Whatdaya say we go around the fire and talk about how great it's going to be to find the fountain and undo the curse and cure Heather? Gabriel, you go first."

"Why do I have to go first?"

"Because I'm team captain and I say so."

Heather rolled her eyes. "Two members of Team Awesome almost died today. I say we nominate a new team captain."

"Hey," Nate said, offended. "The captain's job is to be a leader. Not a babysitter. Okay, Gabriel. What will you do with your curse-free life?"

Gabriel fiddled with a stick. "I would move back to my apartment in New York. Maybe I'd get a pet. Maybe fall in love. Maybe not. Either way, I'm staying away from witches. Permanently."

"If only you'd had that philosophy five hundred years ago." Nate grinned at him before looking at Heather. "What about you? What will do you with the rest of your life?"

Heather thought for a moment. "Try to get into a good college so I can study fashion. Ooh, and travel the world. And try new foods. And get married and have kids and become one of those fun grandma's that always over-decorates for Christmas and constantly smells like cookies."

"Wow. That's…specific," Nate said.

"I also want to eat grass and ride a bear," Heather added with a frown. "But that could be the drugs talking."

"Right." Nate looked at Scarlet. "What about you? What will you do once the fountain makes you mortal and you only have one life left to live?"

Scarlet took a moment to control the ache in her chest at his question. "If I had only one life to live…" She shook her head. "I already had my one life to live in the 1500s when I was mortal and poor and surrounded by love. That was my life and it was beautiful."

Nate exhaled loudly. "Way to raise the bar on the friendly fireside question, Scarlet. How is anyone supposed to follow that?"

"I'm just being honest.," she said. "What about you Nate? What would you do if you only had one life left to live?"

He smiled. "I would find a time machine and go back to when I first met Molly so I could live my life with her all over again. She was the happiest I've ever been. Life after her is just…" he shrugged, "time. What about you, Tristan?" He turned to the very silent Archer beside Scarlet. "What would you do with one mortal life to live?"

"Marry Scarlet."

Everyone stared at him. Including Scarlet.

How could he say that? How could Tristan so openly admit that without hesitating?

Scarlet's heart tore down the middle leaving jagged pieces in its wake. The green-eyed boy beside her wanted to marry her and she was on a suicide mission to save his life.

Nate rolled his eyes. "I'm never playing this game with you or Scarlet again. You're both way too dramatic. Can we go back to the grandma that smells like cookies?" He looked at Heather. "What else will you do with your life?"

Heather smiled dreamily at the ground and traced a finger through the mud. "Dirt is pretty."

Gabriel leaned over and quietly said, "Heather—"

"What?" she snapped her head up and looked around the fire. "What? Was I doing it *again*? Acting crazy?"

No one said anything.

"O-M-G." She groaned. "I'm an addict. I'm losing my mind because I'm a druggie."

"You're not a druggie," Scarlet said. "You were poisoned. There's a difference."

Heather's eyes widened. "But I feel crazy inside. Like I want to scream and laugh and swim in a big pool of chocolate pudding."

"That does sound crazy," Nate said. "And sort of delicious."

"Shut up!" Heather yelled, then gasped in apology. "I'm so sorry, Nate! I don't know why I yelled at you. I don't want to be crazy. This isn't fair. I don't want to die —" Her voice cracked as she covered her face with her hands.

Scarlet scooted off her seat by the fire and walked over to Heather. "Hey…it's okay," she said, rubbing Heather's back. "We're going to cure you and then all of this will go away."

"I'm not crazy." Heather's muffled voice said from her hands. She looked up. "But I might be crazy."

Scarlet nodded sympathetically. "Drugs have that effect on people. But you'll be fine. I promise."

Heather rolled skeptical eyes away from Scarlet.

Scarlet squeezed Heather's hand. "I *promise*."

They sat in relative silence for the next few minutes, everyone shifting uncomfortably and not making eye contact. Nate spoke a few times about the logistics of the next day, but other than that the conversation was stale.

When the fire dwindled, everyone headed off to sleep. Scarlet and Heather shared a tent while Nate, Gabriel, and Tristan slept by the fire, taking turns keeping watch for Raven and her Ashmen.

Scarlet stared at the red vinyl roof of the tent above her, thinking about her many lives and journeys to get to this very place. Funny how she always thought that if she found the fountain, life would be better.

"Scarlet," Heather said. "Are you still awake?"

"Yeah."

Heather's voice had a smile in it. "Remember that time when your ex-boyfriend's crazy ex-girlfriend drugged me with a syringe from her boob purse and then we had to go on a hike to find a magical fountain while being chased by zombies?"

Scarlet smiled, grateful Heather was normal for the moment. "I think so."

"That was good times."

"The best," Scarlet said. "We should totally do it again sometime."

"Totally." Heather shifted. "And remember last year when I swore I would never go camping because it was dirty and uncomfortable and the worst way to have a sleepover. Like ever?"

Scarlet smiled at the roof. "Yeah."

"I was totally right. Camping sucks." She kicked at her sleeping bag. "There's dirt under my fingernails, my feet hurt ,and earlier today something sticky got on my arm and I can't get it off. When we get back home—after I take five showers, of course—we're totally going camping my way. With soft pajamas and ice cream and indoor plumbing."

When we get back home.

Tears rushed up her throat and Scarlet quickly pushed them back. "Indoor plumbing is a nice perk." She smiled. "Do you remember the first night Laura was out of town and I told you I would be fine sleeping in my house alone, but you showed up on my doorstep with ice cream and a butcher knife?"

"Uh, *yeah*." Heather said. "It's in the Survival Handbook for Blondes. Always sleep with a butcher knife under your pillow. Right next to Always Wear Flats When Walking Down Dark Alleys."

"This handbook sounds awesome."

"Oh, it is. I'll bring it to our sleepover next week."

Next week.

Scarlet swallowed. "Remember my first day of school in Avalon, how I was all nervous and freaked out? But then I got to school and you'd taped a bunch of pictures of us inside my locker with cheesy inspirational one-liners on them?"

"Yeah. I think my favorite was *You Are The Po*wer."

"I *am* the power."

"You *are*."

Scarlet laughed. "I couldn't have done school without you. I couldn't have done...anything without you." She turned her head to look at Heather. "You're a really great friend."

Heather rolled her eyes. "That's what I keep telling you. But you still insist on going braless when wearing tank tops, even when I advise you strongly against it." She shook her head disapprovingly. "Friends don't let friends jiggle, Scarlet."

She scoffed. "I hate bras. They're like corsets for boobs."

"Boob corset. I'm going to patent that."

Scarlet shook her head. "I love you."

Heather yawned and her eyelids fell shut. "I love you too."

Scarlet's heart started twisting again and her throat tightened. She whispered again, "I love you."

****

It was Tristan's turn to keep watch but Nate was standing right beside him.

"What's up?" Tristan glanced at him.

Nate shrugged. "Nothing. Just, you know, taking in the beautiful night sky and the cool breeze."

Tristan nodded. "You heard a wolf howl?"

"Yes! Did you hear it too?"

"No." Tristan smiled. "Dude, we've talked about this. There are no wolves in Georgia."

"There might not be any *common* wolves—"

"There are no werewolves either." Tristan shoved his hands in his pockets. "If you'd like to be afraid of something, try armies of Ashmen or evil cousins who have hooked up with Gabriel."

"Okay, ew."

Tristan waited a beat. "So why are you really awake?"

He took a deep breath. "I've just been thinking about stuff. The map, the journals, the magic." He shuffled his feet. "We've been searching for this fountain for five hundred years and it's been this elusive adventure, you know? It's just weird that we're so close to the end." He looked at Tristan. "I'm sure you're happy."

Tristan thought for a moment. "It doesn't feel real yet. I'll be happy when Scarlet is cured and I never have to watch her suffer again." The dark trees swayed with a gust of wind. "She's up to something."

Nate shrugged. "It's probably just nerves. We've got monsters and caves and witches to battle. It's like we're in a real life video game."

Tristan nodded. "And you're the slayer."

"That I am." Another gust of wind came and Nate shivered. "Don't worry about Scarlet. Sometimes people keep secrets to protect the ones they love. You just have to trust her."

Tristan nodded. Right.

His chest started to hurt.

39

The next morning, Gabriel stared at Nate. "What are you wearing?"

Everyone rushed around the campsite, packing up and getting ready for their hike to the Bluestone caves.

Nate looked down at his outfit. "Adventure attire."

"You look like Indiana Jones."

"Exactly—ooh! I need my whip." Nate rushed over to his backpack just as Heather exited the tent.

She looked at Gabriel and turned around in a circle. "How do I look?"

She was wearing a pair of tiny jean shorts and a bright pink T-shirt. Her blond hair was matted on one side and there were dirt smudges all over her arms, legs, and face.

Gabriel hesitated. "Like a Barbie doll that got run over by a garbage truck."

"*Wow*. Really, Gabriel?"

He shrugged. "What do you want me to say?"

"Say something encouraging," she snapped. "Something like *you look like G.I. Jane.*"

"But you don't look like G.I. Jane. And why are you wearing pink?"

She looked down at her shirt. "What color should I wear?"

"I don't know. Maybe a color that doesn't scream *helpless girl in the forest*?"

She narrowed her eyes at him.

"Found it!" Nate stepped away from his backpack with a whip in his hand—an actual whip.

"Why on *earth* do you own a whip?"

"Why don't you?"

Oh dear God.

Flicking his wrist, Nate let the whip sail. It lashed out and made a snapping noise before slapping against his wrist and drawing blood.

Nate dropped the whip and clutched his hand. "I'm a little out of practice."

"With whip usage? I should hope so." Heather crossed her dirty arms over her pink shirt.

Gabriel shook his head. "Why did you even bring a whip?"

"Because Tristan wouldn't let me bring the Thor hammer. Besides, you never know when you'll need a whip. What if we need to climb something really tall or swing across a deep chasm?"

"I seriously doubt we'll be swinging across any chasms."

"Doesn't matter." Nate straightened his shoulders. "I'm still bringing the whip. And you know what else I'm bringing?" He grabbed something from behind his backpack. "This."

He placed an Indiana Jones style hat on his head. Retrieving his whip from the ground, he stood beside

Heather with his hands on his hips and grinned at Gabriel. "Now how do I look?"

Gabriel stared at Indiana Jones and Garbage Truck Barbie.

Heaven help us all.

Scarlet exited the tent dressed in cargo pants and a black tank top with her hair pulled back and a knife in her hand.

"Now, *that* is how you dress for a hike to a deadly fountain." Gabriel gestured to Scarlet.

"A tank top, Scarlet?" Heather looked at her chest. "Seriously?"

"It's comfortable."

"What's the deal over here?" Tristan stopped rolling up sleeping bags. "Why is everyone standing around chatting and wasting time? And why is Heather wearing pink? Come on, people."

Heather rolled her eyes and disappeared back inside the tent, reappearing a minute later with a dark gray T-shirt on.

"Better?" She cocked her head at Tristan.

"Yes. You've just extended your life by at least an hour."

****

The morning sun warmed Scarlet's face as she looked up at the happy sky. Warmth was nice, she decided. The sun, in general, was a happy constant, rising each morning and bringing newness with it. Why had she never seen the sun as such a beam of hope before?

She stretched her hands out and absently let the leaves of nearby trees brush against her fingers, green and soft, cool from the earlier dew, still living while attached to the great tree that brought them life day after day. Another leaf brushed her palm and she squeezed it briefly, releasing it before it was pulled from its life source by her greedy palm.

To her left, Tristan's face was staring ahead, alert and beautiful in the daylight. Next to him, Nate adjusted his backpack as he weaved through trees. To her left, Gabriel walked along quietly, looking every few minutes at Heather by his side.

Heather scratched at her neck and twitched, then looked at Gabriel. "Am I acting crazy?"

Gabriel smiled. "Nah."

It was a lie, but it was a beautiful lie.

Scarlet was grateful for beautiful lies.

Heather would be cured.

Gabriel would fall in love someday.

Tristan would understand Scarlet's sacrifice.

Nate's heart would heal from Molly's death.

Beautiful lies, all of them.

They walked until the sun began to set and, finally, they found the Bluestone caves.

The mouth of the caves looked just like a cluster of boulders, but with bright green vines wrapped around them. The only thing that gave away the caves themselves were the glinting blue stones that jutted out from between the thick vines every few feet.

"This is it," Scarlet said, bringing everyone to a stop.

Gabriel eyed the thorny tendrils that blocked the cave entrance like a giant green gate. "And these are the magic vines?"

The vines were as thick as Scarlet's forearms, covered in thorns, and too overgrown and tangled to see through.

"Yep," said Scarlet. "And they're supposed to be deadly, too."

"They don't look very magical," Nate said. "Or deadly."

"The journal said the vines can only be cut with immortal blood, so," Scarlet took a blood-coated knife from her belt, "let's see if this works." Raising her knife, she swung the blade down on the nearest vine and watched as it easily sliced in half.

Huh.

Heather made a face. "Well, that was anticlimactic."

Scarlet frowned and was just about to shrug off the whole magical/deadly plant thing when the severed vine began to move. It grew new tendrils and pulled itself back together, mending the green gate until there was no longer a gap.

"Now *that* looks magical," Nate said.

Scarlet took a deep breath. "All we have to do is cut through these vines as quickly as possible and enter the caves before they close back up."

"And trap us inside," Heather added with a shrug. "That's not terrifying."

Tristan was already handing out bloodstained weapons to everyone. "If we all swing at the same time, we should be able to make a wide enough hole for all of us to squeeze through before the vines grow back." He gave a pointed look at Gabriel then nodded to Heather.

"Wha—what was that?" Heather lifted a brow. "What was that *hey bro, make sure the blond chick doesn't cut any body parts off* look? Because I'll have you know, I'm an expert with butcher knives."

Tristan pointed at the weapon in Heather's hand. "That's a machete."

Puckering her lips, Heather looked at the blade. "Aren't they the same thing?"

"I'm going to pretend like you didn't just say that. Everybody ready?" Tristan looked around to make sure everyone had their weapons raised. One…Two…*Three*."

Everyone swung and pieces of the vine fell to the side as Team Awesome hurried through the vines and into the blackness beyond.

"Ow." Nate sucked air through his teeth just as the vines started to move back together. He lifted his torn sleeve to show a bloody scratch on his shoulder.

"Watch out for the thorns." He wiped the blood away. New blood bubbled from the wound. He wiped again. Still bleeding.

"Why aren't you healing?" Gabriel asked.

Scarlet examined the thorns. "The thorns have blue tips. Maybe they work like Bluestone."

"Perfect," Gabriel said. "Killer plants."

The vines continued slithering until the vine wall was completely reconstructed and had shut them inside the caves which, Scarlet now realized, were not completely dark.

A soft, blue glow illuminated the cave walls and softly pulsed, as if the caves were alive and breathing. The pulsing blue shimmered with each breath like glowing stardust and it was almost beautiful.

"Oh no. I'm seeing them again." Heather sounded panicked. "I see more sparkles. Like everywhere, you guys. O-M-G, O-M-G—"

"No, no. It's okay, Heather," Scarlet said. "That's just the caves. The walls are actually sparkling."

"Oh." Heather calmed down a bit.

"When you said 'caves'," Nate said to Scarlet. "I had something less sparkly and more bat-infested in mind."

Scarlet stepped forward. "So did I."

Nate said, "Well this is awesome. The glowing walls will make navigating the caves much easier."

Though it was still rather dark, the blue walls gave off enough light for them to find their way through the tunnels without flashlights.

Tristan shifted. "And these caves are supposed to weaken immortals?"

"Yeah. If the deadly plants don't kill you first." Gabriel touched a hand to the cave wall and waited. "I don't feel any different."

"Me neither." Nate scratched his head.

"I actually feel...stronger," Tristan said.

Scarlet felt for him, but nothing echoed inside her soul.

"Maybe the caves aren't as debilitating as we thought," Nate said.

She looked at Tristan and tried again, but still nothing.

He caught her eyes. "What's up?"

"Uh..." Scarlet felt around inside herself. "I can't feel you anymore. Like at all."

Tristan frowned. "Are you sure?"

She nodded. "Can you feel me?"

He shook his head.

"That's weird." Scarlet looked at Nate. "Do you know why—"

Tristan wrapped a warm hand around her wrist, gently encircling it in his fingers and Scarlet turned her eyes to where they were touching.

"Do you feel anything?" he asked.

She felt no supernatural pleasure at his touch. She just felt...normal. Wonderful.

"Oh," Nate said in realization. "That's what the journal meant by deadly to immortals. The caves must cancel out our immortality."

She walked her eyes up to Tristan's. For the first time in five hundred years they were touching without one of them being in danger.

From the look in his eyes, he'd realized the same thing.

And now the hand around her wrist felt incredibly intimate. Warm and safe and *intimate*.

Nate nodded. "It would also explain why you guys can't feel each other in here and why Tristan feels stronger. You're not sharing a life-force right now."

Imagine that.

Tristan hadn't released her wrist yet and Scarlet was absolutely okay with that. For like ever.

"Everyone's mortal. Yay. Now can we get moving?" Heather said.

Tristan ran his thumb over Scarlet's wrist and something about it made her heart leap. It was a simple touch, but it was carefree and unafraid. Tristan hadn't touched her in such a weightless way in hundreds of years and she didn't want him to let go.

But he did. He slowly released her wrist, his fingers brushing the length of her hand as he pulled away and it took Scarlet a moment to get the butterflies in her stomach to behave.

Everyone was staring at them.

"O-kay." Nate clasped his hands. "Who wants to walk through the uncomfortable sexual tension first? Gabriel? Heather?"

"Ugh. Gag me," Heather said. "Wait no. No one gag me."

Gabriel rolled his eyes and walked deeper into the cave, Heather and Nate moving behind him.

Scarlet followed her friends through the glowing caves, staying by Tristan's side as they walked along. His shoulder brushed against hers and the electricity that ran through her body had nothing to do with immortal blood or magic. It was just…real.

She glanced at him, looking at his shadowed profile in the blue glow around them. It had been so long since anything between them had been real. Or allowed. Or safe.

His eyes met hers and held them for a beat before Scarlet faced forward and swallowed. Her throat was dry. Her heart was dry. She missed him. He was walking right next to her and still she missed him. She'd been missing him for centuries.

As if he could still read her emotions, Tristan's fingers brushed the back of her arm and slowly slid to her wrist before slipping into her hand. He wrapped her hand in his like there hadn't been years between them, between their hearts. They were connected at the hand and Scarlet could breathe, really breathe, for the first time since she and Tristan had run in the trees together in her first life.

She lightly squeezed his hand, just to make sure she wasn't dreaming. They were touching and no one was dying. If Scarlet hadn't been so wrecked over what she was planning to do, she would have smiled.

The first hour of their hike through the caves consisted mostly of Nate contemplating the most efficient route to the fountain. The caves split off into dozens of tunnels that went every which way. Following the map, Nate led the way through a series of rather uneventful tunnels and was fairly confident they would get to the fountain ahead of schedule.

But a few hours into their hike, they hit a wall.

It was a wall of vines, but still.

This vine gate was different than the last. It was wide and in constant movement. Stretching almost fifteen feet across, the vines twisted and crawled across the tunnel like a wall of snakes, making a *shhh, shhh* sound.

Through the vines, Scarlet could only see more vines, indicating the wall was very thick, and the blue tips of the vine's thorns glowed in a pulsing rhythm.

According to the map, breeching the wall of thorny vines was necessary if they wanted to continue.

So that sucked.

"Goodie," Gabriel said. "A moving wall of death."

"Think of it like an obstacle course," Nate said. "We just need to hack through the vines and tuck and roll until we've made it to the other side."

"Except for that," Heather pointed to the sides of the cave where jagged stalactites of Bluestone stuck out from the cave walls like thousands of blue knives.

Nate's eyes widened. "Holy crap."

"You know what we need? A chainsaw. Why didn't anyone think to bring a chainsaw?" Heather bit at her nails.

"Next time." Nate pointed at Tristan. "Make a note, dude. Tracking devices and chainsaws."

Scarlet stepped forward. "I'll go first."

Tristan made a face. "Like hell you will."

"Excuse me? I'm the only semi-immortal here. If I die, I'll come back to life."

Nate said, "Unless, of course, the caves *do* negate all immortality, in which case, you're actually just mortal right now so dying could be, you know, permanent."

Damn.

Scarlet hadn't thought of that.

"Why don't we all go in together in a line? If we keep hacking and sawing away, we can probably make it to the other side as a group," Gabriel said. "I'll lead the way and we can put Nate and Heather behind me, then Scarlet and Tristan. That way we'll have two decent hackers in the front and two in the back."

"And the weak, crazy girl who can't defend herself in the middle," Heather said dryly.

"With a *machete*," Tristan said.

A commotion behind them had everyone turning around to see a group of Ashmen charging down the tunnel with their weapons raised.

"How did they get in here?" Heather asked.

"Raven." Scarlet said. "We have to make it through the vines before they reach us."

Everyone lined up and, one by one, they walked into the moving wall of death with their enemies right behind them.

****

Tristan held a knife in each hand as he followed Scarlet into the vines. As a team, they slashed at the snaking thorns and, for the first few feet, were successful. But the wall was thicker than they anticipated and Tristan was soon hacking like a madman just to keep up with the vines Scarlet had hacked a moment earlier.

The Ashmen were getting closer and would soon be entangled in the vines with them. The last thing Tristan wanted to do was fight off rogue plants and dead minions at the same time.

Faster and faster he sliced, blue-tipped thorns cutting into his skin as the vines slithered against him and Scarlet. She slashed at the tendrils lashing out from the walls while Tristan focused on the vines at their feet. The group was slowly separated by rivers of snaking green and forced in different directions.

The first few Ashmen entered the vines.

Like the tentacle of a green monster, a dark vine wrapped around Scarlet's torso and yanked her toward the wall of Bluestone spikes. Tristan swung his blade through the monster, freeing her just as her body reached the spikes.

They hacked their way through the green current, Ashmen gaining on them by the second.

What were the Ashmen after? Raven had the map. What more did she want?

Tristan could no longer see Gabriel, Nate or Heather as the vines knit together more densely, as if sewing them inside. Which would just be perfect.

He and Scarlet reached the end of green web and were soon free from the thorny vines and standing in another glowing blue cave. Alone.

"Hello?" Scarlet called.

"Scarlet?" came Heather's voice from somewhere on the other side of the cave wall. "Are you out of the vines?"

"Yeah. Where are you guys?"

"We're out, too. There must have been more than one tunnel on the other side," Nate called.

"What should we do?"

Gabriel said, "We have to move forward separately. The Ashmen will reach the edge of the vines any minute."

"According to the map," Nate said, "the cave you two are in will lead down a few miles and intersect with our cave at a fork in the tunnels. So when you come to a fork, stop. Got it?"

"Got it."

The dense vines suddenly tightened, sliding against one another until they were a solid mass. They stopped moving, forming a solid barrier between the tunnels. Like a thick, green door.

"Well." Scarlet sighed. "At least the Ashmen won't be getting out of that anytime soon. If ever." She made a face at the scratch marks on her arms. "Agh. These sting."

Tristan looked down at his own cuts. "Yeah, but at least they're shallow."

"Well." She exhaled and held up her knife. "Ready for more cave fun?"

He cocked his head. "Have I mentioned how badass you look with a dagger in your hand?"

She smirked. "Not for a few hundred years."

"Well, I like seeing you with weapons." He smiled as they started down the tunnel. "Even if those weapons are mine and in the trunk of your car because you're *stealing* them from me."

"Borrowing," she corrected. "I had every intention of returning them to you and, if you think about it, I sort of did.

Since, you know, all the bloodstained weapons in the shack are yours." She grinned.

This felt good. Walking next to her without either of them being afraid, conversing like time hadn't bruised them both.

This was living; here in the dark caves where they were mortal and time was precious; *here,* life had meaning.

"Yes," he said. "It was very thoughtful of you to leave all my weapons hidden in a cellar six states away from me."

"Well now they're right next door." She paused. "Why *are* they right next door? How is it that you happened to build your cabin on the same piece of land as mine?"

He shrugged. "I felt you there. After you left New York, I followed you—

"Of course."

"And I could feel that you were somewhere in the forest by the cabin, but since you told me not to find you I didn't. The next day, I felt you start to die…" He cleared his throat. "I couldn't get to you fast enough. And after you were gone, I just…didn't want to leave. The Avalon forest was important to you for some reason, so I made it important to me."

She tilted her head. "I woke up in the Avalon forest last time. Right next to your cabin, actually."

"I know," he said. "I was there."

She stopped walking. "You were?"

He nodded. "You couldn't see me, but I was there the whole time. I wanted to make sure you were safe, even though I didn't want you to remember me."

"Which was *lame* of you. Amnesia really sucks."

"Well after we get to the fountain, you'll never have amnesia again." He smiled.

No amnesia. No curse. Just life.

Her eyes looked pained for a moment and she nodded. "Right."

A thread of unease slid through him.

"What the...?" Scarlet squinted up ahead as the sound of rushing water met their ears.

Their tunnel ended at an underground river. Its lightning-fast current swept through and around a sucking whirlpool, before dropping into a waterfall that cascaded into miles of darkness.

And the only way to get to the continuing tunnel on the other side was to cross the dangerous rapids.

"It seems to me," Tristan said, "that the Fountain of Youth doesn't want to be found."

"You think?" Scarlet stared at the raging waters. "What should we do?"

"Swim?"

"That's your idea? Swim through the deadly whirlpool-waterfall combo?"

"What do you propose we do? Fly?"

"Well, flying would be rad," she said.

He looked at the river. "It's not very wide. If we run and jump, we can probably make it halfway across the river before we'd have to start swimming."

"What about the whirlpool?"

"Yeah." He scratched his jaw. "That might be tricky."

Tristan slid his backpack off, pulled out his bedroll, and removed the tie around it. "We'll tie ourselves together. Give me your backpack."

She shrugged it off and he threw both their bags over the river and into the tunnel beyond.

"Let me see your hand," he said.

She held it out.

He tied one end of the rope around her wrist, and the other around his. "This way, if one of us gets sucked into the whirlpool, the other will have a way to pull them out."

"And if we both get sucked in?" She looked up at him.

He grinned. "Then we'll die together."

She smiled and he saw his thief in the woods. "I like that plan."

So did he.

"You ready?" he asked.

She bit her lip and nodded. "Are you?"

He was suddenly very aware that they might die in the next few minutes. Really die. "Yeah. But just in case this is it for us…"

He pulled her into his arms and pressed his lips to hers. Wild and free, he kissed her fully, holding her face in his hands like he'd so often wished he could do.

He brought her body up against his until she was the only thing he could taste or smell or breathe.

Nobody's eyes were glowing. No one was dying.

It was the least dangerous kiss they'd shared in centuries and it might very well be their last.

****

Scarlet fell into Tristan's kiss desperately. She could touch him—she could *taste* him—without danger and it felt like her soul had been unbound. She wanted to feel his hair and smell his skin, memorizing every small detail she had ever taken for granted.

She went up on her tiptoes to meet more of his mouth and fisted her hands into his shirt, clinging to him unabashedly. He cupped the side of her face, stroking her jaw with his thumb as he deepened their kiss and she pressed into him with a heavy hunger in her veins. Their tongues slipped over one another and their hot breaths wove together.

He lifted her into his arms and pressed her back into the glowing cave wall as she wrapped her legs around his waist. He softly kissed her ear.

She shivered.

He kissed her neck.

She squirmed.

He licked the vulnerable skin of her throat and her eyes fluttered open to a glowing blue. Not from her dying eyes, but from the walls of the pulsing cave that tucked them into its magical glow and let them feel one another without reservation.

She slid her hands into his hair and the rope around her wrist pulled tight. Tristan moved his bound wrist so she would have more room to run her fingers through his hair.

She loved his hair. She wanted to play in it.

He brought his wet mouth back to hers and slipped his tongue between her lips. Sinking a fingernail into the back of his shirt, she ran a line down his back and he shivered. She did it again and he leaned into her.

She tucked her hands under his shirt and slid them up his stomach, feeling the rope pull tight again as her bound wrist moved farther away from his. This time he pulled back on the rope, his hand slipping under her shirt and over her bare skin. Scarlet happily let her bound wrist be pulled from under his shirt and he kissed her mouth and grazed her skin.

She wiggled against him and tried to move her hand back to his hair, but the rope wouldn't allow it. Tristan's hand left the skin beneath her shirt and caught Scarlet's tied hand with his own. Interlacing his fingers with hers, he brought their hands up to the cave wall beside her head and held them against the glowing blue as his teeth softly slid down her jaw until his mouth was back on hers.

Passionate and soft, his lips pressed against hers as he pressed their hands to the wall.

Scarlet wanted to stay right here, bound to Tristan, forever. Behind her were centuries of heartache, and up ahead was her death. But here, in the pulsing blue caves of the very thing that had brought such tragedy to her soul, Scarlet was completely content.

And then the wall rumbled.

****

Tristan froze, lifting his mouth from Scarlet's hot lips.

Another rumble sounded and the tunnel began to shake.

He pressed her against him, pulling her from the wall and tucking her into his arms. The shaking intensified and he realized the tunnel was starting to cave in. Behind them, the tunnel ceiling began to crumble and pieces of blue fell to the ground, one after another, crashing closer to them with each new rumble.

Scarlet shimmied out of his embrace and he took her hand, before turning to face the rapids they'd need to cross if they hoped to outrun the avalanche coming their way.

He squeezed her hand and they ran for the river, leaping into the roaring currents—and possibly into their death—bound together.

For better or worse, they would be together.

This was living.

40

"Are there dragonflies down here?" Heather asked for the third time that hour. She was standing between Gabriel and Nate as they walked along yet another glowing tunnel of Bluestone.

"Heather," Gabriel said. "There are no dragonflies." She'd been going in and out of lucidity all day. Sometimes she was normal, annoying Heather, who said O-M-G all the time. And other times she was crazy, annoying Heather, who talked about invisible insects.

She groaned. "I'm never doing drugs on purpose. This withdrawal crap sucks. All I do is hallucinate. And I have a killer headache. I can't believe I'm seeing dragonflies."

"It could be worse," Nate said. "You could be seeing actual dragons. Dragons live in caves, you know." He looked over his shoulder nervously.

"Dragons aren't real."

"You don't know that." He turned back around. "There could be dragons hidden on some tropical island or living in the deepest parts of the ocean—"

"Oh, I see fish!" Heather pointed at nothing on the wall.

"—or in the Alps or something. They could be anywhere because they're mighty and they're awesome."

"Do you guys not see the fish?" she said.

"You're right." Gabriel said. "I'm sure there's a sleeping dragon just around the corner."

Nate scoffed. "Not likely. It's almost nine at night. Everyone knows cave dragons sleep during the day and hunt at night."

Gabriel took a long, deep breath.

"Do dragons eat fish?" Heather bit her nails, her eyes following an invisible something in the air.

"Depends on what kind of dragon it is," Nate said. "I'm sure a sea dragon would eat fish, but other dragons eat just about anything. Birds, elephants, milk maidens. "There aren't any dietary restrictions for land dragons."

A low sound hummed through the caves and Heather sank her fingernails into Gabriel's upper arm. "Was that a dragon?"

"No." Gabriel kept moving but let Heather keep her nails planted in his skin. "It's probably just the wind howling through a cave hole."

Nate made a relieved noise. "So, *that's* what I heard last night." He looked at Heather and smiled. "Cave holes. Not werewolves."

Heather's eyes widened. "Werewolves are super scary."

"I *know*." Nate's eyes widened as well.

Dear God. It was like traveling with six year-olds.

The sound rumbled again and Gabriel frowned. That hadn't sounded like the wind...

The ground started to shake and the floor in front of them began to split open.

"Ooh," Heather blinked. "I'm bouncing."

Nate looked around. "Is this an earthquake?"

Gabriel started to back up, but the floor behind them was crumbling as well, falling into black oblivion just inches away from their feet.

Heather peered down into the nothingness below and whispered, "Wow."

Gabriel grabbed her arm and pulled her away from the ledge. He guided her forward, hurrying to cross as much of the still-remaining cave floor as possible before the rest of the ground gave way beneath them.

They were almost to where the cracks in the floor were still small enough to jump across, when another rumble shook the walls and the last bits of earth that connected the plane they stood on to the other side of the tunnel fell to pieces.

The shaking came to a quiet standstill and Gabriel surveyed their situation. Behind them was an impossibly wide canyon of blackness, so turning back wasn't an option. And in front of them was a canyon just as wide.

They were stranded on an island of shaky cave floor.

****

Scarlet gasped for air as she struggled to swim above the current that had pulled at her once she'd hit the water. She was being sucked toward the center of the dark whirlpool and couldn't swim her way out of the powerful vortex.

Tristan planted his feet in the waist-deep river water, tugging at the rope around her wrist, every muscle in his body rigid with exertion. Glancing back, Scarlet watched the tunnel they jumped from collapse in on itself, thrusting large rocks into the river. The water began to rise and thrash about with the incoming rocks.

Scarlet was pulled under the cold, dark water and the whirlpool sucked her closer. She was no match for the wild water and the current pressed down on her. The rope cut into her wrist as Tristan—wherever he was—pulled against it.

Her lungs started to burn as she paddled toward the surface. The current kept pushing her down, though, and the whirlpool whipped at her ankles.

She started to feel lightheaded when her wrist jolted a bit then, slowly, her body was pulled away from the whirlpool and to the top of the water.

She broke the surface and gulped in oxygen before Tristan dragged her further away from the spinning waters and fought against the current to hold her steady.

More rocks tumbled into the river and angry waves chopped up the water.

Scarlet started swimming for the tunnel ahead but was yanked under the water again by her wrist.

Tristan.

She pulled on the rope and followed its tension to find Tristan under the water, pinned beneath a rock from the collapsing cave by the river wall. He strained to push it off, but the boulder wouldn't move.

Scarlet dove down and tucked herself between the river wall and the rock, her back against the wall and both feet on the rock.

Squeezing her eyes, she and Tristan pushed against the rock together.

Nothing.

Tristan would not die. He would not die.

They pushed again. Her stomach muscles burned. Her legs burned. And her lungs were on fire.

The rock budged. It was just an inch or so, but it was enough for Tristan to shove out from under it. With their wrists still connected, they swam for the surface of the water.

Gasping for breath, they paddled to the other side of the tunnel where the cave was still intact. The current picked up behind them, racing toward the waterfall, and Scarlet and Tristan reached for the ledge, clawing their way onto the Bluestone floor.

They pulled themselves up and watched the avalanche behind them drown in the depths of the rushing river.

"I think this cave is trying to kill us." Scarlet tried to catch her breath.

Tristan nodded. "I think you're right."

****

Gabriel stared over the edge of the cave island they were stranded on and frowned at the infinite blackness below. At least twenty feet of cave floor was missing, so jumping to the other side wasn't an option. And the tunnel they'd originally come through had caved in, effectively sealing them in.

Yeah.

This was a problem.

"Hmm," Nate rubbed at his chin as he looked across the black canyon before them. "You know what this looks like?"

"A shortcut to Hell?" Gabriel offered, gently pulling back on Heather's arm as she drifted toward the ledge.

"A chasm," Nate said. "This looks like a *deep chasm*."

Gabriel rolled his eyes.

Nate tapped his chin. "Now, what could we use to cross this chasm? Gabriel, do you have anything that could help us in your backpack? No? Perhaps *I* have something that could be of service." He shrugged out of his backpack and riffled through it until he held up his whip in glee.

"Well, look at that!" Nate grinned. "A whip. How incredibly helpful and convenient. *I'm so glad you brought a whip with you, Nate.* Why, thank you, Gabriel. I always try to be prepared."

"You really think that little whip is going to get all three of us across this gap?"

"Across this *chasm*? Why, yes. Yes, I do. All we have to do is find something to latch it on to…" Nate looked up at the cave ceiling and frowned. "Okay, this might be more complicated than I thought."

"I don't think I want to trust our lives to a fake whip you bought at Comic Con." Gabriel clasped his hand around Heather's wrist as she drifted near the edge again.

Good God. The girl was going to give him a heart attack.

"Why does everyone assume I buy all my things at Comic Con? This is a *real* whip."

Gabriel said, "Where did you buy it?"

Nate paused. "Comic Con." He hurriedly added, "But Comic Con sells real whips. Oh! There we go." He smiled as he caught sight of a potential anchor.

Unwinding the whip, he flicked it toward the anchor.

It slapped his wrist.

"Aw, man." Nate tried again and the whip snapped against his leg.

Gabriel stared at him. "Does Comic Con provide whip lessons? Because that would be money well spent."

Nate tried again.

Heather plopped on the ground and laid on her side, her cheek pressed against the hard earth as she drew small circles on the ground with her finger.

"Give it up, dude." Gabriel walked to the ledge and looked over again. Maybe there was a way they could climb down and across?

Heather sat up and bit her thumbnail.

Nate snapped the whip at the ceiling again and this time it wound itself around the anchor and held steady.

"Ha!" he cheered. He looked at Gabriel. "That's thrice now that you've mocked a Comic Con purchase of mine that ended up saving our lives."

"What?"

Nate listed things off on his fingers. "My Zelda sword that saved your ass against the Ashman in the cabin. My Buffy the Vampire Slayer video game that taught me how to slay zombies in the graveyard the other night. And the Indiana Jones whip that will most assuredly get us across this chasm to safety." He looked across the canyon to the dark blue tunnel ahead. "Or death. I'm not really sure what's waiting for us over there. But, either way, this whip will get us there."

Gabriel nodded. "You're right. I'm sorry. Your toys are awesome."

"So what should we do? Take turns?" Nate yanked on the whip to make sure it was secure.

"Sure." Gabriel nodded. "You go first."

"What? Why me?"

"Because Comic Con sells real whips…right?"

"Of course." Nate shook out his arms and legs—weird—then leaned back with the whip with a deep breath. "Here goes nothing."

He kicked off the ledge and swung himself across the abyss, sailing through the air.

And then back.

"You have to jump off." Gabriel watched his friend swing back and forth in terror.

"I know, dude." He swung back. "It's just so high and scary."

"Jump. Off."

Nate jumped off and fell ungracefully to the ground. "Whoo-hoo! I totally didn't die just now. Score."

Gabriel caught the whip as it swung back and looked at Heather, who was drawing circles on the ground again.

"Your turn, Heather."

"This is the worst hike ever," she said, now rocking back and forth on the ground. "Scary witches and thorny vines and nobody sees the dragonflies and Nate's saying words like *thrice*—"

"Hey, what's wrong with the word thrice?" Nate said.

Gabriel held out the whip. "Come on."

"I don't think I can." She scratched her neck. "I think I just want to sit here."

"Yeah, that's not a good idea. So why don't you stand up and we can swing to the other side of this very unstable tunnel and you can sit there. Okay?"

"I can't." Her eyes darted around the cave. "I'm kind of freaking out."

"About the whip?"

"I don't know!" She bit her nails. "I'm just *freaking out.*"

"Okay." He nodded. "Do you trust me?"

"Yes."

"I trust you too," he said. "And I know you can do this. You're Tomb Raider, remember? You're tough."

"I'm not tough." She shook her head and kept chewing on her nails.

"Yes you are. You stab Ashmen with scissors and you take blows to the face and you kick ass in your imaginary pink boots. You're tough and you can do this."

Gabriel was desperate to change the expression on her face. She looked so…lost.

"Come on," he said. "We'll swing over together and then you can freak out all you want when we're not standing on an island of doom, sound good?"

She stopped biting her nails and stood up, nodding as she walked to the whip. "I can do this."

"Damn straight, you can."

They both grabbed the whip and held on as Gabriel kicked off the ground and swung them across the chasm.

There was a cracking sound above and Gabriel looked up to see the stalactite anchor starting to break. They were almost to the other side when pieces of the anchor began to crumble and fall into the abyss.

"Jump!" Gabriel told Heather as the anchor broke off from the ceiling. Their momentum stopped, threatening to send them flying into infinite darkness, as Gabriel hurled his body—which was now wrapped around Heather's—to the other side of the gap, landing on the hard ground with Heather beside him. The whip fell straight down into the black hole.

Gabriel stood and helped Heather stand as well. The three of them looked back at the half-destroyed cave and the chasm of death they'd barely escaped—using a *whip*, no less.

Gabriel shook his head.

His life was so weird.

****

Scarlet bunched up the bottom of her tank top and twisted water from the material. Tristan had pulled his shirt off to wring it out—which was much more effective.

Guys had it so easy.

They had walked until they found a small alcove that was free of deadly vines, rushing rivers, and breaking walls, and decided to camp there for the night.

Tristan's forearm muscles shifted beneath his skin as he wrung out his shirt. The sound of their dripping clothes echoed off the cave walls, but aside from that it was silent and it felt like they were in their own world.

It was a world of man-eating vines and falling rock—so not exactly paradise—but they weren't sharing it with anyone else, which made it seem magical.

In a good way.

Not in a blue-water-evil-witch-curse way.

She caught him staring at the scratch marks on his arms and smiled. "Is it freaking you out to have scars on your body?"

"Not at all. I'm just not used to it. I've been injured plenty of times, but I've never had a wound mark me before." He smiled. "I kind of like it."

"Me too. It's hot."

"Oh yeah? Do I look tough?"

She shook her head. "You look mortal."

His eyes held hers for a moment and wild hope burst inside her. If Tristan drank the fountain water, he would be mortal. And if Scarlet could somehow find a way around sacrificing herself, she could be mortal with him. And they could live a mortal life together and eat pancakes and live happily ever after.

It was such an alluring thought that a lump formed in the back of her throat.

"How's your arm?" He asked, walking up to her and gently turning her arm.

"Fine." She shivered when he touched her.

He frowned. "Your stitches tore open."

She looked down at where her wound had reopened and a thin trickle of blood ran down her arm. "I didn't notice."

He rolled his eyes. "Of course you didn't." He tossed his wet shirt on the ground and retrieved a med kit from his backpack.

"What are you doing?"

"Sewing you back up." He laid out his bedroll. "Sit down."

"I'm fine. Really." Even as she said it, more blood poured from her wound.

"Yes, I know. You're always fine. Sit down."

She sat on the sleeping bag and another shiver went through her.

He smiled and started building a fire. "I can't have you shaking while I'm running a sharp needle through your skin, now can I."

"Not if you want your stitches to look as perfect at Nate's," she said.

"A challenge. I like that."

A few minutes later, a healthy fire blazed before them as Tristan sat beside her and carefully cleaned her arm.

She stared at the red mark around her wrist from the rope, thinking of how easily they could have died in the river today.

She watched him in the firelight. "Were you scared the first time you tried to kill yourself?"

He paused for a moment. "Yes." His eyes stayed on her arm. "I wasn't afraid of the pain—though I should have been because it hurt like hell—but I was scared it wouldn't work and you'd keep dying. And then I was scared it *would* work and that I'd never have a life with you."

He finished cleaning her arm and gently began threading the needle through her skin. She tried not to wince.

"Then why did you keep trying to die?"

He was silent a long time. "Because my love for you was stronger than my fear of being without you." He smiled. "Story of my life, I suppose."

He finished stitching her up and dabbed a numbing cream on her wound before bandaging her arm.

Scarlet stared down at the man who had lived to love her and tried to die to save her, and she was overwhelmed with emotion. "I love you, Hunter."

He smiled at her, his green eyes bright under his dark lashes. "I love you, too,"

Desperation came over her as she took in his sweet dimples and patient eyes, and she leaned into him, kissing him with reckless abandon. Just to feel him without fear, to love him without pain one more time before she left his world.

He kissed her back. Softly. Slowly. His hands slid behind her neck, warming her chilled skin as he tilted her head up to his. She crawled into his lap so she could feel his arms around her as she held his face. The stubble along his jaw rubbed against her fingers as she stroked his cheeks.

She tried to memorize the contours of his face with her fingers, trailing them along his jaw and brow line as they kissed. She wanted her hands to remember him forever. Even in death. Even in nothingness.

Her wet clothes heated against his bare chest as he held her in his arms, his lips soft, but demanding at her mouth. She parted her lips, sharing his breath as his tongue fell deep into her mouth. Hot, wet and wonderful.

She shifted in his lap and gripped at his muscles. He was so warm and strong. She wanted to climb inside him and tuck herself in forever.

She kissed a trail down the side of his neck and moved against his body. He groaned and clutched her hips, holding her to him as his hands slid under her tank top and heated her skin. He pulled the wet shirt from her body, their mouths parting for only an instant as he tossed it aside and went back to capturing her lips with his.

With their bare chests pressing against one another, Scarlet was no longer cold. She was on fire. She brought her hands to his hair, loving how soft it felt between her fingers.

He pressed warm, careful hands on her back and laid her beneath him on the bedroll as Scarlet's hands drifted across his skin, running over hard muscles. His hands slid over her breasts and down her belly and she moaned into his mouth.

If it was possible to burn someone into your soul, Tristan was ablaze in hers, and had been for centuries. Seared into her flesh and permanently marked on her heart.

His mouth moved down her body as Scarlet tipped her head back and reveled in the sensation of his tongue sliding along her collarbone.

They kissed and moved until they were both undressed and Tristan covered her exposed skin with his body.

He gazed down at her for moment with loving green eyes.

He kissed her cheekbone, then her eyebrow; He ran a finger over her lips and touched the shell of her ear. "I love you, Scar. So much."

"I love you too, Hunter. With all my heart."

He kissed the spot just above her heart, his lips resting against the place where a piece of him had lived for so long. Her heart was his completely.

He kissed a gentle trail back up to her mouth and kissed her fully.

Here in Tristan's arms, there were no curses or broken hearts. No sorrow. No sacrifice. It was just love.

Ancient, messy, beautiful love.

They moved against one another in the pulsing blue glow of the caves as their souls collided.

They were Scar and Hunter, the way they always should have been.

****

Nate looked up and down the tunnel. "No falling floors. Awesome. I'm going to go journal."

"You're *what*?" Gabriel blinked. "You're going to go journal? What are you, a thirteen year old girl?"

"Hey, journaling is *cool*," he said.

"Whatever, man." Gabriel sat down beside Heather as Nate walked away.

They had set up a spot to camp for the night and Heather's eyes were growing crazier by the second.

"How are you doing?"

She rubbed her head. "Not good. I feel insane. I feel like a hundred different people and all of them want to scream and cry and die."

She started wringing her hands together and biting at her lip over and over. Then she stood up and started walking around.

"What, uh…what are you doing?"

"I don't know," she said. She paced deeper into the cave in the opposite direction Nate had gone. "I just need to move."

"Yeah, that's probably not a good idea. Why don't you come back over here, where there's less chance of vine strangulation and open gaps in the ground?"

"No." She shook her head. "No, I have to move." She kept shaking her head as she walked farther away.

Gabriel stayed seated for exactly six seconds before following after her.

This girl.

Loud and ridiculous and completely unavoidable.

Gabriel couldn't seem to stop caring about the blond mess. She was so little and vulnerable. And happy. The girl was always absurdly happy.

No one so happy deserved to have anything bad happen to them. Ever.

Gabriel walked off after her and found her pacing along a glowing blue wall still wringing her hands together.

"I'm losing my mind, Gabriel. Like *actually* losing my mind. I don't know who I am or what I want and I'm so, so scared." She shook her hands out. "And what if this fruit thingy doesn't exist? What if we're wrong about everything and there's no cure and I'm just going to be psycho and then die?"

She started to cry in a quiet, fearful way and it did something to him.

He tentatively stepped forward and put his hand on her shoulder.

"I don't want to die," she said.

"You're not going to die." He drew her into a hug and had that same protective sensation come over him.

She tucked her face against his shirt, burrowing like she was hiding from the world in his chest. "Even if I don't die, I'll be this crazy, addicted person forever and have to live out here in the wild with the bears and werewolves just so I can be close enough to the fountain to stay alive." She sniffed.

He relaxed his arms around her and held her more closely. "I'll tell you what. If you have to stay by the fountain for any reason, I'll camp out with you and fend off any bears."

"What about werewolves?"

"I'll fend off werewolves, too. And dragons, if any of those pop up."

She sniffed again. "Okay."

They kept hugging and it didn't feel weird. Gabriel liked how she felt in his arms and how she trusted him to keep her safe.

He liked how she liked him.

It felt real. Maybe it was.

****

The next morning, Scarlet traced the lines of Tristan's tattoo as she laid on his chest. She flattened her palm over the design and he covered her hand with his, slipping his fingers in-between hers.

Scarlet inhaled leather and water and tears burned her eyes.

She didn't want to die. She didn't want to leave him.

He kissed the top of her head. "I love you."

She nodded against his chest and a single tear slid down her cheek and ran over his skin.

It wasn't fair. They'd never had a chance. It wasn't fair.

He cupped the side of her face and tilted it up to him. "What's wrong, Scar?" His eyes looked so pained, so desperate, as he brushed his thumb through another falling tear.

She opened her mouth to reassure him, but her lie got lost in her throat as she looked at him and all the love he offered her. All the love she was about to abandon.

****

The thread of unease that had been weaving through Tristan's veins for the past few days suddenly became a rope of alarm and every instinct inside him wanted to pin her against his body and protect her from whatever it was that scared her so much.

She scooted up and her voice shook with emotion. "If anything happens today, I want you to know that it was worth it. All this. All the crap. All the heartbreak. It was all worth it, okay? And you—you—have made my life beautiful and I will love you forever—"

"Nothing is going to happen." His heart pounded in fear.

Was that what this was about? Surviving the caves?

"Do you not want to go on?" he asked. "Because, say the word and I will stay right here, in these blue caves with you forever. We don't have to go a step farther. We don't have to find the fountain. Hell, we don't need a cure as long as we're in here. So, if you're afraid of dying—"

"I'm not afraid of dying." She swallowed, her blue eyes full and passionate. "We've been a broken, star-crossed mess from the beginning and I wouldn't change a thing." Another tear fell.

He tucked her into his arms, scared out of his mind at her defeatist tone as she buried her face in his chest. "Nothing is going to happen to you or me, okay? We've survived centuries of impossible things. Today—this, whatever this is—is just another battle. And you and I," he pulled back and gently wiped her wet cheeks, "you and I know how to battle. We're partners, Scar. I won't let anything happen to you."

Another tear fell and Tristan was completely lost. He'd never seen her fall apart like this and his heart didn't know what to do with hers.

He wrapped her back against his chest. Speechless. Terrified.

He loved Scarlet. More than anything.

And she was scaring the hell out of him.

41

Heather was feeling better. And by "better", she felt "sane." Her body was still itching beyond belief and she had a pressing desire to chew on her nails, but she hadn't seen any floating fish or dragonflies recently, so she was feeling optimistic about surviving the next few minutes.

She walked between Gabriel and Nate through another long, blue tunnel and tried not to accidentally brush up against Gabriel's ridiculously oversized shoulder. The boy really needed a hobby outside of the gym or bus throwing or whatever it was he did in his free time that gave him those shoulders. They were distracting.

As were his hands.

And his lips…

O-M-G, had she really just been looking at his lips?

Maybe the craziness was coming back. Or maybe she no longer saw him as the oversized, lying, hot guy who had dated her best friend, but rather the oversized, compassionate, hot guy who had carried her through the forest and held her while she cried.

She glanced over at him at the exact same time he glanced at her and things got weird.

Clearing throats, darting eyes, shuffling feet.

Awk-ward.

"So," Nate said loudly. "Does anyone want to clue me in on what I missed that's making this walk so tense and silent? Because I'm starting to feel like I'm traveling with Scarlet and Tristan here. Except with less kidnapping schemes. You do *not* want to know the inner workings of their brains, trust me."

Gabriel shrugged casually. "We're almost to the Fountain of Youth. It's what we've been seeking for five hundred years and it's only a few miles away."

Nate slanted his eyes at Heather, then at Gabriel. "Right."

"...as long as there aren't any other avalanches or tidal waves." Scarlet's muffled voice echoed through the tunnel and Heather stopped walking, as did Nate and Gabriel.

"Did you guys hear that?" Nate cocked his head to the side and followed the sound of Scarlet's voice further down the tunnel, then called out, "Scarlet?"

"Nate?" came Scarlet's voice from around the corner.

Everyone rushed to where the tunnel intersected with another tunnel ahead and Heather almost crashed into Scarlet as she rounded the corner.

"Hey!" Heather smiled at Scarlet. "You guys are still alive. Yay."

Scarlet nodded and smiled back. "Yep. Still alive. No thanks to the cave. It practically fell apart on top of us and forced us through a deadly sea of whirlpools and waterfalls."

"That's odd." Nate scratched his head. "Our cave floor disappeared and we had to Indiana Jones our way across a *chasm*."

"That's crazy." Scarlet sighed. "Well, I'm just glad everyone's safe. Do we know where we're going from here?" She looked around at the four tunnel choices they had before them.

Nate pointed to a tunnel on the right. "That one should lead us straight to the fountain."

There was a moment of tension as everyone looked down the dark, blue corridor.

"Let's do this," said Scarlet.

Everyone headed down the cave and Heather's shoulder accidentally brushed against Gabriel's. He glanced at her.

Okay, this was just getting ridiculous. Suddenly feeling hot and short of breath, Heather moved forward to walk next to Scarlet, where there was less sexual tension and no gigantic shoulders.

"Hey," she said.

"Hey." Scarlet smiled. "How are you feeling?"

"Crazy. But I'm not seeing things at the moment, so yay for that."

"I'm sorry we got separated yesterday." Scarlet frowned. "Were you guys okay?"

"Yeah. I mean, I saw invisible fish and had a total freak on a cave island and then almost fell into the pit of hell—literally—but other than that, it was a pretty smooth hike."

"You had a freak out?"

She waved a hand. "Yeah. But Gabriel talked me down. And then he swung me to safety on a whip." She paused. "That might be the weirdest sentence I've ever said."

Scarlet shook her head. "I'm so sorry for getting you wrapped up in all this What a disaster. I'm glad Gabriel was there for you yesterday."

"Yeah," Heather looked at the ground. "He's a good guy."

Scarlet eyed her for a moment. "Yeah," she said slowly. "And he's pretty hot, too."

Heather felt her pulse rise and tried to give a casual shrug. "Yeah."

Scarlet gasped and her eyes twinkled. "Heather. Baxter."

"What?"

"You're not gushing."

"So?"

"So, you gush over every hot guy—except the ones you really like. Holy cow. You have a crush on Gabriel."

"O-M-G. Shut up." She felt her cheeks warm. "I do not."

"Liar." Scarlet grinned. "Liar, liar, pants on fire—"

"Okay, fine! I think he's sweet. And protective. And he smells really good, like all the time. But I don't have a crush."

"You so have a crush."

"No. I have a crazy kidnapped bonding thing. It's like Stockholm syndrome, but for people who've been kidnapped together. I'm sure there's a term for it. Like the Hostage Hotness Syndrome or something. And besides, he's your ex. Like...yuck."

Right?

"Nope." Scarlet smiled. "Don't you dare try to use me as a crutch. And he's not really my ex. Well, he is. But it's not like that. For sure not now. And Gabriel's totally into you."

"Can we talk about something else, please? Like maybe this bright red mark?" Heather lifted Scarlet's arm and pointed to the red ring around her wrist. "I know why *I* have marks like this on my wrists, but why do you?" She wagged her eyebrows. "Did things get kinky in the caves last night?"

Scarlet pulled her hand back and blushed. "Don't be ridiculous."

"O.M.G." Heather's mouth dropped open and she smiled. "Scarlet Marie! I am flabbergasted...and I totally want details. Was it hot?"

"We're not talking about this."

"Oh, we are so talking about this. Maybe not now, in the death caves. But when we get out of here, I want a play-by-play."

****

Gabriel watched Heather walk beside Scarlet. Her blond hair was a complete mess, but her spirits were high and she'd been lucid for a few hours, so Gabriel was able to breathe easy.

Tristan eyed him as they walked along.

"What?" Gabriel said.

He shrugged.

Heather started biting her nails again and Gabriel's stomach tightened. He really hoped Scarlet was right about the Avalon fruit. If there wasn't a cure, if Heather was going to be addicted to fountain water forever—

Tristan was looking at him again.

"What are you looking at?" Gabriel snapped.

Tristan was trying not to smile. "You tell me."

Gabriel rolled his eyes. "Quit being a girl."

"Hey." Nate squeezed in-between them as they walked behind the girls. "What an adventure, huh? Killer vines, collapsing caves, crazy blonds...I'm totally writing a book about this when we get back. I'm going to call it *Whip Adventures*." He made a face. "Okay, maybe not that. I'll work on the name. So," he rubbed his palms together, "who's excited to be mortal?"

"Mortal?" Gabriel turned to him.

"Yeah. You're drinking the water, right?" Nate said. "It will permanently negate your immortality. Not to mention, heal all those super rad thorn marks on your arms and probably your Bluestone cuts too."

"I don't know..." Gabriel eyed the shallow cuts on his body. He'd never thought about becoming mortal before, and he wasn't sure how he felt about it now.

Immortality was powerful. Unique.

Was he ready to give that up? Maybe.

Maybe if he were no longer immortal, he wouldn't be empty inside.

"Why not, dude?" Nate grinned. "Tristan's drinking the water so the life-force that exists outside this cave doesn't kill him. So *he'll* be mortal. And I'm turning in *my* Immortal Awesomeness card."

Would Gabriel want to be immortal without Tristan?

He glanced at his twin brother.

No.

He wouldn't.

"Come on, dude!" Nate seemed genuinely excited. "It'll be fun. Just think of all the life and adventure and wrinkles and band-aids in store for you!"

"Are you peer-pressuring me into drinking fountain water?" Gabriel laughed. "That's ironic on so many levels."

"Can we take a break?" Heather asked. "I'm starving."

Everyone stopped walking and took a seat in the cave, rooting through their packs for water and snacks.

Gabriel started to move closer to Heather, but froze when he caught Tristan eyeing him.

"What?" he said again.

Tristan raised his brows. "Nothing."

Gabriel shook his head. "Shut up." He went and sat beside Heather.

"Hey, you."

She smiled. "Hey."

"Team meeting!" Nate pointed a finger into the air and everyone looked at him. "Since we'll be at the fountain shortly, I thought it would be best to talk through our strategy. We know Raven and her Ashmen made it into the caves, and we don't know where they are. But there's a chance they're either already at the fountain or on their way there, so I think it's best if we all prepare for a showdown." He smiled. "Hopefully, no one will get hurt. This is your Team Captain speaking. Peace out, Team Awesome."

Nate looked at Scarlet and walked deeper into the cave.

Heather groaned. "I hate Ashmen. They're so mean and they make me lose my pink shoes."

"I know. Ashmen suck." Gabriel looked at her, suddenly afraid for her well-being. "Hopefully, we won't see any at the fountain. But if we do, you have to fight, okay? You can't let the craziness get inside you. You need to be Tomb Raider."

She groaned again.

"I believe in you, Heather. You can do this."

****

Scarlet followed Nate into the tunnel where they had some privacy. "What's up?"

He looked her over with a serious expression. "Are you still considering sacrificing yourself?"

"Yes."

He sighed. "Then I'm going to tell you what I told Tristan when he was trying to kill himself," he said. "You're stupid."

Scarlet shook her head. "I won't let Heather die, Nate. We can't cure her unless I do this. And we can't break the curse and save Tristan unless I do this. I'm not going to let the people I love die. Wouldn't you do the same thing?"

"What about Raven? Maybe we can accidentally push her into the tree and *oops*! she's dead, but *yay*! we have fountain water."

"That's a great plan." Scarlet nodded. "And I'd loved to bring Raven down, but there's no certainty in that plan. We don't even know if she'll be there. I'm not taking any chances."

Nate nodded with pursed lips. "I was doing some reading in your father's journal today and I found out what controls your return to life. It's the Avalon tree. It bares the Avalon fruit once every century, and when that fruit blossoms, it calls you back to life. And when you die, so does the fruit. But if the fruit is eaten, then the Avalon will die."

Scarlet blinked. "Well, good. The Fountain of Youth has never done anything positive for anyone. I hope it dies."

"You don't understand. If the Avalon dies, you can never come back to life. There's no hope of it."

"Okay...? What are you saying?"

"I'm saying, don't die, dammit! There's no safety net here—no chance of you returning."

"I know that. And I'm fine with it."

"But I'm not." He shook his head. "This curse has been robbing you of joy and love for five hundred years. I'm not giving up yet. There has to be another way."

"There is no other way," she said. "And I've already made my decision."

42

Team Awesome walked in silence through a dark tunnel as they neared the Fountain of Youth.

The tunnel fed into a large, open cavern with a tall ceiling that glowed a bright blue just like the walls below it. Dozens of other tunnels lined the chamber, their black mouths looking ominous under the pulsing blue.

And in the center of the chamber, standing tall and majestic, was a large tree.

The Avalon.

It rose from the earth with long, thick roots spreading across the cavern floor and a vast canopy of blue-tipped leaves stretching out over its mighty trunk.

Everything about the tree looked like life. Even the iridescent trunk under the leaves—which, according to the journal, was immediate death to anyone who touched it—was beckoning in its design. Its deadly beauty stood silent; waiting for a heart to give itself over in return for eternal water.

Scarlet could understand now how those who made it this far would be tempted to touch the great Avalon. Even knowing the death it brought, Scarlet couldn't seem to pull her eyes away from the iridescent glow of life pulsing from its trunk.

"Wow," Heather whispered. "It's so beautiful."

"Yes..." Scarlet cleared her throat. "But no one touch the trunk. A single touch is fatal and we are all mortal down here."

Everyone slowly nodded with their eyes fixed on the iridescent beauty before them.

Gabriel said, "Where's the water?"

Scarlet was hoping no one would ask that question.

"It's coming," she said, her insides pulling tight.

She looked at Tristan, then at Heather.

Her death for their lives.

It wasn't even a question.

Suddenly, Ashmen poured from the tunnels around the room, some clambering over roots to get to the tree while others charged at Scarlet and her friends.

Heather bit at her nails.

The Ashmen nearest the tree turned to ash. A few more Ashmen tried to get close to the tree and they fell to ash as well. It was as if there was an invisible perimeter around the Avalon that prevented them from nearing.

Scarlet really hoped that perimeter was Ashman-specific and not another obstacle for her to overcome. The Ashmen heading for Team Awesome gained ground.

"What do we do?" Heather asked, half hiding behind Gabriel.

Tristan grabbed the bow from his back. "We fight."

Gabriel looked at Heather intently. "You can do this." He handed her a knife.

She nodded as Gabriel armed himself with his own knives, and Nate pulled a dagger.

Scarlet turned to Heather. "Stay right by me, got it?"

As the Ashmen closed in, Team Awesome parted ways. Gabriel and Nate went to the left, cutting through the oncoming Ashmen while Tristan headed to the right with arrows already darting through the air and sinking into Ashman hearts one by one.

Scarlet scanned the great, blue room for Raven, but saw no sign of the witch. Grabbing Heather's hand, she headed for the Avalon. She grabbed the bow from her back and quickly drew arrow after arrow, shooting down the Ashmen that stood between her and the tree.

Heather held a knife in her hand as they moved forward and Scarlet tried to keep any approaching Ashmen at bay with her arrows.

Scarlet saw Tristan perched at the top of a large rock on the chamber floor, shooting arrows into countless Ashmen as they came for him. He didn't see the Ashmen climbing up behind him.

Scarlet adjusted her bow and shot down the Ashmen at Tristan's back, before turning back around to clear a path to the Avalon.

At the side of the room, Gabriel was steadily hacking through Ashmen as Nate held his daggers with a happy glint in his eyes.

Scarlet grabbed Heather's hand, leading her over roots and ash toward the tree. But Ashmen continued to pour in from the tunnels, blocking their path.

She pulled Heather back and drew more arrows.

Bluestone axes, knives, arrows, maces…weapons of every type were clutched in the rigid hands of the Ashmen scattering through the cavern as they pressed in on them. Scarlet aimed, released, and retrieved. Over and over, ash falling everywhere.

She glanced at the rock where Tristan had been and found it abandoned. Panic sucked the heartbeat from her chest as she darted her eyes around the room.

She found him hacking through the oppressing Ashmen in the corner. He was steady and precise, but he was one against many, and his body was already covered in blood. A thick gash cut the side of his head and his back was slashed open.

She drew back and shot a few arrows into the Ashmen around Tristan, cutting down their numbers.

Heather screamed and Scarlet spun around as a heavy Bluestone axe came at her head.

She ducked, but not before the side of her face was nicked by the sharp blade. She put away her bow and grabbed two daggers, arming each hand. She started to wildly cut through the Ashmen coming at them. Ash flew through the air, spraying out across the cave floor and over the great roots of the tree.

Heather fought as well, hacking into the creatures coming at her. A blow to the back of Scarlet's head caught her by surprise and she was thrown to the ground.

Blackness shut out her vision momentarily and when her sight returned, Scarlet found herself being yanked up by her throat as an Ashman lifted her off the ground and held her bleeding body above the chaos.

Below her, Heather was overpowered by two Ashmen who dragged her toward the Avalon.

No.

Scarlet kicked and flailed, but the Ashman pinched her throat tighter and she started to grow lightheaded as she watched her best friend being hauled away to be sacrificed.

****

Heather had been afraid—very afraid—when she saw the many Ashmen enter the caves. But Gabriel had told her he believed in her and, for some reason, that mattered.

So she'd fought. She fought to see her family again. She fought to help her friends. And she fought so she could one day buy another pair of pink heels that were prettier than the ones she'd lost during her kidnapping.

And killing Ashmen wasn't so bad. They weren't nearly as messy as killing, say…something that bleeds. And she hadn't felt the need to vomit once. If this had been a vampire fight with blood flying around the room, she would have hurled in the corner.

So no throw up and no blood and Heather was fighting beside Scarlet—who was a serious badass with her bow and arrow. W-T-F was that all about?—and holding her own against the creatures coming at her.

But that was when it was only one Ashman at a time. When two had closed in on her, Heather had been lost.

Whose idea was it to let her come fight in this mess? She wasn't a trained bus thrower like Gabriel, or Robin Hood wannabe like Scarlet, or a ninja assassin like Tristan—she so wouldn't be surprised if that was his day job—she had no business jabbing butcher knives at supernatural creatures.

When she was taken captive by the two gigantic Ashmen—who Raven probably picked up at the bus throwing gym Gabriel went to—she was terrified. So she totally screamed like a girl. She kicked and yelled and felt hot tears push behind her eyes as the Ashmen carried her through the chamber toward the big, pretty tree.

Were they taking her to Raven? Were they going to kill her?

Bile rose up her throat.

****

The moment he saw Ashmen pouring into the chamber, Gabriel wanted to hide Heather in a corner. He didn't know why he suddenly cared for the crazy girl fighting to be lucid, but he did. And he hadn't *cared* about anyone—or anything—in centuries.

Heather was different than Scarlet—she was different than any other girl he'd known. And he'd known a lot of girls.

But none of them made him care like she did. She was light and joy and peace and renewal and if he did anything right in this damn cave, he was going to make sure Heather survived.

It was all he could do not to growl when Scarlet insisted Heather fight by her side. Who could better protect Heather than Gabriel? But he trusted Scarlet, so he'd acted like a man and gone off to fight the bad guys alongside Nate—who had *not* acted like a man.

"Dude," Gabriel had said. "Quit saying *ow* every time you get nicked."

"Nicked? *Nicked*? I have at least three cuts on my body that merit stitches. And one might even be worthy of full blown surgery."

"Yeah. But do you have to say *ow*? Like out loud?"

"They hurt." Nate had glanced over at Scarlet and Heather for the second time since they'd started fighting and nearly had his head chopped off by an Ashman.

"Scarlet's got Heather. They're fine. Concentrate on the zombies, man."

Nate fought for a moment. "*Ow*."

"Dude. Suck it up."

"Well, maybe if I had my Thor hammer or if *someone* hadn't lost my whip, I would be doing a better job. *Ow*."

Gabriel rolled his eyes and a scream caught his ear. He turned and caught sight of Heather being hauled toward the tree by two Ashmen, kicking and crying.

Without thinking, he raced across the roots and discarded weapons on the ground and made his way to her. The Ashmen stopped a few feet from the tree, holding Heather as if they were waiting for something.

Gabriel raised one of his blades as he neared her captors, determined to slice them both in one swing. He started to bring his knife down when a sharp pain split through his back and into his chest.

There was a split second of nothing.

Then Heather wailed and somewhere far away was a roar.

Gabriel looked down at the Bluestone arrow protruding from his body and blinked.

"Gabriel," Heather gasped. "No, no. Gab—" She choked as she struggled to free herself from the Ashmen.

He stared at her tearstained face and something unfamiliar grew inside him. It filled him up as he fell into blackness. Making him less empty.

Oh.

He wasn't empty anymore...

****

Tristan's sole mission today—as every other day—was to protect Scarlet. Especially since she'd seemed so fearful this morning as he held her.

Someday, he was going to make sure she felt nothing but good things. No fear or sadness.

Just love and hope and all the other things he hadn't been able to give her all these years.

After the Ashmen had flooded the chamber, Tristan had stood at the top of his rock and provided cover for Scarlet and Heather, while at the same time taking out the clambering Ashmen at his feet.

But then some asshole had thrown a mace at him—really? Throwing maces?—and it had cut him up and knocked him from his perch. Which of course had left him vulnerable to all the other Ashmen who wanted to smash his head in.

He'd gotten a little roughed up, but then he got mad and started taking out the jackass zombies in bulk. He'd been feeling pretty confident when he caught an Ashman charging at him with a mace—*ugh, not again*—from the corner of his eye.

He turned, but hadn't been quick enough. Tristan braced for the blow, but before it came an arrow cut into the Ashman's heart.

He turned to see Scarlet covering him from the center of the room and he beamed. He loved his thief in the woods. The girl archer who stole his deer and his daggers and his shirts was the keeper of his very heart.

He fought for another minute and a piercing scream cut into the room. Scanning the chamber, he found an Ashman gripping Scarlet by the throat as he raised her body in the air.

With fury in his veins, Tristan drew back and shot two arrows into the Ashman's chest. Scarlet's throat was released and she dropped to the floor, running toward the tree.

Tristan looked to the tree and saw Heather being held captive by two Ashmen and Gabriel running fast to her rescue.

Tristan drew an arrow to give Gabriel cover and then...

Then...

An arrow pierced Gabriel's back, impaling him clean through to his chest.

Something was shaking inside Tristan. Some noise was rattling his insides. He didn't realize he was bellowing into the cavern.

That was his brother bleeding across the room.

That was his brother falling to his knees.

His brother—his best friend—

No.

God, no.

Tristan was moving, but couldn't feel his legs. He searched for the shooter and saw a flash of silver disappearing into a tunnel.

His insides were hollow and cold as he neared Gabriel, who was now in a heap on the floor, dark red blood spilling from his body. He wasn't moving or breathing. He wasn't...anything.

Tristan scanned the cavern for Raven. So help him God, he would rip her jugular from her throat.

He looked back at Gabriel's bloody body and wanted to die.

With stinging eyes, he stood over Gabriel and swung his weapons in madness as his heart tore open.

****

Scarlet stared in disbelief at Gabriel's impaled body.

No.

No.

She ran for Gabriel, but Nate stopped her. Scarlet couldn't hear or see or breathe as she watched Gabriel drop to his knees.

No. No.

A roar sounded into the room and Tristan—murder on his face—raced to Gabriel, standing over his fallen body. He was slicing and jabbing and killing and crying. He was crying.

"Scarlet!" Nate screamed her name and her eyes dragged to his desperate face. "We have to save Heather! Are you listening? I need you to save Heather."

Scarlet blinked and forced herself to keep from falling apart. She charged forward, choking on her anguish, determined to save Heather from this day of hell. This nightmare.

The Ashmen were holding Heather by the tree. She struggled against them, and Scarlet filled with fury. Heather did not deserve addiction or violence or death. She deserved life and love. She deserved to go to college and have a family and smell like cookies. She was the closest friend Scarlet had ever known, she was the reason Scarlet was brave, and she would *not* die.

Scarlet ran for the tree, chopping into any creature that stood in her way. When she reached Heather, she hacked up the Ashmen with malicious glee and set her friend free.

Scarlet moved Heather forward and placed her under the great canopy. "The Ashmen can't get to you under the tree."

Scarlet stared at the iridescent tree trunk and took a breath.

This was it. This was where her love outweighed her fear.

She looked at Heather. "After this is done, the fruit will appear."

"After what is done?"

"Once the fruit appears, you have to grab it and run. Do not let Raven get the Avalon fruit. Do you understand?"

Prepared to set her hand to the fatal tree, Scarlet looked over her shoulder one last time and her heart stopped when she saw Tristan.

Ashmen bore down on him mercilessly as he stood fighting above Gabriel's body. He was sorely outnumbered and cut and broken everywhere as he fought in a rage. There were too many Ashmen, he would never survive.

Knowing Heather was safe, Scarlet ran to help Tristan.

As she neared, she couldn't help but see the boy he was long ago. Laughing in the trees. Smiling in the sun. She saw his green eyes trusting her, believing in her without question, and loving her through time and death all things broken.

She saw hope and love and forever.

She saw everything they'd suffered for, fought for, lived for.

And it was all falling apart right before her eyes as his attackers beat down on him.

He couldn't die.

She wouldn't let him die.

She began to cut through the army of Ashmen surrounding him. She sliced and slashed and growled and cried. And when she finally reached the center of the onslaught, her blue eyes found a set of green eyes and she suddenly knew everything was going to be okay.

Life.

Death.

It was okay. Because they were together.

Without a word, they stood back to back and started to battle against the Ashmen closing in.

They were losing, they were dying.

But they were together.

The cavern began to shake and the ground began to split open. The fighting stopped for a moment as the earth moved beneath their feet. Scarlet looked back at the Avalon to make sure Heather was safe, but froze at what she saw.

Nate had his palm pressed flat against the trunk of the tree, a look of surrender on his face as he stared at Scarlet.

"No!" She pushed out of the Ashmen—who had dispersed a bit with the earthquake—and ran to him, unable to breathe. "Nate!"

She reached him just as his body slid to the ground, his eyes tired and colorless, but he had no remorse on his face.

How did he--? Why would he—? No!

"Nate!" she screamed. "Wh—what are you doing?" Tears stung her eyes.

"I am giving you a chance to live." His breathing was labored and she could see the life draining from his body—she could actually see it sweeping up through his arm and into the iridescent tree, glowing as it entered the trunk.

"No. No!" Her voice cracked as she tried to pry his hand away from the trunk. But the Avalon seemed to have a grip on him somehow and Scarlet's desperate yanking was futile.

"Scarlet," Nate said. "I have lived fully and loved deeply. I'm ready to die."

"No!"

Tristan came up behind her with a horrified expression. "Nate! What are you—"

Nate's face lost all color and his chest trembled.

Tristan crouched beside him. "You can't do this!"

"You need the water." His voice was breathy.

Scarlet kept pulling at his hand and body, tears falling down her face. "No. No, Nate. You can't die."

"Yes," he said with a small smile. "I finally can." He started to gasp. "Heal Gabriel. You all deserve a happily ever after."

Scarlet shook her head and wrapped her arms around him. "Don't die. Please, don't die."

His body trembled in Scarlet's arms and then went lax as the last tremor of life left his heart.

The tree began to rumble, then down lowered a small branch, leafless and bright green with a blue tip. At the tip of the branch grew a small blossom shaped like an apple. Glistening red with iridescent colors of blue and purple and green shining off its glossy reflection, the fruit hung directly above Heather.

Heather reached up to grasp it but was thrown to the ground by Raven. She snatched the fruit from the limb with her gnarled, aged hands and smiled down at Heather. Raven opened her mouth to take a bite and Scarlet left Nate's body and charged at her.

She knocked Raven to the ground, the fruit rolling from her hand as Scarlet grappled to overpower the witch. A hot pain cut into her arm and she winced, releasing her hold on Raven.

Raven held a knife in her hand, wet with blood from where she'd reopened Scarlet's stitches and lunged at Scarlet with darkness in her silver eyes.

The knife came at Scarlet's chest, but Raven's body jolted and the knife fell from her hand as an arrow pierced her heart.

Then another arrow. And another.

Tristan stood behind Scarlet with his bow drawn and anger in his eyes.

"You cannot kill me," Raven wheezed at him. "I have fountain water in my body."

"Even better." Tristan shot her again.

With Raven unable to move, Scarlet snatched up the fruit and gave it to Heather. The ground shook and the cracks in the chamber floor grew wider, but there was still no water.

Scarlet, Heather and Tristan turned from the tree and saw Raven's army of Ashmen surrounding them on all sides. Waiting.

They were trapped.

Suddenly, the ground exploded with water pushing up through the cracks and flying up to the ceiling.

The Fountain of Youth.

The water began to fall down like a great rain, drenching everything in the chamber—including the waiting Ashmen, instantly turning them to ash and washing away their existence.

The cavern shook with more fervor and the water began to flood the room.

With their opponents defeated in one fell swoop, Scarlet looked at Tristan. "Gabriel!"

He was already headed to Gabriel's body. Lifting his brother onto his back, Tristan threw a canteen at Scarlet. "We need to get out of here."

Scarlet quickly filled the canteen and grabbed Heather by the hand, yanking her from under the tree. Raven was lapping at a puddle of fountain water beside her like a dog, arrows still lodged in her chest.

The Avalon began to creak and groan behind them, its massive branches swaying and twisting through the falling water. More water swelled up from the cracks and soon the cavern floor was a pool of blue.

"Run!" Tristan yelled, and they stomped through the rising water, splashing as fast as they could across the chamber to the tunnels. The water rose higher and began twisting with the tree. Faster and faster the water spun, until the cavern slowly morphed into a giant whirlpool.

The glowing blue walls began to dim, growing darker as pieces of the cave began to crumble from above. Tunnel after tunnel, the cave began to collapse, their exit options quickly diminishing. The whirlpool picked up behind them, spinning the air. Scarlet's feet wouldn't move fast enough.

They ran for the only remaining open tunnel as water sprayed up behind them and wind whipped at their faces. They reached the tunnel and a sound louder than thunder boomed throughout the cavern. Turning, Scarlet watched as the cave ceiling broke apart and fell into the whirlpool below. Raven, still lapping at the water like the addict she was, was swept up in the wild waters and sucked down into the narrow darkness of the whirlpool.

A hand snatched Scarlet's wrist and yanked her deeper into the tunnel.

"Run, Scar!" Tristan carried Gabriel's body as they raced ahead. The glowing blue walls grew darker as they ran, as if the cave itself was dying, and pieces of the floor broke underneath their feet.

Water spit into the tunnel, backsplash from the collapsing cave, and chased after them as they ran. The cave grew darker and darker until the pulsing blue was almost completely gone.

The angry water began to rise and push at their ankles, a giant wave building up behind them. Just when Scarlet was sure they'd drown in the massive torrent, she spotted a bright light ahead.

As they neared the light, Scarlet saw it was a narrow opening leading out to the forest. They clambered over crumbling rocks, wicked licks of water and broken earth to reach the light, then climbed out of the cave one by one, bursting into the Avalon forest.

They'd just started running through the trees when a loud groaning came from the caves behind them.

Scarlet could hear the roar of water as the wave that had chased them down the tunnel crashed into the hole they'd just climbed out of. Looking over her shoulder, she watched the great caves explode. Like a glorious geyser, water sprayed up from the hole and shot high into the sky.

Tristan hurriedly set Gabriel's body on the forest floor. Scarlet handed him the canteen and, with shaking hands, he carefully tipped the spout to Gabriel's mouth. "Come on, Gabe." He said quietly.

No response.

Heather was crying as she bit her nails beside Scarlet.

Tristan tried again, lifting Gabriel's head to ensure the water would go down. "Come on. Come on."

Droplets of blue pattered on their heads as they waited with anxious hearts.

Gabriel finally coughed and his wounds began to heal.

Obvious relief ran through Tristan as he rubbed a hand down his face and guided the water back to Gabriel's mouth.

Gabriel took a deep gulp and sat up. "Wha—what happened?"

Tristan grasped his shoulder then slapped his arm around Gabriel in a hug. "Doesn't matter. You're alive."

Now that they were out of the cave, Tristan's emotions were swarming back into Scarlet.

Relief. Loyalty. Joy. Love.

Heather reached for the canteen and started to bring it to her mouth—

Scarlet snatched it away. "What are you doing?"

"I don't know," she said as she chewed on her lip. "I just really, really want some. And I can't control my hands and I feel super crazy right now."

Scarlet nodded to the fruit in her hand. "Eat that and you'll feel better."

Heather took a bite, juice spilling down her chin as she began to devour the Avalon fruit with her eyes closed. "Ah. This is delicious."

Scarlet handed the canteen to Tristan.

He inhaled deeply and took a drink.

Instantly, Scarlet's body began to feel different. As the water undid all the immortality inside his heart, the immortal blood inside her heart vanished as well, cleaning away the curse that had stained them for centuries. Her body became more and more mortal until she no longer had Tristan in her veins.

His battle wounds began to heal as he pulled the canteen from his lips and looked at her. "Did it work?"

She smiled and nodded her head. "We're cured."

43

Scarlet, Tristan, Gabriel and Heather stood in the park at the center of all the Kissing Festival madness. Happy music played from the gazebo and paper stars were strung up everywhere for people to kiss beneath.

The past few months had been bittersweet. The curse was no more, but Nate's death had been heartbreaking. It still didn't feel real, living in this world without him, but Scarlet was no longer confused by his motivations for sacrificing himself.

His life—his heart—had ended with Molly, but he had found purpose in bringing the opportunity for love to Gabriel, Tristan, and Scarlet.

And he had done just that by giving his life.

Scarlet hoped his soul was somewhere beyond, entwined once again and now forever with Molly's.

She looked at Tristan and found his green eyes smiling at her. He squeezed her hand and kissed her forehead.

For no reason. Just because he could.

Scarlet smiled.

"Ooh! They have a love train this year!" Heather looked at Gabriel with true excitement in her eyes. "Let's do it!"

Gabriel stared at her. "I'm not riding something called a *love train*."

"Oh, come on. It's adorable and has all these cute little train cars shaped like hearts." She batted her lashes.

"No. *You* can ride the love train."

"But I don't want to ride the love train alone."

"Then don't ride the love train."

"But I want to ride the love train."

"For the love of God," Tristan rolled his eyes at Gabriel. "Just go ride the train with her."

She batted her eyelashes again.

"Fine." Gabriel sighed. "I have a feeling this next year is going to be filled with batting eyelashes."

Heather said, "You mean filled with awesomeness? Uh, *yeah*. You get to be my New York City tour guide during my first year at college. It's going to be epic! Now, let's go ride the train." She clapped her hands in glee and yanked him toward the red and pink train in the park.

He let her lead him by the hand, a smile on his face, and Scarlet noticed they didn't stop holding hands even when they got to the train. While Heather bounced excitedly at the train-goers, Gabriel tried to look bored. But he couldn't stop smiling.

Tristan nodded to Gabriel and Heather. "How do you think that's going to end?"

Scarlet looked at them with a sigh. "Hopefully without a curse."

A shudder went through her as she thought about all the tragedy the curse had brought them. At least now the fountain was destroyed and could never again wreak such havoc.

Scarlet looked up at him with a smile. "So, Hunter. What do you want to do? Kissing booths? Kissing relays? Creepy dentist?"

He smiled. "Leave?"

Scarlet laughed. "It's like you read my mind."

Still holding her hand, Tristan walked them through the park and into the forest trees beyond.

"I got you something," he said, pulling a small case from his pocket.

Scarlet opened the case and gasped. It was a brooch just like her mothers, but this one was brand new and the etching on the side was the same design as Tristan's tattoo.

"It's a little piece of me and a little piece of you," he said.

She looked up at him and smiled. "It's beautiful."

A loud boom sounded into the night and fireworks lit up the sky. The Kissing Festival finale had begun.

Tristan came up behind her and wrapped his arms around her, bringing her back up against his chest as they watched the fireworks. The finale came to an end and Scarlet could hear cheers in the distance as Avalon celebrated the end of the Kissing Festival.

The fireworks cleared until only twinkling stars remained.

Tristan leaned in close to her ear and whispered, "Is it okay if I love you forever? Even if forever is only for a lifetime?"

She turned in his arms and smiled up at him. "Only if it's okay that I love you back."

He smiled. "Deal."

And while the town of Avalon was busy kissing beneath paper stars, Scarlet and Tristan kissed beneath the real ones. Just as they had centuries ago. Just as they would for years to come.

Avow

EPILOGUE

The forest was nearly dry, save for a single stream of blue water trapped in the crevasse of a boulder. The heavy wind picked up and, slow and steady, blue water flowed down the rock and cut through a small pile of ash before sinking into the damp dirt beyond.

Up from the dirt rose a single, green sprout with a blue tip.

Acknowledgements

This book, and this series as a whole, would not be possible without the people who believe in me.

My sister, Kiele. Without our late night conversations over bowls of ice cream this story would never have been born. You believed in me even before there was a page one and I love you with my whole heart.

My beautiful mother, who has never failed me. Thank you for making my dreams important to you--even when they seemed impossible. My hero and my husband, Brett. Thanks for keeping our world in one piece. You're my lobster. My beautiful children, Kiana and Caleb. Thanks for thinking my job is "cool" and for understanding when I pick you up from school in my pajamas.

My agent, Suzie Townsend, who makes all things possible. Thank you for your endless patience and expertise. You make me a better writer, but more importantly, you keep me sane. And I really love my sanity.

And my heart and soul, Bobbi. Thank you for always being a part of my dreams. I love your guts.

Chelsea Fine

Bugg Photographer LLC

Chelsea Fine grew up (and still lives) in the Phoenix, AZ area where she studied Design at Arizona State University. During college, she also took her first creative writing class, which is how she fell in love with writing. In 2007 while working at a credit union, she found herself staring at a computer screen and bored out of her mind. She promptly opened up a Word document and began writing a story to kill time (she knows she was a terrible employee!). Eight pages and forty-five minutes later, she realized she was having fun. Now, years later (after quitting the credit union, since she wasn't very good at "being on the clock"), she published her first novel *Sophie & Carter*. When she isn't working on her latest novel, she's an avid reader, a lover of music, a Battlestar Galactica fan, a coffee addict, a chronic texter, an obsessive teeth brusher, and a shameless superhero enthusiast.

Also by Chelsea Fine

While other high school seniors are dreaming about their futures, Sophie and Carter are just trying to make it through each day. Carter is overwhelmed by troubles at home as he struggles to support his mother. Meanwhile, next door neighbor Sophie is left to care for her three younger siblings in place of their absent and troubled mother.

All that holds these two best friends together is each other, and knowing that each night they'll sit together on Sophie's front porch swing and escape from their troubles, if just for a while. But as their relationship reaches a turning point and high school graduation nears, what lies ahead for Sophie and Carter?

ISBN 978-0-9885859-1-1, 128pp,
$7.95 trade paperback, $2.99 Nook or Kindle

Made in the USA
Lexington, KY
02 January 2015